The

Jaguar

Hunts

Judith M Kerrigan

All correspondence and inquiries regarding any written works by Judith M. Kerrigan should be directed to: judirose@tds.net
Published by Judith M. Ribbens
Golden Moon Studio
W2445 Main Street
Bonduel, WI 54107

Paperback: ISBN 13:978-0-9857066-4-7
LCCN: 2016950815
Kindle e-book: ISBN 10:0-9857066-5-1
ISBN 13:978-0-9857066-5-4
Amazon ASIN:
Cover design by Paul Beeley,
Create-Imaginations
www.create-imaginations.com

Acknowledgements

Many thanks to my alert and erudite pre-readers who edit my books:

Lois Bergman

Arica Johnson

I am indebted to them for catching many mistakes, misspellings, and those mysteriously garbled passages
I'm sure I did not intend to write.

Dedication
November 12, 2016

I dedicate this book to my daughter, Jeannie Kerrigan, author of *Layla*, her powerful autobiography of her recovery from abuse and addiction. Since January of this year she had been engaged in a battle against pancreatic cancer. She had given her all in this fight and succeeded for a time but after several months it took over and she decided it was time to go. Jeannie's spirit left her body August 24, 2016, surrounded by family and friends in this reality and beautiful spirits in the next, and left us with grace and love. I was privileged to be able to return love to her as she let this world go. She has taught me so much about courage. She is the bravest person I have ever known. Jeannie became, and still is, the Spirit of Love and Light in our lives and the lives of every person she touches.
Today is her birthday.

***

In Memory also of
Bev Nelson
I can only hope Bev found that Great Library in the Sky because she absolutely loved reading while she was here.

The Jaguar Hunts is the third in the Anna
Kinnealy trilogy. The first two books are summarized
below.

Betrayal by Serpent

Seven years after the fiery plane crash in the Yucatan
which killed her husband, Anna Kinnealy believes all the emotional
trauma and financial struggle she and her children have endured will
finally come to an end when he is declared legally dead. She longs
for a normal life.

But there are murders on someone's agenda, bizarre
intrusions in their own home, a police investigation into their lives,
stalking, and a malevolent presence. Slowly secrets emerge that
demand Anna unravel painful memories before she and everyone
she knows become victims of greed, envy and hatred.

In a journey that takes her from Green Bay, Wisconsin, to
unknown and unexpected dangers in the jungle lowlands of the
Yucatan and back, Anna finds courage she never thought she had,
betrayal so painful she can only put her head down and weep, and
depths of rage she never wanted to feel.

Yet even as this happens, she awakens to intense passion
with one man, receives respect and admiration from another, and is
left stunned and grieving as the deep love of an old friend is revealed
in his sacrifice for her.

In Crocodile Waters

When Anna Kinnealy returns to Mexico to recuperate from
the attempts on her life and to continue her love affair with Ramon
Aguilar, she believes all is going well. Sons Cory, Alex and AJ and
daughter Marnie are safely involved in their own lives.

However, unknown to Anna, there is an enemy who has her
every move watched. Greed and jealousy fuel this enemy's vicious
"business plan," a plan of harassment carried out with near-
psychotic vengeance through frightening and cruel attacks on those
she loves most.

Anna discovers the betrayal she experienced so far is only
the beginning. One by one her children, her mother and her friends
become victims, and it takes all the courage Anna can muster to fight
through grief, terror and despair while she offers herself as bait and
walks into the enemy's trap.

Her quest for answers to her question of "Why?" and her
search for her sons send her to Europe, back to Mexico, and racing
home again as she tries to save her children.

For your convenience, I am including a list of characters from each book.

Betrayal by Serpent

The House, Anna's home for many years. It became her safe place and her business office as well. The House came to have a character of its own so I include it in this list.

The Kinnealy Family

Anna O'Neill Kinnealy, age 52 when the first book begins, mother of five children, four still living, wife of Arthur Kinnealy Sr., who died in the crash of his small plane in the Yucatan seven years prior to the beginning of the story.

AJ, or Arthur Kinnealy Jr, age 27, oldest son
Daughter, name unknown, died of SIDS
Marnie Kinnealy, age 20
Alex Kinnealy, age 17
Cory Kinnealy, age 16
The ages of these children when Art Sr. died were 20, 13, 10, and 9.

The Bradleys

Robinson and Caroline Bradley, and their twins, Jake and Jim, age 16, live across the street from the Kinnealys

The Fitzgeralds

Caitlin Fitzgerald and her five sons: Sean, Michael, Andrew, Seamus and Liam. Cait is Anna's best friend from childhood. They live in the west side Green Bay neighborhood where Anna and Art grew up.

Relatives

Katherine O'Neill, Anna's mother, known as MomKat

Carrie Brennan, Anna's aunt, married twice and divorced once, or the other way around—no one really knows—the family "black sheep" and sophisticate

Friends and acquaintances
Old Mr. Houlihan, a protector and friend from Anna's childhood

Big John O'Keeffe, owner of a construction company and friend of Art Kinnealy for many years. Jon O'Keeffe's father

Jonathan O'Keeffe, Art's law partner and co-founder of their firm

Jennifer O'Keeffe, Jon's twin

Mary O'Keeffe, Big John's wife

Boarders at The House
Marthe Grimm, Anna's first boarder at the house and now surrogate grandmother and friend

Lindy Stewart, student at University of Wisconsin-Green Bay who has become like one of Anna's own children. Daughter of archaeologist Ian Stewart

The Law Firms
O'Keeffe, Kinnealy, Soderstrom and Moss. The firm begun by Jon O'Keeffe (Jonny O) and Art Kinnealy Sr. Sometimes called The Firm.

Andrew Moss, deceased partner

Samuel Soderberg, deceased partner

Susan Jane Soderberg, his wife

Wentworth and Foster

Conrad Wentworth, Anna's lawyer

Clayton Foster, his partner

Ardith Seacrest, Conrad's secretary

Abigail Woodman, lawyer from Appleton, WI

Others
Greg Klarkowski, Green Bay Police Department, Detective

Thomas Rudmann, Brown County Sheriff's Department, Detective

Ben Bennett, former classmate of AJ's and now a police officer with GBPD

Mexico

Capitán Jesús Arispe Sandoval, investigator of Art's death

Ramon Aguilar, guide and friend, becomes Anna's lover

Jorge Aguilar, his brother

Adelina Sálazar Díaz, housekeeper, elder, advisor, aunt to Jorge and Ramon, and she became head of the school Anna began

Tomasita, Adelina's helper

Ian Stewart, Lindy's father, an archaeologist

Kevin MacPherson, "Mac", investigator of the drug cartels; Canadian and Native American

Walton Herder, from the American Consulate

Matthew Simoneska, archaeologist with Cross-Cultural Archaeology Institute

Hernan, Jaime and Eduardo. Mexican workers on the archaeological dig. Eduardo is Tomasita's husband.

CHARACTERS added to *In Crocodile Waters.*

Wisconsin

"Iron Mike" DeLorme, Green Bay police detective

Arnold Schwartzkopf, Green Bay police captain

Father O'Doul, pastor at St. Pat's church

Mr. Black, drug pusher

William "Big Bill" Holworth, camp director

Rich Wolcott, sheriff

Vincent Grant, owner of a large security firm. Employed by Grant: Melissa, Stacy Andre, Pete, and Harry

Europe

Gabrielle de Launay, administrative assistant to Robert de la Vergne

Robert de la Vergne, Yvette-Louise de la Vergne, Swiss banker who administers Anna's financial holdings in Europe, and his wife. Her nickname is "Louie."

Aristide Fournier, French politician
Etienne Charbonneau, French count

Ireland
Pat and Jamie O'Reilly, Anna's older brothers

Mexico
The Crocodile, El Cocodrilo, head of his own cartel
El Capitan, head of a third cartel
The Texan, employed by El Capitan

CHARACTERS added to *The Jaguar Hunts*
Green Bay
Abraham Lemke, known as "Big Abe", Oneida Tribal Police

London
Big Tom Kearsley, London police officer
Little Tom Kearsley, son of Big Tom
The Master, former spy, art expert
The man who smokes a bubble pipe, works undercover for Her Majesty's Government

I have not included various minor characters who make very brief appearances.

Wisconsin

One

...journal, 1:37 am....

My nightmares are relentless. Vivid. Brutal. A confusion of past and present that catapults me into stomach-twisting terror and back. Pieces of dreams that bring no peace. Nothing makes sense. I write in the hope of stopping them—a false hope so far.

Always, before, writing in my journal brought me relief, some sense of control, and it became my safe place. Now? That's a delusion! I have no control over what's happening. I don't like...no, I *hate* admitting that! I fear the chaos that would result if I don't control things. I feel... no safety anymore.

Something went wrong with me in Mexico, even before I was lost in the jungle. I stepped off the plane into that strange fey world and, without my awareness, the control I thought I had over myself just slipped away. I've always thought of myself as a sensible woman, feet on the ground, able to face things. Now...I just don't know what this is. Frightening, this loss of control over myself.

When did this start? Before Mexico maybe. But when? Last December when I found Conrad dead? With the attempts on my life? When my mother was murdered? When Ardith began her insane mission to obtain her "legacy" of Conrad's estate by targeting my children?

Yes, I think, looking back, my slow unravelling began with my grief after Conrad's death. After Art was killed, he became my guide, my rock, my connection to logic and sanity.

Except, I have no sense of a "start" really. It's been insidious, creeping around me and through me.

To my great horror, I now think I can kill. I have never, ever wanted to kill before. I'm horrified at that thought! I'm like some kind of animal.

I made myself write that.

Writing did not make that better.

...3:12 am....

The dreams! Oh, god, these dreams! They're destroying my sense of reality...every night...no letup...

...I dream my mother is alive again and crying for Art to come back to save us. He's in the cargo hold of a giant ship in the middle of the ocean searching for drugs while Johnny O, fishing for marlin from the deck, pulls AJ's body from the sea. The whole scene is permeated by the smells of rotting dead fish...

...the recurring dream that Ardith sends large black and red wolves to chase Alex and Cory and Marnie. The chase goes on for days and days, howls ripping the air...screams. First Cory, then Alex, then Marnie drop, exhausted, and are caught. Some horrible creature tears them apart until the dream becomes a red haze of blood...

...the longest dream...I am an animal, ripping the meat off a peccary and gorging myself. It has been long since I ate like this. The

4

pig is not yet dead and screams in pain. I bite through her neck to silence her. A smell...a human coming! I leap for cover in the thick branches high in a tree. The sickening odor that clings to him drifts upward. I sniff and know he is rotting even as he breathes. I watch him for a time from my hidden perch. Two spirits drift with him. The Woman Spirit cries. The Mother Spirit leans over him and sucks his breath in and out to keep him alive. They wander off. I turn my ears and listen. In a far distance monkeys howl, their sound moving closer. I leap to the ground, sink my teeth into the meat and drag it to a small cave. The sounds grow louder. Anger howls. Fear screams. Birds scatter from trees, fleeing from cracking and slashing and breaking branches. Small creatures scurry past, panic in their scent. Noises from angry men whip the leaves of the trees. Raw shrieks tear from the throats of human women and children. Sharp gunshots warn me hunters come this way.

Humans are killers. I must flee. The spirit of the dead woman flees with me. Why does she follow me?

What am I? How did I get this way?

...tonight's dreams...

...I sweat and stumble and hack my way through tangled vines and dripping leaves searching for AJ. No one will help me. I ask. I beg. They all turn away. I am forced to search alone. I meet men who tell me they saw him. I put no trust in what they say. They have red lust in their eyes and greed dripping dirty green from the open holes where mouths once were. They want money, reward, my body. Everyone in the clamoring crowd holds out a price tag. Ardith is among them but, before I can hear the price she demands, the scene changes. As I move over the matted jungle floor, I see it covered with thousand-dollar bills. When I try to pick them up, they dissolve into bloody slime...

...AJ's spirit disconnects from his body. I see it happen. I see the spirit of the woman who follows him. She begs him to help her, to love her, to come to her, and he wants to go but his body won't die. His heart refuses to stop beating. It is not his time to die. I lose sight of him and I panic! He will die if I don't find him! He's my son. I *know* when he's supposed to die. This is not the time! I must find him first, before she takes him forever. A voice whispers to me, "You must join with the goddess and she will help you save him." Rage answers. What goddess? There is no goddess! Only cruel men, sounds of shots, screams of children! I run now, toward them. AJ is there. I must save him...

This is not just posttraumatic stress. I feel haunted.

Slowly, unwilling to move my tired body, unwilling to feel more pain, I come out of the nightmares into the darkness of my room. My bed is soaked with sweat. The ache across my shoulders tells me sleep won't come again soon. Knowing it will become much worse if I don't use

6

something, I sit up, turn on my bedside lamp and reach for ibuprofen and water. I know I dare not use anything more potent. Feeling as I do, I might never stop.

Mac suggested I get a stronger prescription from a doctor. I don't want to see my doctor. All this stress has worn my body down but there's no way I can promise to take life easier. I already know that's what she'll tell me. She has no idea. No idea at all.

I don't know anyone who understands what's happening to me. That isolates me. Who can I turn to?

Mac. He left. He's gone.

I've been depending on him and he's gone. My need for his help is intense and adds to my sense of loss. How will I face this without him? He knows how to deal with these things. I don't. His going left a hole in my life.

To fill the nothing, I'm forcing myself to write the events of last week in this journal. I have to write this or I'll lose touch. More and more, I'm losing touch with time, place, maybe even reality. I'm so scared.

He walked out without even saying goodbye. We disagreed completely on what should be done next.

One thing is now very clear to me. Ardith wants everything I inherited from Conrad and I know she'll do anything to get it. But that's another unknown. Where is she? She's supposed to be in police custody in England. They said they'd contact me. They haven't. I sent Alex and Cory there so they'll be totally safe from that crazy woman. I want assurances that plan is actually working.

If AJ is in the hands of El Cocodrilo, then I believe I can use a ransom offer to free him and bring The Crocodile into the hands of the Mexican Federales. Mac was totally opposed to that. He said that wouldn't work, that it would get AJ killed. He argued that we should go to Mexico secretly and use his contacts to find AJ, to connect with Ramón and Jorge.

He left to do it his way. I am so hurt.

No. More than that. I'm angry!

When I awoke this morning in another cold sweat, it was the eighth straight night of constant nightmares. Every muscle in my body feels weak, drags at me when I try to move. It's not just my own exhaustion and fear. I feel AJ. He's very ill and in terrible danger. I feel the threats to him. I want to be in Mexico looking for him. Every day is one more frustrating twenty-four hours of delay.

...journal...10am...

I cling to some comforts. Marnie is at a Swiss treatment center, safe for now, thanks to Louie de la Vergne. Cory and Alex, in our apartment in London, are watched over by Vincent Grant's security detail. Cory has been seen by a doctor and I'm waiting for the news about what it will take to heal his leg. After that—

8

that one last thing—I must go to Mexico. I can't delay any longer.

And...Great Relief!!! Cait and her teen sons, Andrew and Seamus, Caroline and her twin boys, Jake and Jim, and Marthe—all are somewhere Stacy Andre has sent them—again going through the files Art left so long ago in our attic.

They won't find anything. Greg told me that the clues I found in them led, after a thorough police investigation, to nothing. I'm sure that's one of the reasons Captain Schwartzkopf released the files—because there's nothing there. The real reason is, I believe, to give them a harmless task which has gotten Cait and company out of *his* hair. Apparently, she gave him a large piece of her mind about Ben, in his undercover police role, recruiting her older sons, Sean and Mike, to become confidential informers. Cait has always been a force of nature.

From my point of view, what's best about what they're all doing is that they're out of any possible danger they'd be in if they were here in Green Bay.

Liam, young and so wounded and vulnerable from Clayton's sexual abuse, is out of danger too. Cait got him into a place for the treatment of sexually abused boys. I've had no news on how he's doing.

I've relied on Cait and Caroline for friendship and support. Now I don't have the right to involve them. It's not their fight. If I'm totally honest with myself, I feel a lot of guilt for my part in involving any friends at all in my own problems. Hindsight—the old 20/20. How would I have kept them out? How would I have known, back in September of last year, when this all began, that it would get to this state of affairs?

Anna, if you are completely honest with yourself, didn't it begin long before that, with Art's death almost eight years ago? Or did it begin much farther back?

What was Art doing all those years?

...journal...

A cold lashing rain. October wind rattles the windows. In the dark just before dawn I went out on the garage roof patio and stood there letting it beat at me, hoping it would drive this crazy feeling away.

It didn't.

Again, I just have to write.

Stacy has security around me but Mac slipped away without them knowing it. It sent her into a tailspin. She's doing her best but she's still working hard to recruit more members for her security team. When she broke with Vincent Grant, he sent word out to the security world that she opposed him. Now, finding and vetting out employees of her own is taking more time than she anticipated.

She tried again today to contact Melissa. We will definitely need her to help us in Mexico. She knows that country like we do not. We both want to think she's still there, but we can't help but wonder if she's alive or dead. It's so

10

dangerous there. We don't say that to each other. What has happened to her? She was supposed to leave Mexico with Louie and Marnie.

I must keep Grant's firm as my security team for the boys in London and I feel uneasy about that. Stacy said they'll be safe with his company but I just wonder if there's something wrong with his firm. Stacy said it's him, that he's sexist and very arrogant. She and Melissa both saw that in him. Melissa left his firm because he demanded she marry him. He made a big mistake mistreating them. They're both very sharp women. If Stacy—we—could connect with Melissa, we'd both feel a lot better.

I've tried to contact Ramón and Jorge. No success there either. We'll need all these connections in Mexico.

At least my brothers, Jamie and Pat, and Aunt Carrie, too, are safe here in town. I can be grateful for that. Carrie has her own place to herself now. Jamie and Pat were with her until Jenny O'Keeffe took them into her huge empty house.

When they returned from Ireland, Jenny had to put her mother into a nursing home. The woman, never very stable to begin with, became completely unglued when she came back to that house where Big John abused them all those years. I now believe Big John O'Keeffe abused Mary much more than even Jenny knows and the poor woman couldn't face all those haunting memories. Jenny, on the other hand, has become much stronger and braver. I can sense it in her.

11

I'm not braver. I don't feel courageous at all. I've seen too much. Conrad murdered. Johnny O murdered by his own father. Big John walk to his icy death. My mother murdered. My sons kidnapped. My daughter kidnapped.

I wish I hadn't just written all that down. I can't breathe. I need to lie down...

Night again...no sleep. My brain won't stop. The night drags on. I isolate myself in a small cone of lamplight surrounded and crushed by the weight of tons of darkness. The wind is whining around the house and through the trees, sounding lost, searching for a place to rest.

I'm feeling strange again. Something inside is coming apart. It's more than just lack of decent sleep and the grief I feel at all that loss. I feel irritable, on edge, and strangely dangerous. My senses become so alert I can barely tolerate it. I hear every little sound this house makes and everyone I meet has a pungent smell that marks them as different. It goes on and on and just when I think it won't stop, the odd sensations melt away. Feeling frightened or brave doesn't seem to have anything to do with it. I'm on guard, of course. How could I not be? But it's more than that. What more? I don't know.

I keep losing my sense of time. It's now the first Monday in October. September was all overseas—Ireland and London and France and Switzerland and Italy and Malta—a kaleidoscope of swiftly passing images. Yet there seems to be no time passing, just the unending present.

12

It's disorienting. My sense of place is odd too. I'm here but not really here. I have hours when my house doesn't feel like home. I'm not sure where I'd feel at home anymore.

Events seem long and dragged out, yet it's still less than a week since I've gotten back from all the travels. Or is it? It must be longer. I don't trust the clocks. Even my cell phone seems off. I can't wear my watch. Something about my body throws it off, makes it run too fast.

Sometimes I blank out completely on where we traveled. I planned to write the whole sequence down days ago and then I forgot to do that. Now that I've made a brief list, it still feels unreal.

My dogs are gone. When we left for Ireland I gave them to Sean and Mike to care for and it's kinder to the dogs to leave them with Cait's sons. They're better off where they are but oh, I miss them! I miss touch. I miss warmth. I miss joy. I miss...

This journal is a mess. I have to get my mind and my life in some order.

The worst of it, the very worst—the thing that haunts me most—that sucks my mind into chaotic yet futile and useless speculation—is being told by Ardith that it was not Art's body in that plane long ago. How can that be? How can that possibly be? I can't bring myself to face that at all. It has to be another of her crazy manipulations. It must be! It's got to be!

Don't go there, Anna! Just don't go there!

That brings up the question of how we all missed her craziness for the past umpteen years. How did Conrad miss it? He was smart. He had a knack for reading people. How did he not see what she is? She and Clayton Foster had to have deceived Conrad for years. How could that happen?

This dream is the most frightening of all...

...AJ is being tortured, lowered on ropes again and again into the waters of a cenote, struggling underwater to come up and breathe, yanked up, nearly drowning, at the last minute. When he comes up for air, gray waters pour down on him—a river of sorrow formed from the tears of his brothers and sister. Below him, a crocodile rises from the depths, jaws open. Above him a half-formed figure is manipulating small puppets. The puppets are all of us—everyone involved so far—in London, in Europe, in Mexico, in Wisconsin. The puppet master is Art, screaming obscenities and jerking our strings, hatred oozing out of him in bloody drops of wine. Ardith stands with him, smiling, laughing, her eyes adoring him.

I have dreamed that seven times...so far.

Where is AJ?

Where is Stacy now? Has she gotten the others to safety?

14

Two

Stacy Andre shoved the accelerator to the floor and raced down Highway 8 toward Wisconsin Dells, spraying dark water into the rainy night, hoping no police were monitoring traffic speed at 2:34 a.m., and hoping the driver of the van following her could stay right behind without any other car intervening. *Every second counts now. I sure hope our luck holds.*

She hit the button for the Bluetooth connection and Cait's voice answered immediately.

"We're ready. Caroline and all the boys are packed. So is Marthe. How far away are you?"

"Less than twenty miles. Don't leave your rooms until you hear me outside your patio door."

"What about all the files? We can't leave them. I know you said to just pack us up and not worry about the files, but we got them all into my room. Thank god for four teenage boys who can haul stuff easily."

"You've got them all in your room? Oh, dear god, Cait! That means you're sitting ducks! The files are what they want most. They plan to kill all of you. You're the expendable ones. Let's just hope the leak in the police department hasn't discovered all the information yet, like, what your room numbers are. I don't know how they found out where you are. I didn't tell anyone with GB police."

15

"You underestimate us. They'd have to send an army."

"You underestimate them! They just might do that. Stay on this line with me. I'm closing in on you fast. I have three men coming up from Madison and they should be there right now. Another crew is behind me, just in case."

"OK. See you soon."

Stacy's brain was racing far faster than her vehicle. She played the last days since they had returned from Europe over and over in her mind, looking for cues she should have seen, wondering who the leak in the police department was and how much the person knew and if the information she had was correct and if maybe it was a false lead designed to remove her from guarding Anna. Not for the first time, Stacy wished she had more time to build her business.

How could anyone have found out? I kept that to myself. Did someone hack my computer or my phone? Damn!

True, I can call Vincent Grant and grovel and he'll help me but I'll be victim again to his appalling arrogance. Am I arrogant too? Should I swallow my pride and ask for more help? He's on the case in London and Europe. I can't even begin to cover that.

I can't go back to working for him. Even Melissa won't work for him anymore and she's a lot tougher than I am. I can't go back there. If I could just connect with her! Where is she? Why is she not answering her phone? I hope she's still in Mexico.

News of a leak, of someone within the police department talking about the location of the files, had reached her ears by mere chance. She had been meeting with Greg Klarkowski at the Green Bay Police Department to coordinate her protection of Anna with him and had, out of the urgency of nervous bowels, slipped into a stall in the more convenient men's bathroom. She heard someone come in, a male voice talking, just as she finished and was ready to stand up and leave. She remained on the toilet, instinctively pulling her legs up, locking her arms around her knees, and freezing. She heard someone walk up and down, checking the stalls. He stopped outside hers.

His voice tone was commanding, cold, somewhat muffled, as if his hand was cupped around his mouth, but it bounced off the tiled walls and carried easily into the stall where she huddled.

"That's right. Wisconsin Dells. You have the name of the resort. Three women, four teenage boys. There are boxes of files. Those files are the priority. You'll need a truck."

There was a long silence. Stacy took tiny quiet breaths, fearing the man would hear her breathing, would check behind her door.

"The humans don't matter. Take their bodies to the helicopter at the rendezvous place. He'll dispose of them out in Lake Michigan. It will be months, maybe years, before they find them. Their disappearance will raise unholy hell and keep Green Bay police and press occupied for a long time. That will take attention away from everything we do."

Silence, then someone walking out, the door closing. She stayed in the stall, crouching on the toilet seat, praying it was safe, until she could get her heart to stop racing, calm her breathing down and gulp in enough oxygen to steady her mind and body. Cautiously she uncurled her legs, set them on the floor, stood, pulled up her pants and eased open the stall door. Clear. Skipping any hand-washing, she moved into the corridor, down the hall and, by some miracle, she met no one. Heading back to Greg's desk, it began to dawn on her that she couldn't trust a single person in sight.

It could have been Greg, or any of these men. He didn't sound like Greg, but I can't be sure. Not a woman. Maybe a woman? No. Unless the voice was disguised? I don't think so. Midwest accent. Someone from this area. Well, yes, of course, Stacy! It would be! Get a grip on yourself, woman!

Her face fixed in what she hoped was a bland mask, hiding her fear, she made her way through the busy room. When she got to the desk she was using, she picked up her briefcase.

No sign of someone opening it but that doesn't mean anything. It could have been opened and shut again, but there wouldn't be time to get any info off my laptop.

As her eyes moved over the men and women in the room, her stomach grew icy, frozen into stone. It hit her again, in full this time, that there was no authority—none—that she could trust. *Not one single person in this police department!*

Wait! There's Ben. Technically he's still a cop although his cover is that the department fired him. There's Sean and Mike, but no actual police officer, not even Greg, who I'm absolutely sure I can trust. I'll have to move carefully because if Sean and Ben and Mike become suspected of working with me, we won't have any other resources. Wait! There's Mac. He needs to know this. He'll help. I must, must, must get hold of Melissa! And damn, I'll have to call Vincent! He'll have to know about this.

Detective Greg Klarkowski was draped over his chair, reading a file and running his fingers through thinning brown hair. He straightened as she approached.

"Greg, I'm going back to Anna's house. I hope we're done here. I have more to do to arrange for her trip to Mexico. She's talking about publicly offering a huge ransom for AJ. That's against my advice, by the way, because I just know that will bring lots of bottom-feeders out of every nook and cranny down there. I'm desperately in need of a few Mexican police I can trust."

"Good luck with that! I didn't think that was possible but then again, I hear some of the national police are not corrupted...yet. I wouldn't count on the locals though. From what I hear, money doesn't just talk down there, it roars."

Forehead a washboard of worry lines, he continued, "Can you just let me know if Cait and company are okay? Frankly, I'm nervous that you'll be leaving for Mexico and no one knows where they are. Well, they aren't where *I* know. Will you at least tell me when you go? Have they discovered anything? Captain Schwartzkopf asked this morning if there's anything new regarding those files. He wrote them off months ago or he'd never have let you take them but I think he's hoping fresh eyes will find something."

"No news yet, Greg. I'll make sure they're safe. Don't worry. No promises that I'll tell you where they are but I'll think about it. Please just accept that for now."

"Ok, ok. Maybe I shouldn't worry. It seems the drug scene is quiet here at the moment. We have a DEA guy here, a Texan, as an advisor, so that's a help. You take care and call before you leave, will you? When are you leaving?"

"We haven't decided yet. Mac and Anna and I are having a planning session tonight. We'll leave as soon as plans and protection for Anna are in place for her TV appearance down there. I'll call you. Be prepared for a media onslaught up here as well. Horribly, this is already making international news. There's huge speculation in the gossip press, those bottom-feeders, about how much Anna will offer for AJ's freedom. They're already assuming he's been taken by someone. We don't even know that yet. I don't look forward to this."

"I wouldn't either. I don't envy you at all."

20

Stacy left the department feeling guilty for not telling Greg where she had sequestered the women and boys.

After all, he is Cait's partner, but what if he's the one? What if he isn't but would talk to the person who is the traitor, not even knowing who it could be? Who could it be? Anyone. That's the scary part, and I don't have time to discover who. I have to get them out of Wisconsin Dells and somewhere else. I have no time to waste.

First I have to connect with Sean and Mike and Ben. How? Where? Jenny's! Go there and tell her about this. Let her find them and alert them.

She had driven through some of the streets, watching to see if she was being followed. Finally, she realized that was silly. They all knew where she was staying and that she was working for Anna. She drove to Jenny's, parked in the alley where high shrubs hid her car from the street, and ran in. Jenny promised to get the word out.

Back at Anna's, she warned the three men she had there as guards to watch for anything suspicious and called Mac and Anna into a meeting right away.

It had not gone well.

Three

"Bloody damn and hell!"

"Sorry," Mac said, lowering his voice a few notches. "This just gets worse. They were supposed to be safe, out of this, doing something innocuous, so they wouldn't become targets."

He paced the floor, circling around and around the dining room table.

"You know what this means, don't you? If the files are the target, those women and kids will be collateral damage. How fast can you get someone to them? Stacy, you've got to get them out of there! You know what else this means? You've got a leak somewhere."

Mac's doubts had been there before. Now his concern, that Stacy had not had enough experience or enough personnel in her organization to protect Anna and the others, exploded to the surface in the anger and frustration he'd been keeping under rigid control.

Stacy sat down at the head of the table, bending over her computer to let her long blonde hair cover the hurt, anger and disappointment she couldn't keep from her face.

"I know! I know! Calm down, please! I've got someone on it. I'd already recruited three men in the Madison area who I've vetted out carefully. I called them on the way here and they'll be getting to the Dells later tonight. I'll have everyone moved by tomorrow. Right now we have to plan Anna's trip and, Mac, I want you with us on this."

"No. I won't do that."

Stacy's head jerked up and her eyes widened.

Anna looked up from the chair where she sat. He knew she was unbearably tired, saw the dark circles under her eyes, her facial muscles sagging. He knew her nightmares were coming again and again. She had told him of the ghost of Sheila wailing and AJ following her, stumbling, dying. There were more moments now where she felt she would not find AJ in time, that his death was inevitable.

"Mac? Why not? Why won't you go with me? I need you with me! I don't know how to walk through any of this. I don't know what to do."

Her voice shook.

Mac stopped pacing and looked at her, seeing her exhaustion and feeling like a terrible traitor.

"Anna, if I become known to the press and the police and the cartels down there, I won't be of any use to you at all. Virtually every contact I have will disappear. They won't want to be seen with me. My strength is that very few people really know me, that I can wear dozens of disguises and move anywhere. That's how I'm most useful, how I get information, how I get things done. I'm not good with media, or in the spotlight. I know my limitations."

Anna's face sagged into further disappointment. A gray fog closed around her. She opened her mouth to say something but no sound came out and she forgot to close it, just sitting, staring at Mac as if she had never known him.

"Anna! I'm sorry! I'm so sorry! I know this feels like I'm deserting you but we've had no news about AJ and I feel it's urgent that I get to the contacts I have down there. I can go places and I have connections that no one else has. So far even Ramon and Jorge haven't found him. So far none of us have been able to get hold of Ramon or Jorge or Adelina or anyone. I have to get down there to find out what's going on. I have to do it unhampered by you or Stacy or anyone and I have to do it as quickly as possible."

The phone rang in the library and Stacy jumped, then got up and went through the door to answer it.

Anna didn't move.

Mac stood opposite her across the table, silent, his mouth a thin line, his body rigid.

"Anna, it's the boys in London. They're on Skype."

Anna pushed herself up slowly and, without looking at Mac, went into the library. Both Cory and Alex were in front of their computer.

"Hey, Mom! Look! We hooked up a better camera and you can see both of us more easily." Cory grinned at her. Alex waved.

"You both look great. Tell me what the doctor said, Cory. He's seen your leg. His nurse called and told me that much but she didn't have his decision yet."

24

"Only two operations, not three and lots of physical therapy in between. Piece of cake, Mom. I can even attend school while I do it. I'll only miss a week or two and I've got the name of another student who can tutor me if necessary."

Alex leaned in. "He can do it, Mom. The operations are three months apart and the muscle will heal with little or no scarring and he'll be as good as new."

"What about your internship, Alex? Have you got that started yet?"

"No. Not yet. We got Cory settled first because I didn't know if I'd have to help him, you know, push his wheelchair and all."

Cory punched Alex in the arm and Alex feigned injury.

"See, now I'll have to be seen by the doctor too." He grinned. "Don't worry, Mom. We're doing fine. Our bodyguards are guarding our bodies constantly. Too constantly. It's really boring having them around telling us no-no all the time."

Alex made a face at someone off camera.

"Yes, well, I want you to listen to them. There's still no news of AJ and I don't want anything to happen to you too."

Cory leaned in, looking worried. "Mom, I'm having dreams of AJ and they're not good. He's really sick. You and Mac have to get down there soon."

"I know, Cory. So am I. Having dreams, I mean. We're in a meeting planning what to do right now and then we'll be going there. I'll keep you posted. Will you call Marnie and give her your good news? Tell her I'll call her just before I leave and let her know the plans. Ok?"

"Yeah, we'll do that. Mom, try to get some sleep. You look awful."

"Oh golly, thanks. I just love hearing that. Take care. I love you both very much. I don't want you in harm's way too. And, yes, Alex, I know you want to be in Mexico searching for your brother. I know you both do, but please, no more adventures for a while. I have to know you're both safe. Please, please, stay safe."

"Ok Mom. We will." Echoes of "love you" floated across an ocean and half a continent as the connection dissolved.

Anna looked at Stacy. "Let's get this done."

When they entered the dining room, Mac was not there. Anna called and he didn't answer.

"He must be upstairs," said Stacy. She sat down, booted her laptop back into action and began again on arrangements for their travel.

The ache in Anna's heart warned her as she climbed slowly up the front staircase to the second floor. *He's gone. I know he's gone. He won't do what we want, what I want or need. I'm a drag on him.*

Disappointment and hurt washed through her as she walked into their bedroom. A quick look told her the gear Mac had sorted out and packed the day before was gone. Tears came as she sat on the edge of the bed.

He's deserted me. Us. There is no "us" to him. He's a loner. I should have known. It was

26

his plan all along. I should have known. It's my own fault. My judgment is so off, so skewed when it comes to men. It went off base down in Mexico and I've made such poor choices. How could I have let myself do that?

"Hell and damn!" Stacy swore when Anna returned and told her what Mac must have done. She called in the guards. They had not even seen him leave.

"That's not possible. No one can disappear like that!"

"Mac can," said Anna as she sank onto a chair. "That's why he was so interested in the basement and spent so much time there. He set that up from the first. He told me he reinforced the tunnel in case he had to get us all out fast. I've been so distracted I never even thought that he did it for himself too. He always tries to have an out.

"I hate that he's gone and I'm furious that he sneaked out instead of facing us, but I think maybe he's right, Stacy. He has to do it his way. We'll have to do it ours. I'm offering a ransom of one million dollars. That will make it worth anyone's while to find AJ."

She held up her hand at Stacy's protest.

"Yes, yes, yes, I know it will attract the greediest of the greedy, that it will be hard to control—a press and publicity zoo if there ever was one—but maybe it will also save AJ's life.

"You go! Leave right now! Don't wait for tomorrow. You have to move Cait and Caroline and the others to safety before we go. I'll be fine.

27

The guards here are enough and we'll call police if we need them. I'm calling Robert de la Vergne in Switzerland and selling assets so I have the cash ready."

Stacy began to protest. "Anna, I have to tell you..."

Anna stood up and waved her out.

"Go! Go! Get them safe! I can't bear to leave thinking they're in danger. I'll be packed and ready when you return."

"Anna, you can't call police! Don't you see? I know they're in danger because there's a dirty cop in the police department!" Again, she related to Anna all she had heard. "I don't know who it is and I'm sure the department doesn't either. You have only the guards here."

Anna stood very still and silent, eyes closed. After long minutes, she shuddered, took several deep breaths, walked to the table where Stacy sat, gently pushed her out of the chair, and sat down.

"Go! I'll finish our arrangements for Mexico. I'll be fine. Just please get them all out of there! Now!"

Four

Cait and Caroline huddled on the rug at the foot of the chair where Marthe sat.

"We've done all we can do," Caroline said. "Everything's packed, the files are here, the doors have those heavy dressers in front of them, and even the patio doors are blocked. How far is Stacy now?"

"She's about fifteen minutes away, maybe a bit less. I'm worried. What if we've been watched this whole time? If there's a leak..." Cait's voice trailed off as her mind ran through the police she knew. Then she continued.

"There was supposed to be only one man who knew where we are, where the files are—the captain who authorized it—Schwartzkopf. God! What if he's the one? There's other news too. Apparently, Mac left for Mexico on his own. Stacy said he's disappeared and..."

At that moment, Jake burst in from their bedroom, followed by his twin, Jim, and Cait's sons, Andrew and Seamus. Jake's face told Caroline he was scared.

"What is it?" she asked.

"There are three men out there in the dark beyond the parking lot. They aren't moving or anything, just standing about twenty feet apart. They're armed. I saw the light hit metal and the shape of some kind of gun. Mom, what can we do? I'm scared."

Caroline exchanged glances with the other women. Her throat constricted in fear. She couldn't answer.

"We do nothing right now," Marthe replied firmly. "Stay away from the windows or doors. They might see the curtains move or see one of you move. You don't want to be a target. Those could be the men Stacy sent here. We only have minutes to wait. You know this could all be for nothing. We found absolutely nothing in our first read-through of those files."

"There's not nothing," Andrew declared. "I mean, there really is something. Sort of. We found it."

"What are you talking about?" Cait's eyes widened and she glared at them. "You weren't supposed to lay a hand on those files, let alone eyes. When did you do that?"

Jim and Jake glanced at Caroline, whose eyebrows had risen to new heights.

"It's ok, Mom! It's ok," Jim reassured her. "We didn't mess them up or anything. We kept them in perfect order, but we did find something. You know how Mrs. Kinnealy found a code or thought she did? Well, we followed her line of thinking and figured there might be a code *on* some of the files and *in* them too. And, this is *totally* important, there could be what is called allegorical code as well. I learned about that in ancient history studies. The Hebrews used it and the Egyptians and well, we found there's both signs on the files and a written code within. Or something..."

His voice trailed off as her eyes widened.

Jake continued, his enthusiasm undaunted by her look. "Yeah! Mrs. K was right! On the outside, it looks like nothing, like, old and faded. Just on *some* of the files. Well, actually, on quite a few of the files from the old times but maybe not so many recently. We didn't get through all of them yet."

Caroline found her voice. "Yet? Yet?" she gasped. "You were supposed to be doing homework. When did you do this and when were you planning to continue? What signs are you talking about? We found no signs. Any signs Anna found were investigated by police and led nowhere."

Jake went to his backpack and dug out a book. He handed it to Caroline.

"It's about lost languages of the world. I used it for one of my papers for school 'cause I like writing about weird stuff, old stuff. You know that. I found a copy in Anna's attic when we were hanging out with Cory and Alex early last summer, before they were kidnapped up north," he explained. "It's ok, Mom. Cory said I could borrow it. He said it must have been with his dad's stuff. I gave his back but I got my own from online."

Caroline read the title. *Lost Languages of the World: The Enigma of the World's Undeciphered Scripts* by Andrew Robinson. She checked the publication information inside. "What has this to do with signs?"

Jim deepened his fourteen-year-old voice and tried hard to take on a mature and scholarly look. "Well, Mom, those languages are written in really different scripts. So far, in my research," he stopped as three fists hit his arms, "sorry, guys, *our* research—I found five different symbols that were on the files. Not *in* the files, *on* them, small, faint or faded, down in one corner of the file itself. I'm sure they mean something. So, Mrs. K. was right but she didn't take it far enough. Neither did police."

Cait was opening a box of files. "Show me!"

Jim went to the box and began pulling out files, checking one corner on the rear of each. "No, these are newer."

He went to another box. "These too."

He checked a third and after pulling a few, he held out a file to her and pointed.

"He's right. Which language, Jim?"

Jim opened the book, found a page with the corner bent and pointed.

"I marked that page in the book. There's more. Other scripts were used too. And there's definitely that color coding. It's faint and small, like, you know, on the edges of some files. There's blue, red, and maybe a yellow but we can't be sure about that color. It's so very faint. They're all faded. We know why they're there. There were multiple ways of coding—layers, and each layer is a different set of information.

"So, then Seamus went online and he started researching the names of the people on these files—you know, in census files, for example. Some of the names are, we think, fictitious. Others might have been members of a group, maybe a group who controlled illegal activities or participated in them, and when we read the fake files, there's a kind of weirdness to the legal language that could be that allegorical code, a disguise of what was really..."

A small commotion in the corridor was followed by knocking on the door, and they froze.

Caroline was the first up and moving. She grabbed her own backpack, stuffed the book in, and tossed it to them.

"Boys, go in your bedroom!" she hissed. "Marthe, you too! Push the dresser in front of the door and get in that walk-in closet like we planned. Stay down on the floor. Seamus, here's my phone. Text Stacy what's happening."

Marthe stood up and shoved the nearest boys toward the bedroom door. Once inside, she and the boys followed Caroline's commands. They heard a coarse voice yelling. "Room service! Your food is here."

"We didn't order food, you idiots, and nobody with a voice like that will ever get me to open a door," Cait muttered as she pulled out knives from under the couch.

Caroline stared at them. "You've been busy too, I see. Just how much help will those be? I think whoever is out there has guns."

"Hell, I don't know, but I have no gun permit, don't own one, and don't know how to use one anyway. Neither do you. I know it's silly and probably useless but I just wanted something. Anything."

More pounding and another insistent request to "Open up!"

Cait frowned. "That voice sounds drunk. The hotel bar closed about a half hour ago. Maybe it's drunks wandering the corridor. Or it could be pretense, a diversion to keep us near that door while they come from the back. My phone is still connected to Stacy. I hope she can hear this. She can't be far away now."

Caroline shoved the files back into the boxes and closed them.

"Let's buy time and just keep silent and pretend we're gone. If it is drunks, they might just give up."

Stacy Andre pulled up to the resort, the van following right behind. She raced to the patio entrance of Cait's suite. Three men stepped out of the shadows and stopped her.

"Someone's pounding on their door," said one of them. "We may not be in time."

"I heard it on Cait's phone and got a text from one of the boys. I already ordered my other two men into the corridor. They'll take out whoever it is." She rapped on the patio door.

Cait, peering through the barricade, breathed a sigh of relief. She signaled Caroline to help her and they cleared one side and let Stacy and the men in.

"Get the women and boys out first. If we must leave fast, don't waste time on the files," Stacy commanded.

Caroline interrupted her. "No! The files go first! The boys just told us there's something about the files we hadn't found before. Get them out first. Then Marthe and the boys. Then us. We'll fill you in later."

Cait stood near the door to the corridor, a long butcher knife in her hand.

"No pounding. No sound. There was someone, maybe more than one person, at the door."

Stacy nodded. "I have someone removing them. Leave the barricade up. Where are the boys and Marthe?"

The bedroom door opened and all five came out.

"Quickly. Get this all to the truck and, you boys and Marthe, get all luggage into my van."

"Where will we be going?" Jim asked.

"Only I know that," Stacy answered, "and I'm not even mentioning it until I get you there. We have a long way to go. Move fast! Don't ask questions!"

Her phone beeped and she held it to her ear.

"They were armed? No surprise there. You know where to bring them. Search them and run photos, prints, and DNA on them. Search the grounds for their transportation, and for any other men too. Whatever you do, don't let them communicate with anyone. I hope they haven't connected with anyone already. If they have phones, trace all calls. When you have all that information, turn them over to the FBI. I've already notified them."

She ended that call and dialed a number in Green Bay.

"Jenny, is Sean there? Good. Put him on. Sean, did Jenny fill you in? Ok, here's what I want you guys to do. When your mom and the others aren't found, and it becomes clear they've escaped, I want to know of anyone, I mean anyone, in the police departments, city and county, who are even slightly interested. Who persists in searching for them? Who fishes for information? Who wants their hands on those files? Who makes careful inquiries and appears to tread lightly? I know you might not be able to get that information, but right now you, Mike and Ben are the only ones I can trust."

She listened. "Yeah, there's much more in the files than anyone thought."

Sean Fitzgerald breathed a sigh of relief. He covered the phone. "They're safe."

Mike thrust his fist up and pulled it down and in. "Yes!" He nodded his head, grinning. "Tell Mom we've got her back."

Sean turned to Ben as he conveyed the message and ended the call. "There's something in or about the files they just discovered, but what it means they don't know yet. You were right. One of your police buddies—maybe more than one—must want those files bad. We have to find out who."

Ben's stomach turned over. It was the worst he had imagined. A dirty cop. He had been suspicious for over a month, but had told no one. There was no one, not one person on the force he could tell. He had not said anything to Sean and Mike because he couldn't be sure. *I didn't want to be sure. I didn't want to find out.* Just before Stacy's call, he had told them of his own unease.

"My contact on the drug scene—Mr. 'Black', the guy who's handling me—has too much inside information. He's cautious but he drops little bits and pieces of info that he shouldn't know. He's got an inside contact somewhere. I've been pretending to become more and more addicted and he's careless around me about what he says.

"If I don't find out who that is...well...I'm known to be connected to you both and to have been in on the investigation of the murder attempts on Anna Kinnealy. You're Cait's sons. He's made that threat to kill you. Any one of us is a candidate for a bullet. We'll have to watch our backs 24/7. We need to find someplace secure where we can hole up. My apartment, your apartment, and your mom's house are known to everyone in law enforcement and on the street."

"I know where," Sean grinned. "Anna's house, and I know how to get in without anyone seeing us."

He looked at his brother.

"The tunnel, remember?"

He looked at Ben.

"You didn't hear that, officer."

"I know about the tunnel. I thought Mrs. K had that closed up." Ben said. "And what about Jenny's? Her house is a possibility too."

"She did close it up," Sean replied, "but Mac was busy while he was there. He checked out every nook and cranny in that house and found it. He opened it up and we helped him reinforce it just in case he had to get Anna out in an emergency. That's how he got out so fast and without detection. I love a guy with a mind like that. Devious."

"How did he get past Stacy's security? She had men stationed inside and out."

"Diversion, I guess. I'm not sure how, but he's good...really, really good. I say that's our first choice. I'm not so sure Jenny's would be as secure."

"Let's check out Anna's as soon as she and Stacy are gone to Mexico," Mike said. "Stacy will pull security away. We'll make it look like we're just going to work or school as usual from our own places, like everything's normal, but we can sneak in and, if it feels right, use that as our headquarters at night. I love it."

Ben looked skeptical. Yet..."meeting in the least expected place. It might work."

An old country music song played quietly from the speakers, glassware clinked down the bar where the bartender was washing dishes, and uneven shards of conversation fell in the air around him.

Greg toyed with the lukewarm glass of beer in front of him. For an entire hour he had been running a video in his mind of all the police he'd ever worked for or with in his thirteen years on the force.

Early in the morning he had pulled every file related to the Kinnealys, O'Keeffes, and their law firm, including their dead partners, Soderberg and Moss—and the Foster and Wentworth law firm which included the woman known as Ardith Seacrest. By 4:15 pm he knew something was very wrong. There were too many questions which should have been answered and weren't, evidence that was not fully investigated, reports that seemed to have small parts missing or bits of information left out. *Except what we, Iron Mike and I, did, this is downright sloppy police work.*

Over time, numerous officers had worked on different aspects of these cases so no name stood out. As far as he knew, all had good records. Nothing could be used to convict anyone and there seemed no way to connect the dots but then...*nothing big, just bits that ought to be there in a thorough investigation but they aren't...bits and pieces...*

He had made a list of every missing item he could identify. Then he added another list of all the police officers in the Green Bay department who had been part of those cases, hoping he could find just one name that stood out, that had total access. *Yeah, Captain Arnie*

Schwartzkopf, that was his responsibility, but...I don't want to think that.

At the top of the rank and file he'd put his own name and Iron Mike's, his partner for the last ten years. Iron Mike had just retired. He didn't seem to be living high on his retirement income. No sign that he ever was on the take.

Greg had listed everyone who had retired, knowing he would have to follow any money trails. He had then listed anyone still on active duty, going all the way up the chain of command, ending with the chief's name. He had added to that list anyone he knew in the Brown County Sheriff's Department who may have been on the cases and followed that chain to the top. In the end, he could cross out only his own name and Ben's. *I can't even cross out Iron Mike. I've trusted him with my life but I can't rule him out yet. I'll have to go to IA. God! I hate that idea!*

He couldn't finish his beer. Stress had his stomach churning and his bowels cramping. Try as he might, he couldn't make the label on the bottle read anything but "Dirty Cop." *No. Cops. More than one. For years. At least eight years but probably much more.*

If there are dirty cops, that means Cait and her sons and every single person involved in these families are all at risk. Can I talk to Stacy? She's not in it. She hasn't been involved long enough. But she's gone to get the women and boys to safety and after that she'll be gone to Mexico with Anna. I can't do this alone. Damn, I wish I had Mac here right now!

Greg shoved the beer away, left two dollars and change for the bartender, ran through the cold rain, slid into his Camry and headed north to St. Pat's.

"Do you think he's onto something, that he suspects something? He was buried in our police files all day," the thin man in the booth at the rear of the bar asked.

"Nah! I've read those files. Anything that might have been in there was carefully edited out long ago. I know. I worked on that. No traces left. He wouldn't know what to look for anyway. No one does. Come on. We have a meeting."

They left the bar by the rear entrance and walked south through the alleys to their rendezvous.

At St. Pat's, Father O'Doul, coming from the sacristy, nodded to Greg, bent over and whispered, "Wait until everyone else is gone," kissed his stole and put it on, entered the confessional and prepared himself to hear more of the secrets people unburdened on him.

He was never surprised by what he heard anymore, but the confessions of sinners these days often sent him to his knees praying far more earnestly than he'd ever done for the town and people he served.

Though he would never break the sacred seal of confidentiality, the confessional was always a good connecting point, an unlikely meeting place. Greg, Ben, Sean and Mike now made their point of connection with him.

Five

The land of the Oneida Indian Reservation intermingles sometimes reluctantly, but usually cooperatively with the far west side of Green Bay. Forced from their eastern lands by the white immigrants to North America, it was once a place of extreme poverty and addiction to alcohol. But underneath that oppressive dominant cultural overlay lived the Faith Keepers who kept the ways of the Old Ones and, generation by generation, drew their people upward.

Big Abe had lived his own story of addiction to alcohol and knew chapter and verse of the long story of the work tribal members had to do to lift his people out of that horror. *Not gonna happen again! Not if I can help it.*

When Abraham Lemke stood up, heads were forced to roll back as his six foot, eight-inch frame kept rising until his dark hair was haloed by the clouds in the sky. His square face was scarred and pitted here and there, old pale splotches against his caramel-brown skin. Before he got straight and sober, Big Abe had scattered a rough and colorful swath of mayhem from Canada through Mexico.

He looked at his body in the mirror behind the door.

"Not a Big Belly yet," he mused, but he could see the fat creeping onto his swelling waistline under his tribal police uniform. He didn't like it. He made a vow to increase his

42

exercise in the gym and cut way down on the delicious fry bread his girlfriend fed him.

Even more disturbing than his weight and the heroin invading his tribe, however, was the man he'd seen at the drug training he had attended at the Brown County Sheriff's Department the previous day. Abe had been far back in the long room. He'd arrived late and there were two chairs left, both in the last row. He was seated in one of them when the man, who had stationed himself in the shadow of a pillar at the front of the room, had stepped out briefly to be introduced. It was enough. Abe's chest and shoulder muscles had tightened with both anger and suspicion when he glimpsed the man. Drunk and stoned or sober, Abe had a monumental memory for voices, faces and places.

This particular voice and face was indelibly connected with Mexico and a clear memory of a brawl between two groups of men. Abe had been making his way through Mayan country, delighted by their welcome of this giant indígeno who towered over them. They treated him like one of their gods and he had loved it.

Loved it, that is, until the night the local police had come to the cantina and attempted to force his Mayan friends into servitude for whatever cartel had wanted bodies. His friends told him to leave, quickly let him know he could be killed later, that the cartel intimidated the people in this way, and that, if not killed, he would be tortured and left in the streets to be covered with flies, ripped apart by wild dogs, or

43

die from infections that would enter his body quickly and fester horribly in the hot, humid climate.

He had laughed at the thought of anyone intimidating him.

Perhaps finding additional courage by having this giant in their midst, this group of Mayans fought, and Abe, well on his way to being roaring drunk, chose to fight with them, wading into the police and cartel enforcers with bare hands, picking them up, breaking their spines over his knee, and throwing their bodies back into the bullets that flew from every side. Of course, he had been wounded eventually, but in some miraculous fragment of luck, it had not been serious. The Mayans had won out, for once, and Abe with them.

Abe never forgot the face he saw behind the police, in the shadows, directing them. He also saw the payoff the man made to others and heard his voice, an unmistakably American voice even though the words were in Spanish, in a thick Texas accent.

I'm hearing that voice and Texas accent again. This can't be good. Why is he way up here? Who does he work for?

Abe made careful inquiries. A DEA agent, he was told, advisor to law enforcement. *Crock of cow puckies! No more DEA than I am. But who does he work for? And who can I trust to talk to who won't blow this?*

That was the question. Under the apparent cooperation with local law enforcement, the tribal police were still subject to subtle racism—an issue that would color—he smiled at the pun—his ability to find out deeper information. His own credibility was an even bigger issue. His record of a wild youth was well known, particularly the mayhem he'd heaped on anyone he could fight against in the Green Bay bars. In any surrounding police departments, he would not be given a job. The tribe, however, had watched his recovery for years and when he was deemed worthy, the elder women had given the nod to hire him.

Abe made a mental note to turn his attention to finding out who he could trust. As it turned out, his miraculous luck, or perhaps, as he believed, his guardian spirit was with him.

Temporarily setting the matter aside, Abe proceeded to Northeast Wisconsin Technical College where he gave a talk on police science and cultural issues to the current class. After he was finished, when all the other students had left, he was approached by a black-haired young man who introduced himself as Mike Fitzgerald. As they talked, Mike told how he'd become involved in some police work already.

Guessing correctly that Mike's role was unknown to most of the police, Abe took him to supper at the Blackstone Restaurant and gently probed. *Contact! Thank you very much, Eagle Spirit!*

Mike took Abe to his apartment to meet his brother Sean and Ben Bennett, a Green Bay police officer working the undercover drug scene with the Fitzgeralds. Abe, his instincts in high gear, decided to tell them what he'd seen. All three grew silent. Abe could see pictures of the other cops they knew flashing through their minds. He waited.

"The problem is, though, who can we tell about this guy?" Ben finally asked.

"We should tell Greg Klarkowski first," Mike said.

"Damn!" Sean erupted out of his seat and began pacing. "We can't tell Greg! I don't want to say this, but how do we know Greg isn't in on this? We can't be sure. We don't know, Mike! We don't even know what 'this' is," he insisted, seeing the protest in Mike's face.

Ben nodded. "Actually, I believe Greg's ok. He got suspicious of a leak and did some digging and sent me confirmation of those suspicions through Father O'Doul. Stacy got word to Jenny who got to the priest too. But we can't take chances on anyone else without more information."

He turned to Abe. "Is that all you can tell us?"

"It is for now. The other thing is, the Texan may have made me. In case you haven't noticed, I kind of stand out in a crowd. That fight was over fifteen years ago, and I had a buzz cut back then and was strung out and thinner but..." He shrugged.

"There is one thing I can do. I can use our tribal police channels to see if I can get any other information on this DEA guy. I can inform the feds too. The FBI has jurisdiction on reservations. Let's meet again next Monday night and I'll let you know what I find. Ok?"

Ben nodded. "That's good, Abe. I couldn't do that without attracting attention at the department. Greg either. He's already got some other cops asking why he pulled all the old Kinnealy files. Your involvement will be a big help. The three of us are working the streets of the West side. I'll try to connect with whoever's working the East side too. Public Relations is saying that the drug scene is quiet at the moment but I know the streets and it's not. In view of our information, I don't trust anything or anyone right now. God, I hate this! Makes me sick, thinking there's someone in the department who's dirty."

He sat down and they planned their agenda for a sweep of both west and east sides for any information they could gather.

"We've got a good team here. Three police, Mike and I as two confidential informers, Fr. O'Doul—he's really committed to helping us." Sean said. "Jenny O'Keefe too. Her dad and brother were mixed up in this. She hates that. Her mom's in the nursing home so she's alone in that house. Well, actually, she's not. There's Anna's brothers, Pat and Jamie O'Reilly, back here from Ireland where they lived for years. Jenny invited them to stay with her. Then there's Aunt Carrie Brennan, lives on her own, a real character if there ever was one. Not afraid of anything or anyone. I'd like to keep them out, seeing as how they're pretty old, but given the nature of those three, we probably can't."

Mike nodded. "Rob Bradley too. His wife Caroline and his twins are in danger. He's got a big stake in this."

Abe stopped them with raised hands. "Whoa! Whoa! Who are these people you're talking about? It sounds like you've got an army."

Sean laughed. "We do, kind of. Anna Kinnealy is a woman from the East side who got mixed up in this when..." and he filled Abe in on the rest of the story. "The whole thing revolves around drugs, a drug group that used Green Bay as a route to get drugs to Canada. We don't know exactly why or how Ardith Seacrest, as secretary to Anna's lawyer, became involved but we know it's been operating since before Anna's husband died. Anna and her kids have become the main family involved, and Ardith's targets. We've all been working to discover what it's all about."

Abe looked thoughtful. "Wow! This is more than I ever imagined. Like I told you, the heroin problem is affecting my tribe and it's getting worse. If it's ok with you, I'm in. I'll go talk to our police chief and I can recruit a few guys I know who live in Green Bay, not tell them the whole thing but have them keep eyes and ears open and report to me."

He grinned. "We make pretty good scouts, you know. Give me a few days and let me see what I can set up."

Six

"I don't have the faintest idea where we are, Rob. It seems to be an old dance hall-motel sort of place. Run down, but the furnace is working so we're not cold at night. There's loads of food in a big cooler in the kitchen. The boys are fine although excited about what they found and fighting doing schoolwork. Stacy has us under heavy guard. I feel safe. But, Rob, don't trust anyone. Stacy told us, before she left, that there's a leak in the police department, maybe in the sheriff's department too."

"Safe or not, honey, I want you to take pics of those markings on the files, and hell, everything in the files themselves, the ones that are marked, and send them to my phone. I'm going to go to the FBI with whatever you find. It's the only backup plan I can figure out right now."

"I will. The boys discovered a lot of old connections just doing newspaper and other online searches. Someone in the police department sure didn't do a very thorough job and, if they did, someone else covered it all up. Stacy said as soon as we get them sorted out, she'll have the files turned over to the FBI because she wants to make sure they don't get buried at the police department again and then she says we'll be out of this. We could have that done today. She hasn't told anyone where we are. She calls three times a day to check on us."

"A lot could happen between now and the time you finish. I want that information now. I wish you were out of this now."

"Me too. I love you. I want to go back to our normal life. Part of me regrets even being friends with Anna. I feel like such a traitor to her but this has disrupted our lives so much."

"I feel the same. I'm beyond worried. If the information gets back to the police, what's to stop another person from losing it? What's to prevent..."

"Someone's coming. I have to go."

Caroline reached back and flushed the toilet she was sitting on, slipped the phone into her bra, and opened the door of the stall. She breathed a sigh of relief when she saw Cait but remained wary. Cait didn't know about the connection with Rob.

"What's taking you so long?" Cait asked. "We've got to sort through the rest of those files. The sooner we get at them, the sooner we can get out of here. I'll be glad when this is over."

She walked into a nearby stall.

"I know. I was just taking my time. Cait, when we get done with this, if there's a leak in the police department, how can we turn these over to them? That means the drug group will have access to this information, doesn't it?"

"Yeah. I suppose." Cait came out of the stall and began washing her hands.

"But it won't be our problem anymore, will it? That's a problem for the police. We can wash our hands of it." She waggled her wet fingers in the air as she grabbed paper towels.

"But it still is our problem! Stacy said the man ordered our deaths, for god's sake! We won't be out of danger. Our sons have been on the internet searching for information on all the persons named in those files. Some of it is pretty suspicious. Marthe and you and I know all this too. We could still be in danger just because of that. I want to get back to our lives as much as you but I want some sort of guarantee that we'll be safe."

Cait finished drying her hands and leaned against the wall. "I see what you mean. But even if we know about this and remember a few names, we don't know what they mean, what they represent, we haven't gotten to the bottom of things, to what was really going on."

"Yes, but there will be those who think we have! I think there might be those who want to bury any knowledge altogether, have it all get "lost" along with anyone who knows about them. Cait, we won't be out of danger and our kids won't be out of danger!"

"OK. Well. So. What can we do about it? We need to come up with some kind of plan that protects us from, from...what? Being killed? Damn, that's scary. I don't know how we can manage that."

"I know one thing I want to do. I want to take pictures of each file, each marking, with my phone. If we have a record of them, and that record is in the hands of someone like the FBI, it can't be made to disappear."

Caroline took a deep breath and lowered her voice.

"Look, I have to let you know that I'm in touch with Rob. We have these cell phones programmed only for each other. He can take the information to the FBI for us and that will eliminate the possibility it will disappear. It won't make us totally safe but it will stop the information, and maybe us, from getting 'lost'."

Cait, hands on her hips, eyes narrowed, grinned wickedly at Caroline.

"Well, you sneak! You outdid me for once. Proper Caroline is capable of subterfuge. Awesome! I like it! So, let's get started."

At 11:37p.m. Rob's phone pinged and images began arriving along with the text, "for FBI." He transferred them to his I-pad and made copies. The information came in for over three hours. By eleven in the morning he was at the office of the FBI in Milwaukee. By ten that evening, complete copies of all marked files were made and assembled, and the FBI had contacted two men in law enforcement who they knew were safe.

Stacy, kept up to date on all procedures, let Cait, Caroline, Marthe and the boys know they were done. Their guards loaded up the luggage and took them home.

Sean, Mike and Ben were briefed by a very upset Cait.

"Here's what we think. We know those files will lead to the names of the people who have been selling drugs all along, way back. Some may still be doing that and, even if they're not, some could be indicted for their past activities. This could lead to prominent families who got, maybe still get, their money from the illegal trade. There may be other crimes, like murders, that were committed but weren't investigated or prosecuted. We need protection. And, another problem," she told them. "I don't want to believe it but how do I know that Greg isn't the leak?"

Ben paced briefly, then sat down in front of her and took her hands. "Look. I don't want to believe it either. I can't find it in me to think of him like that, but we need to wait and see. The only person I'm supposed to contact is Schwartzkopf and I can't trust that he's..." He couldn't say it. "We've got the four of us to protect your boys, and Fr. O'Doul and Jenny and Anna's brothers. Let's plan how to set up protection for all of us until we can connect with the police safely. Stacy told you she'd keep the men on your house, didn't she?"

Cait nodded.

"Well then, let's plan what we can do to collect information. The more we know, the better it will be."

"We don't have to do Caroline and family," Cait said. "Rob has already made plans for them and Marthe to disappear."

Seven

"There's a private jet waiting for us at Austin Straubel, Anna. We fly to Cancun with just one stop for fueling in Miami. We'll wait in a safe room there until the fueling is done, just in case there's any attempt to harm you.

"In Cancun, I've set up your press conference with the Mexican and international press corps. You will announce you are there to search for your son and offer the reward. I still wish you'd make it a half million instead of the million, but any money offered will make it a necessity to follow up every lead that comes in so I suppose the amount is irrelevant in a way."

Stacy, who had arrived only fifteen minutes before, stood in the door to Anna's office. Anna, seated at her desk, held her head in her hands, elbows on the edge of the surface.

"Stacy, there's more."

"What more can there possibly be?"

As she spoke, Anna looked out the window at the fading trees, the dying leaves, and more drizzling rain. The gloom matched her mood.

"Marnie left the treatment center in Switzerland and she's off the map. Louie de la Vergne just called. Marnie's missing. She told the people at the center that she was going to London to take care of her brothers. The boys haven't seen her. She was accompanied by the man who helped Louie and Melissa rescue her in Mexico, Count something-or-other. Charbonneau. That was it. Except, Louie found out he's not a count. He's a fake."

Stacy stood silently cursing Vincent Grant, who Anna had retained to manage her European security, *and a pox on stupid flighty girls, and every other person and thing mixed up in this, and Melissa, who still hasn't returned my calls.*

When Stacy's silence grew too long to bear, Anna continued.

"The boys are safe. Ardith hasn't surfaced in England or France or anywhere else. She's the subject of a massive search by their police. I'm completely ready to leave for Mexico now. I'm packed. The money is available. Marnie's made a poor choice, leaving the treatment center, but I can't monitor her every move. I don't sense she's in danger right now but AJ is in great danger. He's dying or may be dead. I have to go there, although I feel sick about Marnie. This is a terrible choice."

Sophie's Choice. Stacy had seen the movie a long time ago. She whispered the words out loud.

Anna stared at her for long minutes.

"Yes. Well, not quite, but something like that..." her voice trailed off.

"All right," Stacy said. "I will be in the deep background behind you. Four men will surround you at all times. I have emphasized to Mexican police that if there is any attempt on your life, the American State Department will be all over this. Vincent Grant pulled some of his many strings and took care of that. The Mexican National

Police seem to be able to stand up to the cartels, successfully in a few cases, but there is always a chance they're corrupted too.

She set an iPad in front of Anna.

"Here's the entire briefing you need to read on the way to Mexico. I want you to know exactly how bad it is. Every cartel there uses massive intimidation and brutality to keep control. The Nogales cartel was supposedly broken up but the trafficking through Nogales still happens. The ruling members of the old cartel moved to a state just north of Mexico City and they're attempting to take over that state through executions of ordinary people to frighten the population into cooperating. It's succeeding.

"Cartels hold 'ceremonies' using drugs as the attraction and from those ceremonies they recruit 'soldiers', cannon fodder for their wars with each other. And they do use cannons. Or rather, tanks with huge guns, military equipment they get from illegal and legal arms dealers, any kind of firepower they can get their hands on.

"The cartels will compete for this reward money. They don't care if AJ is alive or dead, although if he's alive, they can and will ask for more. My information is there are two main cartels in the Yucatan. Los Cocodrilos, who, we are pretty sure, took over the Mexican portion of the cartel that Ardith ran. You have met The Crocodile. He hates it that you escaped and will try his best to bring you down any way he can. I haven't ruled out Ardith from this picture because of her psychotic behavior prior to this,

56

and because the British think she may be trying to revive her cartel. She accumulated loads of money. Some of that money British police and Interpol traced and seized, but I would bet she has much more stashed close at hand to Mexico. They emphasize strongly that she may be crazy but she's very, very smart. There is a rumor of a third cartel. I can't find any more information on it yet. I'm still looking."

Stacy's face was grim.

Anna nodded. "So you're sure Marthe, Cait, Caroline and their boys are completely safe?"

"Yes, absolutely, Rob has that covered for his family and Marthe. But Cait, well, she's staying in her house for now with her two younger ones. She's a fighter, isn't she? I'll have men on her house though. I insisted."

She hesitated. "However, your brother Jamie is going with you. He refuses to stay here. Pat and Aunt Carrie are staying in Green Bay."

"But that's absurd! He's in his seventies!"

"Well, he's the toughest seventy-something I've ever met. It seems he got involved with the IRA for a while and learned a thing or three—no, make that ten—before he entered that monastery, like how to use some very lethal weapons. In fact, he might have served a prison term if he hadn't gone to the God side first."

"Jamie? Seriously?"

"Oh, yeah! I had him checked out very thoroughly. Pat is a quiet one but Jamie was a terror with the IRA for a few years. If he hadn't entered that monastery years ago, he wouldn't even have been allowed back in the USA. I've asked him to remain in the background in Mexico. His first job will be to pose as a wealthy sponsor of archaeological digs and find out everything he can about and around Ian Stewart. You'll be the public figure, the diversion, for the activities of the rest of us. You do have a legitimate reason to contact Adelina though— that school you started. You will 'visit' there to check on one of your philanthropic interests. You will play the public role, the very distressed rich American mother searching for her son. The press will follow you while the rest of us go hunting. I hope Adelina will get us to Jorge and Ramon."

"I've tried to contact them—the school, I mean. No response. Have you heard anything about Lindy?"

Stacy turned back into the dining room and fussed with papers on the table.

I don't want to tell her the truth.

"Stacy?"

"Yes. She's disappeared. She had gone to her father's camp. I don't know where she is now. Ian Stewart's official story is they fought over his continued cooperation with the cartels and he told her to leave. Apparently, she did. Of her own free will, he says, but I don't know if I believe that. When he speaks about anything at all, he emphasizes only that he's digging a site that will be the most extensive in Mexico and has the cooperation of everyone, government and police and cartels, all 'for the good of Mexico'. I'm hoping Jamie can find out about her too. The problem is, I'm not sure just what the story is. We'll have to see what we can find out when we get to Mexico."

"But, Stacy, we've got to find her! I'm responsible..."

"No, Anna, you're not. She's a grown woman. You can't be responsible for everyone. Keep in mind that Mac will be down there soon looking for information too."

Stacy saw disappointment, fear, and hurt flash through Anna's eyes. And then anger.

It was the anger that remained. Sly, calculating anger.

"All right. Let's smoke them out."

Eight

The Texan was angry. This risk was not in the contract he'd signed.

We had a clear understanding. I am not a killer or drug runner, and I can't run an entire network of drug dealers. I don't want to. I'm a spy, an investigator, a recruiter of judges and police and politicians who can be bought. A Texas good ol' boy. He's going to get me killed.

That's when it occurred to him El Capitán might be doing just that.

Is he setting me up? Is he going to see that I'm killed after my use to him is over? Is he going to leave me to take the fall? No one does that to me! No one!

The Texan stood at the window of the second story office on the West side of Green Bay that Ardith had used, above the still-open import shop which the police now used as a front for gaining information. Across the room, a thin man stood in the shadows. Another bulkier man stood behind him.

"I hope ya'll are with me on this. The boss would be mighty disappointed if this don't work. We need to be up and running again full speed ahead as soon as possible."

"And if we're not?" a rasping voice asked.

"He sends in an enforcer to weed out any weak links," the deep voice of the bulky man barked out. "He won't mess around. There's no room for error. No hesitation. He wants results. By my calculations, this is nearly a billion dollar a year operation when it's running full on to Canada." Suspicion reached into his voice and dragged out edges of sound that cut through the room. "Are you backing down?"

The thin man whirled. "I am the one watching our asses, you fool! I am the one taking the chances supervising the drug scene here and making sure it works so you can get your money. Don't anger me."

"Boys! Boys!" the Texan soothed. "We're all a little tense. Let's get this plan up and runnin'. Ya'll gonna be feelin' a whole lot better when we've got it all in place. Ya'll goin' to be a whole lot happier when you've got your money from the whole operation safe in a bank. Just think about that.

"Now let's get to plannin' here. Here's the maps. Here's the means." He laid a sheaf of papers on the table in the middle of the room. "Here's the plan." The three men bent over the papers. When they were finished, all three nodded in satisfaction.

The thin one stated unequivocally, "We'll have no strong-arm tactics if we can help it. I can keep the lid on this easily. I see to it our cops out there have small drug busts, small potatoes, just enough to look like progress. There'll be the occasional big police bust when we've got a well-oiled organization working. Drama made to satisfy the politicians and media and the law enforcement departments. I'll warn you of those.

61

"We'll keep that connection with Mexico going with that Crocodile guy as the source for your people's activities," he pointed to the Texan.

"What about the Kinnealy woman and the reward. It's all over the news. What's that all about up here, anyway?" the Texan asked.

"We, the police departments, have to look like we take it seriously. Her husband was well known around here and so was she. That would be a liability, except it's working out for us. I can be sure my department uses that publicity to cover what we're setting up. It's our diversion— an ongoing diversion which buys us time. I'll get you the files on that family so you have some background."

"You keep files on the whole family?"

"We've kept files on them since her husband was alive, from the time Art Kinnealy and Jonny O'Keeffe partnered up in that law firm. We didn't think it was drugs back then. We thought Big John O'Keeffe was using that firm to back up his underhanded dealings in the construction business. We never could get any proof. Nothing Anna herself did ever was suspect. She was just a housewife.

"Then I discovered there was someone in the department that kind of let everything slip. When I figured out who was on the take, I made it my business to become his successor. He disappeared off the map a long time ago, probably into some country where he's lived high on the hog under some other name. I never wanted to know. I just want a very comfortable retirement out of this. A policeman's retirement pay doesn't make up for all the years of aggravation, in my mind."

The burly man nodded assent to that. "We keep this just between us. So far, no one has caught on and we're careful. Very careful. We make sure there are just enough arrests to show we're actively working at stopping drugs, but our lines run smoothly, for the most part.

"There's that Marinette-Menominee area with the traffic bottleneck over the interstate bridges but the sheer volume of truck traffic through there—we've clocked a high of as many as one hundred trucks per hour over that bridge—and the fact that it's a major drug usage area, actually works in our favor. To expand, we infiltrated three trucking lines that make regular runs through Upper Michigan. Two owners don't even know we use their trucks to run contraband. We make sure their companies look good. If anything is discovered, a driver is the one who will go down for it. We set up 'evidence' of that. There are even fake inspections of those trucks to 'help' the owners avoid usage of their businesses by drug runners. We've got it covered completely." The smugness in his voice was undisguised.

The Texan nodded, satisfied. "Well, gentlemen, I think we've got a very good thing going here. I think we can all look forward to retirement in fine style too. I'll be off now. Thanks for your help. I look forward to doing more business with you."

The other two listened in silence to his footsteps fading out down the stairs and the alley door latch clicking faintly.

The thin man watched from the window. "Is a file set up on him too?"

"Of course. We want as few people as possible to know and remember what we do here. He will have 'retired' to some quiet spot of ground as soon as we can gain control of it all. An accident, or a disappearance. Whatever."

"Can we do that without those files? The names in them would help us track down those from the old times."

"For now, we have to. The FBI have them. We daren't make a direct attack on the women and boys who worked on them but I would consider setting them up to fall somehow. I really don't understand why or how Anna Kinnealy has so many friends who get involved."

The thin man made no reply.

The burly man left after a few minutes of silence.

The thin man listened to the footsteps down the stairs as his partner left. It occurred to him that there is indeed no honor among thieves. He was now in possession of the "evidence" of his own participation that had been assembled by the aforesaid burly man. He also had his own files on that man.

If anyone is the last man standing, it will be me.

Is all this worth it, I wonder?

This was not the first time he'd asked himself that question. It was not the first time the answer came back an unequivocal *Yes*.

It would be millions worth of *Yes* before it was over.

Perhaps more.

Mexico

Nine

Ian Stewart stood outside his tent at his dig. He awarded himself a fat Cuban cigar, a gift from the local cartel soldier in charge.

My dig! Yes! It will rival Chichen Itza. It will rival Teotihuacan, Tulum, any of the major sites. My name will make history.

He gazed at the high mound swelling from the jungle floor, still only partially cleared. Then he turned to look at the next huge hill—another large building, maybe another pyramid—part of the complicated map now being formed in detail from aerial flights, ground-penetrating radar, *all the newest methods at my disposal. I can afford the best equipment now.*

In the tent just across from his, he could hear the quiet tears of his daughter, Lindy. When Lindy had heard how he'd sold out to the cartel, she left Anna's house in Wisconsin, contacted her mother in Paris to tell her what Ian was up to and both of them had tongue-lashed him for his compromise with the cartels who trafficked around the site. He had dismissed his ex-wife's arguments, on the phone from Paris, as shrewish, but he was unable to entirely ignore, face to face, the terrible disappointment of his daughter. They had been close.

They were not close now. He ordered her kept under guard. *To save her life,* he

69

rationalized. *If the cartels hear of her opposition, they might kill her. It's better this way.*

Down separate paths, under cover of the trees, he was watched by two people. One, a cartel soldier, had orders to watch Ian for any signs he would not cooperate with them.

"I want to know of any sign he is wavering," El Cocodrilo had ordered, "or if he is doing anything that is not related to this dig. We must protect this or we will have national police on our backs. Because it is part of Mexican heritage, there are powerful people who want it preserved. There has been much publicity about it. I do not trust him."

The cartel soldier heard Lindy's furious arguments against what her father was doing. When his relief came, he would go directly to The Crocodile and report.

A second watcher, Eduardo, watched them all. He had already sent word to Jorge and Ramón Aguilar. The girl would be killed if she was not removed from here. He was well aware that her father would also be killed if The Crocodile wished it so.

Eduardo had even more on his mind. He had been contacted by a man from a small village near Felipe Carrillo Puerto with a message from a curandera. Adelina had also sent him a message. El Cocodrilo was looking for AJ. In addition, a gringo who was very ill had been picked up by the Croc's men and brought to that village. Then the people from that village disappeared. That village did not exist anymore. The gringo was with those people

"Where are the people now? Where are they fleeing to?" he had asked. The man was not sure. He sent the man to find them with instructions to get them to Santa Anita. He sent word he would also get Stewart's daughter if he could.

I wish Mac was here now. I need help. Where is he? He would be another ally to help us all. This is getting very dangerous. Tonight, when Stewart is asleep and the guards are smoking marijuana, I will see if I can persuade the girl to leave. We both need to get out of here.

Light from a small campfire flickered over Lindy's tent. She slept, exhausted by the conflict with her father and her disappointment in him. She did not hear the soft rip of the fabric as Eduardo, hidden by the darkness behind it, cut the back wall of her tent.

His first main concern was how to awaken her without her crying out. He would then have to persuade her to leave and, most dangerous of all, they would have to get away safely.

I could use a long diversion right now. Wishful thinking. Just do this.

He put his hand over the girl's mouth and shook her awake. As soon as she made a sound, he put his lips to her ear and softly begged her to be quiet. Lindy froze.

"I beg you not to speak. You are in terrible danger. So am I. We must leave here. The cartel plans to kill you."

71

When she remained frozen and didn't cry out, he continued.

"If you want your father to live, please do as I say. They will kill him too if they think he is influenced by you. You must leave."

He felt her body relax slightly. She nodded. Cautiously he removed his hand from her mouth.

"Eduardo, I know this is true," she whispered very quietly. "I know my father has been corrupted. This dig matters more to him than his life or mine. I know I must get away."

Eduardo breathed out his relief but it was a very short breath. Two moves down, one to go.

"Get dressed and put your boots on," he ordered.

"I have them on. We can go."

Lindy grabbed the canteen of water from under her cot and followed him, creeping to the back of the tent and out the long cut.

Holding on to his shirt in the blackness, she carefully set each foot down as quietly as possible. Once a small twig snapped under her and they both froze. When nothing happened, they continued.

It was impossible to tell how long and how far they had gone when the hand went over her mouth and the cool knife-blade bit into her throat. She heard a scuffle ahead of her. Then she heard nothing. The smelly rag that covered her mouth and nose collapsed her into unconsciousness.

Eduardo fell forward with his attacker on his back. He rolled instinctively and hit out, felt his fist slam into a solid object and heard the crack as they connected. There was no more movement.

He turned to try to find Lindy. There were no telltale human sounds. He dared not speak, call her name, for fear there were more attackers. Carefully he felt around him in a widening circle. No Lindy. He found her canteen but his search revealed nothing except the man he had knocked out. He killed him.

The man had night vision glasses. He took those, put them on and looked around. Nothing.

In the morning he watched, hidden, as Ian went to her tent, found her gone and raised the alarm.

Whoever had taken her had not come back to the camp. Eduardo returned in daylight to scour the place where they had been ambushed. He found a trail where someone had walked through the brush and some footsteps made by a heavy person—*or someone light carrying a heavier burden*. They disappeared after a time.

I have been watched by someone, maybe for a long time. His usefulness at the camp was compromised. He left to follow the rumors of the sick white man and to join Jorge Aguilar.

El Cocodrilo smiled when he heard the news.

"Good. We have a stronger hold over Stewart. Let him know this. Remove the girl to my new northern headquarters."

El Crocodrilo had profited well from Ardith's loss of her Mexican influence. He now had the home which had been Wentworth's and then Anna's: many new soldiers, new politicians and police Ardith had bought who were now in his organization, and even the island she had used as her main headquarters. The national police had vacated that island after their meticulous search. Then a national politician had commandeered it. Then the politician had disappeared under mysterious circumstances and The Crocodile spread the word it was haunted by the ghosts of the people she murdered. Now, he had a luxurious private headquarters. The latest technology made it perfect.

Lindy woke up to find herself in the home she knew as Anna's, north of Cancun. Her sudden feeling of hope died quickly to be replaced by terror when she found herself prisoner of The Crocodile's men.

In his tent, Ian Stewart sat with his head in his hands. The realization of what he had done washed over him again and again. The deflation of his ego took hours but when it was over, he had regained some of his old ethics. He compared the courage of his daughter to his own and found himself woefully wanting. That old part of him would not be silenced. "Too little, too late" it repeated over and over, mocking him.

But I will find mine again. It will look like I'm cooperating, but....

He walked out of his tent and began giving orders for the day's work.

The watchers thought they were seeing a man who had not even changed with the loss of his daughter. A cold man.

Ten

His hot feverish brain impaled by the memory of his crucified wife, AJ, arms spread open, trembling legs splayed apart, lay moaning and shaking on his own crucifix of stinking feces piled in the dirty alley where men, dogs, and other animals had relieved themselves.

Bits of memory made their whirlwind path through his mind again and again...

...stumbling through the roots of dead trees in a thick muddy syrup of swamp, and a brief struggle with a python which lost its life to his fierce rage and bare hands...

...falling exhausted into the cool waters of a swift-running river that dragged him through rapids and left him bruised and battered...

...kneeling on a path under large dripping green leaves in thick jungle sobbing wildly and uncontrollably...

...hearing Ramón call his name and, throat swollen and choked with some strange infection, unable to answer...

...drinking in the gloom of a smoke-filled cantina surrounded by short dark men. One man—white, far larger than the others, wide meaty shoulders hunched over the bar—the one who bought him shot after shot of tequila, who listened as he poured out his anguish.

Most cruel of all, Sheila, her hands and feet impaled in the side of an ant hill, body slashed with cuts, legs open and the trails of blood and semen still dribbling from her mouth and vagina...

Sheila, raped and dead...

Sheila, her ghost following him...

Sheila, her spirit whispering, or crying, or screaming or...oh god, the ants...

AJ did not feel the rough hands pick him up and throw him in the back of the old truck. He did not hear the drivers gloat about the money they would receive when they brought him in for ransom.

He only vaguely heard the loud crackling bursts of gunshots and did not feel the truck swerve into a rock, its driver dead. He did not see the man who stumbled from the passenger door and ran for cover into the jungle.

AJ did feel hands drag him out of the truck, but only because they let him fall to the ground. He passed out again before they got him into a second truck and, gunning the engine, raced down a dirt road. He could not hear the men planning the next move for him.

One of the men held a cell phone to his left ear, plugging the opposite one so he could hear.

"Bring him to Felipe Carrillo Puerto. We'll pick him up from there," said the flat hard voice.

"Sí, Señor. As soon as possible. I will call when we are near the city."

He paused to listen.

"In about three or four hours. We are far to the southwest and are still on dirt roads."

He listened for some moments and then hit the button to end the call and turned to the driver.

"El Cocodrilo says there will be a ransom to collect for this gringo. He will pay us ten thousand dollars when he collects from the man's family. We will be rich men!"

"Sí, and dead men if we do turn him over to that animal. He does not keep his promises. He will have us killed to cover his trail. We must find a way to turn him over to his family."

Fear flooded the other man's eyes.

"If we do not give him to The Crocodile, he will send his killers after us. We must do it his way."

The driver glanced at the body slumped in the rear.

"If we do not get him to a curandero, there will be no one to ransom. A dead man does not command any price. We must find a healer first."

"Es verdad. He is very sick, hot with fever. There is a curandera in a small village just west of Puerto. She is very good. She cured my sister. We can stop there. We can tell El Cocodrilo we have to do this and that this man is dying. It is not far from the truth."

He reached back and felt AJ's neck for a pulse.

"Muy malo! I can hardly feel the beat of his heart. We must go as quickly as we can."

The driver hit the accelerator and the truck lurched forward, churning the dirt of the road up and spraying it backward, leaving only the fumes of gas and oil hanging in the hot and steamy air. Small animals nearby froze, waiting as the rough motor sounds slowly faded. When all was still again, they shook themselves and crept away from the sickening smells.

The small hut of the curandera barely covered AJ's long body. She had two young boys lay him out on the bare ground, took herbs and copal, lit it and, with a fan of macaw feathers, waved smoke over him from head to foot and into the air around him.

Coming out of the hut slowly, tiny, bent over and wrinkled, she looked up at the man who waited and shook her head from side to side slowly.

"Muy malo. Muy malo. You should have brought him in days ago. Now, I do not know if..."

"You will do this and fast. We must bring him to Puerto as soon as possible," the man ordered, crossing his arms and looking down his nose at her.

"It will take me at least three days," she said as she held up four fingers, waving her hand slowly from side to side. Across the small fire a boy saw the gesture and departed silently.

The men looked at each other and contempt for her fleeted across their faces, then changed into stern and threatening glares.

"I will send helpers into the jungle to collect medicines. One of the medicines is a half day away. I will do my best." She smiled and called for someone to bring the men food to eat.

79

"He is followed by a very bad spirit, a bruja. If you do not want her to follow you, you must sleep in that hut at the edge of our village. It will be safer for you." She pointed to a wooden shack just beyond the perimeter of the village. "I will put protection around you there.

The men took their food and moved themselves and the truck as far away from her as possible.

When they awoke, they found no people, no food, no clothing, no medicines, no curandera and no AJ. They did not know it was four days later.

A black feather was tied to the rearview mirror in the cab of the truck.

Their cell phone, after they charged it using the truck, was filled with demanding and then threatening messages. They threw it into the jungle, an evil thing, hoping the curses inside it would be eaten by the worms and bugs on the forest floor.

The men left, took the nearest road to the highway going to the far southwest of Mexico and disappeared into what they hoped would be a land totally beyond the reach of El Cocodrilo.

Eleven

The aging Mexican man stood in front of the Nogales border guard, his papers in hand, his eyes cast down. He shuffled a bit from foot to foot, hitched up pants which were loosely held by a scarred and worn leather belt, and then scratched his unwashed salt and pepper hair. Sweat beaded his forehead in the hot, dry early Texas evening. The day's heat of ninety-plus degrees hung imprisoned in the air, unreleased by the slight suggestion of an evening breeze. Smells of dust and the exhaust of dozens of vehicles waiting in line to be cleared in their passage to and from the United States and Mexico thickened that air to choking levels.

"Where you heading, old man?" the guard barked, squinting his bloodshot eyes. A hangover pounded inside his head and the noise from the streets clanged and grated from the outside. He felt like hell. The night before had been a wild ride on tequila and two women.

"To the home of my daughter in Monterrey, Señor. I have been working in the fields. My papers are very good, sí? I have come and gone across this border for many years, Señor. Do you not remember me?"

"If I tried to remember all you pee-ons, I'd go crazy. Ok. Ok. Just wait until I have another guard look at these."

He walked over to a second guard and said, "Does this look good to you? I'm too new here to recognize this man. Is he familiar to you?"

81

"He looks sort of familiar to me, but honestly, after a while, they all look alike. Don't worry, he's going *back* to Mexico. He don't look like no mule to me or no coyote neither. It's the ones going *into* the US that we have to really check out. Just let him go but take a good look at him so you'll know him next time. If there is a next time."

"Thanks."

The border guard returned to the old man, took time to look him over, and passed him on. Lifting two fingers to his brow, the old man saluted the guard, and shuffled on slowly. After a time, the guard looked over into Nogales. The old man was gone. He had already forgotten what the man looked like.

Ninety-six endless hours after he left Green Bay, Mac slipped into a café in Nogales he knew would have a bathroom and a back door. In the bathroom, he quickly changed clothing, hairpiece and shoes. Leaving the old clothing in the garbage bin, he slipped out the back door and disappeared into a maze of shacks, adobe buildings, and debris until he came to a main road with much pedestrian, burro, auto, truck and other traffic. Looking now like a tourist over the border for the day, in jeans and a casual blue shirt, his sienna skin and black hair blending into the Mexican scene easily, he headed into the long and crowded market plaza.

Twice women approached him with offers of sex and he was tempted to bargain with them just to see how far down they would lower their price. Once before, in Nuevo Laredo, he had done just that and the price had gone down to twenty-five cents. He had nearly been attacked when he refused that. He smiled, remembering. It was almost a half hour later, browsing through the market stalls slowly, when he finally came to the woman he was seeking.

Easing up to her stall, filled with fetishes, strange objects, herbs, and pouches of unknown content, he nodded his head and murmured, "Mariana, it is a good day for love potions."

She looked up slowly, furtively. A small twitch of her lips and a nod were her silent response. She turned to look over her shoulder. With her eyes and a very slight jerk of her head she indicated the rear of her stall.

Careful to check if he was being watched, Mac moved down the tables of her merchandise, making a show of examining items until he became sure no one was watching. He quickly disappeared around the back and crouched down in the shadows to wait until the cooling darkness deepened into late night, when Mariana would be free to help him. Opening the backpack he carried, he took out a bottle of brown cream and began rubbing it on his face, neck, and arms. He took off the baseball cap he wore and rubbed the cream into his scalp. His Native American skin, a light copper color, was too light to risk the activity he planned. His brown-black eyes would do. His aim was to look burned dark from the sun, like a field hand. An allover dark, in case he was forced to disrobe.

His stomach growled. He had eaten little these last days while he made contact after contact to get him over the border as fast as possible. The journey, which he had made so often and so easily, had dragged into four frustrating days. He had planned to be in Cancun or, better yet, in contact with Jorge or Ramon by this time. *Stacy and Anna are there by now and here I sit.*

Instead, he was facing what now looked like a long journey south and east. Still, Nogales would be a good place to pick up information. Mariana would be the best contact for that.

It had been dark for more than two hours when Mariana threw him a crumpled brown paper package. He disregarded it until a tempting smell rose from the package and his stomach sent out urgent demanding noises. Grateful, he gulped down three tasty burritos.

Finally, the market became quiet. Mariana closed her stand and packed her merchandise. When the trunk of her ancient Chevrolet had been tied down over her packages and the right front seat and half of the back seat were also loaded, she pointed to the right rear seat and Mac crept in, staying low. Mariana took off through the streets to an edge of town where she stopped, unloaded her merchandise into her house, locked it and came back to the car.

"What do you need this time, Señor Mac?"

Through the darkness, he could see her white teeth gleaming softly in a grin. "It is good to see your smile again, Mariana. It has been too long. What I need is entry into a ceremony—the drug ceremony of the Nogales cartel. I need to have much information about all the cartels operating in Mexico. Someone up here on the inside must have that."

He couldn't see Mariana grow pale in the dark night but her smile disappeared and her voice came out of the blackness full of fear.

"Mac, you will be tortured and killed if you go there! Everyone who attends is known. You will be marked from the minute you enter the door."

"I know this danger, but I must. The life of a friend depends on gathering this information. I need your help turning my skin darker. I need some medicine to counteract the effects of the drugs they will want me to use. I need help in arranging passage through Mexico all the way to the Yucatan and I must do this as fast as possible and without being caught. You are the only one I know here who has the contacts, the medicine and the knowledge."

There was a long silence. Then Mariana pulled him out of the car and into a small shack next to her house.

When he left, Mac's body was dark all over, his clothing that of a Mexican peasant, and his backpack had been exchanged for something more fitting a Mexican field worker—a threadbare old carpetbag. Mac had much information he needed, a thick oil to coat his stomach should he have to take the drugs he knew would be forced on him in the ceremony, and an antidote should the oil not be enough.

He also carried guilt at the satisfaction in his groin and, indeed, throughout his entire body. Mariana's original skills had not diminished since he had met her many years before. She had not forgotten what he liked and had not forgotten what he liked to do with her in earlier days. She had demanded payment in two forms.

Mariana was a good bit wealthier and very sexually satisfied when he left.

The drums had been pounding for over an hour while Mac stood in the shadows outside the ceremonial building checking the security and watching who entered and left. Armed guards lurked back in shadow, their cigarettes and reefers glowing from time to time in the darkness. Men and women and even two or three small children entered and left as he watched, unmoving. He saw his chance when a large group of people came from some way down the road, all of them stoned and possibly drunk. As they passed him, he slipped into their midst and staggered with them into noise, into smells of sweat and sex and sin, of dangerous air filled with the turgid crawling energy of evil unleashed without restraint.

Crashing into him, throbbing incessantly, the beat pounded through his body, mind and spirit, and he had to fight to keep his focus on what he wanted. Pot smoke was thick. The smell of copal was thicker. Dancers whirled around him. Chaos reigned. He staggered his way to the rear of the room into shadow. Mariana had described the man he was to contact but Mac could not see him in the low light and in the constantly moving crowd. A packet was pushed into his hand and the man who gave it to him shoved Mac's hand up to his mouth. Mac pretended to open his mouth and shove the packet in as he grabbed a glass from another man and drank. He grinned and the man who had given him the drugs grinned back. Mac clapped the man on the back as he dropped the packet on the floor, stepping on it so it would not be noticed. The man wandered off and Mac turned.

He found himself staring into the barrel of a rifle, his shirt grabbed in front and a large hand propelling him to the wall.

"We need some more soldiers. You will come with me," came the gruff order. Within two minutes he was in the back of a large truck with other men and the truck drove off. Through all of this he had clung to the carpetbag. Now greedy hands reached, yanked it out of his grasp, opened it and dumped it out. The bottle of oil and packet of medicine lay with scattered clothing, a pair of well-worn work shoes, and a pair of old flip-flops. Mac waited, expecting they would search him and find the papers he had taped to his lower back. To his immense relief, it didn't happen.

Instead, the oil and medicine were grabbed by the next man and he demanded to know what they were for. Mac gestured to his groin, pointed to the oil and made an up and down motion in front of himself. The man snickered. Another man grabbed the bottle of oil, opened it, took out his penis and poured it on, massaging himself into a hard on. Men laughed and clapped and the bottle was passed around until it had been used up.

The medicine packet was ignored in the joking and Mac retrieved it, picking up his clothing, covering it and returning it to his bag, laughing and joining in the coarse jokes with the other men. As each one came to orgasm, the noise subsided and Mac began a careful conversation.

In the several hours that followed, Mac learned there were now three cartels operating mostly out of southern Mexico and the Yucatan. They were said to be headed by The Crocodile, by a woman whose name no one knew, and by a man, a gringo maybe, whose name had never been known. It was rumored the woman had lost control but then one would expect that of a woman who had no business taking over a cartel. A gringa, at that!

One by one he obtained names of men who were known to associate with the Crocodile and the names of places to get further information. He even discovered the routes taken by some of the activities. At that point, Mac decided this was working for him.

Mac told them he had heard many rumors. "I am happy to have you correct me. It is clear that my information is very bad."

When the conversation finally died, Mac had much more information than he expected on two cartels and much more to learn about a third.

So. A third cartel. No, a second, now. The Croc is taking over, maybe already took over the woman's organization. Mariana was right about that, too, but this information is just not enough. This still means a trip to Puerto Felipe Carrillo. I have a long way to go. AJ has to be embroiled somewhere in this, and where are Jorge and Ramon? How dangerous will this be for Anna? Ardith is probably clearly out of the picture here. If the Crocodile is in control now, he'll target Anna. He'll want that ransom!

What he still did not know and what he most needed to know at this moment, was how he would get himself out of this very dangerous captivity.

Most of the men didn't know where they were headed but "we are going to the south. Maybe we will even be near Monterey and you will be close to home but we will have to fight for the cartel soon, so you must pray to Los Santos you are not killed first."

They rode through the remains of the night. In the very early morning they stopped. Cooking smells drifted faintly through the cool air. The men were ordered out, allowed to relieve themselves, given a plate of rice and beans, and that was when Mac realized they were part of a small caravan of trucks. They were joined by a tank-like vehicle and three more trucks of armed men. Mac did not know where they were, only that the rising sun was to the left—obviously east—and they were going south and slightly west on dusty roads. He did know they were nowhere near Monterrey or the Yucatan.

"How will we fight? We have no guns," he whispered to the man next to him.

"They will arm us when we get there. They do not give us guns in case we want to get away and might shoot them. That has happened, but it is not a good idea. Those who try to get away are shot as they run. It is better to do as we are told. It is more likely we will live if we do."

The man looked at him with a skeptical eye.

"Have you ever shot a gun? You don't look like a cartel soldier to me."

"I have, but not those rifles I see our guards carrying."

"How come you were at that ceremony? How did you get there?"

"The woman I was with told me to go there because she said I could get some drugs," he lied. "I had a good time with her and wanted more. She was with me but I don't know what happened to her."

"Ha! I do! She is being screwed by the men we left behind. That is what happens to women who go there. She will be there for days. She will be used and then put out to recover, like all women should be."

90

Mac could not keep from frowning.

"Do not be upset. She will not be killed like in some ceremonies. In some, the women and children are a sacrifice to the gods. The mayor of that town does not approve of that. It deprives the men of sex when they want it. In one town, there were no women and children left and the men had sex with each other. That is evil, so that had to be stopped."

Mac nodded and turned his face away. The man tapped him on the shoulder. "You will forget all that when you can kill. Killing is a better high than sex and drugs. Soon you will know that."

They were herded into the truck and, with shouted orders and a few gunshots, went on their way again.

I am in deep trouble here, more than before.

Mac pretended to nod off as he began to think of how he might escape. He could think of nothing but Anna.

I have made a very stupid mistake.

Twelve

Except for those who loved killing, whose eyes had the look of predators waiting for a feast, the other men around him had become quieter, more solemn, withdrawn into themselves. The smells of sweat and dirt changed to the smells of fear and lust. Released by fear rising to terror, the smell of pee and shit grew stronger. The truck stopped for no one and nothing.

Mac knew they were in central Mexico, somewhere north of Mexico City, on the way to a village. Their work, they had now been told, was to kill all the villagers who had resisted the cartel. In effect, that would be everyone, since there was no way to tell who was a resister, who was telling truth or lie, who was friend or foe. Therefore, they were all foe.

We will be there within a half hour.

It was coming on night again, dusky evening, and hot, sticky. Mac was soaked with sweat from heat and fear. He was acutely aware, as were all the men in the truck, they would be shot if they tried to leave.

We'll all be shot anyway when this is done. A cartel wants no witnesses to its murders, especially not the murderers themselves.

They were still unarmed. They would not be given arms until they were in the village, he was told again.

"How are we to see what we are doing?" Mac asked the man on the other side of him.

"I do not know. I have not done this before. I have never killed anyone before this. I do not want to do this but what choice do I have if I want to live?"

"I do not want to do this either. Even if we survive, I do not think the cartel will allow us to leave. Do you think this also?"

"Sí." The man choked back what sounded like a sob.

Mac felt time slow down and drag its feet. The half hour became endless. He waited, hardly breathing, and in a while the truck slowed and he heard shouts. Gunfire began even before the truck jerked to a stop and snapped his brain into high survival mode. The back flap of the vehicle was ripped aside and they were being yelled at to "Move! Move! Move!" and guns were slapped into each man's hand. Mac held back, hoping to see what was happening in the street before he jumped down. He could see nothing. Black holes and moving shadows imprisoned him. Yelling continued and more shots and screams, cries and begging and pleading and more screams and shots. Mac's head spun with the sounds of pain and terror from the victims.

He hit the ground ducking and tried running to one side as a rifle was slapped into his hands. Rough hands grabbed him and hurled him back into the line of men. The world became darker and all Mac could see were the two or three men closest to him. He felt for the trigger of the rifle and shot into the air, hoping that his dodging and weaving looked like he was doing what they wanted.

Someone grabbed his neck from behind, pushed him forward, and he found himself looking down at a very small child who was shaking with fear.

"Kill him now!" a voice ordered. Mac felt the nausea rising in his stomach and froze.

"Kill or I will kill you, bastard!"

Mac pulled the rifle up to his shoulder and, twisting around as fast as he could, he slammed the barrel into the man's head, then aimed it at his face and pulled the trigger. Human flesh and blood splattered over him and a faceless body dropped to the ground. He slung the rifle on his back, turned, scooped up the child and dived for the nearest cover. Then he was up and dodging from shadow to shadow, hugging the child to him, sounds of screams and shots behind him, slowly fading, fading. Finally, he heard nothing except the pounding of his own heart. Still he ran and dodged and scurried and stumbled through an eerie silent landscape of night where leaves he didn't see slapped at his face and roots tripped him and stones dug into his feet through the old shoes he wore.

Mac didn't know how long he went on. The only thing that stopped him was the complete loss of all energy. It simply stopped. He couldn't move any more. He dropped to the ground, laying there, the child under him. He didn't move again until he saw light coming through the trees and bushes around him. Dawn slowly registered on his numbed mind.

He rolled on his side and looked at the child for a long time. When the child didn't awaken, he sat up.

Dawn revealed Her terrible truth. The child, a girl, lay still.

No bullet holes. Oh! God no! I smothered her with my body! He gagged, turned his head away and wretched but nothing came up.

He began to shake all over. The sun was high overhead when he finally regained control of himself and looked around. There were only morning sounds—birds, maybe some animals.

He smelled badly—fetid sweat, acid pee, rotten poop and rancid fear.

His body jerked when he heard a shot in the distance.

He wandered, dazed, through the trees and brush collecting all the flowers he could find and covered the child's body with them.

Then he turned in what he hoped was south.

Creator, forgive me.

He could not forgive himself.

He never looked back so he never saw the little girl stir, tremble all over, sit up, and gaze in wonder at the piles of flowers on and around her.

Thirteen

Jamie O'Reilly, as Anna's oldest brother, had been determined to protect her and had learned early and well in life with his drunken and abusive dad, and later, his stepfather, how to fake anything. A fake Irish tourist-investor interested in archaeology was a no-brainer.

All the years on my knees and God hasn't taken that character defect from me. Well, then, I'm supposed to use it for a while yet.

He grinned in anticipation and sent a silent salute to Jesus, whom he regarded as a Jewish revolutionary of a Roman-dominated Holy Land who would surely understand what Jamie had to do.

All the years in the monastery had also taught him language skills, not the least of which was a very good understanding of Latin and of no less than three of its successor languages— French, Italian and Spanish. If anyone here were to use Spanish in front of him, assuming he didn't understand, well, that was their mistake. Mayan was not one of those skills of course, but that could be turned to his advantage as well. He would be expected to ask many questions. Not so dumb probing questions disguised as dumb tourist questions.

And Ian? He'll be a piece of cake!

"So, tell me now, sir, just what you hope to find here? How can you be so sure this is the great site you say it is?"

96

As he listened to Ian Stewart expound on the vast extent of the dig still unrevealed and how the discovery had been made, his eyes counted every worker and took in the guards with rifles who stood just under the canopy of the thick jungle surrounding the dig. He noted the tent placements, the other equipment and the open tent which had a slit at the back.

Jamie had not wasted his time in the plane on the way to Mexico. He had devoured maps, collected information from Anna on Ramón, Jorge, Adelina, Melissa and any other connections and made himself a plan. Jamie would be the contact for each of them. With Anna in her prison of bodyguards, police and reporters, she would not be free.

By agreement with Stacy and Anna, he waited in the plane until all reporters and others were gone and then slipped away to the south with a well-paid guide hired to show him "all the archaeological sights."

"I'd like to know as much as possible," he told Ian, as they stood at the edge of the excavation, "I have a wee bit of money to put toward a worthy cause," and he mentioned a "wee" figure which made Ian's eyebrows lift, "and I'll be wanting to know if this is something that will pay off. I'm looking at a site in Turkey, in Anatolia to be more exact—mysterious country, that—and the underwater site off the old city of Alexandria. Would you mind if I spend a day or two here? See how things are done? Have a look around at the unexcavated parts?"

"Oh, yes, yes indeed! Make yourself at home. I'll designate a worker to accompany you and there's an extra tent you can use and I'll make time to give you a tour personally of the whole area. I have some matters to attend to right now. Later, then?"

"Certainly. I am very happy for your hospitality. I've taken the liberty to have some good food catered in. Just a bit of thanks in return for your valuable time. I hope you don't mind. There's a truck on the way. A bit of good whisky and cerveza we can all enjoy too."

Three days later, Jamie had spoken and listened to workers, tramped his way through the site, and, using the connections Stacy had given him, three men had been hired to add to the staff, at Jamie's expense, to "help you with your survey of the site's potential" and they would be doing a thorough mapping of a fifty-square-mile area for Ian.

Jamie just forgot to mention that one man was an undercover police officer with the Mexican national police. Another was an expert tracker who just happened to work under deep cover for Interpol. The third was a grizzled old IRA acquaintance whose love of trouble had gotten him a bit of time in Kilmainham Gaol in the old days. He had also spent time as a treasure hunter, a drug-runner, now and then a thief, could drink anyone under the table and possessed a few other talents useful to certain people who paid well. Jamie had saved his life once. He was repaying the favor. He was to infiltrate the cartel if he could. The men would funnel Jamie, national, and international law enforcement any and all information they could ferret out.

It didn't take long to ferret out the story of Lindy's kidnapping, the disappearance of Eduardo and the finding of the dead man in the jungle just after they disappeared.

With eyes and ears in place and more information than he even expected to get, Jamie left Ian with broad hints of his further interest in financing the dig. Ian left Jamie with the strong hunch, though he didn't actually say so, that Ian would much rather be cooperating with this wealthy Irish tourist than with any cartel and that he would do whatever he was told to get his daughter back safely.

On a strong hunch and a vague rumor, Eduardo, risking his life, had returned to observe it all from the jungle. With a satisfied smile, he connected with the grizzled old man and then with Jamie.

Two days later, Jamie drove into Santa Anita.

Jorge smiled with satisfaction as the gears of another battered pickup truck screeched in protest when its driver braked in front of what had been the infirmary where AJ and Sheila had practiced their healing.

"More food supplies and more weapons. More very much needed information," he said to his odorous and disheveled companion.

The protests against the cartel incursions were growing. The intimidation tactics were backfiring as more and more of the common people—mostly Mayans—became fed up with the torture of men, rape of women and killing of children.

His smile faded instantly and his heart hurt as he thought of the women and children. At the same time, he felt relief that Ramon's children were still safe in their mountain village.

Ramón had gone in search of AJ and returned three times. He now stood next to Jorge, sipping hot coffee. His hair and beard were long and he had a haunted look. He had just stepped out of the jungle and smelled of sweat and an acrid rotting odor of total discouragement.

"We hear a rumor but when we get there, it is old news or false or not enough to follow. The last one I heard, a week ago, is that he was in Felipe Carrillo Puerto. We have not gone into that town yet. I wish we could talk to Anna. She may be able to sense him, sense where he is, but she is surrounded by guards and reporters follow her wherever she goes. I tried once but failed. Even Adelina is unable to approach her."

"I know this. Adelina called me. A man who says he is the brother of Anna is here in this camp. I am not quite sure I trust him yet. I do not know anything about him except what he tells me. I will let him come and go at will but I will have him watched. What do you hear of Mac? I need him."

"Nada. He is not with Anna and has made no contact with me or anyone I know. Where is Eduardo?"

"I do not know that either. Information has been slow to reach us here. He sent the news that the girl, Lindy, has disappeared. If Eduardo is alive, he will be gathering information. I hope to hear from him soon. If he is dead, we have lost one of our best."

"I heard rumors of these things. So it is true."

Ramón closed his eyes and pictured Lindy as she had been at the dig before all this happened. *A brave young girl. Full of life. Has she lost that life now? And what of Eduardo? We need him.*

"Mi hermano," he said. "Where will all this lead? We will not be supported by national police if we fight the cartels. They fear we will want our freedom from Mexico, our indigenous lands returned, our own government. They remember we have tried to regain that before. They will do nothing to keep the cartels from destroying us."

Jorge shot his brother an angry glare.

"Do not talk like that! We have only two choices—to become victims of the cartels or to fight them in any way we can. Are we not as brave as the women of that little town in Guatemala who stopped the cartel there? We must be like them. We must be more than they are. We were great warriors once. You know our history. You taught that history. We must be warriors now! We must!"

His eyes flashed dark fire at Ramón.

"I am sorry, mi hermano. I am very tired and hot and dirty. Before I leave again, I must have some rest and food." He lifted his arms and made a face at his own smell.

"I can smell the hot and dirty," Jorge agreed. "Go swim in the cenote. I will have someone bring you food. When you have rested, I want you to meet this brother of Anna. I want your opinion of him."

Ramón left as the driver of the truck approached Jorge.

"I have a lead on El Medico," he said in a low voice.

Jorge lowered his head and scanned the immediate area. No watchers. No one he did not trust completely. "Sí?"

"A driver of a truck was found dead, shot, and his truck was wrecked. A shot through the windshield. A small child saw it happen. A second man ran from the truck after it crashed. The child then saw two men drive up, haul what looked like a dead body from the rear of the truck, throw it into their vehicle and drive off. She said it looked like a gringo—that dead body. She knew nothing more. This happened outside a very small village south and west of Puerto. She said everyone has also heard a story of a gringo who is very ill. She thinks it is the same gringo."

"How long ago?"

"Four, maybe five days. The girl was so frightened she could barely speak and was not remembering clearly."

"She was sure the person was dead?"

"Sí."

"Madre de Dios!" Jorge's heart beat painfully hard in his chest and tears stuck behind his eyelids.

"But there is more. He may be alive. El Cocodrilo sent men to search that village for his body but there was no body, no village, nothing left. We questioned others from a village nearby. The curandera told them she is sending a gringo here to you, that he is ill. The people of her village are somewhere out there heading this way and the doctor may be with them."

Two hours later Ramón and the messenger left to search for them all and bring them to safety.

Jorge did not tell Jamie.

Jamie left after a call from Stacy, satisfied that he made at least a first contact with Jorge.

The driver who took him to Cancun was most accommodating and promised he would help Jamie with anything he needed.

Those are Jorge's orders. Good, even though he doesn't trust me yet. I wouldn't trust me either.

Fourteen

"Where is her son, the doctor?"

Far out to sea east of the South American continent, El Capitán, naked in the tropical sun, phone at his ear, lounged in his most comfortable deck chair enjoying the gentle lift and fall as his immense yacht rocked on deep blue ocean waves.

"We don't know. The rumor is someone found him very ill and he has either died and his body rots somewhere or he is still lost. Our information was that the Crocodile had someone bringing him to Felipe Carrillo Puerto but he did not arrive."

"Find him."

"Yes, sir. We think he'll turn up in Puerto and we have men there now searching."

"Good."

This will mean leaving the ship eventually, but it will be worth it. I will have a working drug line to Canada again and more police in my pay. And I will have my revenge on them all.

El Capitán looked at ease. He was not. His adrenaline was rising. Revenge had become his favorite drug years ago, when he had lost control of that line to Canada to the men who looked down on him, discounted his abilities, and shoved him aside. The men who, in his mind, betrayed him, betrayed his friendship and cooperation. And there were still two men in particular who stood in his way from very early on. *If they're still alive, and my information says*

104

they are, they won't be after I get to them. I'll make them regret every hour they have lived.

Mentally he tallied the merchandise he now bought and sold. The illicit animal trade. Sex slavery of women and children. Drugs. Gems. Arms. Slave workers. Mercenaries. Politicians who would make laws favoring his "clients"—the huge corporations who wanted guaranteed profits.

Anna's children will bring in at least a million each. She'll bring in Conrad's art collection too. Priceless. Then there's the property: two houses in Green Bay, the apartment in London, the house north of Cancun, the villa in Italy. I will get rid of the houses. Not to my liking, but certainly profitable. My wealthier friends will take them off my hands.

He watched the call girl in her bikini, caught her attention, and signaled her to take it off, then grinned and nodded as she did so, slowly and with many seductive movements.

For a little kid from Green Bay, I've done magnificently. I'll control them all. It's time to pluck the threads of this web.

First, El Cocodrilo. He must die. Next, acquire his business and what's left of the line that Ardith ran. Then expand the line to Canada. That one will be the trickiest. Far too many honest people involved. Good connections so far. Must have the Texan watched though. He doesn't like to get his hands too dirty.

His mind swept back to that long past time when he controlled just a small part of his world.

I will have my revenge on all bastards who stopped me. For that, I need Anna Kinnealy as bait.

Fifteen

Days after they arrived in Mexico, Anna finally stood, feeling numb, at the podium, facing the room full of reporters again. The shock of the news of the boys and Marnie—that they had been taken again by Ardith—had just reached her.

None of the press knew that part, thank god, or it would be sheer mayhem. It was bad enough already. There had been delay after delay trying to get full cooperation from the police and then between them and The Crocodile. Anna felt vindicated in her course of action, however. The Croc had let police know he had AJ. Now, finally, she had announced the ransom from the script Stacy had prepared for her.

Her guards stood behind her, flanked by Mexican national police.

She felt sick, nausea rising in waves as questions stormed her ears.

"I'm just here to find my son. I'm only here to find my son," was all she could manage to say in reply.

She turned to one of her guards.

"I think I'm going to throw up. I have to get to a bathroom."

He took her arm and hurried her out.

Mac stood outside the window of an old hotel in an even older small town watching a very ancient television screen on a wide windowsill set into the filthy gray wall of the bar across the street. A few men and two women also stood near

107

him in the street, watching the TV. Most had some money for cerveza and a taco. Mac was hungry but didn't dare bring out any money. He needed to remain as unnoticeable as possible. There was no telling who might be an informer for a cartel.

He had heard Anna's voice and thought he was hallucinating. He forgot his hunger when he saw her face. Gaunt. Frightened, maybe. But fierce. Fierce was the only word for the look in her eyes.

"Hey! You look at the gringa like you want to eat her, man. Maybe you do, eh? Not for the likes of you and me. Forget it. That puta will not be yours."

It was all Mac could do to stop himself from hitting the man. He turned and shuffled away. Shame and longing flooded through him. His heart broke and he felt its pieces drop with every step he took. *I must get to her. I must!*

Green Bay

Aunt Carrie Brennan's mouth was set in a grim stony line. She had just watched the coverage of Anna's announcement in Mexico.

There must be something I can do. I can't, I won't let Anna down. I may be old but I'm not helpless. I'll go for a walk. That will help me think this through.

Her phone rang as she was dressing to go out and she almost didn't pick it up.

108

"Carrie, me girl, I need a wee bit of fresh air and a devious mind and that made me think of you. Meet me at that restaurant in the old railroad station. You'll be buyin' me lunch."

Pat O'Reilly, finishing his cup of coffee at Jenny's kitchen table, had been thinking. *I can't go gallivantin' down to Mexico like that daft brother of mine, but there must be more I can do here.*

He decided to go for a walk. It would be good to refresh his memory of the West side. It had changed so much since he was a boy. Aunt Carrie could bring him up to date. A good talk later with the priest wouldn't hurt either. So it was that Pat and Aunt Carrie joined forces.

Father O'Doul had seen the news. He called Jenny O'Keeffe who came over for some of his good Irish tea. Sometime later, he welcomed Pat and Aunt Carrie in and they discussed matters. When they left, all were smiling.

The Texan was watching Anna on the news when the call came from his employer. When it was over, he looked sick.

"But I'm not a killer. You know that," he had protested to El Capitán. "I haven't any experience running a network like this, or killing. You've got to send a pro to do that."

"I have faith in you. You'll do it. Or you'll never see that money you have deposited in Geneva. I want access to those files immediately. We'll use those to rebuild the network. The files will lead us to people who were in that network.

They may even tell us what type of contraband they ran, who their contacts were or are, who the traitor was—because someone was—and who had to, or might still have to be eliminated. Get in touch with the officers and get that line running full on to Canada. You will do whatever it takes to make that happen. Whatever it takes."

The unsaid threat was "or you will be dead too." El Capitán never made that threat outright but no one who opposed or failed him was ever seen again.

Mike, Sean and Ben went online to watch the constant reruns of Anna's news conference.

"Geez, she looks like hell." Sean breathed a long sigh. "I'd sure hate to be in her shoes."

"I think AJ is dead, frankly. They should have found him by now," Mike said.

Ben hung his head.

"Damn. We really need to catch a break. You know, there's one thing that puzzles me. Why this family? Why them? There's a lot we don't know yet. We need more information. More people working on this. A lot more."

Vincent Grant stood in Anna's London apartment watching the news replay of Anna's announcement, feeling for the first time in his life like an utter failure. That feeling made him furious. The demand for ransom of the three Kinnealys fluttered from his hand to the low table next to him.

London

Sixteen

Days earlier...

Louie de la Vergne lifted the receiver on the antique phone in her boudoir, a direct line to her husband, Robert.

"Mon cherie Robert! I am patiently waiting for you to be here. You are so late tonight. What is happening?"

She listened and her mouth dropped open in astonishment.

"Oh! Mais non! She is free? How did that happen?"

Louie listened. "Oh, this Ardith woman is a force so terrible! So her lawyers freed her on bond and she has disappeared? She has outwitted the police of all Britain. That is very bad news.

"Oui? Anna called you? And...one million for AJ? Oh, that is not good! That will cause a feeding frenzy among every human shark in the world. Anna does not know how to handle them. Even I would tremble at that thought. Where is she? What are we to do? How can we help her?"

She was silent again, then picked up a pen and began writing on a small note pad.

"Oui. Oui. I will put this in place at once. If Anna is on her way to Mexico, we must help her here. I will contact this Vincent Grant and fortify her villa on Lake Como even more than Stacy did. I will also have our own little chateau set up as an alternative."

She listened again. "Yes, Marnie too. I am on it, as the Americans say.

"Darling, have you eaten? Have you taken your heart medicine? Put your secretary on. I'll have her look after you. When will you be home?"

A pause.

"Tres bien!"

Another pause.

"Tres bien. Oui. Merci beaucoup, my dear Gabrielle, for looking after him so well. Call if you need help."

Louie set the receiver down slowly, looking fierce.

Oh, yes! She will look after him so well. Yes, my dear Gabrielle, I know your ambitions. I also know my Robert. He is quite capable of playing you for all it is worth, and we have a history, he and I, which welds us together more than you will ever know.

It occurred to Louie that Gabrielle could become a breach in their security if she was offered enough money to supply information. *This is a war and the opposite side will use whatever they can to sabotage us, including, if they can, our own people. We must have all precautions in place.*

She called Robert back.

"My dear, are you alone? Oh, never mind. No matter. But just listen. I ask you to remember 1959 and the episode of September in Paris and the woman Antionette who could...yes. Because this Ardith woman has money to buy anyone."

She stopped to listen.

114

"You are so clever! You see it all."

She laughed, a long silvery cascade of delight.

"Why do I ever worry about these matters? Because I love you. Yes, yes. I will have more faith in you. Au revoir, my love."

Louie dialed the treatment center.

"I wish to speak with Marnie Kinnealy, please."

Her usually animated face grew still as she listened.

"When? Did she say where she was going? Who was with her?"

Louie listened impatiently for many seconds.

"But of course. I understand. She will not be allowed to return because this is the second time she has left against advice. Oui. Oui. "

"Stupid child!" she hissed as she hung up the phone. "Charbonneau! She went with Charbonneau! He is a fake, not to be trusted. I should have told her this but I thought he was out of her life."

Louie had ordered her contacts to investigate him after meeting the Count de Charbonneau during the rescue of Marnie from Mexico. True, he had been a great help. True, he declared he loved her. True, he had...*but something was wrong there, something I could not quite put my finger on*...and Louie had been correct in her hunch. He was not a count, not a Charbonneau at all, and much of his past was clouded. Robert now had his own contacts digging ever more deeply but nothing more had been unearthed yet. *That, in itself, is suspicious. Is this man under deep cover? If he is, then who does he work for? If not, then what? Was he after her money? Well, very likely. And if he did not get that, he can be bought by anyone who offers him money. Has he done this before? He has to be on someone's radar.*

Hurriedly she entered her closet, tossed off her peignoir and nightgown, and slid into old clothing—jeans, T-shirt and hoodie. She added smart suits and accessories to a garment bag and scooped up toiletries.

She made another quick phone call to Robert.

"No, mon cherie," he said. "We have no more news regarding Charbonneau. Patience, my love. It will take time. However, here is another phone number. You know this man as well as I do."

He gave her the man's undercover name.

"Oh, yes, I remember him. He is still working? Amazing! I will call immediately."

She took down the information from Robert and dialed.

He remembered her as well. "You were my favorite, cherie. If Robert hadn't married you, I would now be your husband. I would not have taken no for your answer."

Louie smiled to herself, seeing him as he had been long ago. "I am so happy you are available. I need you to find where this man is and who is with him." She gave him the name and

116

description of the "Count" who had picked Marnie up from the treatment center.

"He seemed reliable when we rescued her in Mexico but he is not. I thought then that he is an opportunist, after her money. That may still be the case. Expose everything of his past and present that you can find. You have the news on television? Oui. I am sure it is part of that case. The woman called Ardith was let out of the British prison on bail and she has disappeared. I am wanting to know if she bought him."

Louie listened for his reply.

"I am very sure she is psychologically unstable, full of revenge, and she has a lot of money to fund her psychosis. Killing is nothing to her. He may be working for her. He has just yesterday picked up Anna's daughter from the treatment center where she is supposed to be recovering. I am very worried. I'm leaving right away for the London apartment of Anna Kinnealy but I still must stop to see another of our underground contacts. I am setting up my own security protection here for two chateaus, just in case we need them. I think there is much more to this than meets the eye. If you cannot reach me, call Robert. I will keep him up to date on my every move. And thank you, thank you again."

She listened.

"But yes, mon ami, this is not nothing I ask. This is very much I ask of you and it *is* dangerous. There are two cartels out of Mexico mixed up in the lives of these people. They will stop at nothing. They have European contacts and we do not know who they are but, after I swept through Mexico in my countess role, I suspect they know very well who we—Robert and I—are. I will fax you the information on those cartels."

She hung up and a very sly smile crept across her face.

"They do not know who they have as an enemy. It is good to feel this adrenaline rush again. I have missed this."

Her childhood days as a spy at the end of World War II and the operations during the long Cold War played in her memory as Louie checked for her legal passport, scanned the other passports and papers and chose the ones she might have to use, took money from a small safe in her closet, checked her credit cards, loaded her backpack, pulled her hood over her head, and backed out of their garage into the darkness in the old car she kept for those occasions when she didn't want attention.

Darkness. My safe place. I became one of its creatures and it always welcomes me.

I will outthink this woman. She will be in England. That is where she has access to the boys. And if she has the girl, that is where Marnie will be also.

I hope.

Seventeen

Cory's leg was throbbing. The first operation to repair his calf muscle had been pronounced a success by the doctor but physical therapy demanded agonies of stretching and turning and twisting that left him gasping for breath and longing for drugs to end the pain. Nothing they had given him had taken it away.

Alex, watching him, nodded repeatedly off to sleep and then jerked awake again. They were home at the apartment but he swore the three days in the hospital had been a week. Cory's nurse had gone an hour earlier. Their day guards had been replaced by a night crew, one inside and two outside.

There had been no news from Marnie but they had not expected her to call them.

"Alex, try Mom again. See if you can get her."

Alex hit Anna's cell number and put the phone on speaker. No answer. No voice mail.

"She must be where there's no service available. We need to wait for her to call us."

"Is it time for my pain pill yet? My leg is bad. So bad."

"Another hour yet. Would it help if I massage it like the physical therapist did?"

"Maybe. Try it."

Alex pushed Cory's pants leg up, got out some oil, spread it on his hands and began gently manipulating the long calf muscle, carefully avoiding the incision area.

When the doorbell rang, both jumped.

They waited and it rang again.

"Where's that butler? Where's our guard?"

"Maybe it's Marnie." Cory struggled into a sitting position and moved himself into the wheelchair next to the bed.

"Why would she ring? She has a key." Alex stood up and wiped his hands on a towel. "Why isn't she in Switzerland?"

It rang again.

"Something's not right," Alex said, "and I don't like this.

They waited. When the bell didn't ring again, Alex walked to the bedroom door, opened it and listened. There were no further sounds. "The guard should have come in here by now. Something's off."

He pulled out his phone and punched the number for Vincent Grant.

"Mr. Grant, we've just had someone ring the bell at the apartment three times. Neither the butler nor a guard answered those rings and we don't know if anyone is even here with us. Can you get someone here fast?"

Grant swore under his breath.

"I'll get on it right away. Sit tight."

Alex slid his phone into his shirt pocket. "I've got to go see if there's anyone here."

"Well, don't leave me alone. I'm following you, wheelchair and all."

They made their way down the long hall to the living room and paused in the entryway. No one. There should have been a guard. A maid. A butler.

"We're alone here. This is weird. Why are we alone?"

"Because I want you alone," a voice behind them snarled.

Ardith Seacrest walked out of the dining room, a gun with a silencer in her hand.

"I'm not finished with you yet. I'm not finished with your mother yet either. I deserve that money she inherited and I will get it, one way or another. She will pay every penny she has to ransom her precious children.

"Bring her out here," she ordered someone behind her. Marnie was pushed out from behind her by someone Alex and Cory had never seen, a man with a tired, cynical look, his mouth curled in a sardonic smile.

"The Count de Charbonneau, at your service," the man stated.

She broke free from him, ran to Cory and threw her arms around him.

"I'm so sorry! I'm so sorry! I thought he could be trusted. He helped rescue me in Mexico. I thought he was on our side. I'm so sorry!"

She burst into tears. Alex pulled her off Cory and held her. Cory, angry, tried to stand but failed when sharp pain shot through his leg.

"Keep your gun trained on them," Ardith ordered the man. "I'm going to make sure there's no one else here."

"Where are our guards?" Cory demanded.

"Where they won't be a bother to me," Ardith snapped.

She walked swiftly through the apartment and came back.

"All clear. Get them out of here. Grant will have police here soon. We'll go through that empty apartment on the other side of the building."

Cory, struggling to rise, was shoved roughly into the wheelchair and Alex was ordered to wheel him ahead, a gun in his back held by a second man who had materialized from behind Ardith. Marnie was shoved along by the Count with a gun at her back and Ardith brought up the rear.

No one intercepted them. The hall was empty of any other persons. The vacant apartment was locked behind them and a car waited outside the rear door.

Cory was yanked from wheelchair to car, Marnie and Alex pushed in, and their captors followed quickly. A faint clang-clang of a police car grew louder and then faded again as the doors were slammed shut and they drove away.

When Vincent Grant and the police arrived, they found the wheelchair on the sidewalk.

Four dead men, the butler and three guards, were laid out in the basement. Bullet holes were placed neatly through the backs of the men's heads.

There was no sign of the maid.

A note, demanding ransom of Wentworth's entire fortune including the art collection, was on the dining room table.

Ardith had added, "You cannot stop me. I have an international organization. Anna has one week to hand over my inheritance."

Instructions for deposit of all monies to a bank in the Cayman Islands ended the note.

Grant swore for a good fifteen minutes after the note fluttered from his hand.

Eighteen

Ardith Seacrest, or whatever her name was, was not altogether immune from bad luck. The kidnapping of Alex, Cory and Marnie had not gone unnoticed. Another man had witnessed the transfer from wheelchair to car and had seen the guns.

Little Tom Kearsley—as opposed to Big Tom Kearsley, his father—had wandered the streets of London since he was five, and he knew dirty work when he saw it. He had the build of a great football player—soccer, that is—and had won a scholarship to college for his prowess. He had won many fights in the streets of London as well.

Little Tom had been on his way to see Cory and Alex, having heard about the blokes from America who were mixed up in some sort of mess back there and might want his help making their way safely in British society.

Little Tom was not altogether altruistic. He had also heard those blokes had money. A scholarship was not enough to pay his entire way through college but, being street-wise, he knew a good opportunity when it presented itself. He had ridden his motorcycle to the apartment building and had only just parked about twenty-five yards down the street behind the building when he saw the gun jammed into Marnie's back as she was forced into the car. His instincts told him to drop and he did, but he kept his eye on the scene. When the car left, he hopped on his bike, looking like any London resident on the road, and got close enough to see the license plate. He then dropped back a discreet distance and followed.

At first, he was covered by other traffic but that became less and less and he had to dodge to the curb now and then, use his encyclopedic knowledge of the streets to sort out where the car would be going. He would then cut through alleys and back streets to pick it up again.

There came the time when, however, he had to stop. But he knew. *Oh, yes, I know bloody well where they are now!*

That's when he phoned Big Tom, who happened to be a police officer in a London suburb.

"Dad, you know those American blokes I told you about. Well, I went to ask for a job and..." He gave a detailed description of what he'd seen, including the vehicle and license, and where he was now located and what he suspected.

"Stay there. I'll make some calls. If something's up, I'll get information on it. Do you think you can find out where they are?"

"Already done, Dad. It's the old neighborhood where we lived when I was eleven. Know it like the back of my hand." He described where he was.

"Keep watch. I'll ring you back."

Little Tom parked his bike where he knew it wouldn't be stolen—the yard of an old friend. Putting his phone on vibrate, he walked down the street in his workman's clothes until he got to the buildings he remembered, a small old red brick storehouse that butted up against a much bigger abandoned warehouse. His familiarity with locks and how to pick them served him well and he was in and through the small building in minutes to the old door that connected both structures.

"I hope I'm not wrong. I could have it all wrong. God help those boys if I am, and that girl too."

He opened the door between. A dark wave of silence emanated from the gloomy cavern of the old building. No sounds at all.

Little Tom could barely see but there was enough light to prevent him from tripping over debris on the floor and bumping into boxes and pallets and other obstacles. It took too many minutes for him to make a thorough search of the first floor. As he was about to take on the next floor, his phone vibrated and he had to make his way out to answer it.

"It's me. There's been a kidnapping from a fancy apartment." He gave the address. "Three people. Two boys and a girl. That what you saw?"

"Yeah, dad. That's it. You remember the big warehouse three streets over from our old house? That's where I am. Nothing on the first floor. Everything's silent now. If you and the others come, it better be on the quiet. They might kill if they hear sirens."

"They would. They left four dead men, killed execution style. You be damn careful. I'm heading that way. Leave me a mark if you have to go, like we used to do when I was teaching you to follow someone proper."

"Will do, dad. Goin' back in now. There's three more floors to check out."

Big Tom shrugged into his coat, called the station where he was based, took out the gun he rarely ever wore, checked it to be sure it still worked and dropped ammunition in his coat pocket. Besides Little Tom, he had two more sons he had trained in survival on the streets. He called them to "Go hunting" and they responded.

Little Tom crept back into the large building, carefully easing up the stair edges to keep from making noise by stepping on a creaky board. The second floor gave up no more than the first and he began to seriously doubt that this was the building.

Have to be sure though.

As he eased up the next flight of stairs the hair on his arms and back rose slightly. *Something. There's something. I can feel it. Bad energy.*

That floor proved to be a series of smaller rooms, former offices. *I just know. I just know.* Some smell. Some creeping crawling energy. Some infinitesimal sound that shouldn't be heard here.

Smell. Very faint. Perfume? The woman is here? Then, above him, far off footsteps, high heels, walking away down another staircase. *Other side of the building, that is. A man's quieter footsteps too. That leaves one to guard those kids, if these are the people in that car. The odds just got a lot better.*

He crept upward. More small offices.

He heard the girl's furious voice first.

"You bastard! She's bought you! You won't get away with this! The alarm has gone out through London. All over Great Britain and the continent. In the end, she'll kill you too."

"I have known her for years. I will come out of this a very wealthy man."

The man spoke with a French accent. "If you had married me, you would not be in this danger. We could have stayed out of this on your money. We could be anywhere else in the world now."

A young man's voice joined in.

"You won't get out of this. She'll kill you just like she's killed many others. She's crazy. Psychotic. She likes to kill."

"Shut up! You know nothing about this. You are a pair of stupid young boys."

Little Tom peered very carefully around the edge of the door where the voices came from and ducked quickly back. The man with the gun had almost seen him, was almost facing in his direction. The younger men couldn't see him, but maybe the girl did.

If only I can get past this door and to the one around the corner where they can see me and he can't.

But how to get around the corner without being seen?

He heard the girl's voice get louder. *Too loud. Why so loud? A sign to me? Did she see me?*

"Etienne, you told me you loved me. Why are you doing this? As you just pointed out, I have money. If you want money, I can provide that."

She sounded like she was moving, her voice changing directions slightly. Little Tom risked a peek. She had seen him! She had made the man turn!

Little Tom flashed past the door and crept around the corner. Again he heard her voice from another direction and peeked around the doorjamb. The man had his back turned completely. *Both boys can see me! I'm closer and I can tackle this guy! They see it too.*

One of the young men, facing him, lowered his eyelids and raised them, acknowledging Little Tom's presence. The younger boy lowered his hand to one side. One finger, two, and three.

It was over in a flash of movement. On three, the young boy stood, then dropped with a cry, clutching his leg. *Brilliant!* Distracted, the gunman began to turn. The other young man grabbed the hand with the gun, pushing it skyward while Tom dived in and tackled the man at the knees. The girl hit the gunman with a chair to his head and he dropped, unconscious. Not, however, before he had gotten a shot off.

Little Tom scrambled to his feet and told them, "We've got to get out of here! She could have heard that shot and be on her way back. My dad is coming and we'll get you to safety somewhere."

That's when he realized that the boy who had collapsed was truly injured and couldn't walk.

Alex and Marnie attempted to get Cory to his feet. Little Tom pushed the girl away and got Cory's arm over his shoulder. Marnie grabbed the gun on the floor but it was clear to Little Tom she had no idea how to handle it.

They were limping down to the second floor when they heard the woman's voice shout to someone in the building.

"If you must shoot, shoot to kill. I'll just have to ransom their bodies."

Little Tom grabbed the gun out of Marnie's hand and motioned her to take his place next to Cory. As Alex, Cory and Marnie struggled carefully down the steps, Little Tom followed them, twisting back and forth, waiting for the woman to show her face. They were three steps from the bottom when they heard furious cries.

"They have to be here or near here! Get them! Now!"

They heard the stomp of feet from above. More than one person.

Little Tom got them out the door and was astonished when he saw the van and heard an old familiar voice.

"Hey! Tom! This way! Saw your bike! Your dad called. Figured you to be in trouble again. Let's go."

As they piled into the van, Little Tom pulled out a black crayon and left a sign on the cement building before he jumped in and the van took off.

"Message for your dad?"

"Yeah. Lettin' him know we got away."

He turned to the three in the rear of the van. "So what's your names, anyway?"

Cory, hands around his calf, gasped through gritted teeth. "Oh shit!"

"Dumb name for a Yankee," Little Tom replied and smiled with satisfaction.

Nineteen

"This has to be the worst tea I've ever had!" Marnie choked as drips of the liquid dribbled down her chin. She grabbed a cloth and wiped her face and T-shirt off but stains remained on the shirt.

"It could be worse, sister dear. You could be dead. Or dead drunk. How could you be dumb enough to be led on by a creep like that?"

Alex was feeling mean, angry, frustrated, impatient, and, the truth he didn't want to admit, very scared. He paced a parlor furnished in ancient English décor in a small house in some unknown part of what he thought was still the city of London. It could have been anywhere for all he knew. The ride had been long, with many turns and twists. That much he knew for sure.

Marnie glared at him.

"I'm very much aware of that. Where are we? Who are the people who got us out of that warehouse and why aren't we being brought back to the apartment? What is this place and what is going on?"

"Haven't the faintest, sister dear, except one of them is apparently connected to a police force in some small part of London. I think. Maybe. I don't know. All I know is we're safer than we were. That Ardith woman is just plain bat shit crazy. She won't give up her weird idea she's some relation to Conrad Wentworth and that mom owes her his fortune. I personally think she'll keep hunting for us. I wish we could get hold of Mom."

"Alex, stop the sarcastic sister dear stuff! Cory, try again with your phone." Marnie ordered. "Try Sean Fitzgerald too. We need to get some kind of news from them and get some news out to her."

"My phone's dead. Now, if one of you had thought to bring a charger, we might be able to do that."

Cory lay on a couch with his leg propped on some embroidered cushions. *I bet if Mom saw this she'd make me take my foot off them.* He wondered where she was and if she had found AJ and if she knew the woman tried to kidnap them again.

For the moment, the pain had subsided but he had gone through nine hours of throbbing hell before he could rest. Now, his leg had stopped hurting but he had a pounding headache. Any pain meds were back at the apartment.

The men in the van had grinned and reassured them but it was not comforting. He heard them talk about the butler and two guards being killed. Where was the maid who was supposed to be there? Was she dead too? Was she in on the whole thing? Had she been Ardith in disguise? *That's a creepy thought. How did Vincent Grant screw up our security so bad? At least Marnie's with us and not out there alone somewhere.*

Alex's thoughts ran in a similar vein. They were interrupted by the entrance of Little Tom and the driver of the van. They carried bags of food.

"Time for a bit o' traditional British hospitality, blokes and blokette." He held up the bags. "We got us MacD here too. Thought you might like a taste of home."

Little Tom grinned. His speech did not include the letter h. He had said 'ere and 'ome. It wasn't that he didn't speak proper British, he explained to them, but "this 'ere is me 'ome territory and when at 'ome, speak as the 'ome boys do. But I'll drop it so you can understand me proper."

"Now," he announced as he distributed bags and another man came in with trays of drinks, "I am here to offer my services and that of my blokes...uh...that means my brothers and friends. That was what I was up to when I saw them take you out of that building. I followed the van you were in and knew where they took you—well, I guessed at that—but, you see, that was old territory where I knew my way around and so I knew that was the most logical place you would be. Quite right I was, too. My father's a copper with local police in a suburb and I called him and he got on it and here you are, safe and sound."

He looked at Cory. "Well, almost sound. We've got a doctor comin' soon, man, so you'll be none the worse for wear in just a little while. Let's start with you. You're the one called Cory. Just what is this that you got yourself into, anyway?"

134

Cory looked at Alex and Marnie with the question on his face. *Can I tell them? Should I?*

"Tell them, Cory. Begin at the beginning and just tell them," Alex said.

Marnie nodded assent.

Two hours later, the first bags of food gone and more sent for and eaten, Alex and Marnie had added their parts in the story.

Little Tom and his two companions, and his dad, Big Tom, who had entered just as Cory began, looked at each other with amazement. Who would have thought these three from some far-off, small size Yankee town would be caught in the nets of international poisonous spiders whose sting had been felt in Ireland, Britain, France, Switzerland, Italy, the U.S., Mexico and who knew where else?

Big Tom had become more and more solemn and thoughtful as he listened. Having raised three boys to survive the streets, he automatically took the measure of the young people. *The boys have been tested and they are fighters. The girl, maybe, maybe not.*

He would pass that on to his super who would pass that on to higher powers who had let him know they had a strong interest in these three Americans and had a plan they had outlined briefly to him. The Yard wanted this woman and all who associated with her. They needed bait.

Big Tom leaned forward and, without mincing words, laid out the situation and the plan.

135

When he finished, it was Cory, Alex, and Marnie who were astonished.

Alex ran his hands through his hair. "I thought it was just us, just our family. Maybe because of our dad's illegal activities from long ago. Or just that crazy woman wanting our money—Conrad's money."

"It is much, much more than that, young man. The running of drugs, human slavery and prostitution, sale of children to pedophiles, arms dealers, sale of ivory and black diamonds, illegal animal sales. You name it, it's out there. That's what you are caught in, what we're all caught in now. Human greed results in billions of dollars of revenue for individuals and corporations run by sociopaths and psychopaths. You three have been caught in one small section of an immense web. My government would like you to help us unravel the threads a bit.

"Cory, since you are the 'injured animal', you become the primary bait. Alex, you and the lads here," he nodded at Little Tom and his friends, "become the ones who do the legwork on the streets, and you, young lady, will work with another woman in the upper echelons of society. This woman is very experienced. In fact, you know her. She rescued you from the escapade in Mexico."

"The countess? What experience does she have? How do I know she can help me?" Marnie's memory of the "countess" role Louie had played was sketchy, just scenes here and there. Her memory of Louie's placement of her in the treatment center, however, was not pleasant. Louie had not minced words at the time.

Big Tom gave Marnie a list of Louie's accomplishments.

"And those are the ones I can tell you about. The rest are still top secret. You will be in good hands and can learn much from her. If I were you, I would jump at the chance to learn from this woman.

"The Yard will give you a day to talk this over but, frankly, you will not be able to give us a 'no' for an answer. I have been told my government will use your presence in this country to the maximum advantage we can.

"You will not be allowed to tell your mother or any others what is going on. Your government will only know that you are cooperating with us. If that upsets you, I'm sorry. However, I do have some comfort for you. My sons will be supporting you.

"Because we lived in some London neighborhoods where there was much crime and because I was a policeman and engaged in dangerous work, I taught my children to survive on their own from a very young age. They are experienced in survival in this urban landscape. It's the reason you are alive at this time. Little Tom recognized what was happening to you and he rescued you using that knowledge. He has agreed to continue. Do you have any questions?"

Alex stood, arms folded in front of his chest.

"So. We are being kidnapped by the British government. What if we refuse to comply?"

"Your visas will be pulled and you will be returned home immediately. Without protection. On your own. All family financial assets under British control will be frozen. Vincent Grant will have his business closed in this country and in all other countries with whom we work, which includes most of Europe."

Little Tom stood up, a shocked look on his face.

"Dad, what is this? Why? They're being treated like criminals. This is unfair. How come you're telling them this? On what authority?"

"On the authority of Her Majesty, the Queen's, government. There is a great deal you don't know about my job all these years. There are things I could not and cannot tell you. There are reasons I am doing this. Parts of London and all of England are experiencing a massive drug epidemic right now, with all the crime and violence that accompany them. The decision has been made at high government levels to do all in our power to stop it.

"I must go. I will be back tomorrow for your answers."

Big Tom left. Little Tom and his friends withdrew. The shock on their faces told the Kinnealys they had not known about this.

Alex, Cory and Marnie were left alone. A feeling they had just been abandoned washed over them.

Alex still stood, a stunned look on his face. Cory took his leg down off the couch and sat up, confused and frightened. Only Marnie could move, her eyes flashing rage, her fists clenched.

"Those S.O.B.s!!! Those arrogant unfeeling conscienceless obnoxious uncaring sons of bastards!!! So we can go home without protection? Well, then, I say we go! Let them ship us back home! They can run their own drug busts without three American guinea pigs. I wonder if our government is actually cooperating or if he was lying. You saw his son's face. Little Tom didn't even know about this. Even he was shocked. Cory, you can get just as good medical care back home. Mom brought you both here to keep you out of trouble, not into more. To keep you safe. This is not safe. This is setting us up to be killed just so that they can smoke out their criminals. I say let them do their own dirty work. I'm calling Mom. It's none of their business what we say to Mom. I say she needs to know this. I say..." Marnie stopped and pulled out her phone, tense lines around her thinned lips.

She was only partly through dialing when Cory struggled to his feet, gently took her hands in his and stopped her.

"Marnie, stop, please. First of all, your phone's useless too." Unshed tears waited in his eyes for him to blink. The blink never came.

"Second and most important of all, I'm scared. I'm seriously frightened. But not of the British. True, they are being assholes, using three Americans as bait for their predators. I'm more scared this will go on and on and on. I'm scared this will get us all killed. Only a couple weeks ago I was facing death in that cave and I wanted to live. I wanted to have a long life. I still do. I want to be an actor, a singer, a musician, a...well...whatever my life will bring.

Ardith would have killed us with only the thought that we were worth less money dead than alive. Or she would have sent someone else to do it. She still will. It doesn't matter if we go home or stay here or even go to Mexico to help Mom. She'll follow us. We're prisoners of the circumstances of our lives and I don't want it to go on. I want to face it. With or without the British, it will go on unless something, no, *we* make it come to an end. We can go, but I think we'll have more resources if we stay. Please, both of you, just think it through first. Please. I just can't face this going on and on."

He sat down, wincing as his leg twisted and crumpled under him.

Marnie knelt and gently pushed his pants leg up. She pulled the bandage away from the incision and air hissed in through her teeth.

"Whatever we do, Cory, you have to have medical help right now. This is infected."

Alex stood over the two of them.

"Ok. I say we stay. I'll get Little Tom in and demand medical help. They have to do that if they want their bait."

"Wait!" Cory whispered. "Listen close, both of you." He gestured them into a huddle.

"Remember when we were kids and played 'One O'clock the Ghost is Here' and figured out how to win more games than all the kids in the neighborhood?"

Alex grinned and nodded. "Yeah, we cheated. We changed the rules of the game. We weren't being fair but it got us lots of wins. Lots."

"Think about it, Alex, we won because we controlled the territory!"

Marnie slowly nodded her head. "Yeah, but I don't see how we can do that here. True. We controlled as much of the setup as we could. True. We knew the territory better than anyone else. We even disappeared..." An evil smile crept across her face. "It *is* a possibility. Yes, it is!"

"Alex," she said quietly. "Cory's right. We controlled it all. The obvious fact is, we can set up more control with more cooperation here than if we go back home. Back home is a mess—an unguarded house, a neighborhood and town that thinks we're drug pushers, a crazy lady who'll follow us there, and can we trust the police there any better than here? We don't know that. Here we have the British government all the way to the top invested in using us. Let's take that day they gave us and set up our own operation. Operation Stay Alive and Fight, fair or unfair.

They looked back and forth at each other. Wordless agreement.

"We'll set up our plans tonight," Alex said, "but first we check this house for bugs and get that medical help. I also want to have a heart to heart with Little Tom. I think he might be at least

141

partly on our side. He looked really shocked at the way his dad acted.

"You do the thing with Cory's leg," he ordered Marnie. "Quick! Cover your leg back up, Cory. Marnie, look totally worried, horrified even, when you uncover it, but don't overdo it. Only enough drama to justify getting help. Let's see if we can get them to take us back to our apartment and your doctor, Cory. That'll be the test. If we can make them do that, we know we can set up our own scenes."

Twenty-four hours later they arrived at their London apartment after Cory had been seen by his physician and given strong antibiotics. They were accompanied by Little Tom, hired as their bodyguard and recruited by Alex to teach them the "lay of the land", so to speak. They were met by Louie, in her very rich, very commanding countess role.

Another twenty-four hours and they had a team, Louie included.

Anna had been reached via Louie's phone. Marnie explained they were "just fine", reassured her about Cory's leg, gave her details of the visit to the doctor, and told her all about their reminiscences and how they were remembering their childhood games, like "Run, My Good Sheep Run" and especially how much they enjoyed "One O'Clock the Ghost Is Here."

Anna, in her hotel in Cancun, was very relieved to hear from them and a bit puzzled but her senses were acutely tuned in.

Another hour of remembering and she got it. Not quite all the details but she got it. She called Louie's secure phone and got the full details.

"Anna, you must be satisfied with this arrangement for now. They have British police solidly behind them. Better than nothing at all. You have devilishly clever children. I love the way their minds work. Much like mine. I can teach them tricks I haven't used for years. Do not worry. And now, what of AJ?"

"Many false leads. One possible. It's being checked out. I can feel he is still very ill. I don't know any more. Negotiations with The Crocodile are slow—very careful, of course. Well, dragging, really. I'm in a glass cage which I feel will be shattered by the least misstep."

"It will come together soon. I can feel it. Au revoir, my dear."

I have lied to her. A white lie? This will not come together soon, none of it. The manipulations of those who are addicted to greed do not stop. They continue. They escalate.

Louie phoned Robert. "My darling, I have some ideas for you to think about. The art collection. What if..." and she laid out those ideas.

Twenty

"My leg is feeling better. I have pain in the muscle when I stretch it but otherwise, I'm OK."

Cory's legs were stretched out on the floor in front of him and he was exercising the muscle by moving his foot inward to touch his opposite knee and then stretching it out with toes pointed down.

"You look like you're doing ballet exercises. Cute!" Alex commented.

Marnie joined in with her own comment and the banal conversation went on until the police officer got a phone call and left the room.

Immediately the three sprang together.

"What's our next move?" Cory asked, in a low voice.

"You and I are going with Little Tom," Alex explained. "He's taking us over the territory covered by the map he brought us last night. We're about to learn how to navigate the streets and back alleys of London, one neighborhood at a time. He persuaded his dad that if we're both to be bait, we at least should have a fair chance at survival if things go wrong. Cory, you're going to listen and learn the sounds of British. All the different accents. We need a bloody translator. See. I'm even picking it up. Everything's going to be bloody this and bloody that."

"I'm going with Louie." Marnie said. "I'm to be the" she wiggled her fingers in quotation marks, "visiting heiress and model, the one who's in the public eye, while you guys are ferreting out or drawing out Ardith. I'm going to get to know every single person around us. Louie will get me files on everyone. She says there's always the chance that Ardith has people planted in the police department or, well, anywhere. She also says there may be other drug cartels looking for an 'in' to Ardith's group, so we have to know everyone's background as much as we can. She'll purchase prepaid cells exclusively for each of us so we can always connect with each other. We want some way to keep in touch all the time. We have to learn a lot, maybe more than we need to know, because she says you never know what will be useful."

"OK, in the meantime, sneaky sister dear, you learn this map. I want to know you know your way around too."

"I'm on it. Louie brought me a map of London and it includes the subway. She's making me learn it all. She's the sneakiest person around here. She's one person in front of police and then changes her personality to her spy role the minute they walk out of the room."

"Where is she now?" Cory pulled his pants leg up and began massaging his calf.

"I don't know but she left in her countess personality so I guess she's with police or Scotland Yard or something like that."

"Something like that" was not police or Scotland Yard. The countess role had been her cover.

145

"I will be doing shopping for clothing for Marnie," she had told Big Tom Kearsley very firmly. "She will have to dress the part if she is to be bait. I would take her with me but I can do this most easily alone. We don't want to use her unnecessarily. Time enough to bring her out in public when we have everything in place. I also insist she learn more about London in this role. If she sounds too stupid, she will not fit in with the people she must meet. I have assigned her homework."

Big Tom Kearsley was developing a growing dislike of this woman. The person he was seeing seemed at odds with the information he had about her past. *Her past success has gone to her head. Imperious bitch, she is. Doesn't know her place in this modern world. Still thinks there's a Cold War. That blonde hair of hers is from a bottle. I bet it's all white under that color. Too old for this, I think.*

The police stationed at the apartment had been ordered to watch her carefully.

Vincent Grant agrees with me too. Grant's cooperation was assured. He had been brought down many rungs of his own ladder of success by the failure of his men to protect this family so far. *Not totally his fault because that Ardith woman is a loose cannon. There's no predicting what she will do or try.*

Obsession is the only word for it. Without doubt extremely dangerous. Unpredictable. Psychopath, the profiler said. Psychopath with unlimited money and she employs people just like her.

Louie was aware of the police officer following her. A man. *A woman would have been better. She would be able to follow me into a bathroom, or the dressing room at the couturier's. No matter. I will be rid of him soon.*

She was.

Louie spent three hours choosing clothing for Marnie, giving measurements to the designers, choosing fabrics, ordering accessories and making sure her follower saw all she did. When she finished, she ditched him and travelled by back ways to meet the messenger Robert was sending. The messenger turned out to be an old acquaintance and they had a nice tea at a lovely old hotel dining room.

Robert had warned on the phone. "He has all information you asked for, my dear. I have marked the places in London which would be safest for a confrontation with this woman but you must never underestimate her. She will insist on choosing her own places to make a stand. On one hand that may be turned to your advantage. Remember Paris, 1956. On the other hand, it could be extremely dangerous."

The old man had remembered Paris too. They discussed possibilities.

"It is time I reappear at the apartment," Louie sighed. "You think you can find out where this woman goes to ground?"

"I think so. There are four of us on this. Just so you know, the police are having a fit right

147

now looking for you. Look for me among the pack of reporters when the police set the girl up as bait. The seamstress from the couturier who brings the clothing is one of us too. She's old but she's very experienced. You can pass information to her."

"Merci beaucoup, mon ami. Au revoir. Now I must finish my shopping."

Louie took a cab to Harrod's, made purchases of delicious foods, window shopped along the streets of London until she was sure her follower had found her again, but not before she had purchased certain electronic devices on the sly. She arrived at the apartment in a cab loaded with purchases just in time for the delivery of several dresses from the couturier.

She smiled sweetly at the thundercloud face of the man who had been assigned to follow her who now stood across the street, wiggled her fingers in a lovely greeting and swooped in with her purchases, all of which were searched.

Louie was not.

There followed a lengthy fitting of clothing for Marnie, observed closely by a female officer who did not see Louie slip a device into the pocket of the seamstress. The officer also missed the transfer of said device into the case of sewing tools and supplies which had already been searched by said officer. Said officer was aware that the seamstress, hurriedly checked out by police, had been on the London stage for a time. She was not aware that the seamstress had been part of a magic act using sleight of hand. Picking pockets was a skill the woman had acquired but never listed on her resume. The transfer of said communication device into Marnie's room was a piece of cake. Louie slipped the other devices into the boys' rooms.

Dinner that night was most pleasant. Louie spent much time educating the young Americans in proper British etiquette for formal dinners. Marnie would surely need it. The boys were included just in case they might need it too. One never knew.

Alex, Cory and Little Tom Kearsley had ridden motor bikes through much of the London suburb of Camden, including all back alleys and shortcuts. They had been taken along all routes to the warehouse and allowed to walk over the crime scene and were grilled again by a man from the Yard and Big Tom.

"How's your leg holding up, man?" Little Tom asked as they stood in the door of the apartment.

"Fine. Using the motor bike is brilliant."

Cory's speech was taking on British words and an accent. To Little Tom's amusement, he was evolving into an American Harry Potter with Ron Weasley's ginger hair.

"Walking around makes it hurt but nothing like it did."

"Good. We have the doctor coming in the morning to check it again to be sure it's healing right. We need you in good shape in case you

149

have to run. Tomorrow is more of the same. Study the maps. Be prepared."

After retiring to bed, Marnie installed the device from Louie that would block their conversation from anyone and called her brothers to her room where three grown up brats from the East Side of Green Bay, who had cheated at games as children, schemed to know and rule as much of London's territory as possible.

"Do you think this will really help? Cory asked. "It seems so little."

"It's all we can do right now, Cory. We just have to hope what we learn will help us," Marnie replied.

"It can't hurt," Alex added. "It's better than just sitting around waiting. But I wish I knew how Mom is doing. And AJ."

"Me too," echoed both Marnie and Alex.

"For now," Louie said, "it's best not to call. She knows you're safe. She can put all of her attention on ransoming AJ."

Twenty-one

Marnie swayed as the sudden intense longing for pot hit her. The hunger, the desire, the need, the powerful impulse to suck in huge lungfuls of smoke and wait for the peaceful sensation as it spread through her body—all of that had slapped into her consciousness with the speed of a bullet. She was totally unprepared for it. This was the second time it happened. She thought it was over, that hunger, but it flooded in accompanied by a memory of her father, laughing with her, adoring her, along with the awful loss that had emptied her heart when he never returned all those years ago, as if she had done something terrible and he didn't want her any more.

Louie, watching the fitting of the formal gown, saw it. She signaled the seamstress to leave, zipped Marnie out of the gown, letting it drop to the floor. She took Marnie's hand, gave it a shake, and Marnie lifted her foot and stepped over the pile of shimmering fabric, a dazed look on her face.

"What drug are you wanting? Heroin, cocaine, what?" Louie asked as she slipped a loose silk caftan over Marnie's body.

"How do you know?"

"I have been in many situations in my life from which I longed for relief. In some instances, I got it. The price was very high, but I got it."

"I don't believe you."

151

"Well, you should. You may be able to benefit from my experience."

Louie's memory flashed a panorama of painful events from her own life—her aunt who cared for her after her parents disappeared into, so she had been told, Stalin's prisons. The uncle who took over when her aunt disappeared, and then the life on the streets of East Berlin beginning somewhere around the age of eight. The Soviet soldier who took her in and fed her and clothed her...for a price. The cigarettes the "uncle" gave her to calm her down when he wanted her body. The day she killed him. Robert finding her stealing his supplies and sending her to an orphanage until she was old enough to help in the long Cold War. The day she begged Robert to marry her, knowing she could never let another man touch her, ever, and knowing she would never feel safe with anyone else. His protests that he was too old. Her protest that she could not bear to be apart from him, that if she was, she knew she would return to the streets and the drugs and the horror, drawn to it as she was. She had not told him how close to suicide she was.

The fairytale myth they had concocted about how they met, so delightful, so sweet, so untrue.

"Sit down. I will get you some juice and water. You must drink more water. It will cleanse your system."

Marnie sat, stunned at the power of her hunger. Others in the treatment center had tried to describe it but no description she remembered was adequate. She had felt they were exaggerating, creating drama to call attention to themselves. She had felt contempt for them. *Now, oh god, I* am *one of them!*

A wave of deep disgust and disappointment swept over her. *Oh, god, I am one of...*them!

She pulled her knees up to her chin and curled into fetal position on the couch where she sat. Shame assaulted her.

Unaware that she was speaking out loud, she whispered, "How did I get like this? How did I sink so low? How did I become an...an..."

"The word is addict. Addict. An unpleasant word. I have never found it an easy word to hear or say. It is replete with shame and cruelty and sickness, at least in my experience, anyway."

Louie lapsed into silence until Marnie stirred, uncurled slightly and looked up.

"My dear, drink your juice and just listen. Perhaps my story will help you. Perhaps not. But I am going to tell it. At the moment, it is all I have to offer."

Sometime later, Louie returned to silence. Marnie watched the slow tears that ran down Louie's face. She reached for some tissues, leaned forward, and wiped then away.

"Merci, my dear. Merci." Louie took a deep breath. "It is a long time since I have spoken of all that. Many years. Only Robert and one other ever knew the whole story. The other person is long dead. I hope it gives you hope too, that you will know you can find healing."

"Yes. If you could find healing after all that, I can. I can. But how do I get myself and my brothers out of this mess? I don't see what I can do to help this along. I'm not talented at any of the skills you have. I'm not subtle and don't know how to deceive and..."

"Ah, but you do! Addicts are good at deception. I will show you how to take the ability to deceive yourself and others and turn it outward and use it in a good way, for the good of your brothers and yourself and your family. In fact, you'll fit right in with the British upper class. They are so good at it. For that matter, so are the French, and the Germans, and the Americans. Upper classes almost always love to deceive themselves and others about their worth. Entitlement. It's how they justify what they do. The trick is not to get caught into believing your own or their deceptions.

"Now, are you still wanting marijuana? No? Of course not. Lesson One: that too passes, and quite easily at times if you do not give it power by giving it attention. My story drew your attention away. That is one reason why twelve step programs work."

Louie stood and drew Marnie up off the couch.

"Now let's get that dress fitted. It is stunning and you will use it at the dinner tomorrow night at the embassy to draw attention to yourself. We will see if you can smoke out this

154

crazy woman who craves your mother's money. Puns intended. She is as much of an addict as you and I have ever been.

"When the dress is done, we will again go over dinner table place settings and what to use with what course, and then we have pictures of people you will meet and information about them. Do not worry. I will be at your side most of the time. I am to introduce you to this society. But there will also be a half hour when I will appear to leave your side. We hope that if the woman wants to get in touch with you, she will take advantage of that time. That will be the pattern for all our forays into society. Just think of it as an extended runway and you want to attract a buyer."

Despite the motor scooters they rode, by mid-afternoon, Cory's leg was aching.

"I've got to get to physical therapy or this won't work, dudes," he told Little Tom and Alex. "I can't skip it. We've got to work around that schedule. My leg is pounding."

"Right! Sorry, mate! I should have taken that into account. I got so eager to teach you how to get around here that I forgot about your injury."

They were having afternoon tea at a pub in the district where the old warehouse stood. Both Cory and Alex had played cat and mouse through the streets and alleys, and learned shortcuts through shops until they completely escaped Little Tom. He was very pleased.

"We'll do more of that in other districts and neighborhoods. You'll be able to escape anyone who tries to kidnap you but even more important, you'll be able to lead anyone after you into the arms of police. Dad says there's been some feelers out that undercover coppers reported. He thinks she's got a plan in place. He said they're hoping that because she's so loony, she'll screw up somewhere along the line and they'll be able to round up a good part of her crew."

Alex nodded in agreement.

"Right, and I just want to come out of this alive. Now, Cory and I would like you to help us learn more. The place we need to know next and best is all that territory around our apartment. We think that might be a good place to lure her into our trap. She didn't hesitate to break and enter the place before."

"Sure. We can do that. It makes sense to me. I'll get us police maps but you can use Google Earth tonight to learn the main streets. In fact, let's go there now. I'll call in the physical therapist for your leg, Cory, and tomorrow we can work that area."

He turned away to signal a waiter.

Cory looked at Alex. Both smiled.

Twenty-two

Cory was in a state of shock.

"God! You're beautiful! That dress is awesome on you. Your hair, it's so pretty! You smell good too."

Marnie's black hair was piled high on her head except for one long black curl that curved down her cheek and lay on her white shoulder. The strapless dress, in turquoise, molded her figure until just below her hips where it flared out to the floor, with the tiniest of glittery crystals winking in the light. Her nails matched her dress and had one small crystal on the tip of each. Diamonds dripped from her ears and lay in delicate swirls around her neck.

"Cory, your compliments would be great if you didn't sound so utterly surprised that I can look nice. And smell nice."

"Well I don't mean it that way. It's just that you look so, so high society, and I'm not used to thinking of us in that league. You'll fit right in."

"I don't know about that. I'm pretty nervous. I can't even remember if I start with the outside silver or the inside silver at dinner."

Louie glided into the room, a form-fitting cobalt blue dress undulating with every step she took. Alex's jaw dropped and he gulped a bit for air.

"I wish I could escort both of you. Why couldn't I come too? I'd like to see all those glamorous people. I'd like to be one."

Louie smiled.

157

"Perhaps there will be a time but right now you do not have the proper evening wear and you do not have an invitation. Nor have I trained you enough. I will consider your request however. And now, my dear," she turned and adjusted the long black curl, "we will see what will be attracted by such lovely bait."

Marnie stood at one side in the room where the dancing was to begin. A very proper and pleasant older couple had just left her. Louie was nowhere in sight. This was the time when they hoped someone would approach. The dinner had gone well. Seated near Louie, Marnie could watch which silver to use. Too nervous to be hungry, she sat through an uncounted number of changes of plate and food, picking at whatever lay in front of her while talking to the men on each side of her in turn. By the third course, she had forgotten their names and was too embarrassed to ask again.

The music had begun and still she stood alone. When it became clear she was being ignored, she turned and left the room.

If I am to be left alone by these society people, at least I can wander through the other rooms and look at the art. Maybe someone will make contact then, away from the crowd.

The building she was in was huge, with great portraits in the halls and objets d'art carefully placed on tables, bureaus, and shelves. Taking a glass of something from a waiter, she slowly walked along the walls, allowing herself to enjoy every beautiful object.

The drink smelled of alcohol. She set it down on a table.

After ten minutes of wandering, she found herself in a long library. Halfway through, browsing through book titles, she heard a door close and a click. She turned and a man in formal wear stood just inside the door. A small nugget of fear formed in her stomach. Looking the other way toward a far door, she saw a second man in a waiter's clothing close that door. The nugget grew to baseball size. Panic rose from stomach to lungs to shoulders, up her neck, across the back of her skull and froze her face.

I'm trapped.

Slowly the men came toward her. She picked up a large vase to defend herself.

"It is of no use, Miss Kinnealy. Please do not be so foolish as to fight us. We would not like to tear your clothing or subdue you in any violent way. We will, however, do that if you fight."

First Man had said all this softly, with a smile on his face. Second Man came toward her slowly but said nothing. He had his hand in his pocket and as he neared her, he pulled out a cloth. Marnie could smell the strong anesthetic on it and gagged.

Suddenly, there were noises behind the men and people were moving swiftly into the room toward the piano at one end. Louie appeared and, with a smile, neared Marnie, phone out and aimed at the men.

"Darling, let us get our selfies taken with these wonderful guests. You, sir," she aimed the phone at one man and took his picture, "and you, too,' she aimed at the other, "we will want to remember you and everyone here." She flashed the camera in all directions, taking pictures one after another.

The men retreated carefully and melted into the now-crowded room. Someone was playing a jazzy tune. Dancing began. Voices and laughter filled the air. Glass and ice tinkled.

Marnie, feeling frozen in a cube of airless space, carefully set down the vase and slowly eased herself into a nearby chair. Louie, not skipping a beat, began to dance with a young man nearby and then brought him over to Marnie, pulled her up out of the chair and shoved them at each other.

"You young people must really dance and have fun. I am too old for this."

She sat down in the chair and sent the pictures from her phone to the police.

So now we know two of them, but where is she? If Ardith sent them to this affair, she can get her people into anything. She must be nearby. I have to be more careful and follow Marnie more closely.

She watched Marnie. The girl's mouth smiled but her eyes still held the fear that had so recently flooded her face.

The movement of dancing had been Louie's goal. Movement would bring Marnie out of the frozen shock. *Tomorrow I will process*

160

every second of this event with her. When she is done, she will know more about how to manage these situations. This lesson will strengthen her.

Alex and Cory retreated to Alex's bedroom with the small drawings they had made of the basement and upper rooms of the apartment house during the night. Cory paced the room.

"We can keep those old boards in your closet loose," he said, "but we'll have to make sure they look like they're in solid. We got in and out tonight easily and this old building has lots more nooks and crannies to explore. Nothing like an old British building for odd spaces. I say we make a place where we can keep someone captured if we need that. Or hide out when we don't want to be found.

"The thing is, do we want to let Little Tom know we can do this? And, where else in this neighborhood can we create hiding spaces? I want options. I want plans A, B, C and D. We've got to have options. What if we need to hide Marnie to keep Ardith from her? Do we let Louie know about this? Boy, she's an odd one, isn't she? One minute I feel like I should bow to her and the next I'm scared of her. She's been around."

Alex gulped his soda as he stood thinking about that.

"I trust her. I think she's on our side totally and I agree she is an odd one. But I'm not ready to tell Little Tom about our ventures out of here. The thing is, I don't quite know how all this will help us yet. How will this save us? How will this get us free of surveillance by Ardith or the British police?"

Cory rubbed his temples. A headache was starting. "I wish we had Mom here and AJ and, actually, I wish we were back home and all this could be over. Or, better yet, I wish I could just take my acting classes and finish high school and live my life."

"Me too, Cory. I wonder what Mom's doing now. Can you feel her? Can you feel AJ?"

"Sort of. Actually, all I feel is lots of anger—rage really. Ugly. Dark and creepy sick. As much as I'd like to find AJ, I'd rather be here. I don't like what I feel."

"From Mom too?"

"Yeah, especially from Mom. I don't want to be around her right now. Remember that time long ago just after Dad was killed and Mom and AJ came back from the Yucatan and we got up one night and she was pacing the dining room and she looked like an animal? Like she was going to eat someone? Do you remember? We sneaked down the back stairs."

"Yeah." Alex looked up from the maps.

"Like that."

Alex sat on his bed, drew his legs up, elbows on his knees.

"It was days before she calmed down. I never saw her lose it like that again. You mean she's like that now?"

"I think so. Something's happened to set her off. Something bad. Why don't you see if you can phone her? See if you can make a connection, Alex. Or maybe Louie can."

"That won't make any difference. She can't help us and we can't help her. We have to get ourselves out from under this situation."

"Alex, I want to see if we can find a way to fly out of here, to have some sort of air transportation set up if we need to leave. I know that sounds impossible but we just have to have a way out of this country."

"I agree, but I sure don't know how. We have no connections for something like that."

Another hour of talk and discouragement set in. They fell asleep and didn't hear Marnie and Louie come in.

After Marnie was in her room, Louie slipped into Alex's bedroom. She examined the notes. "Naïve and careless to leave these here. But they are right. We certainly do need Plan E/F—Escape out of here by Flight if necessary," she whispered to herself. "Yes. That must be ready."

Twenty-three

"Robert, my darling. I need to set up the plan we used to get out of the Netherlands in 1965. Is Jacques still alive?" She paused to listen. "I will wait while you contact him."

Another longer pause.

"He is? Right here in London? Why, then I will visit him. He is still at his old club? I can easily shake the British police to do that. Another shopping trip should leave them thoroughly confused. Yes, this would be a last-minute, only if absolutely necessary, plan.

"I love you too and...

Louie listened.

"Yes, two men showed up but I did not give them a chance to take Marnie, thanks to the guests I herded into the library. Our crazy woman certainly has high connections though, to get the men into that particular party. That told us a lot about her sphere of influence.

"Yes, darling, I will keep you up to date. Au revoir."

Three hours with Marnie and Louie felt the girl was much more able to handle the next party. One hour and several cabs later, Louie had visited an old gentleman's club for tea and escape by plane was in place should they need it. She decided not to tell the boys.

Little Tom stood across the desk from his father, hands on hips, legs spread, his face twisted with anger.

"I don't believe you! I don't believe these boys have had anything to do with that woman. Yes, she was secretary to Anna's lawyer. Yes, she lived in the Green Bay area for years and yes, she knew their mother, but how could anyone who was a child know about events so secret even the police had no clue? These were kids, Dad! They have no connection to what their father might have done. They are victims. Their lives have been at risk just because of who their father was. I can relate to that. It's the same for me and my brothers. Our lives were—no, are—always at risk because of what you did. Do. The difference is that you've been on the good side of the law. True, you taught us to survive, but you lied to us just as their father lied to his sons. You lied to us about the whole extent of what you've been doing. You lied to Mum. I don't owe anything to you. If it comes down to it, I'm going to get those boys out of here. They don't deserve to be used as bait."

He turned and stalked out.

Big Tom Kearsley stood, head bowed. *I deserve it. I knew it would come to this one day. The lies won't be repaired soon. Still...*

He picked up the phone and called a special number.

"My son won't go along with this. Put on extra men, but in the background. The Americans will probably try getting out of the country and Little Tom will help them. Stop them until we can

165

ferret this woman out. Set them up so she can get at them easily. The girl too. And that arrogant French-Swiss woman. Put someone on her from whom she cannot, dammit, slip away!"

Louie saw the extra men—passersby on the street, sitting in the cafés, street maintenance, even a new apartment maintenance person—and the woman who followed her shopping and into the loos. *So obvious! Subtle as a sledgehammer, as the Americans used to say. We were so much better at this back in the fifties and sixties. They do not know how well I remember faces.*

So. They have added more on. That means they expect Ardith to act, or is it a setup? Or, they expect the boys to try to get away. Well, we shall just have to be more clever. This next party at the French embassy will prove interesting.

She sailed through Harrod's, the woman tailing her and trying to keep up.

Ah, but I know so much more about these stores than she does.

Louie, bags hanging from her arms, left one door and quickly entered another, a tobacco shop, where she moved swiftly down the aisle, past the door to the storeroom, out the door to the alley and immediately into the next building. The woman following her figured it out, but was too late. Louie had disappeared.

The woman held a phone to her ear. "She's done it again. I know she's close by but there are five doors within fifteen feet of here and she could have gone into any one of them. I can't imagine what she's up to now."

What Louie was up to was her search for a safe place for Marnie and her brothers if they would need it. The old man she had met at his club would be the one to provide it. When she saw her chance, Louie hired a cab to deliver all her packages to the apartment, slipped into a bathroom to change into sweats and sneakers, and got herself to the London suburb where the man lived.

He listened, sucking on his pipe, which bubbled with every breath he took.

"Oh my dear, with my connections I can set up a half dozen places you can hide the girl and her brothers if you need it."

The pipe burbled.

"Don't worry on that score. I, however, am much more interested in this woman, this strange person who pursues these children and believes she must get their money. And," he sounded much amused, "who has been able to stump the British government. My contacts have apprised me of this case. I ignored it until now. If I had known you were involved, I might have taken a greater interest. Now, I'm loving it."

The pipe gurgled with happy juicy noises.

"Fill me in on your role in this. Then I will check my street connections and see if I can find out where she is."

The embassy party led to nothing. Marnie remained quite safe the entire evening. The next

167

day British society pages featured a picture of her with an earl and countess and the headline "Beautiful Heiress Wows London Society."

Cory and Alex had spent another day learning the London underground and a fifth suburb, as well as the very posh neighborhood in and around Buckingham Palace, the Mall, Westminster and its environs.

"The powers at the top have pulled away the obvious security around you," Little Tom told them, "but they have more people following you still. They want to smoke her out. Not such a bad idea, really. The sooner we do this, the sooner you can get back to your lives. Two days from now the police will announce they have information that she has left the country and the focus of their search is, therefore, France. They will announce that they no longer are interested in the American connection and all contact with you has ended. It won't have ended, of course."

Louie sat in the old man's parlor.

"She's in the suburb of Chiswick. That is only one of her lairs, however. She's too smart to stay only in one place. She has six men around. She pays them exceedingly well so they will do whatever she tells them. Two of them are hired gunmen and will kill on her orders. They were not the two who were at that party so that tells me she wanted Marnie alive. The other four are armed but are more for security than killing. However, she demands their absolute loyalty and if they have to kill, they will.

"I couldn't find out how she plans to get the girl and her brothers but there is no doubt she's after their money. It's my guess she'll kidnap them again as soon as she can and demand a higher ransom. Perhaps she'll take them out of the country to a place she controls."

"Where is that? I have to know."

"I don't know. It's impossible to say. I'm sorry. I couldn't gather much more information on such short notice."

"This is more than I expected, mon ami. I thank you. We will be on our guard. Please keep on with your activities. The more we know, the better."

Louie was far more nervous than she showed as she straightened Marnie's jacket collar.

"All right. Today you will go shopping on your own. I will not be with you. There will be a guard but he will stay far back. He will not be able to rescue you unless you delay any attack on you for at least five minutes or more. Do not hesitate to use the grab and pull move I taught you if you get a chance. Do not forget the high heel to the kneecap. Do not forget the back doors and even the rooftops.

"Alex, you are visiting a bank today to interview for an internship. Little Tom will be following you. You are the most likely to be her focus. Cory, you are off to school, which is relatively safe as long as you are there. Then you are off to your acting lessons, which we also think

169

quite safe. The same warning applies to both of you, however. Your guard may not be able to save you."

Louie said all this in front of Big Tom and Little Tom and their attending officers in what they had told her was a secret meeting. When the police left, by a back door which she knew was not at all secret, because she had "the seamstress" watching it—*again, subtle as a sledgehammer*—she drew them into Cory's room, after making sure there were no listening devices and cameras.

"I would like to catch this woman as much as the police do. She is a monumental inconvenience in my life and yours. However, not at the expense of your lives. She will kill or order you killed on a whim. She has temporary headquarters in the suburb of Chiswick, a place none of us know. Yet. Tomorrow we will see that you do. If you are captured, try to get away before she takes you there or anywhere out of town. Here are phones programmed only for me. If they capture you, they will take them, which is good. I will be able to track them. As much as possible, keep in touch with me."

"And if we lose contact with you is there some place we can meet, like a rendezvous place? A pub or something?" Alex was rocking from one foot to another, like a prizefighter nervous about the impending fight.

"Yes. Get to Westminster Cathedral. Remember, if you use the underground, get off at Victoria Station. Hide near the northwest corner of the cathedral—inside—until I can find you.

170

You are dressed warm enough. You have credit cards, money, papers and your London travel passes. Let us hope this is the only time we must do this."

"I'm looking forward to this," Cory declared. "It's been a bore having someone with us all the time. I'm finally off to school and acting lessons. This is what I came for. I'll see you all tonight." He waved as he set off, slamming the door behind him.

"I'm not. I want my brother back alive and well. When I get done with that interview, I'm going to his school. He's overconfident. Little Tom, you and I will see that he's ok coming home."

Alex stood in front of Cory's mirror, straightened his tie, gave his hair a quick comb-through and he and Little Tom walked out.

Marnie buttoned her jacket.

"Well. I'm off to shop and to interview for a modelling job. I bet she won't have anyone try anything. I bet she knows the police will still be watching us."

Louie watched Marnie leave, then went to her own room and called the old man.

"They are all off. I have done all I can.

Now we wait, and now I know how Robert felt when I went on a mission."

Twenty-four

Marnie returned first, just at lunch time, reporting no trouble.

Alex came in at two, worried. "I missed Cory at school because my interview extended into lunch and he never got to acting classes. I don't know where he is and he hasn't used his phone. Little Tom is at the acting school trying to find someone who might have seen him, or he was when I left him."

At four, Cory had not come back.

Louie tried to contact him. No answer.

Both Marnie and Alex tried their phones. Nothing.

Little Tom returned. No luck.

"Let us get to the school again, to find out if anyone saw him leave," Louie said. "There could be teachers and maintenance people still there."

Louie was in her old clothes, no countess now. She thought quickly of changing, thinking maybe the countess role would open doors. *No, this is better if we need to search the streets or follow him to her headquarters.*

They returned to the apartment at six. Cory had been in morning classes but no one remaining at the school had seen him leave. The search ordered by Big Tom Kearsley had, so far, led to nothing.

Louie called one of her contacts. Cory had not been seen at the place where Ardith was and she was there. No unusual activity had been observed.

Cory had been standing at the second story window of the classroom. His last class of the morning was taking a short break and it was almost over when he saw a man across the street slide into a tobacconist's shop doorway and wait there. At first, Cory thought the man might be waiting for a bus, but when two buses came and went within seven minutes, and the man did not get on, suspicion inched its way into Cory's brain.

He's waiting for something and it's not a bus.

Cory backed away from the window.

I'll finish the class and see if he's still there.

He was.

If there's one, there may be more. He moved into other rooms, now temporarily empty for the lunch period. With care, his eyes searched every doorway and alley entrance. He found two more possible watchers. *I'd better call Louie.*

When he tried to call, the phone wouldn't work. Fear tugged at his stomach. *OK, this is what we've been training for. Think this through, Cory, slowly. There are three watchers, east, west, and south of this building. What about north? Is there a north exit from this place? Would they have someone watching there too? Scout out all the doors from the main floor and the basement.*

173

Cory made his way through the main floor. He found no exits he could be sure were not watched. In fact, two of them were clearly under surveillance. *Are they her men or police? I can't know if they're safe or not.*

The basement of the building had eastern and southern exits and a stairway leading to double doors *just like our cellar door at home.* Cautiously he lifted one and peered out. An alley. *No watchers. No exit I can see either. Doors leading to other places, yes. Will this be a trap? I hope not.*

He lifted the door and slipped out. The alley seemed about a city block long. Cory tried to remember what shops and buildings were on the streets behind the school but he couldn't. *Damn! I should have learned this place too.* He went from door to door, opening them to see if they led into a shop and then into the street. He knew from the direction he went that the watchers were on the other sides of the school. Finally he found a pub door, entered, and with a smile and a salute to the bartender, who looked a bit surprised, he left the pub and turned to the north. A quick glance around reassured him he was not followed and he began walking.

He tried the phone again. Nothing.

OK, somehow I need to get to Westminster Cathedral or to the apartment. Where am I now?

One car cut him off in front and the other pulled up behind. The man who hopped out of the one behind jammed what felt like a gun into

174

Cory's back and pushed him into the car in front and they took off. They didn't notice that Cory dropped the phone to the ground. It was all he could think to do. He hoped someone would find it.

Someone did. A boy, riding his bicycle through a side street, saw the kidnapping and saw the phone slide under the front car. He waited until the cars were gone, got the phone and tried to use it. When it didn't work, he took it home, stole his brother's charger and plugged it in. Several hours later, the phone's light shone out in the darkness and the boy tried again.

Louie's phone rang and she grabbed it. "Hello?" No answer. "Hello? Who is this?"

"I'm Artie. Who're you?"

Bit by careful bit Louie extracted information from little Artie, including his address. As she repeated the address, Little Tom phoned his father and police were dispatched.

Covering the phone, she looked at the assembled group in the dining room of the apartment.

"Someone has Cory. Men forced him into a car early this afternoon."

Twenty-five

"You're not going anywhere without me."

"Yes, Alex, I am. I don't need you as my babysitter. We both need to get ourselves out there. Two potential victims are better than one. We know how to get around this place now. We have to smoke that batty woman out."

Their quarrel had gone around and around for over an hour.

Marnie stood up. *Guinea pigs on a wheel. Wasting time. Enough of this.*

"I'm going shopping. Let's see if she sends someone after me. You go to the next job interview or whatever you're supposed to do. The police are covering Westminster Cathedral and that area in case Cory shows up."

Alex went to the bathroom and threw up. Even to his sister he couldn't admit how scared he was for Cory.

When he came out Marnie was gone.

Last night police had come and gone. A police search had led to nothing and Alex spent most of the night without sleep.

Louie was gone. She had not told anyone where she was going nor did Alex know when she left. No one knew.

Their guards said nothing. Occasionally one would walk down the hall or go to another room to take a phone call. Mostly they kept outside the door of the apartment. Little Tom had not called this morning as he had said he would. Alex hoped he was out tracking Cory.

London was in a soupy fog, cold and grey and muffled. *My brain feels like this weather.*

Alex had nowhere to go. There was no interview, no reason for him to go out. Yet to remain, to do nothing, to just wait. *Not possible. Not an option. I'm giving our watchdogs the slip and I'll go to Westminster myself to see if Cory made it there. After that I just don't know.*

He made it out easily through the passage they had discovered in the basement. Walking swiftly to the closest underground station, he caught the train to Victoria Station.

The main doors of the cathedral loomed out of the mists. He couldn't see the spires and rooftop. Fog obscured everything twenty feet above the ground. Before he went in, he walked the entire perimeter, noting all doors. With no sun to guide him, Alex realized he was confused about which direction was which. To find all the exits was the best he could do. Whether they were open or not, he didn't know. He didn't try them. Where they led inside was a mystery he didn't feel like solving. Returning to the main doors, Alex tagged along with a group of tourists entering the cathedral.

Interior lights were on. Tourists still came, although it was October but only a few groups wandered here and there, listening to their guide. Others were there in twos, threes, and a few single persons walked slowly around the walls. Worshippers sat or knelt. Those far up by the altar looked tiny, so far away. A wave of immense loneliness washed over Alex.

He gawped, speechless, at the immensity of the place. A shroud of grayish darkness covered the high arched ceiling but gold leaf still shone through it, giving hints of heaven. Passages led to crypts, side chapels, and unknown smaller caverns. For a brief time, Alex forgot his loneliness and fear as he slowly wandered down the main aisle. Then his memory of St. Frances Cathedral in Green Bay came into his mind in the only comparison he knew, and he felt crushing guilt. *I shouldn't have let Marnie go.*

He returned to the main doors and began a systematic search to his left in every nook and cranny he could find. After an hour, he began there again and did it to the right. No Cory.

Except. Except there was a small crude sign, as if some child had been playing on the floor with sidewalk chalk, in a crypt, behind a raised marble coffin, where it couldn't be easily seen.

Does that mean something? A figure eight, on its side. Infinity.

Another. The letter P, in green. *Packers Forever? Not! That's dumb!*

We never set up any signs between us. If this is supposed to mean something to me, I don't know what. It makes no sense. We should have set up signs, like Little Tom and his family use.

Alex tried his cell to call Marnie. No reception. He went outside and tried again. No answer. Finally, not wanting to return to the apartment, he wandered the district. No one came near him.

178

He got a sandwich, crisps and soda in a pub.

Taking the underground to the district where they had been held, he found the warehouse and went through it again, looking for any clues.

Nothing.

For a while he stood outside Cory's school.

He wandered through the darkness in the districts where they had learned the streets, at a complete loss. For the very first time in his life, he felt he had no family, no friends and that he was completely alone in a strange and hostile world. Even the loss of his father had not left him this lonely. There had always been family. He had assumed there would always be family.

I want to go home and find they're all there and this isn't happening. I want my brothers and sister and mother there. I want friends there. My father too. Even my father.

The cold drops of fog in the air blended with the tears running down his face.

We have to go home! We all have to go home! We have to go home!

This became his mantra as he made his way back to the apartment.

He stood in front of the man guarding the door and told him, "You blew it, man. I got out and I've been out all day and half the night and you didn't even know it. Tell your boss that. Tell him to find my brother so we can go home."

He walked in. Marnie was not there. Louie was not there. Mind and muscles rigid with

179

tension, he went to his room and opened his pocketknife and began slowly scraping the skin on his left forearm until drops of blood oozed out. One of the girls at school last year had told him this relieved feeling stressed. He'd watched her do it over and over, wondering, and worrying she'd cut too deep.

I never thought I'd feel like this. This must be how she felt.

It didn't work. He couldn't feel the cuts. He was numb. No feeling. No emotion. Just dead inside and out. Unable to think, he lay down on his bed. Thoughts of suicide drifted through his mind. Temptation. End this all now. So much easier. They dissolved as he drifted off to sleep.

Alex shot awake from a nightmare at 1:27 a.m. by the clock. The dread in his chest spread to his gut, to his lower abdomen, through his pelvis and down his legs. He almost peed in his pants but made it to the bathroom. There was a light in the living room down the hall and he stumbled into it. No one there. Sick with fear, he turned and made it to Marnie's room. She wasn't there. She was not anywhere in the apartment. Neither were any guards. Not outside the door. Nor in the building.

We've been their bait. They've been using us just like they said they would. Louie must be in it with them. She's not here either. How long will it take for Ardith to get me too? Why hasn't she done that already? I've been alone here. Why hasn't she come?

180

Alex dressed and searched the apartment and the building twice over, thinking Ardith might be waiting for him. He found nothing.

All attempts to calm his mind failed. He paced the long hall, unable to plan or think logically or even feel his system. He was frozen again. Feelings, sensations—all frozen except for a sickening sense of impending dread.

Go home! You have to go home! Home, in his mind, became the place where his dad had been, where AJ probably was by now. He didn't even think the word *suicide*. That wasn't it at all. It was to not be here. Not be here. It was *home, go home.*

What saved him from further despair was the most absurd thought. The phrase from *The Wizard of Oz.*

There's no place like home. There's no place like home.

Toto barking. Ruby slippers. He looked down at his feet and laughed—a high, silly, giggly laugh, just like he had when he first saw the movie as a boy.

He raced for the bathroom and threw up the little food he had left in his stomach. The red haze that blocked his eyes as he stood up exploded into rage. He smashed his fist through the glass of the shower door. Splintered shards stabbed his arm and one hit his right cheek.

Breathing heavily, Alex stood before the mirror in the heart-pounding silence that followed and watched the blood trickling down his cheek. After an unknown time a slow drip,

181

drip, drip caught his ear and he looked down. A red pool was forming next to his right foot. His wrist and forearm were slashed with cuts.

Little Tom found him in mid-morning sitting on his bed, the bedding bloody, his face pale, his eyes blank.

"'ere, 'ere. We can't 'ave this. Don't worry, man. Me mates is lookin' for yer brovver and sister. A doctor's comin' an 'ere's the thing. You got to pull yerself togevver an' 'elp."

"That there Swiss lady is 'elpin'. Me da is 'elpin'. Told 'em they was all effin' stupid to do this, I did. Now we got two missin' and not a bit to go on. But we will, we will. Now what I got to get from you is what you been doin' all this time. Right from the top, the whole tale."

Slowly Little Tom dragged the account of Alex's last thirty-six hours from him.

"The sign was infinity and a P? You're sure? That's a good sign, mate! That's a small bit to go on. I'm 'opeful, I am. But we got to make connections. I got to. You got to pull yourself together. Something's afoot but who and what, I don't know. I've got to find out what."

His English became less accented as he paced.

Alex sat, his eyes following Little Tom back and forth, back and forth and for some odd reason, he began to feel calmer.

"Now, here's what I want you to do. I want you to pack up your brother and sister's stuff, your stuff, and be willing to leave at a moment's notice. I want you to have it right at the back door of this building. Don't leave here! I want to know you're here. Wait for me to come back. Ok?"

He didn't wait for Alex to reply.

Twenty-four hours later Alex left.

I've been abandoned again.

He locked his brother's and sister's things in the apartment, shouldered his duffel bag, grabbed his carryon, and took a cab to the airport.

I must, must find Mom. I can't be alone anymore. I'll help her find AJ. I can't manage anything here anymore. No one is helping here. No one is even calling me. No guards, no security, no police, no Little Tom, no Louie. Where are they all? That crazy lady has isolated me from all help, that's what she's done. I'm cut off. If I can get myself to Mexico, I can at least get some help from Mac or someone.

At the airport, Alex got out of the cab, paid the man, picked up his bags and headed toward the doors. Suddenly he was flanked on both sides by two large men who pushed their shoulders into his. Another man glided into place ahead of him. A man behind him ordered him to keep walking. They went in one door and the group turned and headed through another door. Alex was ordered into a black car with dark windows.

The car sped toward an airfield which held smaller private planes.

The gun held at his head was black. The men's clothing was black. Black shiny shoes. Two of the men were black-skinned. Blue black when lights hit their skin. The plane they walked toward was black with silver stripes.

Her suit was red. She stood in the door of the plane, unsmiling, but nodding in satisfaction. Ardith stood back to let him pass. He turned to his right to enter.

Cory and Marnie sat, tied to their seats. He stopped in astonishment.

She gave him a push.

"Sit down." She turned to her henchman. "Tie him like the others."

"You're my bait now."

Mexico

Twenty-six

Melissa sat in the small boat waiting for the turn of the tide to flow inland.

"If Stacy and Anna could get out this way, we can get in," she told Jamie.

He had encountered strange and scarcely believable luck when he returned from the dig. Dismissing the man Jorge had sent with him, he had literally run into this woman while testing rusty old skills on his newly-rented motorcycle. He had decided to go north up the coast to check out the house Anna inherited.

Melissa, crossing the street near the market in downtown Cancun, head averted, eyes elsewhere, had not seen him until after she had tumbled right across his cycle and to the ground.

He had stopped, apologized profusely, aided her to her feet, and they had attracted quite a few pedestrians.

"Stop fussing!" she had hissed. "Let me go. Don't attract so much attention!"

Her actions could only have been described as furtive. His curiosity aroused, he had kept firm control of her arm as she stood and he insisted on taking her to a doctor.

"I don't want any more attention than you do. If you come quietly, I'll get us out of here," he muttered to her.

She looked at him sharply, recognized the fugitive look, decided maybe he might be useful, and went quietly.

187

An hour of guarded and cautious talk later, at a tiny out-of-the-way outdoor café, they had not even exchanged names but they had found common ground. He needed help to find a young woman and get her to safety. She needed a safe phone, information, and money. Lots of money. It was when he told her where he had heard the young woman was being held that her interest shot up.

"But that's Anna's house!" she blurted, then froze, looking from side to side, afraid she might have compromised herself.

Jamie gazed at her, sizing up the situation. *I'll never find Lindy if I don't take this chance. How she knows Anna is anyone's guess but I am definitely going to find out.*

"Anna's my sister. My name is Jamie. I'm here to help her. The young woman is the daughter of an archaeologist and I need to find her. She may have information about a missing friend." *Not quite true but close enough.*

"Is your name by any chance Melissa?"

He watched as the woman's eyes turned to ice and both her hands slowly gripped the edge of the table. *Damn! She's going to bolt or shoot me!*

"Stacy's looking for you. She's been calling you. Why haven't you answered?"

"You're Anna's brother? You know of Lindy? Stacy? I've avoided all contact with them so the Croc can't make a connection between us."

Carefully they told each other more. When they were finished, Jamie had much information about the Crocodile cartel, more than he ever

188

expected. Melissa had an ally with money and a way to contact Stacy safely.

"I'll help you get Lindy back if you can safely get me in contact with Anna here, with people in Wisconsin, and especially with Stacy, and we can find out what else is going on," Melissa said.

"It's a deal. Stacy's staying way in the background so she can keep things moving. I had no idea the Croc cartel was that extensive."

"Extensive isn't the word for it. This place", she waved her hand to indicate Cancun, "is crawling with his people. He picked up more soldiers from that crazy woman's cartel and her property here in Mexico too. He took over Anna's house up north.

Jamie nodded. "That's where I was going. I wanted to check it out because I'm wondering if Lindy could have ended up there. Anna told me she's been there before. I was thinking it's a long shot but it's worth a look-see.

"I think Lindy knows a lot about what her father is up to, who controls him, and, most important, who we can contact. Mac told me he had a contact at the dig but no name and I wasn't able to find out who it is while I was there without raising suspicion. I'm not supposed to get anywhere near Anna. She's under heavy guard by the men Stacy hired and both national and local police and those damn reporters follow her bloody everywhere. They just today followed her to the school she began. I think it must have been set up as a PR thing, what do they call it now?

Putting a spin on things? No. maybe not. Doesn't sound right. I watched from the crowd, disguised as a tourist curious about what was happening. I think she saw me. I hope she did. She gave no sign. Stacy told her to keep all eyes focused on her so those of us who want to help can do that without anyone focused on us."

Melissa thought about that.

"Then I'd better not call Stacy in case her line is bugged or someone listens in somehow. This place is truly swarming with the Croc's people. Like I told you, I've been gathering every bit of information that I can on him and his cartel. He's making sure he's secure here and then he's going after that line through the USA. I think Lindy knows who Mac's contact at the dig was. She may not know she knows, but I need to pry as much information out of her as possible. I'd also like to scope out that place and see what El Cocodrilo has set up there."

"Then let's do it. Can you get me an AK-47?"

"How do you know how to operate that kind of weapon?"

"You are a bit young to remember, but ever heard of the IRA?"

Melissa leaned back, her face a mask.

"Let's go." She stood and pushed back her chair. Jamie followed.

At the same time, several customers at a café down the street also rose from their seats and left their tables. One of them carefully folded his newspaper and tucked it under his left arm.

Across the street, another made the same gesture, rose and followed Jamie and Melissa. The remaining person carefully folded up and tucked away a listening device which picked up conversations over a distance and phoned his employer.

"Ok, the tide's turning. Let's go. We have a long way to row, then a long walk over mangrove roots and through water, then a cliff to climb and last, but not least, an open yard to cross. I hope you can do all that, old man."

"I hope so too. I'm in pretty good condition though. I kept up the exercise all these years." Jamie didn't tell her that the exercise had been gardening and that the most strenuous thing he'd done was dig up potatoes.

The rowing, the walk through swampy water, and the tangled roots were not a problem. The cliff was another story. Darkness had descended, making any progress a matter of feeling their way blind, hand over hand, foot by foot. Melissa had done much rock climbing and she moved easily. Jamie's arm and leg muscles were in pain and quivering before they were a third of the way up. He forced himself to feel above his head for the small places his hands, one after another, could hold onto, and then do the same for each foot, hoping he wouldn't slip and fall. Those times his feet slipped out from under him, times that were all too frequent, made his heart rate rise, made him shake in alarm and pain, made him force his way ever upward with a massive act of will. It was clear to both of them he was a liability. Melissa lifted the weight of the gun off him.

"If my arms and legs don't hold me," he gasped between moves, clinging to the tiny hand and footholds, "then you have to go on alone. Don't wait for me if you see a chance."

"You have to make it. I need backup, old man. Besides, you'll make too much noise if you fall and splash into the water. Keep going! It's less painful in the end if you keep moving. At least it was for me when I was learning this."

"And when was that? When you were ten?" Sarcasm eased the pain somewhat.

At the top it was all Jamie could do to haul himself over the edge and lay, shaking, on the ground. Melissa lay next to him under the brush that covered them.

"Safe for now. Just wait. Rest. We want to do this about 2 a.m. Thanks be to Mother Nature we have no moon. It set early tonight."

"Wouldn't you know? First time in forty-five years I'm layin' next to a woman and I can't do a feckin' thing about it. Damn!"

Melissa grinned into the darkness, leaned over and kissed him thoroughly. "But that's all you're gonna get from me."

"Da-a-a-m!"

They lay in silence until "Up!" Melissa ordered. Muscles silently protesting, Jamie dragged himself to his feet.

He took the gun from her. "I can do this now," he said and he meant it. *I can, by the saints! I can! I'm dying from exhaustion but I will!*

They slid through the tall vegetation to the edge of the open space. The pool and yard were lit by bright spotlights.

Melissa stood frozen under the leaves. "No crossing that," she breathed. "There's a lot more land here than we can see. If we go to the right, we'll be able to work our way around under cover of brush and trees. There are patio doors at the front. They'll have lights there too but we can get closer."

Backing off, they edged their way through the night, sliding from shadow to shadow. At the front a garden space with low bushes still had to be crossed.

"They're over-confidant. The patio door is open." He pointed his chin at the house.

"They have to have guards. My info is that they have lots of electronic equipment, a very modern cartel headquarters. They must have guards. Where are they?"

"We had best wait. This could be booby-trapped."

An hour later, no movement had been detected.

"I don't like it. I think they're onto us." Jamie squirmed slightly. He had been holding back, waiting for action. He was impatient to find out what they faced.

"Melissa, let me go in. If someone's waiting, let it be me they take. You need to survive to help Anna. Let me see what's happening." Jamie could see faint traces of dawn in the eastern sky.

"No. We go in together or not at all. I don't like this either. There should have been movement, something. Let's crawl slowly, inch our way."

On elbows and knees they crept silently toward the doors. Nothing changed.

Without standing, they eased themselves over the sill and into the room. No movement. They stood then and made their way through the entire house, all the way to the top and the bedroom on the roof, then back down.

"This isn't right. No one would leave all this unguarded. We've gone through it all." Jamie's suspicions had increased with every step, his skin shivering and creeping as his apprehension grew.

"There's one more room, a gallery in the lowest level. As far as I know there's only that door." Melissa pointed to the steps leading to a door at the bottom.

"We're in the fryin' pan. Might as well check if there's a fire," he muttered.

They walked down the stairs and opened the door. Melissa flipped a switch and soft light flooded the room with spotlights where paintings had been on the walls. At the far end Lindy lay huddled on a couch. Melissa moved swiftly the length of the room and felt her neck.

She turned to Jamie and shook her head no. He sagged against a pillar and looked away to hide the tears.

Both of them jumped when they heard the flat brutal voice.

"I see you have taken my bait." He gestured with the hand that held the gun on them. "Don't bother to shoot. You would be dead before you could raise your weapons."

Three men stepped from the door, guns raised.

"It will be interesting to find out just who I have captured and how that will bend Anna to my will and bring me the money for the body of her son."

Melissa lowered her gun carefully to the floor, remaining silent. *He doesn't remember me. Good.*

Jamie looked at the man and knew the type instantly. It was the kind of man who made him choose to leave the IRA. The kind of man who loves to kill, who no longer lives by the ideals of a political movement or organization or religion, who lives only for himself. The kind of man he had almost become.

He too slowly lowered his weapon. *The kind of man I will have no trouble killing when the moment comes for Melissa to get away, as she must, even if I have to die. Especially when he speaks of the body of her son. Bastard!*

The van turned north when they left the house. Jamie's wrists were bound, as were Melissa's. In the rear seat of the vehicle, both of them facing backward, he mouthed to her in the very faint light, "Watch and wait." She blinked.

Salsa music played quietly from the radio at the front. One guard drove, one road shotgun, and the third sat in the middle seat, gun at the ready. El Cocodrilo had ridden off in an armored car to the south, commanding his men to take the prisoners to his island.

If we get on that island, we'll be tortured, probably killed. We'd better make our move soon. Anna told me of that place. Jamie's eyes roamed the floor at his feet. There was nothing he could make out in the dark space there. He could see the glow of the guard's cigarette in his peripheral vision mirrored in the window on Melissa's side of the vehicle.

That means he's directly behind me. If she ducks, there will be a split second where he'll fire and she might live, even get out, if I could find a way to get that door opened. It will have to be from the outside. How can I get them to open that door?

His mind ran scenarios again and again, looking for a way. *Dawn will be coming too soon. We need to act while it's still dark.* He shifted his weight to look at her and tried with his eyes to indicate he was up to something. Her eyes widened slightly.

He felt her boot nudge his and looked down. Slowly she raised the toe of her boot until he saw what she was aiming at.

This is one of those cars where the back door opens from the inside too! Never saw one of these when I was young. We can't be that lucky. We are that lucky!

He watched as Melissa's boot slowly rested on the handle and began pressing down. As the car rounded a curve, he took the advantage and leaned against her slightly and stopped her.

"Hands first," he mouthed. She faked a coughing fit, turning from him enough to show him she'd worked the thin ropes loose.

I won't make it but I can set it up so she does.

He nodded at Melissa as she turned back and her boot pressed the handle down as far as it would go. Jamie, waiting for it, heard the latch click loose, slammed his booted foot against the door and it flew open. He lifted his body, yelled, "Go!" and threw his body upward against the barrel of the gun. The shot deafened him. His inner ear tore apart in pain. He saw Melissa dive and roll and disappear into the darkness behind the car. Brakes screeched. He aimed his own body through the door, felt something slam into him and that was the end of his consciousness.

Jamie came to with head pounding, his body numb in some places, throbbing with pain in others. There was silence all around. He heard nothing. His left hand crept upward to his face and head through thick debris. He made a weak attempt to brush himself off and move the mess away and felt something liquid and sticky on the side of his head. He was bleeding from one ear.

He was alone, buried under debris.

They must have thought I was dead.

Did Melissa get away?

Twenty-seven

El Cocodrilo slapped the messenger across the face with the leather whip he held, rage driving him to do it again and again until the messenger passed out and dropped to the floor. The skin of his face hung in strips.

The man at the door of the room wanted to run but his body was frozen into shards of icy fear held rigid by the thick glue of terror. He and his companion had brought the news of the escape of Melissa and Jamie.

One of the men was dead, the one who had been passenger in the front seat, killed when Jamie hit the gun with his body and it twisted. The driver lost control when the blood and bones of his companion splattered into his eyes. The gunman was thrown backward and before he could recover, Melissa and Jamie had rolled, one after the other, out the door. When they recovered, and daylight gave them clarity, the two men returned and found no trace of Melissa. They found Jamie's body and dumped him into a hole in the ground, then threw in leaves, branches, whatever they could find.

There was no place for the man to run. He stood in the doorway of the island home El Cocodrilo had taken over from Ardith. There was no escape, he knew, from the sharks who hungered for the humans fed to them in the harbor. The sharks came promptly at feeding times and, swimming slowly in circles, waited for that great delicacy—human flesh.

The Crocodile's rage was fueled by the news that AJ had yet to be brought to Puerto. Where his body was, no one knew. The two men supposed to be bringing him had also disappeared.

It is the Mayans, the ones who are sabotaging my lines. I must contact those in government who I pay. They are not doing enough to put those little vermin in their place.

He stood, watching the shark fins circling out beyond the shore, as he tallied his scores.

The good news was that there were now tentative arrangements for the transfer of Anna's money. The police were cooperating. Anna seemed to be cooperating. Only his part was not working to plan, thanks to stupid men.

The ruse to draw out the brother of Anna, and the silly woman who fancied herself a bodyguard of Anna, had worked. They had been easy to spot for the men who worked the streets of Cancun and the men who kept him informed about Ian Stewart and the dig. The girl, Lindy, had been easy—well, mostly easy—to kidnap. He had found out about Eduardo, the informer for the Aguilars, and the men Jamie had hired for the dig. One of them had been recruited already, the tough older one. The information he provided had been worth the bribe paid. *Money rules. And the other two will be dead soon.*

The bad news: one man dead at the site: one man dead taking Melissa and the unknown man she was with to the island: Melissa had not been found: AJ was still missing, along with the two men who had been bringing him in.

I need the body of AJ. Alive or dead, I need that or I won't have any ransom deal.

He called down to the harbor with orders to throw the men who had failed to the sharks, sent others to continue the search for Melissa, ordered his helicopter to be ready, and strode out.

Twenty-eight

Mac walked slowly closer to the outskirts of an unknown town, knowing only that he was bone tired and had been walking and catching short naps in trees for what he thought might be two days. His mind had grown foggy about time. He had stolen food and shoes from unattended huts and the food stalls of an open market that was being held in one town. Now, behind a cantina where he had gone to pee, he lucked into an old auto with keys in the ignition. He clicked the key forward one notch and was pleased to see that there was at least three-quarters of a tank of gas. Scouting the near vicinity, he saw no one who could effectively stop him, and with silent apologies to the owner, he got in, started the engine and took off. Faintly behind him he heard cries of outrage, but they faded quickly.

By the time the gas ran out, he made the far northern outskirts of Mexico City.

He stole a clean shirt and pants from a clothesline, took money and one of the credit cards from the packet still taped to his back, got himself a shave and haircut at a barber and checked into a small hotel where he gave himself the luxury of a long shower. Then he went out and bought a prepaid cell phone.

Big problem. The craziness of the last few days blocked memory and he couldn't recall the phone numbers which had been programmed into his old phone. He finally remembered one number. He thought about whether or not to call her. Guilt at leaving her forced him to take the chance.

"Anna, this is Mac. Contact me at this number." He did not know if she had that phone, or where she would be now. It was all he could do. Then he got some food, returned to the hotel room and lay down for some much needed sleep.

Twelve hours later, he woke. *Daytime.* Standing carefully just back from the window, he noticed a man staying in the shadow behind a small billboard across the street below.

Did they trail me? Was her phone bugged? Can't take the chance.

Mac slipped out the back, checking for suspicious bystanders. He found a clothing store, bought a suit with one of the credit cards he held in another name, found a car rental place and left for Cancun.

Using those cards might trigger something but I need to get the hell out of here. Maybe out of the frying pan and into the fire but staying put is out of the question.

He decided to approach Cancun from the north and drove long hours out of his way north and east on national highways, then turned south down the coast road. *I'll check out Anna's house on the way. Maybe she's there.*

When Jamie had slammed his foot into the door and it flew open, Melissa was already aiming her body out and down into a roll. In the dim light, she couldn't see where she landed but it hurt. Something was sticking up and jabbed her left shoulder as she hit the ground. Instinct and training took over and she kept rolling off and to her right until she felt plants slapping her face and the vegetation became thicker. She rolled on her knees and tried to crawl but her shoulder screamed in protest and she almost screamed out loud. As quickly as she could she crept as far as possible into the brush and then, hearing shots, yelling and cursing, she kept on going, praying Jamie was doing the same.

She thought she had heard Jamie hit the ground but that was more of a wish than a fact. Could he have gotten out too? She could not admit to herself he might be dead. When she heard men searching for her, they were speaking Spanish. Jamie would have been swearing in Irish. She kept going.

Morning filtered with extreme care through the trees, as if aware that all was not well. Melissa knew she had to go back to find Jamie if she could. Only bird sounds now. A raucous parrot overruled the others, screaming indignation at some unknown annoyance. Melissa could only guess at the direction she had come from until she realized she had broken plant stalks in her progress.

Oh, god! If I can read my trail, so can they. We were on the main highway going north. Maybe there will be other cars passing. No, maybe not. It's not that well-traveled this early in the morning.

It took until the sun was well above the eastern trees before she located Jamie.

She found the site of the shooting because of the glass on the road. No car. There was the gruesome sight of one faceless dead man, dragged into brush twenty yards off the side of the highway. Not Jamie. She walked south on the eastern side of the road, just under cover of trees. No Jamie. She walked north, searching that same side again, farther into the trees, then switched to the west side of the highway and went south a second time. No Jamie.

If he isn't on the roadside or just off it, it means he might have crawled away like I did. Then again, maybe they found him in the dark and picked him up and took him with them.

She felt like she had been walking forever when she heard the Irish swearing in the trees becoming louder and louder.

"What a feckin' lot of shite this is! Can't move my bloody arm. Where the hell is that woman?"

Jamie staggered out of the trees into the middle of the road and stopped dead as he saw her. One side of his face was scraped raw and had bled down his clothing. His right arm hung uselessly at his side and his pants had a long tear down one leg.

"Well, don't just stand there, woman. Get the hell off the road before a car comes and we have to answer questions."

Melissa grinned and did just that.

"You still got yer cell phone? Sure and we could use that right now. I figure we're about fifteen miles north of that house, maybe more.

We could maybe call Anna for help. Or something," he finished lamely.

"It's gone. I ditched it under some brush before we entered the house. Turned off. Didn't want anyone to see the numbers. It looks like we have a long walk."

"Hell!"

Melissa estimated they had walked less than a half mile when it became clear Jamie could not continue. His hip had taken a vicious beating in the fall from the car as his body had bumped its way to the roadside.

"Look, girl, you've got to go on. If you can get to somewhere for help, you do that. I'll just have to rest. If my hip gets better, I'll walk south. Somewhere just off this road is where I'll be, watching. You go ahead."

"Ok, but stay off the road in case the Croc sends searchers. I'll come back for you as soon as I can. Stay west of the road and in the jungle."

A half hour later Melissa, walking along the roadside, having thrown caution to the winds after no cars had come by, was startled as a car raced past her, then braked abruptly, tires screeching, and backed up. She was already thirty yards into the jungle when she heard a familiar voice yell her name. Surprised, she turned back and saw Mac running toward her. A wave of intense relief swept through her.

When they picked him up, Jamie, trudging very slowly, was enormously grateful.

"Mac, Lindy Stewart is dead," said Melissa. "I found her body in the art gallery under the house. I felt for her pulse. There was none."

"No! Not Lindy!" His stomach turned sour and his chest felt as if it was ripping.

"I'd like to see if we can recover her body, but the house is the Croc's headquarters. There are armed men."

"Look in the glove compartment."

Melissa did and found two pistols.

"Ok. These might help even the balance a bit. How do you see us doing this?"

"We walk in and take them as they come. I'm in no mood to fool around."

"They let Jamie and I walk in and walk through the whole house. They were waiting for us, saw us coming. I should have been more suspicious."

"I don't have a better plan. Do you?"

Jamie snorted.

"Well, I do. You give me one of those pistols and I get out and hide in the jungle across the way and shoot at every window and door I can see. They think it's coming from there. You sneak in under cover of my fire and take them one by one. Just don't take too long to do that. I hope you have enough ammunition."

Mac laughed. "Well, why the hell not? It just might work."

Melissa nodded. "Mac, you take the other pistol. When the fire draws them upstairs, I'll get down the stairs and get Lindy's body. Just keep them busy for ten or fifteen minutes."

206

"That's a plan."

Lindy's body was not there. Two men lay dead from Jamie's fire, one behind an upstairs window and the other inside the open front door. Mac took out two more inside. Melissa walked through the entire house disabling every piece of electronic equipment as she looked for Lindy. Jamie limped his way around the grounds, disabled all security cameras. He found no burial evidence. Mac searched the cabanas and went as far as the cliff to see if her body had been thrown over. No evidence of that. Twenty-five minutes later they left.

They had planned to stop at the school in Puerto Juarez to see if Adelina was there. When they drove by, a sign in front stated that it was closed for repairs. One side of the building was blown out, scarred by fire. All three sensed the spirits of dead children calling for help.

In Cancun, Mac checked them into a small hotel he had used before, where he hoped they would be secure.

Twenty-nine

Anna paced the elegant hotel room incessantly. More than restlessness, she felt caged, a captured animal. The smells she remembered from wandering in the jungle were coming back in full force, stronger even than before, "as if I'm out there somewhere," she said to Stacy.

"I hear sounds, of birds, of animals, of rustlings in the air. I feel the air around my face when I'm not even outside. I'm hallucinating. I need to get out of here for a while. I can't just stay here. I want to get out and run. I want to move constantly. I can't sleep soundly. I wake up at the slightest noise. Swimming in the pool is the only place I feel sane. I don't know how to explain this."

"Anna, it's understandable. This is anxiety. It's the stress from this waiting. I feel it too but we must wait. The National Police have been contacted again by El Cocodrilo. He's agreed to the ransom amount and to bring AJ to a meeting. They just have to be sure it's in a place where the exchange is safe. It's being taken care of completely."

"No. It's not. I feel AJ. He's somewhere else. He's still in danger but not from Cocodrilo. From himself. He's angry and...I don't know what this is. I've never felt this from him before."

"Anna, I know you often feel your children but, really, it's this situation. It's just this terrible situation. It's the horrible news of the children at the school—that explosion that killed two of them and wounded so many others. The police are still investigating but it really seems to have been an accident."

"No, Stacy! It was not an accident! I know this beyond any doubt. I know this. I know..." Anna sat down in a chair but her right hand kept picking at the padded arm under it.

Useless. It's useless to argue with her. There's no way she can understand. I'm sensing all of it now, feeling all the evil and the hate and The Crocodile's cold rage and AJ's bitterness, and Cory's pain and Alex's frustration and Marnie's what? She's the one who feels most healthy. Her iron determination to do something, her intense focus on getting through this. I feel it all. And more. Ramon is close but holding himself back. Jorge—I don't know. He's become a mystery. Jamie. He believes he's supposed to leave this world. My brother is ready to die. I can feel it. There are other deaths too. Who else has died? I know someone has. More than one. Many are dying or dead. This is a brutal war zone.

"Anna, I know you want to fight them but you must wait until the exchange. Please."

"Yes, of course. I will. I'll swim again. Maybe that will help."

In the water, Anna scarcely could admit to herself what she felt was happening.

I feel like an animal. No. I feel like my mind and body get taken over by this animal. I felt this in the jungle when I was lost, but never

*this strong. Never like this. It's this cursed
tropical atmosphere. It has to be. This is
abnormal. Down here, I become something I'm
not. If I get us all free of this place, I'll never come
here again. I hate this!*

Stacy stood at poolside, watching Anna
breaststroke her way across, sleek and gliding
like a long fish.

God! I hate to do this to her!

"Anna, the police have called. They want
you at the meeting place for the exchange."

Anna's stomach turned and she felt a wave
of nausea fill her. She dived underwater, feeling
the cool slide of liquid over her head and body.
Coming up fast at poolside, she pulled her body
up and out onto the deck, slipped into her robe
and walked quickly to the private elevator. *I wish
I could have stayed under, just never come up.*

As she went past the back window she
glanced up and caught her breath. A man was
sweeping the patio about twenty yards down the
hill. The man was Ramon! He turned toward her
and on his T-shirt she saw the letters. AJOK. He
turned away just as quickly and walked out of her
sight.

Anna stood still, taking deep breaths. She
knew Stacy had not seen that. *Ramon and Jorge
must be involved somehow. They've gotten word
to me. It will be all right. OK. It will be OK. The
Crocodile will let AJ go.*

Relief swept through her.

One hour later Anna stood at the edge of
an open parking lot, all sense of relief lost, all

210

tension back. Police vehicles were on each side of her, one bodyguard at her side, another behind her. The money exchange was to be electronic, to a neutral bank where their instructions were to deposit the sum to yet another bank until it reached a bank in the Caymans who would confirm it for the Crocodile. Robert had called. He had assured her the transfers were ready.

Across the way were two armored vehicles and one long black limo behind them. When the final bank signaled receipt of the money. AJ would be turned loose.

Seconds of silence felt like hours. A shiver carefully clawed its way up Anna's spine.

A police officer gave a dramatic gesture and the door of the limo opened.

It's wrong! It's all wrong. AJ isn't here. It's a trick!

The armored vehicles opened fire, a sack was thrown out the door of the limo and it and the other vehicles roared off, followed by the screams of wounded men and then silence. Anna and one of her bodyguards, the man directly behind her, were the only ones left standing.

Anna looked to left and right and saw only bodies on the ground. *This was deliberate! All murdered except me. Oh, no! Oh god, no!*

Anna ran to the sack and zipped it open. The body inside was Lindy Stewart.

Thirty

The brutal scene in the parking lot had been the final blow that broke Anna out of her glass cage. When the last shot rang out and the silence fell and the body bag was opened and Lindy's white and bruised face was revealed, Anna lost all faith in police and bodyguards and vowed to face the Crocodile head on. Fury took over.

"If he wants me, then let him come and get me and I'll be as visible as I want to be, go where I want to go, do it my way!"

Anna had called a press conference, revealed what had happened—against the protests of the police and Stacy—and challenged the Crocodile to be as good as his word and produce her son. She had then rented a car and, in a deliberate public show, had Lindy's body placed in a hearse and they drove the long roads to the site of the dig, a conspicuous caravan followed by cars of reporters, photographers and police.

Ian Stewart, slumped on his cot, held his head in his hands. Anna stood before him, fury radiating from her, the body bag opened at her feet.

Bright, happy, beautiful, sweet, loving Lindy, whose loyalty and love for this selfish man has led to her death! I have no pity for him. No pity at all.

"Where do you want me to have her body taken? When and how do you plan to inform her mother?" she demanded, not telling him she had already called Lindy's mother in Paris and had called Louie to go to the poor woman and help her.

Most of the workers, when they saw what Anna brought, had deserted the scene, afraid of the spirit of the dead girl.

There were three who waited to see what would happen. They looked at the woman who had brought the body and decided not to call attention to themselves if possible. Her eyes were fierce. Her jaw hard. They did not want to cross her. But they had been hired by Jamie and would report to him, if they could find him. He had given them a means of contact in Cancun, if they could get there. It did not occur to them that this woman was his sister. He had not told them his whole story. They had no access to television or internet.

Ian Stewart did not answer her questions. He didn't even hear her. Anna had brought him the body bag, laid it at his feet and opened it. He was now in an unreal world of living hell where he realized he was one of the devils.

Mexican authorities paced a few yards away, waiting to take over and close the dig. They made it clear they planned to send Ian on his way as soon as the intense publicity died down.

Publicity had increased. More cars of "reporters" arrived, chosen carefully by El Capitán to add to the chaos.

El Cocodrilo's watchers followed Anna's every move, waiting.

El Capitán had the Crocodile's every move watched as well.

The predators of the human jungle waited for their prey to make a false move.

The hunters of those predators drew close. In Cancun, Mac and Melissa and Jamie sensed something was about to change.

Melissa connected with Stacy, to the relief of both of them. Based on Melissa's information, Stacy came to the realization that any security she could provide for Anna would never be enough to cover the coming war.

"You take over here in Mexico," she had told Melissa. "I have to do something about building up my ability to provide security for everyone up north. I'll try to see if I can work with Grant or if he'll work with me. I'll try to persuade Anna to leave. If she won't agree to that, I'll get her to Cancun and then you just stick with her. Keep her alive."

Mac set up plans with contacts to fly Anna out of Mexico "just in case" he told Mel.

Ramon had found the people of the little village and AJ and sent them on to Jorge. He had gotten the news to Anna as best he could. Now he gathered information in Cancun, disguised as a food vendor.

At Santa Anita, AJ practiced firing a gun. Jorge, unable to break through AJ's wall of grief, watched as the man he knew as a healer turned himself into a killer.

214

Jamie resolved not to let AJ go into this without someone from his family with him and so he practiced relearning the skills he'd used with the IRA and prepared himself for death.

Privately Stacy was worried about the plans. *I don't trust that this will all work out. I just don't trust this. It's unravelling. I have to get Anna out of here.*

Thirty-one

Anna glared at the uniformed man who stood before her, a haughty look on his face.

"You have failed to find my son! You have failed to protect the people with me! You have failed to catch El Cocodrilo! You have failed to help me! You! Have! Failed!"

Her voice, although deadly quiet, saber-slashed the air with every word.

"You no longer have any credibility with me. From now on I will be doing this my way. I will go wherever I choose. I will be leading the search for my son. Please leave.

"Señora, if you continue to travel wherever you wish, I will have you deported."

"No! You won't! The United States Department of State has been informed of the fiasco you commanded, of the murder of my security people and your own men. They are informed of your failure to keep that area secure. They are informed that you allowed El Cocodrilo to take control of the exchange, and to escape, and that you failed to have men in place to follow him. I have filed a formal complaint that asks that you be investigated for bribery and collusion with that drug cartel. I will do everything in my power to make this an international incident. To that end I have again called a news conference to report on the failure of Mexican police to protect me and to find my son. I am informing them that an innocent young girl has been murdered by the

216

head of a drug cartel and you have done nothing to capture her murderer."

"Señora, I will place you under arrest if you do not become quiet."

The voice behind him was icy.

"No, Capitán, you will not. A representative of the United States Embassy in Mexico City is on his way. You will leave now. I am in charge now."

The police capitán whirled around, ready to protest. It died on his lips when he saw the man behind him. The man spoke a short phrase in Spanish.

"Sí, sí, Señor. I will leave at once."

He did.

"I am very sorry for this terrible state of affairs, Señora Kinnealy. I am Francisco Escobar. I am a commander of the National Police. I have been fighting El Cocodrilo for many years. He has been a great threat to Mexican people as well as to you and your son. I understand your concern. I have had to move my family to the United States, with the cooperation of your country, to keep them safe. I cannot be bought and that has made me a target of the Crocodile also. I will be taking over here. You may leave the animal to me. In the meantime, I have had a search begun for your son and the murderers of his wife. But I must say, this will be difficult. It seems the Mayan people who knew your son are very protective and I have had little success in getting information from them. If you can come to trust me, would you help us?"

Anna paced. She was silent for a long time. The man waited patiently. Finally, she turned to him.

"Señor Escobar, I have no trust right now in any police in this country. I will visit the Mayan people I met the last time I was here. They will help me. You find El Cocodrilo. I will find my son. When I have done that, I will leave this country. I hope never to return.

"I believe my son may be lost somewhere in the state of Quintana Roo. As you know, he had a clinic there with his wife. If he is anywhere, he will be there. Please do not have me followed, or spy on me. I have a bodyguard and my brother to assist me. Right now, I must make the arrangements to send for the mother of the girl who was murdered. When she arrives, I will be sure you are contacted. She will be flying here from Paris, France. Now, please leave."

Escobar hesitated, then bowed slightly. "As you wish. I will see to the Crocodile. I leave you my card. If you want my help, I offer it. If not, I wish you good fortune. I think you will need it."

He set his card on a nearby table and left.

Anna sat down, head in her hands.

"You can come out now. He knew you were here, you know. He's had me watched."

Melissa, Mac, and Jamie walked out of the bedroom.

"If it's any consolation," Mac said, "my probing bears up his honesty. He's one of the few police who have an unspotted reputation. He was telling the truth about his family. They live in

218

Dallas and he flies back and forth every week to see them. He's trying to keep this region clean but he's fighting a difficult—no, an impossible battle."

Melissa sank down into a stuffed chair, her legs stretched in front of her.

"My information bears that out too. You can trust he'll do what he says. I also think he'll watch you and us if he can. If he wants the Croc, he'd be a fool not to watch you, Anna. The Croc will go after you just for the fun of getting you, of lording it over you and in the end, killing you."

"Jamie, stop prowling. I've been doing enough of that for both of us."

"I'm restless. I'm like you, Anna. I can feel the threat. I can feel the hate. I can feel the fear. My own, and others as well. I didn't join the IRA because I was a saint."

Jamie stopped his pacing long enough to stand in front of Anna.

"I'm not going with you to find AJ. I'm going after the Croc."

"Jamie! No! This isn't..."

"Yes, it is. I'm makin' it my fight. Years in that monastery and I never lost the desire to fight. I left the IRA disillusioned by the brutality some of its members used and how they justified their actions. I couldn't make myself into them. But I know a good cause when I see one and this is one. This Crocodile is just like the worst of the IRA and the Orangemen. He's murdering people right and left, innocent people. Innocent children! That's the real reason I left the IRA. I

219

saw the innocent children on both sides murdered in the streets of Londonderry and Belfast. I saw their souls murdered by years of seeing and hearing violence and brutality."

He sat down next to Anna and put his arm around her shoulders.

"We're both fighters, Anna. You go find AJ and get him the hell out of here. If I survive, and I'm pretty damn good at that, I'll follow, but not until I get that pond scum. Melissa, can you help Stacy set up escape for Anna and AJ? Then, can we set up a plan to lure that crocodile out of his swamp or trap him in it?"

Anna put her hand on his arm.

"Wait, Jamie. Just listen. I have to connect with Ramón and Jorge. I know Ramón knows where AJ is."

She told them about her brief glimpse of Ramón.

"But, even on my trip to the dig with Lindy's body and my return, I've been impossible for them to make any contact because of the press following me and the police and...I must get to them, to Santa Anita. Maybe even Felipe Carrillo Puerto or Chetumal, down on the border of Belize."

"I wouldn't advise Puerto or Chetumal, Anna," Melissa said. "My information is that Puerto is crawling with soldiers of two cartels— the Croc and one other, headed by a man who is an unknown entity even to police. All they have are rumors about that guy. The man is gringo, or he's not a gringo, Hispanic or white, lives aboard a yacht and never sets foot on shore, or has his headquarters in the USA, or controls a huge network involving Eastern Europe, Africa, North and South America or, he runs a small operation. He is said to be American by origin but again, rumors, not facts."

Mac turned from the window, where he'd been watching for watchers.

"I agree. Felipe Carrillo Puerto is very, very dangerous right now. I can get you to Santa Anita. I got some information in Puerto Juarez about Adelina and Jorge. She's safe but the bomb that went off at the school has sent her into hiding. Jorge is at Santa Anita. He's commanding Mayan guerillas who are sabotaging the cartel lines running through the states of Yucatan, Campeche and Quintana Roo. Ramon was there, so if he appeared here with that message, he may have seen AJ or have heard of him. He was originally the one Jorge sent in search of AJ."

At that moment, Stacy came in, slamming the door behind her.

"I am so pissed! So pissed! National police have gone over the island where Cocodrilo had his headquarters, have gone through your house, Anna, with a fine-tooth comb, or so they say, and have gone over the place where you met for the exchange, and have nothing. Nothing? That's just not possible! I know how to examine crime scenes. I know what they have available. I know the US has offered help. Stupid, stupid men!

"And, Anna," she continued, "I'm so sorry but I have more bad news. The Brits have lost

Cory, Alex, and Marnie. Literally. Lost them. Can't find them. Have no idea where they are."

Anna shot up off the couch.

"What?"

She paused, remembering the oblique message from the boys.

"Well, maybe, and maybe not."

She explained to the others about the games and the reference to making the game go their way.

"It's entirely possible my sons and daughter are running a con on the British. It's entirely possible that Louie de la Vergne is aiding them. I can try to phone her but we agreed we would keep communications to a minimum due to the snooping devices being used by both police and possibly Ardith. Stacy, can you see if you can get more information before I try that?"

Stacy nodded. "I can. In fact, I'm going to love calling Vincent Grant, considering the news about your kids. I also have a car available and we can leave for Santa Anita whenever you want to do that. Mel, can you go with us?"

"No. I'm going hunting with Jamie for the Croc. I know that man. He'll want to kill Anna. He'll kill any of us. We need to find him, or make him come to us. Let Jamie and I take care of that."

Mac spoke. "I'm going with you, Stacy. If we must track AJ, I'm the best at that. I have good contacts down there. I can get us information. I can even cruise the bars of Felipe Carrillo Puerto if need be. That's where I was wanting to go for information from the beginning. Melissa, you cover this area and we'll stay in touch."

"Anna?" All eyes turned to her.

"We have a plan," she nodded. She went to Jamie and hugged him for long minutes.

"I don't want to lose you again. I love you."

"No enemy gets near me without a fight. I'll see you again, my girl."

Melissa stood up.

"Jamie and I will go get our car. We'll be back in about an hour if all goes well and we can ditch p&p—press and police."

She grinned at Jamie and punched his arm. "Come on, you old leprechaun! Let's go."

With a wave to Anna, the two left.

Stacy moved into the bedroom, on her cell phone.

Mac and Anna stood staring at each other.

Anna saw the guilt in his face and knew he had done things he was ashamed of. She waited.

"There's a chasm between us of my own making, Anna. I can't cross it right now."

She nodded. "I can't either, Mac. I'm another person inside. I..." Her voice trailed off and she looked away. "I'm hunting. I'm every bit as much an animal as the Crocodile."

She stood, arms at her sides, tense, alert, feet apart, the silence broken only by the faint voice of Stacy on her phone in the bedroom and Anna's own breathing.

"Mac, just get me out of here without the police and press."

223

Thirty-two

Jamie, with no explanation, had changed his mind. Mac thought it might be guilt at leaving Anna. Jamie had returned. Melissa had not returned with him. He didn't know where she had gone. "To hunt croc like she said."

"Like it or not, Mac, I'm goin' with you to feckin' Carrillo Puerto. I can pick up info on the Croc there too. Besides, you'll need me in the bar fights. I'm just as good as you at pretending I'm someone I'm not. An' given the state of mind you're in, I mean to get you out alive. You're acting like a Dublin street vendor who couldn't sell the wares he had so his kids could eat. Whippin' yourself with guilt, you are."

Jamie's head was turned away, watching the jungle as it passed. His voice was soft, so the women in the rear couldn't hear.

Mac, driving, gripped the steering wheel hard enough for his skin to turn white where the bones jutted up. His mind was in turmoil and he was only half listening.

I could be driving the one decent woman in my life to her death. If the Crocodile finds her, she'll be tortured and killed. If she goes back home, there's the mess back there. If she goes to Europe, that Ardith woman will be after her. There is no escape unless we...no, I'm not part of that any more. It's like Jamie said. I'm guilty. I betrayed her for my own survival, to get my own way. I can't expect any more of her. Can even Jorge and Ramon protect her? Will they?

Their own people need help. Adelina is in hiding, for god's sake! They're in daily danger from the cartels and from the Mexican government, who treat them like insurgent slaves, like second, third, fourth class citizens.

"We'll be at Santa Anita in about an hour. Let's hope AJ is there. If he isn't, we'll have to do a search for him before we get anywhere near Felipe Carrillo Puerto. We may never even get there."

Both men retreated into silence.

Then very quietly, Mac added, "Frankly, I don't think he's alive."

In the rear seat, Anna had heard the murmur of their conversation. She sensed what they discussed. Her sensors were so finely tuned she almost shook from the energy surging through and around her.

I've been thinking I'm going crazy but maybe not. This must be what animals feel like normally, or when they hunt. I can even sense the animals in the jungle as we pass them. I just saw that small herd of peccaries through the leaves. Sensed them and saw them. I'm a human. How can this be? This isn't supposed to be possible. If I search for AJ, will this help me?

Almost nothing is hidden from me. I know Mac had sex with another woman. I feel his body remembering. Strange. I feel so detached from that. With all that's happening, I can't find a reason to care about what he did. We are all in this strange life-threatening reality. What would I have done? Well, I did. I had sex with

225

both Ramon and Jorge last time I was here and loved it. It's odd that I don't feel any shame for that.

Jamie wants to kill. He loved killing. He left the IRA because he was afraid of the person he'd become. Ashamed, he was. Now he has a cause again. He's dangerous now. Maybe that's why he changed his mind. Or is it because he wants to die. Why would he want to die? Did he do something that he doesn't want to remember?

Stacy is stretched to her breaking point because she wants so much to succeed at this. Grant used her. He used Melissa too. And London! Are my kids safe? At least Grant's not in charge there anymore. Louie is there. She has resources I could never have. I must hope they'll be ok until after I see AJ and get us out of here. Will he go?

Lindy. Poor innocent Lindy. That's the real tragedy. Her terrible death. I can't bear to think of that for long. She...Stop!

Anna forced the picture of Lindy's dead body out of her mind. Another just as disturbing took its place.

So, El Cocodrilo is not the only cartel operating here. There's another. All we've got are rumors but...it would have to be incredibly well organized. An iron fist would have to run that. This scene is chaotic though. How can anyone keep an organization together in this maelstrom? Justice does not prevail. It's kill or be killed within and around the cartels. Mac said

226

the northern cartel is trying to take over closer to Mexico City. He was caught in it.

Death runs through the Yucatan the way the underground rivers do. The undertow reaches up and sucks down the innocent and the guilty alike. It feeds on the blood of women and children. It drips from the tree branches and stains the old roads. Tourists come and tourists go and they don't see it, don't see the shadows of fear and pain, not even in the eyes of the Mayans who wait on them every day in rich resorts for twenty-five cents an hour. Every day is The Day of the Dead and there is nothing to celebrate.

"Anna, we're here," Mac called back to her. "This is Santa Anita."

A sick feeling came over Anna.

"Mac, something's wrong. It doesn't feel right."

Anna leaned forward, hoping against hope for a glimpse of AJ, or for someone she knew. There were four men seated on a log at the end of the street. There was one woman hanging out wet shirts on a line she had strung from tree to tree. The dust of the road was settling behind them where their van had kicked it up. Mostly, there was silence.

Stacy looked back and forth.

"Isn't this where Jorge has his headquarters? Where is he? Where is everybody? Why are there so few people here?"

"Mac," Anna said again, "something's off here. Jorge's not here. Neither is AJ. I wish

Melissa had found Ramón before we left her. We could have brought him with us."

"Stay in the car. I'm going to talk to the workers over there."

Mac slid out of the car slowly, taking his time. He made sure the men saw his hands free of any weapon. He walked to the hood and opened it up, fiddled with the engine a bit, closed it, turned and waved to the men.

"Ola, Señores. ¿Es Señor Jorge aquí? I have much to tell him. I bring news for him."

One of the men stood. All three were armed with pistols strapped around their waists. The man made no move to use his but he waved his hand in an eastern direction and offered, "That way."

The men looked at each other. Their faces were closed books. The one standing half-turned away.

Mac heard the car door shut behind him. *Oh no, she's doing it her way!*

Anna walked directly up to the men.

"My son is the doctor who was here and my daughter-in-law was the nurse who was with him, and she was his wife. I have come to find them. Please help me find them."

All four men rose and bowed their heads to Anna and one of them stepped forward.

"Señora, your son was here but he is not here now. He is with Señor Aguilar and they are checking on the families in a village to the east. The cartels have been threatening the people there. Your daughter-in-law is dead. You know this, sí?"

Anna nodded.

"If you wish, I will show you her grave."

"Yes. I wish that. The people in the car are my brother—that old man—and my guard, that woman, and our driver, Señor Mac." Anna pointed to each one as she spoke. "Please allow them to sit and wait for me."

The men nodded and one went and brought some chairs which he set near a fire pit.

"Muchas gracias," Anna said and waved Stacy forward. "This woman will accompany me to the grave. Please lead us there."

Mac was tense. "Anna, maybe..." She cut him off with a wave of her hand.

"Mac, the atmosphere is tense here because there has been an attack on that village he spoke of by cartel soldiers. Don't ask how I know this. I just know. AJ and Jorge and the others are returning but it will be some time before they get here. Even the animals in the jungle around here are upset. That's the tension we feel."

Jamie had remained in the van. Now Anna called and motioned him over.

"This is my brother, Jaime. He has been a fighter also, like you. Please welcome him."

Jamie wondered if these men remembered or even knew of his first visit. They gave no sign of recognition.

229

"Jaime, I am going with this man to the grave of the wife of my son," she said in Spanish. "You can come with me or stay here as you wish."

Jamie, trusting none of them, looked at Anna as if she was insane. "Well, if Stacy goes with you, I can stay here. I just want you protected."

He had replied in Spanish.

"Señor," the man with Anna said, drawing himself up as tall as he could, "your sister will be very well protected."

"Señora y Señorita," he said, "This way, por favor."

He led them onto a barely discernable jungle path to the north and they disappeared beyond large dark green leaves.

The Mayans sat down on the log. They did not invite Jamie and Mac to do so. Mac and Jamie returned to wait at their vehicle.

Silence reigned.

Anna knelt at the grave of the daughter-in-law she barely knew.

Another innocent. Like lights being snuffed out. That's the tragedy now. That the innocent—the light-bearers—are being killed. That we have all been forced to lose innocence. What's the line from the song—"what's too painful to remember we simply choose to forget." Well, I won't forget. I can't forget. And AJ, he won't either, but how has it changed him?

Anna picked some leafy debris off the grave and softly smoothed it over. She sat listening to the silence for a long time. Stacy moved a few feet away and sat in silence also.

"Mom."

"Oh, god!" Anna whirled and clawed her way up his open arms to her feet, bursting into tears.

AJ, holding her while she cried, felt a very, very small piece of the ice within him melt. His eyes burned but he refused the relief of tears.

Jorge signaled to the men with him to go on. Stacy remained. He caught her eye and signed her to follow him, stopping some twenty feet away. Stacy pulled out her ID and gave it to him. He read it and nodded.

"We have some news," she said.

"So do I."

"Anna's brother is at your camp, too, and Mac. I understand you know Mac."

"Sí. I have met her brother also. He was at the dig. We must talk. We must all talk."

"Yes. When they are ready.

Dusk came and there were no lights in Santa Anita. Jorge had ordered them off. No fire. Cold food. Only necessary movement was allowed. The vehicles had been covered with tarps to stop any reflection from the moon or stars.

All talk was done in a closed house with a small pinpoint flashlight set in the center on the floor of the room.

Jorge began.

231

"I am very happy to see my friends, Mac and Anna, and to welcome Jamie and Stacy. We would have a better welcome but I must tell you that the cartel soldiers have come within fifteen miles of here and we are taking many precautions to avoid having them discover us. They attacked a village twenty-two miles away. It is near one of the old roads and the villagers did not want to cooperate and so they were punished. I am sorry to say that many did not survive. We must move our headquarters as soon as possible. We will move deeper into the jungle. I would like to know what news you bring."

"Mac, you go first," Anna said. "Tell how you got back to Mexico, what happened to you."

Mac, his voice low and quiet, told his story up through the search of Anna's house and the discovery of Lindy.

"Jamie, you go next."

Jamie added in all he had seen and done. He also told of his time in the IRA and in the monastery.

"Stacy, tell them what happened in Wisconsin and the plan we had for here."

Stacy did and included all she knew about what was happening in London, which was not much.

"Now I will fill in the rest." Anna left out nothing. She wanted AJ to hear it. She knew he would have to make a decision to stay in Mexico or come with her. The pain that streamed from his eyes and face in spite of his stone-like mask, the grief that poured from his body, the pull of

232

the spirit of Sheila, told her more than he would or, perhaps, could ever say in words.

He wants to die. He wants to be with her. I understand that. I can't make his decision for him but he must and will know the whole story first.

When she finished, thick silence tore at the night. Finally AJ spoke.

"I'm staying here, Mom. I know you want me to go home but this is my home now. Where she is. This is my home. I love you. I love my brothers and sister, but...I can't go."

In the darkness, tears streamed down Anna's cheeks.

It feels like someone just reached in and tore my heart out of my chest. I never felt this before. It wasn't the same when Art died. It was awful but not this. He's a grown man, Anna. Not my little boy, not even my grown son. He's his own person and he must do what he must.

Jamie's voice came out of the dark.

"Anna, he won't be alone, without family. I'm staying here. This is the reason I came. I'm supposed to be with him."

In the dark, his hand found hers.

"I'm a warrior. So are you, but your fight is for the rest of your kids. AJ and I will be fine. Just fine."

At the hint of first light, Jorge ordered the village stripped of everything his people could carry. When they were done, it looked desolate, as if no one had lived there for a long time.

Anna and AJ stood next to the van. Mac and Stacy waited inside. Jamie was gone. He said his goodbyes and left with the people. Jorge waited at the edge of the jungle.

"Mom, I have to tell you one more thing. It confirms a rumor I heard while I was ill, when I had wandered into a bar one night. There's a cartel that's headed by a white man and I think whoever it is has connections to Wisconsin. I'll try to find out more but the person keeps a very, very big wall of mystery around himself. No one except Jorge believes this man is operating here. If what I heard was true, he has a world-wide operation. Marnie, Cory and Alex could be his victims just as much as they are of Ardith. If there's one thing I've learned, it's that they all manipulate each other and there are layers and layers of their activities. That's two things. One more. It's all about greed. All about money. If that drug line through Wisconsin to Canada makes money, they'll all want it. Don't let your guard down. Trust only those you know. And, Mom, you may have to get the hell out of Wisconsin. Don't hesitate if that time comes."

"I won't. I love you."

"I love you too, Mom."

Anna climbed into the van. AJ moved to join Jorge.

Anna closed her eyes and remembered every bit of his hugs and his goodbye kiss and heard the question that never left her mind—*will I ever see my son again?*

She also remembered Jorge finding her in the dark last night and laying down and cradling her in his arms as she wept silently, and his last kiss before light broke, and the empty space when he left.

Mi amor.

His whispered words floated in her mind.

Her memories were painful. The other nagging thought was not. It nudged and pushed at her until it broke through the pain.

A white man? A connection to Wisconsin? Who? No. It could not be. Impossible! But, Ardith said the corpse wasn't his body. Not *totally impossible, Anna. It could be possible he survived. How do you know whose body that was?*

As Stacy drove them away, Anna sat silent, shocked at the waves of anger and bitterness that flooded her entire body.

I don't love him. I do not love him.

Then...

I hope he's dead! I don't want him in my life anymore!

Thirty-three

"You were right, Anna. Publicity is your ally. Don't avoid it. Use it. All the publicity you can get. I'm staying here. I can't get you out of Mexico. I can't stay with you. I'm a soldier of fortune, a wanderer, and a spy. I'm going to disappear into the jungle as soon as we hit a small town and you and Stacy are going to get to Cancun as fast as possible. You get yourselves out of here. The Mexican government will be glad to see you go. They'll escort you to the airport, put you on the plane, and celebrate with tequila when you're gone."

"Mac, you jerk!" Stacy exploded, pounding a fist on the steering wheel. "How can you desert us now? We need you to get to Cancun. We could be followed even now. We don't know those few cars behind us aren't after us. At least get us to a tourist zone—the Zona Hotelera or, if you won't go that far, to Cozumel. I can have someone there to help us get out. I can call the embassy in Mexico City and have them fly us out of here if necessary."

"If I go to Cancun or those tourist zones, I run the risk of someone recognizing me. I've been with you too much as it is."

Anna shook her head, disgusted.

"Stacy, let him off in the next town like he asks. We'll make it to Cancun or one of the other tourist spots along the way. He can make his way to Felipe Carrillo Puerto and get himself killed. Let him go."

Anna's anger ripped through the air but she controlled her voice.

"No. Take him to the outskirts of Puerto. He's on his own from there. We'll go north as fast as possible."

Mac said nothing.

They dropped him off at a gas station on the edge of Puerto and continued on their way. Anna, hurt and angry, remained silent. After a while, Stacy broke the long silence.

"It'll be OK, Anna. Even before we left Cancun, Mac gave me the names of three men who can fly us out in a private plane. I set it up just in case. I even had our clothing packed and sent to the airport. It was Plan B. We can go directly there. I'd like to pick up some food at Chetumal though."

Her eyes had been glued to the rearview mirror while she spoke. Anna half-turned in the seat and gasped.

"Stacy, that's just like the limo at the shooting! But, how would they know?"

"Don't panic! It could be some rich tourist in a limo going to Cozumel. If it turns off there, we'll know it's not tailing us."

They rode on, hypervigilant, both watching the cars behind them. As they neared Cozumel, a tour bus and several other cars added themselves to the line behind them, making it difficult to see the black vehicle. Neither woman thought of stopping for food as they had planned.

Stacy gulped a deep breath as they passed the last road into the town.

"I think we're clear. I don't see it anymore," Anna said.

"Neither do I, but check all the cars behind us."

"I'm seeing a gray car about a mile behind us that looks sort of official. Those in between are old. I think we're clear."

"Maybe, and maybe not. Sometimes these people operate as a tag team. One leaves and another takes its place."

Mentally, Stacy counted the weapons on hand. Two pistols in the trunk, one in the glove compartment, and a knife under her seat. Not much ammo.

"We haven't enough ammunition to defend ourselves for any length of time. We have to hope no one tries to harm us. We'll aim to make it to the airport."

She tossed her cell phone into Anna's lap.

"I have Mel on speed dial. Call her for me."

Anna did and hit the speaker.

"Mel, Anna and I are alone driving up from Santa Anita. We're just past Cozumel by about three or four miles. Can you meet us at the airport? Did you connect with those guys to fly us north? And bring more security?"

"No problem. The plane's set up to get you out of Mexico. I'll have them watching for you at the airport entrance and come up ahead and behind you. In fact, I'll send a car down that road to meet you. It will be the camo jeep. You know the one."

238

"I do. Were you able to check out the whereabouts of the Crocodile?"

"I have feelers out but for some reason he's laying low. I'm having the house up north watched but so far he hasn't shown up, nor have his men. He's plotting something and I know the reason. He's hornet angry right now. I found out from Louie de la Vergne that her husband pulled strings with high banking connections in Europe, Anna, and your money is back in your account. It was transferred out of the Croc's bank last night. He didn't deliver your son. He doesn't get the money."

Anna gasped. "What? All of it?"

"Yup. You have some very influential friends, woman. And I wish your brother had stayed with me. He's a crack shot. Did you know that? I'd hire him anytime."

Stacy broke in. "Did you find out anything about that other cartel and if it's a player in this game too?"

"No. It's strange. I have a few of my sleazier acquaintances making the rounds of bars in four towns—Cancun, Puerto Juarez, Chetumal, and Felipe Carrillo Puerto. It's all contradictory, rumor, vague. I'm beginning to suspect the confusing rumors are being spread on purpose. It would be a good tactic."

"Keep digging. With some luck, they might keep the Crocodile's attention while we get out of here. Will you be at the airport too?"

"No. I'm chasing down some rumors myself. Don't worry. The contacts you make are

239

those Mac recommended. Anna, he said he got you out of Mexico that way before and it can be done again."

Anna nodded. Stacy said goodbye and the call ended.

"Do you know who these people are that Mac used before?" she asked.

"I think I'd recognize one of the pilots, maybe both. I do know what end of the airport Mac used. It's the farthest from the main area as anyone can get without being in the jungle."

"Ok. I'm a little nervous about Mel not being with us but she and Mac do have great contacts."

Ten miles south of the airport they were joined by the camo Jeep and they were escorted to a secure area where bags were waiting. Two officials met them, checked their papers and waved them on. Their bags were whisked away. One of the men from the jeep handed them both large paper cups of coffee, accompanied by his equally large grin.

"Mel said you might appreciate these. Bon voyage, ladies." He waved them down a short corridor. "It's the last door on the right. Your baggage has been stored in the plane and you can be off."

Anna was in the process of saying it was almost too easy when she heard another voice, male, call Stacy back.

"Go ahead, Anna. I'll just see what he wants and be right back."

Stacy turned around and called, "What's the problem?"

Anna went through the door, over a short stretch of tarmac and up the stairs. The cabin was empty but her luggage was in one corner.

She sat down and buckled her seat belt.

It wasn't until the door of the plane slammed shut that Anna realized something was off.

Stacy! Where's Stacy! We're moving!

She unbuckled her seatbelt and ran to the door of the cockpit, pounding on it. Her yelling went unanswered. The plane tilted into a fast takeoff and Anna flew backward, rolling along the floor of the plane, slamming into the stationary seats. She pulled herself upright and into a seat, then to a window.

We're flying in the wrong direction. The sun should be in the west, on the left side of this plane. We're flying west! Why are we flying west?

Anna stood, steadied herself, walked to the rear and checked the toilet and a closet-like area. She returned down the aisle and checked the front. No one else was in the plane. The cockpit door was locked when she tried it. Again she pounded and yelled. No answer. The plane was still gaining altitude.

Betrayal! Who? Mac? Melissa? Stacy? I've been kidnapped!

Thirty-four

"It's time. She's on her way. Her children in London are out of our way. I've had them watched and made sure Crazy Woman kidnapped them. My pilot has Anna on a plane heading to my airport just north of Mexico City. Unfortunately, her brother escaped us but I will have him found and sent north also.

"When he leaves the plane, the pilot will be eliminated. I want no one to trace her. I have the computers set to convert the plane to a drone. Her papers will be processed by the time she sets down in the US. The current cover story is that she's been my guest here. The word in Mexico is that she has left on her own. Her bodyguard is effectively neutralized."

The Texan stared out the window at the cold rain pounding the streets of the West Side of Green Bay, trying unsuccessfully to figure out what this meant for him.

El Capitán could picture him doing just that.

"Your job won't change. I still want you to move plans for expanding that drug highway to its highest financial return. You do that and there'll be a nice bonus for you in that account of yours in Geneva. Maybe in the one in the Caymans too."

"Yes sir! You bet! It's comin' along. I got me a small plane and flew up the highways all the way to the border and all along the border. Got some good maps for ya'll to look at to choose

242

more border crossin's and got a few more truckin' companies that might fit your plans. Our police buddies and I have got an idea for maybe settin' up them Kinnealy boys fer aidin' and abettin'. Along with that Crazy Woman maybe."

El Capitán rolled his eyes skyward. *Sometimes this man gets the silliest ideas.*

"Just put that on hold until we have the line at its peak production. Then we'll talk about it. I should be able to be up that way sometime soon. I'll keep in touch."

"Yes sir! I got it! We've got some other good ideas too..." he stopped talking when he realized he was on a dead line.

El Capitán stood looking aft at the small yacht approaching his ship from far to the south. He was expecting a delivery of several young girls for the entertainment at his meeting with the Colombians and Venezuelans. The man who was delivering the girls was a new contact in the sex trade. He came with high recommendations but El Capitan wished to check him out personally so he had insisted the pimp come with his girls. The advantages of having meetings on his own boat were many. Anyone who was his guest knew they would have to do as he wished if they preferred not to swim long distances in shark-infested waters. It made negotiations so much easier.

The revenge I get will, however, make it more than worth it to visit Wisconsin.

In Wisconsin, the Texan sat down at the desk and thought long and hard.

"It's time I got out of this," he said out loud. No one heard him. No one was there. "It's time I put the plans in action."

He called his bank in Switzerland and, giving a prearranged code, had them move half of his money to a numbered account in Dubai, where banks were even more careful. He did the same for the account in the Caymans. He closed out all the credit cards under his current name and activated two others under the new name he'd chosen.

There would be a plane waiting at Appleton airport to fly him to Detroit, then an international flight to the Far East to a beautiful resort he'd bought long ago in still another name.

He felt some regret knowing he'd never see his beloved San Antonio again, never walk the River Walk again, but the beauties of his new country were even better, both the scenery and the women.

With that in place, he left for a meeting with the two police officers who also would want out if they couldn't keep their secret lives secret.

He had a "retirement plan" for each of them and he hoped it was an offer they couldn't refuse. It would allow them to leave in a blaze of glory.

They would take the credit for capturing a dangerous group of young adults who worked for the psychotic woman responsible for many deaths, youths lured into this group by drugs.

Among these boys were the Kinnealy brothers and their sister, and their friends, the

Fitzgeralds, with a little brother who could be a sex pervert, and the Bradleys, those half-black, half-white boys.

An equal opportunity drug bust. Mulattos and poor white trash, that's what they are.

246

London

Thirty-five

Eight days earlier...

"Well, where the bloody hell are they? Yes, they could be in England. Yes, they could be in the United States. Yes, they could be in Europe. Why don't you all just admit you have no idea? You blew it! Totally screwed this up!"

Vincent Grant paced the living room of Anna's apartment, attempting to blame this second kidnapping of his clients on the British to avoid looking at the massive failure of his own security company and the deaths of two more of his men, found, as the others had been, laid out in the basement of the apartment building.

Big Tom Kearsley, for his part, silently agreed with the man but was not about to admit it. *We're the police. We should have been on it.*

Little Tom, withdrawn to the far end of the room, was still unable to shake the huge disappointment in his dad, whose dishonesty about his activities through the years left him wondering what else he didn't know about his father.

Louie de la Vergne, finished with her bout of disgust at the lot of them, had moved on. She had retired to her room to think it through and dress for action in well-cut, expensive jeans, blouse, and sweater, which would take her anywhere.

United States and Canadian officials have been alerted. My contacts in Europe have not seen or heard anything. Therefore, it is best to assume they are still in this country. Then the question is, where? Three young people and a crazy woman would not go entirely unnoticed for long, especially when she has an entourage of at least six men who do her work for her. I mentioned to them about leaving signs, but did they? Would they have had any chance to do that? We should have worked that out in much more detail. Has anyone thought to look for that? But no. Of course they have not. Not in this place. Not at Westminster. Not at the art school.

Louie walked from her room, feeling quite discouraged. Big Tom and Grant had gone. Little Tom sat in the large sitting room, slumped on a sofa, head in his hands.

"I wish we had taught them to make signs as you learned to do," she commented. "There might have been some clue to help us if we had."

She wandered around the room, turning over papers or books, feeling it all useless.

Little Tom raised his head slowly, thinking.

"Signs? There was a sign in the cathedral. Alex saw it there but it didn't mean anything. I pretended it did and I went out later to talk to my street contacts to see if I could find out what it meant but there was nothing. No one I know could figure out what it meant. If only I'd gotten back sooner. It took so long."

"What sign? What was it?"

"The number eight on its side, like infinity. With a green P. I thought it might be a dirty joke

250

or something sarcastic, like 'peeing forever.' Something some bloke left there so 'e could brag later to 'is friends about a dirty joke in the cathedral."

The skin on Louie's back began to crawl. Bits and pieces of long ago memories began to surface. *Who knew they were told to go to Westminster? I'm not sure. I told them that here. So someone did? Someone with the police? With Grant? Did they overhear? Were we recorded somehow? Is this even related to what's happening?*

"Where in Westminster did he see that?"

"I don't know for sure. Off to the side somewhere. I can't remember what he said. I didn't think it was important."

"Come on. We are going to find that sign."

The weather was still cold and damp, the cathedral was even more so. Louie shivered, as much from apprehension as she did from the cold.

How do they heat such a monstrous building? For that matter, how do the French heat Notre Dame? Irrelevant. Get your mind under control or you will miss the details.

"We will begin to our left and inspect every inch all the way around. We must and will find this."

They did. It took over an hour. Louie had brought a flashlight and was using it but even so, they almost missed it. The sign was on the base of a large stone tomb. Louie found another older one farther on, nearly faded out, on the base of another tomb.

"Does this sign have something to do with who's in these tombs?" Little Tom asked.

"No. It does not. I have seen this sign but it would have been used a very long time ago. I would not have thought it is still in use. It was used during the Cold War by a man who was dealing in arms, supplying them to Russia. He supplied other things as well. He was a very evil man."

An involuntary shudder shook her and a wave of nausea followed. She took a deep breath and leaned against a nearby pillar.

How would anyone know of this? He was killed in Italy. That is what we were told. We celebrated with champagne when we heard that. We heard nothing of him after that. His spy network fell apart. The question is, why is that sign in Westminster? Is it in use now? It can hardly be left over from way back then. Is it just a coincidence? Is it a joke, as this young man thought? Is she using it?

"What is it? What's wrong? What does this mean to you?"

"Oh, my dear young man. It is a tale too long and too terrible to tell. We will check every part of this place for more of these and then we must leave here and go to see a friend of mine as soon as possible. You must come with me. I must know you, at least, are safe."

The pipe bubbled and gurgled as the man drew in air slowly. He blew a long drawn-out plume of smoke before he spoke. Little Tom watched the chubby and finely wrinkled face of the old man sitting in the pool of light from a tall lamp.

"I remember him. I came face to face with him once and nearly didn't survive. I was in Poland, behind the Iron Curtain, when I heard the news of his death. It was a great relief and I cried real tears because I knew how many people would be safe because he died.

He drew on his pipe again and said softly, "I had not cried tears for a long time before that.

"I cried because I knew you would be safe also, my dear. I called Robert and he promised he would take care of you. I am very grateful to Robert for that. Petrovsky could not take you and sell you to his sadistic clients who wanted young girls and boys to torture.

"Now let me see what else I can remember. His network was mainly across Europe, and not so much in Britain, although there were rumors he tried. He created smoke and mirrors to hide what he was doing. He was a master at it. Rumor had it he was married and supposedly a 'model husband' but then so were some of Hitler's henchmen. Mm-hmm. Jekyll and Hyde."

The pipe gurgled again for a time. Little Tom could not bring himself to interrupt the old man's thoughts but he had a thousand questions racing through his brain.

253

"There was a rumor he had two children but I don't know any more about that. I hope to God they never knew the side of their father you and I knew, mon cherie. I wish I could tell you more but you know the man we called The Master. You have visited him recently. Yes," he said, seeing Louie's eyes blink and her startled look, "I still know what goes on here and there."

His smile twinkled at Louie and he chuckled, sounding exactly like his pipe.

"Go see him now. I'll give him a call to expect you. He has access to archives and memory I don't. You must be very wary. If someone has taken up the 'business' this man had, you are in grave danger. But you know that. I will call Robert for you too. Do not use your phone until you have it checked. One more thing. MI5 is involved in this. They have vetted you out thoroughly. They are happy you are here to help us. They are asking your husband to help too. He'll call you tomorrow on that."

He held out a tobacco-stained hand to Little Tom, who happily shook it.

"I'm very pleased to meet you, young man. Come back again and I will answer some of those questions falling out of that brain of yours."

Big Ben had chimed one in the morning before the next meeting was over. Little Tom's head spun with tales about WWII and its aftermath that were in no history book.

Louie and Little Tom sat in the back of a large black SUV which The Master had offered to return them to where they wanted.

"My father needs to hear this but I don't think he'll believe it."

"I agree." She laid her hand on his arm. "Don't be so hard on your father. I won't be surprised to learn he is, and has been for a long time, involved in this. He will listen. It helps that you have witnessed all that we have just discussed.

"If I know my husband, he will be here in the morning. He never could pass by a good episode of intrigue and leave it alone. He also has never failed to keep me safe. We will have his help too.

"We are not returning to that apartment. It's not safe there. I know a wonderful little bed and breakfast. The owner is a former friend of mine, also from the old times. She can tell some tales, but I will forbid it. We both need sleep."

The meeting at one in the afternoon was well attended. Little Tom looked around and saw not only The Master scrunched in a wide wooden chair, but also Robert de la Vergne and Louie holding hands, the gurgling pipe emitting smoke curls, and his father frowning at him. There were also various blokes who he guessed were from higher-up levels of government. He relaxed. He knew his father would not reprimand him in front of them. He was very pleased. He would have lots to tell his brothers. Not that he wanted to gloat but...*Yes, I do. I'm going to love telling them all this.*

He had been unable to sleep and was happy with the very strong English tea now being served.

All stories got told again and the questions came thick and fast.

The Master had been silent, letting others field the questions. Finally, he stirred.

"There are three things we need to find out. What is the real identity of this woman? What is her connection, if any, to Petrovsky? And where are those young people? If we don't want to find them dead, that is the priority question."

The pipe gurgled. "I've got feelers out. She hasn't gotten them off this island. Every small plane that goes up is monitored and no one tried flying under the radar."

Big Tom nodded. "Every large plane too. All airlines have been watched, searched, and monitored."

Risking annoying his father even more, Little Tom spoke up. "But if she couldn't get a plane in the air, what about boats, the ferries to the continent, to Ireland, to the Isle of Man, sea traffic up or down the coast, and the Chunnell?"

Little Tom was aware that it was next to impossible for police to check every mode of transportation available to the inhabitants of an island nation. He knew the others knew that and, even though he was somewhat intimidated by the presence of such experienced men, he wanted to know how they would do that.

He continued. "I say the best bet is to hope those young people can get one of them free. They're fighters, they are, and clever too. How can we set it up so they can get to a copper wherever they are without alarming that crazy woman? How can we use the fact she's crazy to lure her out? There must be a way. She wants their money. Maybe that's the way."

His father was now double-glaring at him.

Robert stood up, squeezed Louie's hand, and pulled a map of London toward him. He had spent a sleepless night doing much homework.

"Oui, young man. Money is exactly what she wants. She will remain here until she gets that money. So, we must lay our plans with great care. Remember, she is very clever. I have an idea where she might have taken them and I have control of enough of Anna's money and property to lure her out. To begin, there are six possible sections of London and the suburbs where they might be. These were sections which we think might have had connection to Petrovsky long ago. They were reduced to almost total rubble back then and have only been partially rebuilt. Three are completely abandoned places still. Any search of these areas must be very subtle, almost unseen, but very thorough. That will take time.

"To gain us time then, we will need the use of a private gallery, a building where she can approach and monitor the entire scene freely, so that she will feel safe enough to view a very large and valuable collection of art. Anna's collection is being packed and will be on its way today under extreme security.

"This woman will, I am very sure, be lured by Anna's paintings and the objet d'arts which she believes belonged to her 'brother' and she will demand to know this collection is not fake. She will want very badly to see them. She will want to have 'experts' of her own choice examine them. We will offer her the name of the best, a pristine reputation. Right, sir?" He smiled at The Master, who smiled back and nodded.

"We must make her believe we agree to that and to any of her other terms."

The men and Louie gathered around the maps and discussion began, Little Tom included.

He knew the role he wanted to play. He wanted to be the rescuer of the "princess" Marnie.

Thirty-six

Fake fingernails make good picks. Marnie had used up three of them before she knew she had loosened threads on a section of her rope. Days had gone by...three, she thought but couldn't be sure. Sleep had come at the oddest times and she'd lost track. The windows had covers over them. She couldn't see if it was day or night. Two lamps had been on the whole time.

When it became clear from Ardith's growing irritation that flying out was not an option, they had been removed, finally, from the plane. There was a long ride through the London streets blindfolded. She had been walked into a building, still blindfolded, tied to a chair, and the blindfold removed. Her guards had taken the ropes on and off for eating and for bathroom breaks and were getting careless with her, but she couldn't tell where she was except, "it seems like a small house and I'm on the ground floor." She had begun talking to herself out loud just to keep from feeling so isolated, so hopeless.

"They think I'm harmless. Model thin, so no threat there. Young and pretty, so no threat there. Arrogant asses, and their arrogance will undo them. I'm better at this than they are. Yes, I'm arrogant too. Takes one to know one and takes one to outwit one...or two. Or maybe more. I am not so arrogant I'll underestimate them. Now to disguise these loose ropes and be sure I can be totally free in an instant. I hope Alex and Cory have the same idea."

She could not know where they were. A building of course. Nearby? "I can't hear them at all. I wish one of them would yell or something."

She had tried singing at the top of her lungs but had no response from her brothers. When she persisted, they tied a gag around her mouth. They took it off later and, when she remained quiet, just left her alone.

Fear came. "I'm all alone. No! Don't go there! Ok. It's loose. Now fix it so it looks tight but falls off. There. Practice it now."

And she did. Whenever her guard went outside, which he often did, she explored. She found herself in a small cottage, with two floors. Four rooms were on the lower floor and one large room above. One other door seemed solidly boarded up on the outside and all windows were blacked out and boarded up.

She was alone.

Alex and Cory were not together. On the paranoid but correct premise that if left together, all three of these young people would plot against her, Ardith had divided them up among some rundown and unused cottages in a neighborhood in London mostly abandoned years ago by anyone except the homeless and hapless. Her men made sure those creatures were gone. In size, it was relatively small, perhaps four to six city blocks in length and width, but its boundaries were made up of abandoned shells of larger buildings that masked the old dilapidated cottages within, like a small ancient town within walls.

Cory was hungry, and emotionally alternating between fury and fear. He had succeeded in loosening his bonds, set a trap for his keeper, attacked him, but lost the battle, was subdued, tied even tighter and left alone since that time.

Alex was fed, but Cory's attempt to escape meant Alex was also bound tighter, handcuffed to a pipe before he was fed, and then tied again afterward.

Both had yelled themselves hoarse and could hear each other, but after a time, both realized it didn't help.

Both thought about whether or not there was a ransom demand made. When Ardith did not appear to either brag about how she had their mother searching for them or to announce an exchange for money, they began to lose hope and believe she had collected the money and abandoned them entirely. The continued presence of guards was the only sign she might still be interested in them.

Despair was eating small bites out of any hope.

Homeless people mostly just mind their own business. Old Anse, short for his proper name of Anselm, was one of those. Old Anse, however, did not like anyone disturbing the peace of this cozy little area he called his castle. So, after getting kicked out, when his favorite member of the London police came tooling along on a bicycle around the perimeter of the wall of buildings, he stopped this officer to complain about the shouts and yells and presence of men who didn't belong there. He told of voices calling names like Cory and Alex and Marnie.

"Now this be me 'ome, and I deserves some peace I do, an' these fellas is most disturbin' an' I want some service 'ere."

"Well, I agree with you, Anse and I'll be looking into it," said the officer kindly. He liked Old Anse.

Unfortunately, other crises, in a neighborhood that had a minimum of three per day, took the officer's mind off that report and another day went by before he remembered. It was an email that brought him to his feet and sent him to his supervisor who hurried to another especially secure phone.

That was the day Ardith sent her second ransom demand. The note, in the severed hand of some poor soul, was delivered to Anna's apartment. The police quickly determined the hand did not belong to the young men or the girl, but the cruelty underscored their belief that Ardith was badly over the edge.

"She's demanding eight million in cash, more than she demanded before, and all the paintings in Anna's possession, and the titles to homes in Green Bay and Italy," Robert told them. "She has gotten the message we sent out. That means we have her close attention. The fact that she is demanding the homes means she is not thinking straight. She's delusional if she thinks she will ever be able to use or sell them."

"I've learned that Anna is not yet home from Mexico but is, somehow, still the target of a cartel, so no help will come from that quarter." Big Tom shook his head. "This woman won't be satisfied with anything but destroying Anna financially and I believe she will certainly kill those young people once she gets what she wants. We must find them."

Cory found an out. He got very bad diarrhea. He was not faking it. The food they finally brought him was atrocious. The guard, with some dismay, was ordered to take care of him. The alternative to having him mess his pants and having the putrid smell waft gently past the guard's nose at unexpected times, was to release him from his bonds and leave him to his own devices within the small house.

Diarrhea had never stopped him from doing anything as a small child and it was no different now. Discovering a pile of junk in the basement and a walled-in back yard, he quietly made a sort of tunnel to the wall, found a loose board, loosened it more, and left a fragrant pile of underclothing stained with the product of said loose bowels in the house so the guard would not miss him.

Finding where they kept Alex was not hard. All he had to do was look for a small structure with a guard sitting outside. It took perhaps an hour to slowly search the area and then several hours more watching the guard's habits.

He takes a magazine in with him and stays longer. That's when he goes to shit. If I go in when he's sitting there and he doesn't see me, I can hide until he goes outside again and then get Alex free.

It worked. They got out but only just in time. Cory's guard raised the alarm. They watched as four more men arrived and a search began.

"We've got to find Marnie. We can't leave without her," Alex said as he surveyed the area from the third story of one of the perimeter buildings. "She doesn't even know we're still alive. We don't even know if she's here. Or if she's still alive, and if she is, is she ok, or hurt, or..." he broke off, unwilling to continue.

"She's ok. I can feel it," Cory said, "but...I've got an idea but we'll have to split up for a time. Now listen."

The faint singing came from a perimeter building about three football (American football) fields to the east. Two of her men were dispatched to investigate.

Slightly louder singing came from the south. Two more went in that direction.

A brief time later the north echoed to the sound of music. Literally. *The hills are alive...*and so on.

Marnie listened. Her guard stood outside in front of the cottage and she heard the directions he gave to the others.

"I think it's just some locals from out there," he pointed to the outer world, "but we'd better check it out." He dispatched another man in each of the three directions.

Another came running up just after they left. "My bird flew the nest. The other one too. Where's yours?"

He checked inside.

"She's ok. Let's go. I'll bet it's those boys doing that singing."

The men split up.

In seconds Marnie was darting from cottage to cottage, but had no idea of the direction in which she was headed. She had only the thought that the guards were off in other directions.

It has to be this way. I sure hope this is what they wanted me to do. I hope they can get away. It was Cory singing that one song. Didn't sound very much like Alex on the other songs though. Too far away to tell. Don't make noise! Move fast! Don't stop!

She kept up a steady stream of pep talk and made it to and through a large three story building and stopped dead. To her great surprise, the street on the other side held people going about their business.

It's another world on this side! Do they know about the world inside? Do Cory and Alex know about this? They can't. I have to go back

265

for them. We've been so close to help. What do I do? Get help first or find them first? If police go in, they'll be shot first. I just know that woman will give orders to kill. They didn't leave me. I just can't leave them.

Marnie looked up and down the street, making sure she could recognize landmarks—a pub on the corner with a wolf's head on the sign, a small warehouse across the street with a bright blue front, another pub far down on the right, an old house next to it—dirty green color.

She turned and went back into the old building.

The bobby on the bicycle caught her movement out of the corner of his eye and thought it strange that a young woman would go into that old place, then thought about the singing and yelling someone had reported just before he left the station, then thought about the alert which had come in yesterday. He made a U-turn and headed back to the station.

"We have the location," Big Tom announced to those at the station where he had been following the search. "It's one of those areas on the map we singled out. But it's confusing—a bit odd, really. There's been singing heard and a young girl was seen walking *into* a peripheral building—not a good description of her but slim, dark hair. We'll be going in from all sides, hoping to find them."

Marnie raced in and out of one building after another hoping she would see Cory or Alex.

She was afraid to yell, to sing, or to make any noise.

I know it was Cory's voice. I just know it. He must be somewhere in these buildings. God! I hope he's not in one of those little houses. I'll have to search forever. Maybe I should go for the police. But then there'll be sirens, and they could be killed before the police ever find them. How can I get their attention without getting them killed?

Oh, god! There are sirens wailing out there. Yell! Take a chance!

She ran up the nearest stairs, got to a second floor, ran to the inside circle and looked out over the houses. Brief movement—far across the houses she saw a man run from one house to another, gun in hand.

"Coreee! Aaaalex!" She repeated their names over and over, shouting from behind the empty cement frame of a window that was long gone. A man ran out of a house and started toward her, firing a shot that buried itself into an inside wall. Another ran from a small house halfway across the scene, stopped, listened, and came toward her.

Marnie waited until she saw them about fifty yards away and then moved quickly back to the other side of the building and down the stairs to the ground floor. She was about to step out of the building when she was grabbed from behind.

"Marnie!" Cory spun her around. "The attention's off Alex and on us. Let's get help here!"

"This way then! The street will be busy outside of here." They ran out and stopped. No traffic. No people. A dead end.

"This way! This way!" Marnie ran back the way she had come.

"Holy shit!" Cory yelled. "The guy behind us has a gun. Go back into the building. Duck! Dive!" He made it into an opening as a bullet hit the cement wall he had just passed.

"Sirens! I hear sirens! Come on!" Marnie yelled and dived out one door, running for the next. "Cory! Come on!" She made it into the next, seeing only two buildings ahead of her and cars, pedestrians, a street. No shots rang out and she darted out and to the second last building. When no additional shots followed, she risked a look back.

"Cory! Cory!"

There was no response from Cory. No Cory appeared. No sounds at all. No pursuers appeared. Nothing.

Marnie dashed for the street and began yelling for police. "Help! I need help! Call the police!"

Bystanders either dived into doors and shops or ran, but one man yelled at her and pointed to a police vehicle rounding a corner.

Two officers jumped out as it screeched to a stop.

"My brothers are in danger, in there!" She pointed to the building complex.

"Are you Marnie Kinnealy?"

"Yes! Please! Help me find my brothers! We were held in there. I saw two men. One had a gun and he shot at us. My brother and me. Cory. He was behind me. He should have gotten out. He was right behind me. Please! You've got to find him, and my other brother, Alex! They're still in there. Please!"

The driver, inside the van, was transmitting to someone. Marnie heard her name mentioned. The two officers were speaking to her but she barely heard what they said. She turned back and began to run the way she'd come.

"No, Marnie, no!" one officer shouted and started after her.

A shot hit the police vehicle as it was turning to follow Marnie. The second officer dove for the building.

Alex ran as fast as he could, not looking back. He hit the street, saw police and yelled for help. Slowly, police surrounded the entire area. Creeping through the perimeter buildings, they left at least one shooter wounded. Another man was captured.

Cory was found and carried to an ambulance. Alex was brought to him. They waited.

Five and a half hours later, the entire area had been searched again and again.

Marnie was not found.

Thirty-seven

"We got four of her men. Three are alive and talking," Big Tom stated, as he looked down at Cory on the sofa, his leg now in a firm brace. Alex stood across the room, leaning uneasily on the mantle, trying to keep himself from pacing the entire length of the apartment.

"We found how she got out with Marnie. She apparently has used that place for some time and she had a short tunnel opened through the basement of one of the perimeter buildings. It may be one of the old underground places used during the blitz. We also have an eyewitness who saw an older woman and black-haired young girl leave a small hotel in the district west of there, and a description of the car they used. That's more than we've ever had."

Robert walked over to Alex. "Do not look so worried, young man. This woman will be her own undoing. We want you and your brother to play another part that will contribute to her capture. It will be dangerous. We will want you to be at the gallery when she is there. The bait she can't resist, you see. The police are staying far back. We will use her insanity, her crazy thinking, to get her to release Marnie for the two of you. That is what she thinks will happen but that is not all that will be happening. We will have another person—you know him as The Master—our art expert, who will walk with her, talk with her, and distract her using his knowledge. Once Marnie is safe, we will close in and extract you. We have

270

used this before, years ago. It will work again. What do you say? Are you in?"

"Of course I'm in. I want my sister safe."

"Same here," said Cory. "When does this happen?"

"The art is hung and we are waiting for her to accept that we will give her free reign to inspect the entire area for safety. We hope that will convince her to inspect the art and have it authenticated, as well as have it packed up and removed to wherever she wants it to go. We want her to bring Marnie with her but she may not agree to that. We do think she will have Marnie close by because she would have it set up to have Marnie killed if we thwart her in any way. You will be the live bait. We'll have you record a message that your mother is ill and she has authorized you to represent her and she agrees to the ransom. We will have you negotiate for your homes in Green Bay, just to make it feel more authentic. Don't worry!" he said as he saw the protest on their faces. "We'll give you a script to follow and coach you. We must convince her that she'll get her way. So, the police will not appear to be part of this at all. However, we have someone who she may want very much to meet."

He turned to the man Alex and Cory knew only as The Master.

"I knew her father. There are not many remaining alive who can say that," the Master told them. "She apparently idolized him. As you may already know, she believed Conrad Wentworth was her brother, the one who was

271

given to a German couple who escaped Nazi police. Conrad was not her brother but they had similar stories. She came to believe they had the same parents because she was also, apparently, given to an adopting couple. They were not so lucky that they escaped to a free country. They did, however, tell her glorious stories about her father and she believed them. The truth is that her father abandoned his child and fled to Russia and ran illegal arms and human trafficking for many years. The sign that you saw was the one he used. We think she may have been using that as well."

"But, how will she even want to meet you. She doesn't know about you, does she?" Cory asked. "How will she know?"

"Don't worry, young man," he said as he saw Cory's face. "We have made sure she gets a hint of who I am. We will get your sister out of her clutches. We will not let you be harmed either. We are quite experienced at this. I actually am an art expert, among other things."

The Master, the man with the bubbling pipe, Louie, and Robert moved to stand together.

Cory felt a shiver run up his arms and down his back. *I wouldn't want to face them. There's something menacing about them, the way they stand and the look on their faces. I think they've seen and done things I don't want to know about.*

Big Tom's cell phone rang. He put it to his ear and listened, nodding.

"Good! Withdraw all police. Make it very obvious we're not there. Her radar will easily enable her to spot any watchers. We will have them in the area but she won't know any of them.

"She'll take our bait," he announced to the group.

Four days later...

Big Tom rang off his cell phone and looked around. "Finally it begins. Art appraiser, you go first, with your secretary."

The Master nodded and left with Louie, who gave a long look at Robert as she went.

"And now the two of you will join the packaging and moving company she has hired." Robert, in well-worn overalls, and the man with the bubbling pipe, similarly dressed, left together.

"And finally, Cory and Alex, as we have arranged, there is a taxi waiting outside to take you there."

Little Tom had edged his way out of the room. He made his way to the back of the building, got on his cycle and waited at the corner.

"Dad may have to stay out of this, but I don't," he muttered to himself as he watched the taxi edge its way into traffic. He followed at a discreet distance.

In the car, Cory and Alex looked at each other.

"This is it, bro," Cory said. "I can feel it."

"Can you feel how it will turn out?"

Cory blew out a long breath. "I wish."

A taxi drew up to a long single-story building and Louie alighted from it, looking very secretarial in a plain navy blue pantsuit, white blouse underneath showing a bit of ruffle at the throat, hair in a chignon. She turned to help the old man easing his way out behind her. Together they removed a briefcase and a small black rectangular case as well as a small cart. Louie put the items on the cart, reached in for a computer and closed the door, indicating to the cab driver he could go.

They entered the main door.

Moments later a second taxi arrived and Alex and Cory entered the building as their vehicle drove away.

From her nearby hidden location, Ardith watched a small screen. She and her two men had scoured the entire neighborhood from one end to the other, and had her own hidden cameras in place. She was quite satisfied that the police were holding off but still suspected there might be undercover agents.

In the days previous to the arrival of the old man and his secretary and the two boys, Ardith had sent men into all the shops and finally, she herself had visited them for a third time in the role of a tourist souvenir hunter. None of them had seemed anything but what they were.

The garrulous aging woman in the flower shop, in an atrocious floral print dress, had looked like and spoken like she'd lived there for years. She had given Ardith a tour of her place, extolling the beauty of the flowers in the Queen's Garden, reciting their genus and species, and assuring Ardith she could have those very species shipped to her own garden in America. Ardith declined.

The old man in the tobacconist's shop she had visited two days ago had allowed her to smell several of the blends, described them in great detail, recommending them for her husband, and was quite surprised when Ardith said she didn't have a husband. He attempted to flirt with her a bit. Quite clumsy at it, she thought, and put him in his place quickly. The last sound she heard from him was his own pipe bubbling. She thought him a harmless old goat.

And so it went. Ordinary Londoners all, she was quite sure. When Ardith arrived at last, alone, she was confident that two men were at the rear of the gallery awaiting her orders, that Marnie was nearby but guarded, that Marnie's guard had orders to kill her at any sign of surveillance, and that she herself would be able to walk out with her acquisitions and leave unharmed. The moving company had been checked out and staffed with her own people who had then hired just two extra workers so the transfer could be expedited swiftly once authenticity and evaluation had been finished.

At the same time, a transfer of money would be sent to Ardith's account in a Swiss bank. That would also include the deed to the property on Lake Como in Italy. She had agreed to let the United States houses and the London apartment go. She hadn't liked it, where it was located, or the décor. *Let it all be a drag on what's left of Anna's income. She'll have to get rid of it, of course. I don't want the American properties either, even my brother's. I'll never be going back there. We will see about Mexico, after I kill the Crocodile.*

Arrogance is a double-edged sword. It can make a person very confidant, which helps when making bold moves or having to take chances. It can also lead to over-confidence and overlooking the obvious. Ardith's judgment of the area and its people was happily assured when, as she alighted from her car, she saw the large, wildly flowered rump of the flower woman, who was bent over a pot on the walk outside the shop. *Good! Business as usual.*

The flower woman, on her part, touched the button on the electronic device in the pot and alerted police, whose undercover men and women, moving carefully and thoroughly disguised, went about the activities of the day that go on in many neighborhoods in London. Business as usual.

Ardith was watching as Cory and Alex entered. Two men entered immediately after and escorted them to the rear of the gallery where they were ordered to sit. The men stood behind them. Ardith then entered the gallery by a side door.

"You are here to assess this art?" Ardith asked, looking the old man up and down.

"But of course, Madame. May I present my secretary, Louise."

Louie extended her hand. Ardith nodded but did not take it.

"You are prepared, I hope, with black light, cameras, and a computer program so I will have a thorough assessment and inventory when we are done."

"Of course, Madame. I propose we begin with the objet d'arts, since there are fewer of them. Then we can proceed to the paintings. Louise will photograph everything, measure it all, and packing can proceed piece by piece. Are the persons from the shipping company here?"

Ardith tapped the phone in her hand and asked someone if they were at the gallery. "They have arrived at the back of the building. We can begin."

Three hours later numerous packaged items had disappeared, one by one, out the rear of the building. The old man was clearly tired, or so he seemed. He had kept up a running commentary on the art and Ardith had been impressed at the depth of his knowledge. Her guardedness melted a little.

The last of the paintings was photographed and measured and described into the computer program. Louise began to pack up the equipment and she had turned away from the old man.

"You are not American, are you?" he said as he faced Ardith.

She stiffened. "I was not born there, no."

"I knew your father, Little Mouse. That was his nickname for you, was it not? I remember a little girl who loved to climb on his lap. Yes, his little mouse. It has been many years but I recognize you. You have his eyes, his nose, and his mouth. I never thought I would see you again." The old man's voice was soft, melodic, lost in the past.

Ardith's hand went to her pocket, stayed there. She looked wary, but not unconvinced.

"That is not possible. He died years ago."

"That is true, my dear, but I did know him. Petrovsky. He had a sign he used. The infinity sign, on its side, with a P under it. Did he teach you that? Did he ever tell you what he did for a living?"

Ardith retreated three steps away from him, her back toward Cory and Alex and the men behind them.

"Who are you really? What is your name? How did you know him? What happened to him? I have searched. I could find nothing. You could not have known him. I...I believe he went back to Russia."

"Yes, my dear, he did. He left you, gave your brother away, and he left your mother and you and went to Russia. That is where I met him. Italy is where I killed him. He was a monster and I killed him."

Ardith's hand came out of her pocket holding a small gun.

"He was not a monster." Ardith's voice rose. A muscle in her cheek began to tic. "He was

278

my father. He loved me. He promised he would come back and he did, several times, and then we heard nothing. If you killed him, you are the reason he didn't come back. You are why my mother died, why I was orphaned."

Cory and Alex risked a glance at each other, assent in their eyes, waiting...

Louie stood, unmoving, sideways to Ardith, gun in hand on the side Ardith couldn't see.

"No, my dear." The old man stepped closer, sadness in his eyes. "He was going to kill you both. You were, after all, Jewish. You knew too much about what he did. Remember the children you saw? The ones you saw in the trucks? He told you he was taking them to orphanages, or to their homes, or to where they would be safe. But you saw their eyes, the pain and fear in their eyes. You saw his lies and you questioned him, and he slapped you, and ordered you never to speak to him of that again. He slapped your mother too. You saw your mother's tears."

The old man's voice continued softly, hypnotically, and Louie, face down but eyes turned to the side, watched Ardith's face and waited, seeing the memories return, bit by bit, piece by piece. Cory watched and felt the tension building in Ardith.

Get her to tell us where Marnie is. Please, get her to tell us where Marnie is.

"Yes, my dear, it does seem as if all children are a mockery, doesn't it? It galls you to

279

see happy children. The children are what took him away from you."

Ardith nodded, her face registering rage. She brought the gun up to his chest level but didn't shoot.

"You found your brother after such a long search and then he told you his mother and sister died in the camps. A lie. Your brother lied too."

"He wouldn't believe me. He went back to Europe again and again, searching. He even went to Eli Wiesel. He couldn't find any record. How did you know my father? How did you meet him?"

"We were spies together. He was working for Russia. I was working for Britain. At first, we were on the same side, but then the Cold War began and he worked against the Allies. I worked for NATO and Britain. He erased all trace of being Jewish. He turned against all good. He made his money selling arms and secrets and children. He sold children to men who loved to torture them. He turned evil."

Ardith screamed, "That is not true!" and shot. The old man clutched his chest. Louie turned and shot Ardith as Cory and Alex threw themselves back against the men behind them whose hands rose to shoot. Both grabbed the gun arms and grappled with the men as bullets shot wildly into the ceiling and walls.

The room flooded with police.

Cory rolled off the man he had brought down and stood up, shaky, his leg aching and wobbly. Alex crawled away from the man he had downed and looked at him. The man was dead. A police officer stood over him, gun pointing downward. Alex bent over until his forehead hit the floor, his hands over his eyes, a visual picture of Marnie dead in his mind.

Louie knelt over the old man, her hands tearing at the two bullet-proof vests she could only hope had stopped the bullet fired at such close range.

"It is a shoulder wound. He needs medics, now!" she shouted.

Medics came. He was stabilized and carried out.

Big Tom strode in.

"Where is Marnie? Where is my sister? You've got to find her! She didn't bring Marnie. Where is she?" Cory's face was twisted with anguish and anger.

"Turn around, son." Big Tom pointed.

Cory turned and Little Tom swaggered in with Marnie on his arm.

Thirty-eight

Louie, in her role as countess, demanded a thorough debriefing. Backed by Cory, Alex and Marnie, she got it. At the apartment, a cadre of servants, brought from the de la Vergne home in Switzerland, served high tea, scones, small delicate sandwiches, and other stronger refreshments to those who needed a bit more fortification after such a difficult day.

Marnie, Alex, and Cory sat together on a couch with Little Tom on the floor at Marnie's feet. Louie and Robert sat close to each other on the loveseat. The sound of a bubbling pipe came from a stuffed chair in a corner now growing shadowy with evening. Vincent Grant posed himself by the fireplace. Big Tom pulled a straight-backed chair in front of the young people, sat down and began.

"We found your sister even before you went in but we couldn't let you know in time. When we decided on that neighborhood, we had our people contact every permanent resident in the area, all vetted out and on our side, and then we also planted our own in the shops, so we got constant information as you were on the way. Marnie," he nodded at her, "was a real hero. She kicked the gun out of one man's hand and we did the rest.

"The Master, and he'll be fine, by the way, had his people there as well. When the truck pulled up at the back, his men took down hers

282

and they were the ones who packed up everything. It's all on the way back to Switzerland as we speak.

"We hoped to capture Ardith alive. Louie shot to wound but the bullets from your guards' guns" he nodded at Cory and Alex, "went astray and one hit her fatally. She died on the way to hospital. Please realize you did not cause that," he added as he saw the boy's faces.

"However, we have enough information to take her network apart here and in Europe. We have informed Mexican national police. Apparently, she has no more influence there either. She had an informant, the maid who was here originally, who placed listening devices in your rooms at the apartment. Regarding the sign she used, apparently she'd been using that before. She had a network of couriers and informers that used many spots in London and left that sign. We will be able to track down those places little by little and to identify many of those in her employ.

"I have, on your behalf, informed the FBI and Green Bay police that you are all safe. We have not reached your mother yet. The last news is that she had seen your brother and was on her way out of Mexico. We will try to arrange a Skype call for you when we establish communication."

Big Tom carefully kept to himself that Anna was missing and no one knew where she could be. Her bodyguard was also missing.

"And, police tell us that the threat to your family is not over in America. I assure you again that we will keep you safe should you choose to remain here.

"Actually, this has gleaned a lot of publicity and I have an invitation for the three of you to meet someone who would like to congratulate you on your bravery and she wants to assure herself with her own eyes that you are none the worse for wear. She would like you to meet her own grandsons."

He handed each of them a thick cream-colored envelope.

"Little Tom will be your escort should you wish to accept the invitation."

Alex looked at the inscription on his envelope. "OMG!" he breathed softly.

"Do not worry. I will teach you how to curtsy," Louie chuckled.

"Would you like a cup of tea, my dear?" Louie asked as Marnie drifted around the apartment after the police and the others had gone.

Something's different. She's changing. She is no longer the frivolous girl who demanded her own way at the expense of her family and her own health. Good! It is time.

"Yes, thank you. I need to talk." Marnie launched right into it. "My mother is still in danger. I just know something's not right and so do my brothers. What do you think is going on?"

Louie set a cup of tea on the coffee table in front of Marnie and took her time stirring honey and lemon into her own cup. When she finally spoke, they were words that were completely unexpected.

"Tell me about your father. What kind of man was he?"

"My father? Why my father? He's dead. He's gone. That's it. Isn't it?"

"Perhaps, and perhaps not. Even when people are gone, their influence can change the lives of people for many years. What do you remember of your father?"

"Well, I was pretty young when he died. I was devastated. I was his little girl, his only girl child. I thought he would be there forever. It was the first time I felt deserted, abandoned, not loved. I didn't know what death was then. I never saw his body. I was only told that he was burned. It was gruesome to imagine. It was horrible. Part of me felt like I had died too."

Marnie, sitting on the couch, had folded her legs up, chin on her knees, and was hugging her legs and rocking slightly.

Fetal position. Rocking. She is still hurt by his disappearance from her life. She tells me nothing of him, only of what is in her own heart.

"What was he like when he was alive?"

"Oh, he was fun! He would come home when I was little and lift me up and toss me in the air. He would tease me, in a good way, you know, about my uncombed hair or my torn jeans. Because I had brothers, I wasn't quite a girly-girl type. He played ball with me just like he did with my brothers. I...he..." Marnie buried her head in

285

her arms. Her breath came in short sharp intakes and shuddered out again.

Louie waited until the emotion spent itself.

"If you had to look at him now that you are an adult and have some experience with other adult men, what kind of person would you see?"

Marnie looked off at the light coming through the curtained window. It was a long time until she answered. Louie thought she might have shut down, but waited through the silence. Her answer came as a surprise.

"He was a selfish man. I know that he worked long hours and I thought that was what all fathers did. I thought that was what he was supposed to do. But now, I see that even when he could have been—was—at the gatherings of people at our house, he wasn't really there. He wanted what he wanted when he wanted it. He could accommodate to others if he had to, but he would escape as soon as he could get away with it. He would go in his office at home and shut the door and shut us all out. He stayed at the office downtown for long hours. Mom used to call him and remind him of our family plans and he'd make some excuse and so we'd just go ahead with them and he wouldn't be there.

"My brothers and I got used to it. Cory even made a joke of it. He was just a little kid but he saw it. We got a TV with a remote and he joked that Dad was the remote for our family. When he finally came home or back to our reality, the

286

"remote" changed the menu. We all thought it was funny then. It isn't funny to me now."

Marnie unfolded her body and took a deep breath. "Maybe he was better when he and Mom were first married—more attentive then or more—something. I don't know. But, underneath that façade, he was emotionally gone from us when I was growing up. I don't think I'd be able to see that if I hadn't gone to treatment and been confronted with my own emotional distance, and seen it in others. They said it's an addict thing but I don't think it's just that. Or maybe my father was addicted to something else."

Marnie glanced at Louie and, startled at her face, stared at her intensely.

"What? What are you thinking? What are you seeing?"

"At my age, my dear, I have become very good at reading between the lines of human thought and behavior. I will not mince words. I think your father left a dangerous legacy for all of you. I think he must have been involved in affairs he would not have told you or your mother about. Yes, very dangerous affairs. And what he did is still affecting all of you. As you said, your mother is still under some threat. So are you and your brothers."

"We think so too. Well, we think Mom is in danger but maybe not us. Definitely her. Alex and Cory want to go to Mexico and get AJ and then go home to help Mom. We haven't planned how to do that yet but I think they're right."

287

"I agree with you, which is why there is a private plane available for you to fly out of England. I have had it arranged since I realized how serious your situation has been. I advocate that you meet the queen and then announce that you will be returning to America, after a vacation, including a visit to your brother in Mexico."

"That's a lot of publicity. Won't that make it harder for us to protect ourselves and Mom?"

"No. It will make it harder for anyone to attack you and get away with it. Come. Let us talk with your brothers."

Louie rose and held the door to her room open for Marnie.

It will make whoever is orchestrating this take notice. It will make it harder for someone from their past to use them as a front, or set them up again. Ardith was the tip of the iceberg. The Crocodile was a Mexican problem. However, Robert's investigations are correct.

There is someone who has built power for many years, carefully, meticulously, and with little or no regard for human life. A very cold man. Perhaps even her own father.

It is not over.

Thirty-nine

Louie had a phone call from Robert and excused herself. Marnie heard her brothers talking and walked into their room to find a very agitated Cory.

"We have to get out of here. We've got to get to Mexico and drag our brother home. I know Mom's in real danger. We have to call someone in Green Bay and find out just what's going on. Not just what they want us to hear, but what's really happening."

Cory had no more tolerance for waiting. The night before, he'd had a monumental and crazy nightmare, where his father murdered his mother and then turned into a monster who forced Marnie to begin stalking AJ in the Mexican jungle.

"Cory, we still have to meet the queen. We must play the part of being safe, of it all being over over here. Aren't those the words in an old song? It won't be over 'til it's over over here. There. Wherever." Alex, trying to keep it light, was wishing it was truly all over, but he knew better.

He turned to Marnie.

"I agree we've got to get out of here. What about you?"

Marnie got up and walked to a window and stood looking out. She turned around, hands on her hips.

289

"We will. Louie arranged it. Stop!" She held up her hands as they both jumped up and began speaking at once.

"Sit down and listen! Please! I know we have to go. I agree with you. However, we need to do it so that we control the attention to ourselves. We're in a spotlight. As long as we have that meeting with the queen on our schedule, we will remain in that spotlight. If we don't do that, we run the risk of insulting the British people. We might lose our protection. You have to be patient."

"You stop!" Cory interrupted. "When did this all happen? How is it you know this and we don't?"

"I just found it out when I was talking with Louie. She found your notes the night we went to the embassy. She agreed with you and set it up. She's coming with us. I may be a drug addict in your eyes, Cory, but I'm recovering and I'm not an idiot, nor have I abandoned my mother. I've caused her a lot of pain and worry. I know that. Louie will try to find out what's going on both in Mexico and in Wisconsin. She has connections we don't. I wasn't going to tell you until she had more news.

"So here's what we do know. There's a rumor the Crocodile is dead and his network was taken over by someone else. That someone else may be American. We know Ardith is dead and her network is crumbling. The Croc had tried to take over her scene in Mexico. That's all I know, but it's enough. Think about it, guys, an

290

American. Who are the Americans who knew about the drug scene long ago?"

Cory got it first. "Our own father, but he's dead! He's dead!"

Alex began pacing. "We never saw his body. AJ said he was burned to cinders in the crash. He saw the body. He was a med student. He knew what he saw. But..." Alex couldn't make himself say it.

"But the body could have been someone else," Marnie finished his sentence. "I'm not saying he's alive and running the drug scene now, but it could have been, *he* could have been alive back then. Look! This is all conjecture. I want to be there, in Green Bay, and find out just what's happening and if it is our father who is the American, I'm going to kill him with my own two hands. If my father did this to me, to us, I...I..." Marnie burst into tears. "I was so hurt, so very, very hurt when he died. When I *thought* he died. How could he do that to us? How could he leave all of us?"

"Marnie," Alex sighed, pulling her into his arms, "we don't know the truth yet. We don't know if that's true. We'll find out. We will."

He pulled up the edge of his t-shirt and wiped her tears. "Where's Louie now? When will she be here?

"She was on the phone with Robert when I left her. I heard her say she's going to a meeting. They're gathering all the information they can. They set up the plane for us. She didn't want me to tell you everything right away because she thought you'd give it away somehow. You're impatient. She and Robert have a lot of contacts. She wants us to act normal, be the focus of publicity for a while yet. After we meet the queen, the word will go out we're going on vacation to the Caribbean."

Cory looked insulted. "Why does she think we would give it away? We can keep a secret."

"Cory, everything you feel shows on your face. It always has."

Alex grinned. "True dat."

"Not 'true dat.' I'm an actor. Just watch me. I'll sail through this with flying colors. And please don't use that phrase. You're way too white for that."

Just before leaving, Robert and Louie had a final tea with the Master.

"These cartels affect us all, you know," he said to them. "Britain is having a crisis of heroin addiction. We're all threatened by groups who are supplied with arms sold on the black market. The eastern countries of Europe have had many girls gone missing or lured into sex slavery. Refugees are pouring out of Syria and North Africa. And, behind all of that, there are men making billions of dollars off the misery of others. We can't stop it all but we can do what is possible. We must do what is possible!

"I have very little news from Mexico. No one has been able to get hold of Anna or Stacy or Mac or anyone down there.

"I do have the names and phone numbers of a few men who worked for Stacy up north, courtesy of an FBI friend who is aware of the situation in Wisconsin.

"Most importantly, I have information on the American who is supposed to be directing this drug line. Either Anna's husband actually survived and he is the one, a very unlikely possibility, or there is another man from that area, an older man, perhaps one of the original men involved, who began his own cartel years ago and is trying to take over that corridor to Canada. I have the names of seven men who might be candidates.

"The third possibility, one we can't rule out, is that there is someone no one knows or suspects behind this. Just to get this much information, I have pulled all the strings I have here, on the continent, and in Canada and the USA. I'm sorry it is so little."

"It is more than we expected, sir. Louie and I are grateful for your help."

Robert rose and picked up their coats.

Louie leaned forward and squeezed the Master's hand. "Thank you so much. We must go. We are meeting Anna's children and we fly out in an hour."

She rose, leaned over and kissed the Master on both cheeks. He smiled. His hand rose to his face and he touched each place where she kissed him.

"Keep me informed and I'll keep Her Majesty informed. She loved meeting them."

The plane was well over the Atlantic before Louie briefed them.

"I have connected with Melissa and she will meet us at a private airport at Cozumel but there is a serious problem in Mexico. Stacy is missing. Mac and Melissa have been searching for her. They've arranged for us to go by helicopter to a safe place north of Santa Anita and from there by automobile to Jorge's headquarters near the border. Thanks to Ramon we'll get there and back safely but you will only have one chance to do this. It's not safe for you there. It will be your job to persuade your brother to come with us."

Louie looked at the three young people. "Do you think he'll listen?"

Alex, Cory and Marnie looked at each other.

"We don't know," Alex answered. "We don't know what he's been through really. I think he must have been awfully shocked by his wife's death. He's sort of a mystery to me. I mean, we've been apart for a long time, since he went away to school. I can't say what he'll do."

"He'll do anything to help Mom, I think," Cory said. "If he knows she's in danger, he'll come."

Marnie was silent until Louie asked, "And you, Marnie? What do you think?"

"No. He won't. He's been independent for much longer than we have. His ties aren't with us anymore. His ties are where he chose to go to practice medicine. His ties are where she's buried. He has his own life."

Louie raised a hand to stop the brothers' protests.

"Well, we shall see."

"Where is Mom? Is she with them?"

Louie cringed inside. "She's en route home at this time. We'll wait until we can report to her about AJ and then contact her."

And an addict is very good at lying, even one with years of recovery. I can only hope she is somewhere safe.

Forty

Anna felt the plane lose altitude but when she tried to determine where they were, thick gray cloudiness enveloped them until just above the night-dark earth. The plane taxied past a series of metal buildings partially obscured by smog. Small planes stood here and there. Lights shone from large doors in a few buildings and workers could be seen, blurred black ants scurrying to and fro. Her plane taxied slowly on and on into darkness and Anna began to lose any hope of being near other humans.

Her anger was at a peak when movement finally stopped. Had the pilot or anyone walked in on her, she was prepared to fight them, with bare hands if necessary. No pilot emerged into the body of the plane. She could not determine if anyone even left the plane at all. She tried to free the door and failed. She paced from cockpit door to tail. It was clear she was a prisoner and no one had come to free her.

Where is the pilot? How did he get out? Did he get out?

The lights in the plane shut off. Anna fought deepening terror, bouts of rage, and finally burst into tears of frustration and exhaustion.

Ardith! This must be Ardith's doing! No, she can't be in London and here. It has to be El Cocodrilo, to get back at me for the loss of his money. He would do something like this. If he could murder Lindy, he wouldn't hesitate to

296

kidnap me and leave me here. But why? I'm more use where I can get him more money, where he can force me to pay him.

What happened to Stacy? Is she alive? No one knows I'm here. Wrong. Someone does know I'm here. Someone engineered this, set this up. Who can possibly have the power and influence to do something like this? Someone with more money that I can imagine. Someone who dominates, who has no conscience.

Feeling her way around, Anna tried again to free herself from the plane, looking for tools she could use to break glass, jimmy a door. Nothing.

Food is gone. One bottle of water.

The toilet. If I use it, maybe it will be dumped on the ground. Is that what happens? Or is it stored somewhere in the body of the plane until it can be cleaned? I don't know. If I flush it, will anyone notice?

She did that and then realized she was wasting water she might need if no one came.

No one came.

The Caribbean Sea

"Where is her plane now?"

"At your private buildings, Building 18, to be exact."

"Good. That will keep her out of the way. It's time to put our plans for the Crocodile into effect. Have we secured the house in the North,

297

the one that belonged to that lawyer, Wentworth? And the island?"

"Yes, sir."

"Then go after him. I want him alive. I want to be sure I have access to all his holdings, to every man, woman, and child he has working or slaving for him, to every bank account, every bit of land he owns, everything. Tell my men there will be a bonus in it for everyone."

"Yes, sir. Thank you, sir. Will that be all, sir?"

"Set our course for the island. Once we have him subdued and have the takeover in progress, take the drone with the Kinnealy woman to Albuquerque. The usual way—under the radar of course. Our cover story with US security is solid. No need to deal with that. Leave her in the plane there, door open, with a ticket for Delta Airlines for Green Bay. Have a porter come for her luggage and convenient transportation to the correct flight desk and have her watched to be sure she's on her way. And, oh yes, double check to be sure that pilot's body was disposed of, will you?"

"Yes, sir."

El Capitán made his way to the large stateroom he used as his main office. Two long and wide tables stood in the center of the room. One held a three-dimensional topographical map of North and South America. The other held the same of Europe and the Middle East, including much of Asia. Colored lines were strung from city to city, country to country. Three colors. His, in gold. El Cocodrilo, in black. Ardith's, in red. Carefully, beginning in Colombia, through Central America and Mexico, north to the Mexican border, with meticulous care, he began removing the black and red and replacing them with gold. He paid particular attention to extending lines out of every major city to the small towns. When he was finished, he smiled.

"My web," he murmured with satisfaction. "I believe I ought to be known as The Spider. Now for the good old US of A."

He touched keys on his computer. In a few minutes Skype had a picture of the Texan.

"You rang?" came the Texas drawl.

"I did. I am in a particularly good mood. I am in the process of doubling my network here and it's time to triple it. What is your news?"

"Well, then sir, I do believe I've got a bit more good news for you. We got access to them files. The information there gave us, us meaning our police friends and me, access to the good ol' boys who ran this network years ago and two are on board with us already, and I have been able to find one of them without usin' them files and he still loves his money comin' in and it ain't comin' in fast enough to suit him right now and he is on board and he is the head of a truckin' company. We got us a great line to Sault Ste. Marie. And, I..."

"Good! Good! What can they tell us about the others?"

"They can't. It seems that most of those who were in on this back then were kept in the dark about each other—told no more than they needed to know. It was Art Kinnealy who knew the whole picture, and we know he kept his own record in and on his files. Layers and layers of information, the FBI guy said. They'll be uncovering it for weeks, maybe more. There was this construction guy, Big John O'Keeffe, but even then no one was sure just what he had going in this, and his son, who was a bit of a loose cannon, and ..."

"I know that story. What's out on the streets now?"

"Not a whole lot other than what we passed out there. The police have been on the whole drug scene like ferrets, both city and county, sniffing out anything that smacks of drugs. Police in the next county found a meth lab run by some amateurs and that's closed now. With all the publicity stirred up, law enforcement is lookin' good. That wasn't any part of your line and that bust takes attention away from us. Our contacts in both departments are solid, so far, and..."

"I want you to dig deeper. Find out about every undercover cop out there. Run a check on all the money held by anyone involved—police officers, civilians, anyone who might be part of this—where it is and how much and if they've made any purchases of property anywhere in the world, or any investments. I want to know their spending habits, their current income, their debts, anything financial. Then I want to know everything personal—girlfriends, wives, children, where they live, what they eat, when they piss. Get the idea?"

"Yes I do. I already got a start on that with this Detective Greg Klarkowski. Turns out his girlfriend, Caitlin Fitzgerald, is a friend of Anna Kinnealy and she is one o' them what was lookin' through the old files for clues to what went on and if there's anything relevant to today and..."

"Is this Caitlin Fitzgerald from the west side of Green Bay?"

"Well, yeah. Is she familiar to you? You know these people?"

"Send me her file and every file of anyone associated with her or Anna. As soon as I've taken over the Crocodile's line I'll be up there. Anna will be on her way up there soon. Watch for her. Don't approach her. Just keep her under surveillance."

"Yes, sir. Will do."

The screen went blank. The Texan blinked. The tight feeling in the pit of his stomach got tighter. *It's all goin' to hit the fan up here and when it does, I do not plan to be part of the shit.*

But there was no way he could see to back out at this moment without being a dead man.

El Capitán sat himself down in a comfortable chair and mused on the coming scenes he would control.

It has been a very long time since I have been in Green Bay. I return in triumph. To see the look on their faces...

Priceless. Beyond priceless!

Forty-one

After two days of captivity, during which she had grown irritable from hunger and thirst, had searched in vain for tools to escape, and grew hoarse from futile shouting, Anna had finally fallen asleep from exhaustion. When she awoke, it was daylight and the plane was in the air. It was a sign of her exhaustion that she had not even felt that.

She was puzzled when she looked outside. They were flying low over what looked endless. Sometimes desert. Sometimes mountains. Sometimes green hills. It dawned on her after a while that they were flying north. The sun was in the East. Then, they were over water.

Another unmeasured time passed and they were over land again, over small buildings like farms, a small town or two, and after a while, more and more buildings. *We're flying awfully low. Too low for this plane. I can see...*she sucked in her breath as she realized that, on the roof of a building far below, she was reading an American word.

I think I've been flown to the US! I think I might be out of Mexico!

Her hopes rose as she realized they could be landing at a major airport. The plane gained altitude for a time and then began circling. Then it began to descend.

Albuquerque!

What's happening and who is doing this? Was this all arranged by Mac? If it was, I'll kill

302

him when I see him for the sheer fear and horror I've had to go through to get me here. I am so angry! If not Mac, then who? Stacy didn't do this. I just know she didn't. Oh god, I hope she's not dead!

The plane landed and taxied slowly farther and farther from the main buildings where large airliners were hooked to telescoped entryways.

Anna paced. When her own plane finally came to a stop, Anna could see a man outside with one of the vehicles used to ferry baggage and people around airports. The door to the aircraft clicked, then opened and the stair electronically lowered itself to the ground. The cockpit remained sealed. Cautiously Anna moved toward the open door. The man she'd seen on the cart bounded into the cabin with a smile and a steaming cup of coffee.

"You are Mrs. Kinnealy, I presume. I have been hired to welcome you here and assist you on your way home. I have a ticket for a plane to Green Bay which leaves in an hour and a half. You have time to eat a light breakfast and then I'll get you to your gate. First class. Delta. This coffee is yours, two creams and a bit of honey is, I was told, just the way you like it." He paused to take a breath and handed her the cup with a flourish.

"Welcome to Albuquerque!"

Anna's face registered suspicion, disbelief, and astonishment as the man held out the ticket and the coffee. She read the ticket, took a sip of the coffee.

Ok, I'll go with this and see where it leads. He doesn't look dangerous. In fact, if he's over twenty-one, I'll be very surprised.

"Is it ok if I take your bags? Then I'll assist you down the stairs and we'll go find some food for you."

"Yes, take the bags. I can walk down the stairs unassisted, thank you very much. I'll need a place to freshen up as well as breakfast, and I need to get my phone charged."

Which is what she got.

His name was Todd and he was extremely attentive. She had even gotten money at an ATM in the airport as he "guarded" her.

"I do apologize for the stop, but we couldn't get you a direct flight. You'll be in Green Bay at 4:39p.m. We have transport waiting for you to your next gate in Minneapolis."

An hour and a half later, teeth brushed, hair combed, clean underwear, blouse and skirt on, she was seated in first class and took off to Minneapolis. Todd had had no answers to the questions she fired at him. He was clueless.

Waiting in Minneapolis, Anna tried her phone, calling Caroline—no answer—and Cait, who did.

"OMG, where are you? How are you? Where's AJ? What have you heard about Marnie and the boys? What's going on?"

"I have no idea what's going on. I need someone to meet me at the airport. It's all a mess, Cait, and call Greg. I want police with me."

"You can't go to your house. Someone's been there, maybe living there and whoever it is, the police have been watching, including Greg, but they don't know who or why. Unless he's gone already. Then maybe they're searching. But maybe not. Well. Um, I'll pick you up and we'll go to Jenny's. No! Wait! If I meet you, then people will know you're back. I'll have Mike pick you up where the luggage comes in. Wear sunglasses and old clothes."

"Cait! Stop! Someone already knows I'm here in this country. Someone kidnapped me and put me on a plane and had me taken here. Stop!" she interjected as Cait began to speak again. "Don't ask! I don't know why or who. It won't matter how many meet me. Someone, maybe more than one someone, knows. Why can't I go to my house? Why haven't the police gone in and removed whoever is there? If anyone is there, I want them out. Now."

"I'll call Greg. We'll meet you. Oh, what the hell! We'll probably all meet you."

Forty-two
The Place of the Talking Cross
Eduardo told Mac the story.

"Long ago, in the middle 1800s, my Mayan ancestors were fighting for our land. There was much injustice and mistreatment of los indígenos. That was called the Caste War.

"We were about to give up when a voice came from a cross here in Puerto, urging us to continue and guiding us to eight years of victories. We were free from Mexico and the Spaniards, Then, sadly, the cross was stolen and we were overrun. We have tried twice since to be free again but we have been under their whip since the 1950s. Very few are still trying. The Spaniards, now the Mexican government, have defeated us every time.

"But we honor the cross every year on Tres de Mayo, the Day of the Holy Cross. Back then we called this village Chan Santa Cruz. It was our headquarters.

"Felipe Carrillo was the name of a governor of the Yucatan. He was not so bad. He was called 'progressive' by some so then they changed the name of the city to honor him. Others who governed us, well, they were not so very 'progressive'. More like abusive. Brutal.

"It is still a small place, a gateway from the sea to land through the Sian Ka'an Biosphere Reserve, a swamp-like smuggler's paradise. From the south to the north as well, on the old

306

sacbes that run through the jungle, and even on the main highway, it is a crossroads.

"The Well of the Talking Cross is still here but there is no power, except perhaps the power to find out much from the devils of the underworld in the small cantinas. I will fit right in. You? Maybe, but Felipe Carrillo Puerto is a dangerous place. You have darkened your skin, but you are too tall to be Mayan."

"I can fit in. I've been here before. I have my favorite places to collect news. We'll do fine here."

Mac parked the ancient truck they had "borrowed" for the occasion and looked at Eduardo. "Ready? It's dark enough now. We'll meet at that old well—yes, I know where that is and yes, I know I must remove my shoes in respect—after the cantinas close."

They parted.

Mac's satisfaction at the news he'd picked up turned to nervous apprehension as the dawn light crept into the entrance to the well. Eduardo was long overdue. The old truck would be an object of interest and if that happened, they would have no way to escape the town.

I can't wait any longer. I can't be found here.

He crept out of the cave where the well was, stopped in some bushes to put on his socks and shoes and made his way silently to the truck. He met no one, but he knew that didn't mean he wasn't watched. He felt his knees begin to give way when he discovered Eduardo's limp body in the bed of the truck. Touching him brought a wave of relief. *Warm. Drunk or drugged? Can't wait to find out. Get out of here!*

Ten miles north he stopped on the side of the road and examined Eduardo thoroughly. *No wounds, but he smells of alcohol. The whites of his eyes are red. Probably other drugs as well. He'll live but he's going to have a terrible hangover.*

Mac turned the truck toward a village west of Puerto. *Let's hope the people moved back after she doctored AJ. They were all risking death by caring for him.*

He had to search for people and it proved to be deserted except for a young boy who looked to be about eight.

"My friend is ill. Is the curandera here?"

The boy said nothing but signed them to sit. An hour later Mac was ready to leave when the boy and two people emerged from the jungle with a litter for Eduardo. He followed them through thick vegetation on an almost imperceptible path to a small hut.

The curandera examined Eduardo, grinned, remarked on the size of the headache he would have and slowly dripped some medicine down his throat. His swallowing reflex was the only one he had left.

"They can always swallow more," she said, "even when they are at death's door."

"He is that close?"

"Sí. This was intended to kill him. How is it they did not do this to you also? You are good at this, Señor Mac, but you are not indígeno."

"We were working separately. He thought I would be the easy target."

It was two days before Eduardo could move. Mac chafed at the delay. He was to meet Melissa at the ruins of Tulum as a tourist and he was late. He could only hope that all was well, that Stacy and Anna had made it to the United States, that Jorge, Jamie, AJ and the others found a safer place and, that he could find a place to charge his phone which no longer worked.

Eduardo remained with the truck as Mac changed clothing and began the tour of Tulum. No Melissa.

Checked into Mac's safe hotel in Cancun, he plugged in the phone, left Eduardo to cleanse his body with herbs and water, and made his way through place after place. No Melissa. No contacts at all.

He was walking through the lobby of a small hotel on the edge of town looking for a man who might have some news when the words "El Cocodrilo" caught in his ears. A television was on in the bar and the words *es muerte* made him stop in his tracks.

He was murdered? He's dead! Good! One more who could harm Anna is out of the way.

He listened carefully to the report. Murderer unknown. On his island. Body was found torn by unknown animals near the shore but identification was certain.

"Good riddance to one more parasite!" the bartender remarked.

"Why is that?" Mac asked.

"The man was a drug dealer, head of a cartel. They are all dirt. My brother died from an overdose. I wish national police would just kill them all but that will not happen," he said as he polished a glass with a towel. "Someone else will just take over. The police are all corrupt."

Mac returned and Eduardo was asleep. Mac tried to get Stacy. No answer, but luck was with him when he tried Melissa.

"Thank the gods you're alive and well!" she breathed. Her voice was low and he could barely hear her. "All hell broke loose even before the Croc was killed. I can't find Stacy. She was separated from Anna at the airport. I have no news of Anna either. I haven't been able to make any contact in Green Bay with them. I'm afraid to call the police there because the last I heard, someone in that department is dirty. I don't know where Jamie is or AJ or Jorge or Ramon. I had contacts in the Croc's network but they've been totally shut down. There's some kind of takeover going on. Just tell me quickly where we can meet. It has to be off the map, hidden, because I may be a wanted person. I don't know."

Mac gave her directions. "Ten p.m. No lights. You know this place?"

"I do. Thanks."

The Aguilar hacienda was enveloped in a dark and brooding silence. As Mac walked through it he thought he could feel the presence of a sad spirit but told himself he was imagining things. The moon came up and dim light filtered through trees and shone in slivers through the windows. When Melissa arrived, it was on a bicycle. Almost no noise. They had just greeted one another when a car pulled up and low women's voices floated on the night air.

"That's Tomasita!" Mac whispered. "I hope, I hope..." His hope materialized inside the front door as a woman entered, lantern in hand, breaking blackness into shadows.

Adelina called out, "Señor Mac, I have been waiting for you."

"How did you know it was me?"

"You have a smell of your own and the woman with you is having her monthly time."

"How does she know that?" Melissa asked him sotto voce.

Mac laughed, "Because even I can smell that on a woman."

"Jeez! I so need a bath."

Melissa scarfed down three of the burritos Tomasita brought out from the basket she carried.

"Sorry. No food for the last two days, more actually. I'm so hungry," she said between bites and chewing. "I've been in hiding. Had to. The police might come after me. I was there when the Croc died. I was waiting for him. I knew he couldn't resist coming back to that island. He's got...had...an ego the size of the whole Yucatan. He couldn't resist playing King of the Mountain

311

there. The man was almost delusional. No, I think he was—some kind of megalomania. I wanted information from him. I knew I could get him to brag about what he did. I am terribly scared he's murdered Stacy.

"Well, ok, I'd better tell you the whole story," she amended as she saw the puzzled looks on their faces. "The Croc did brag about all his exploits. Then he told me how he killed Lindy. He tortured her. I lost it. I threatened him. He pulled a gun and fired but he missed the first time and I shot him. I dragged his body to the beach and left it there. The sharks hadn't been fed in a long time. They came near the shore and something—maybe a croc, I'm not sure—tried to drag him into the water and he got caught on a snag and then a boat came into the harbor. The sharks must have thought they were going to be fed and most of them left and I dragged his body back because I wanted him found. Which he was.

"The boat wasn't a police boat. I don't know whose boat it was. I ran and hid and made my way off the island that night. I had a kayak hidden. That's how I got there. Farther out to sea was another much larger ship. I could just barely see the lights but it wasn't a cruise ship. I don't think anyone searched for me but I don't know how they could not have seen me even from that distance.

"I've thought and thought about who was there. It could have been Colombians or someone else from South America. I know there are those who wanted him dead and those who wanted to still make deals with him. Well, that's not possible now. But who is taking over? I've only heard rumors."

Mac watched her with some concern.

"You did the right thing by saving the body. You probably provided the police with the knowledge they needed and they're now warned that a takeover is in progress. They'll be looking for someone in another cartel as his killer. How are you feeling right now about all that?"

Melissa looked surprised at his question. She hesitated, looked down, looked up with a puzzled expression on her face, mouth open.

"I'm numb. I don't feel anything."

"You're on adrenalin overdose, otherwise known as a killing high. I know the feeling. I've killed too. When you start feeling again, it's going to be bad. Don't run from it. Let me know."

"I have a medicine for that," Adelina stated, "but first I have news. Jorge, Ramon and the people of the town are safe. AJ was with the people so he will be there now. Her brother, Jaime, is there also. Jorge moved everyone from Santa Anita to a safer place.

"Mac and Melissa, you must go north again. You must protect Anna. She is still in danger. I am not sure she has gotten home safely. I do know she intends to make herself the bait and there are many forces against her. Very powerful forces. I have news of the third cartel. The man who rules it is most definitely a gringo. This I know for sure."

Mac nodded. "Good. Then it's true. I heard that in Puerto. So did Eduardo."

"Eduardo! You know where he is?" Tomasita grabbed Mac's hand.

"Sí. He is fine now. He has recovered from the drugs and alcohol they gave him. I will send him here when I return to the hotel. He is safe for now."

"What hotel? I must find him. I must." She glanced at Adelina, who smiled and nodded.

Mac told her and she left.

"What was that all about?" he asked, puzzled.

"She is pregnant with his child. They are husband and wife. Life goes on around you, Señor Mac, and some things you don't even see. It is amusing." She chuckled.

"Excuse me, Señora, but I've been a little busy."

"Es verdad. You are excused for that."

"I heard a little more about the gringo too," Mac said. "I heard he's definitely American. I heard he is in the process of taking over the Croc's network and that he has connections far and wide, maybe world-wide."

"Sí. He has been very careful to hide behind many others. He has been so cautious they say he has never even set his feet on the lands where he operates, that he lives on a large ship in the ocean and controls from there. A myth, that sounds like. A myth maybe he makes sure is told again and again. When I go into spirit, I see only a large spider's web. No. More like one

314

web over another. He plucks the web and everyone along it jumps."

Adelina was drawing radiating lines and connecting lines unconsciously in the air as she spoke. Mac and Melissa could see she was only half present, in some other reality. They looked at each other. Melissa motioned for him to speak.

"What do you see?" he asked softly.

"What I see...Anna. There are large dark spaces around her and they are moving toward her, whirling around each other. Something is using her. She is changing. She is at the center...whirlwinds of hate...revenge. Yes, much revenge. Out of control."

"Where is she? Is she home?"

"Air...air surrounds her...I cannot see..."

Adelina choked, coughed and blinked. "What did I say? What is wrong?"

"You were in the spirit world. You told us that Anna is in serious danger."

"Sí. Es muy verdad. Muy verdad. You must both go to help her as soon as possible."

"But I have to find Stacy. She's in great danger too, if she's not already dead. I have to look for her. Can you tell us where she is?"

Melissa's jaw was tight and her hands clenched. Mac could see that she wouldn't leave without answers of her own.

Adelina looked at her for long minutes and finally said, "You must begin where you left off. That is all I can tell you."

Mac knew she would not say any more.

"Melissa, come back to the hotel and get some sleep. You're nearly exhausted. I'm going to prowl the cantinas again to see if I can learn more. Adelina, where can I drop you off?"

"I am sleeping here in my own bed, and Señor Mac, do not worry," she added when she saw his expression, "I am well protected. They are all around me."

"They?" asked Melissa.

Mac stood up.

"That's how she refers to her spirit helpers. Don't ask for details. You won't understand. Just know she'll be ok. Come on. I came on a motorcycle. Leave the bicycle here and ride with me."

He leaned forward and hugged Adelina.

"My grandmother, I will see you when I see you."

"And I will see you wherever you are. And you, Melissa, I will call you if I learn any more about your friend."

Forty-three

Morning light was still creeping in from the East when Melissa and Mac stood drinking coffee in the motel room.

"Keep in touch with me and don't worry. Adelina will help you find Stacy. There's much more to her than meets the eye. Here's two contacts at the airport." He handed her a piece of paper. "Start there. It's the place where you "left off" like she said. Someone there knows something. I guarantee it."

"Thanks, Mac. Tomi called. She and Eduardo said to tell you thanks as well. They're picking up Adelina this morning and then will return to pick me up at the market. I'll see if I can find out anything about Anna too. I'll keep you up to date."

She left him standing in the middle of the hotel room, well away from the window, which was where he was still standing, drinking coffee, a half hour later when the window shattered and a bullet whined past him.

"Yes. I thought that would come. We've been watched. Or I've been watched. Time to go."

He moved into the bedroom. Shortly, a maintenance man, in a threadbare uniform, left the room through the door into the hall. He pushed a small cart, with broom, mop, dustpan and rags attached, down the hall and disappeared. The man who came out of the elevator saw an old man at the end of the hall

317

shuffle round the corner and thought nothing of it.

The man searched the room and it was empty. It looked like no one had even been there, except for the shattered glass on the carpet.

Mac stood outside the building in the shadows and watched the person who came out. *No one I know. Part of the takeover? Who knows?*

He considered his options carefully. He could follow the man, or there was Monterrey, or...

He decided on Cancun.

I'll stay in the frying pan where they least expect me. I need to know who's trying to create the fire. The Croc is dead. Why attack me? My cover has always been tight here. How and why is it coming unraveled? Or was it Mel they're after? Hell and damn! I need a lot more information before I can leave. In any case, we've got to find Stacy.

Mac changed to a very small hotel on a back street. It was not one he knew well but he passed as Mexican easily. Safely hidden, he ate the breakfast he'd bought from a food cart and contemplated his options again.

Anna. Before I do anything more I have to know if she's safe. Making a phone call to her will be too risky. Who can I call? His mind ran through the people who surrounded her. He rejected a call to Greg. *Too easy for someone to overhear. Cait? Tough and cooperative, but no.*

Not the women involved. Cait's sons. No phone number available and maybe not safe. OK! Yes!

Rob Bradley's tone was cold, suspicious, and anger anchored his words underneath the polite façade.

"I'm trying to back away, for the sake of my wife and sons. I don't want to go any deeper. I don't want anyone to know I have had a phone call from you and I can't be sure this office phone isn't being monitored, even though I've had it checked over and over again. I also know you deserted Anna when she was here and when she was down there."

Mac was silent for several seconds and Rob was about to hang up on him when he continued his original plea.

"Look, Rob, I don't want to involve you and your family any more than you do but I have to know what's happening up there and who it's safe to talk with, who I can call. If you think it's been bad this far, I can assure you worse is coming and everyone there will be swept up in it. Someone very powerful has taken over both the Crocodile cartel *and* the cartel run by the woman who was Conrad's secretary. I'm sure he'll be extending his sway over whatever he can get his hands on up there. I just need one contact, just one, who will know what's going on.

"If you think the drug scene is bad there now, wait until this man takes over. I guarantee you it will be ten times worse. Your boys won't be able to leave the house safely, much less walk on the street. If you don't believe me, talk to people

319

who have to deal with the effects of drugs—ER and medical personnel, judges, the FBI. Go find out the facts." Mac was unable to keep the exasperation and urgency out of his voice.

"I do care about Anna. Is she safe? Are her kids safe? I do care that the rest of you are at risk. That's why I'm calling." Mac could think of nothing else to say and fell silent again.

Rob had talked to the FBI. He had also spoken with a client who worked at a hospital ER and he had contacted Greg.

"Ok. Here's Greg's private cell phone number." He rattled it off. "He's the one you should contact. There's a dirty cop somewhere in the police department. Don't, whatever you do, call him at work! Here's the Milwaukee FBI number."

Again he barked out numbers. "I've been in contact with them and I think they're clean. Anna arrived here safely. She's moving into her house as we speak. Making a public show of it. I'm getting my wife and kids out of here as soon as I can. I don't know anything about her kids. This place has turned into an effing ghetto. Don't call me again."

The phone went dead.

"God, am I glad to hear from you! When will you get up here? I sure could use your help!" Greg exclaimed.

"Two days, I hope, but no promises. I need to find out if Stacy Andre is alive. I want her to come with me if she is." Mac, looking like a prosperous Latino businessman, a porter trailing expensive luggage behind him, was walking swiftly down the tarmac at Cancun airport toward a sleek private plane. He had not heard from Melissa and decided to make a quick flight to Monterrey to connect with the man in the National Police to see what they had. He didn't want to leave but calling the man was far too risky for both of them.

"What happened to her?"

"I'm not sure." He filled Greg in on Stacy's disappearance and Melissa's failure to find her and his failure to connect with Melissa. "Wait. I have another call coming in. It may be news."

"Yeah?"

"I'm at the airport. I found her." Melissa reported. "Someone locked her in a shack out here at the southeastern edge of the runway. She's in bad shape—bitten by who knows what bugs, no food or water since Anna left, and she was beaten on her legs to the point of flayed skin to keep her from walking. They're infected. She needs medical care badly. Where are you?"

"You have great timing, woman! I'm just approaching my plane. I'll get my pilot to taxi to where you are. Put out some kind of sign. We'll pick you up and get you both out of here. Be ready."

Mac punched back to Greg.

"Greg. I have a crisis here and I'll have to get back to you. Make that three days. Stacy's hurt and desperately needs a hospital, and not any in this place. We'll head for Monterrey but may have to go to Texas. We will get there. I promise."

Greg found himself listening to a dial tone.

Mac tapped his phone back to Melissa but there was no answer.

He raced up the steps into the plane and leaned into the cockpit.

"Roberto. Slight change of plans. See that shack way off there?" Mac pointed in the direction Mel had given him. "We're going to pick up two women and it might be a problem. One is badly wounded. I don't know what to expect. You'll know them when you see them. Rafael and I may have to go in for them. Be prepared to take off fast."

Mel could see through a crack in the wall of the shack. She watched a small plane grow larger as it taxied slowly over the tarmac.

"Ok, Stacy, time to get you out of here. This is going to be painful. I just hope there's no one around who'll try to stop us."

"Mel, I can't walk." Stacy's mouth was dry and she could barely form the words. She sounded drunk. "My legs...stiff. Hurts. Skin rips."

"Focus on something else, Stace. Anything. Keep your mind off them. Just long enough to get you out of here. God, it's hot in here!! You've got to be so dehydrated. Think of water. You'll have water soon. Come on, girl! Arm over my shoulder."

Mel succeeded in getting them out of the door but the sun hit Stacy's wounds and, whimpering in pain, she slid down. At that point, a shot whistled overhead.

Mel hit the dirt, pulling Stacy with her, and rolled both of them to the protection of the shack's other wall. Pulling out her gun, she crawled to the edge of the building and peered into the jungle. *It's airless, no wind. Any movement will be the shooter.*

She waited, motionless, and movement came. Mel aimed swift shots back and forth through the shifting vegetation...down, right, left, back to center. Movement stopped.

"Mel, we're here! Cover for us!" Mac and another man picked up Stacy and raced for the steps. Mel followed, walking backwards and shooting.

"I think I got whoever that was," she yelled as she topped the steps and got out of the way of the closing door.

"Get us out of here," she shouted to the pilot as the engine got louder.

"He will, Mel. Here! Help us get her into a bed."

The three of them got Stacy up and onto clean sheets. She tried to say something but could only gesture toward her mouth.

"She needs water. Her mouth is so dry she can't talk." Mel grabbed a cloth and wet it and dripped water into Stacy's mouth. A look of intense relief spread over her face.

When she could speak, she signaled for attention.

"I have news. I overheard men talking on a phone before they locked me up. They were on speaker phone. The man who ordered this is American. I heard his voice. Midwestern accent. He took over the Crocodile's cartel and he says the Croc is dead. His men found him dead when they went to his island to kill him."

"I know. I killed him," Melissa said. "Did anyone call this man on the phone by name?"

"No. They called him El Capitán, but not to his face. It was just 'yes, sir' and 'no, sir' on the phone. Mel, I'm in so much pain and my legs are infected. Am I going to lose my legs? Am I going to die?"

"Absolutely not! No! I've got some stuff from Adelina that she's always given me in case I needed it. It'll knock you out for a while and I'll work on your legs when you can't feel it. I'll clean out any infection then."

Mac leaned over Stacy. "We've got antibiotics with us. We're heading for Monterrey and a hospital. We should be safe there."

An hour later, with Monterrey in reach, Melissa finished.

"That's very, very bad, isn't it?" Mac said softly as he looked over Stacy's wounds.

"Yes. She could lose her left leg. Her calf is horribly flayed, badly infected. Mac, we need to get her to the US if we can. We don't know how far this man's reach is, but we can't leave her in a hospital anywhere in Mexico where he might be able to finish this job."

"I'm on it. We'll land safely in Monterrey and pick up a doctor and supplies and then go north for Dallas. We'll have protection. I know a guy. Actually, he's high up in the Federales and no one has been able to corrupt him so far."

Greg felt his cell phone vibrate. A text began coming online.

"Go thru list of men frm files. Fnd 1 who lft GB long ago. C if U cn follow $$ or trvls any1 still alive or mayB alive. Prsn of intrst male, Mdwestrn. Start w/any frm west side GB. Heading 2 Dallas. Mel, Stacy on brd. S bdly hrt."

Greg placed a call to the FBI, and then headed for work.

Forty-four

"How did they find this place? We're supposed to be secret." AJ threw himself down on the ground next to the fire.

"Ramón." Jorge answered. "Mac found him in Cancun and connected him with Anna's children. He said they have news for you. They are here to ask you to go home with them, of course. They have been through much danger too, AJ. You must at least listen to them. They are your family. I did not tell them you are here, but, mi hermano, I think you must listen to them."

"What news is that?"

"I did not ask. It is their business, and yours."

Jorge knew what news they brought. Ramón had told him of the possibility that Anna's husband was alive, that Art had not been the body in the burned plane. Ramón thought it very unlikely but, still, it was a possibility. The police officer on the case back then was indifferent at best, lied at worst, and was now dead. Jorge did not want to even think about that possibility. He had told no one, not even his own brother, that he truly loved Anna.

"How soon will they arrive?"

"This afternoon."

"I will not be here." AJ rose and walked into the jungle shadows.

Jorge shook his head. *Stubborn gringo! This is not his fight. He needs to go home.* He could think of no way to persuade AJ to go other than to order him out entirely.

Jorge stood waiting as the car drove into the compound. Mayans who were in camp stood behind him. Jamie waited just inside the edge of the jungle.

Ramón emerged from the driver's seat and Louie, Cory, Alex, and Marnie exited from the three other doors and stood waiting.

"Mi hermano!" Ramón put his arms around his brother in greeting and quietly spoke in Mayan. "I am bringing you supplies as well as our guests. I will introduce you to them all. Where is AJ?"

"He walked into the jungle. He refused to meet with them. Jamie said he will find him if we must do that. Jamie is just behind me in the trees. Will you get him and ask him to come and sit and find out what they have to say?"

"Does AJ know his father might be alive?"

"No. I have said nothing."

Ramón drew away from his brother and introduced them all, then left to find Jamie.

"I am happy to meet the family of AJ and Anna. I welcome you here. Please come inside and sit down and I will have some tea made for all of us." Jorge led them into a small house where a table and chairs had been set up.

"Where's my brother? Where is AJ?" Cory asked.

"He is in the jungle and I have sent someone to find him."

"Eduardo and Ramon are searching for him," said Jamie from behind him. "In the meantime, tell me what's goin' on. I don't think you'd come all this way without good reason."

"We didn't. There is good reason," Alex said. Cory and Marnie made signs for him to continue.

"Tell him," Marnie said.

When Alex finished, Jamie questioned the others, especially Louie. He was most interested in her information.

Jorge turned to Jamie. "Do you know this man who was husband to Anna? What kind of man was he? Would he be the kind of man who would do this?"

"I don't know. I left long before Anna married. To me, he would have been just another neighborhood little kid. Frankly, I don't believe whoever is involved is Art Kinnealy, or anyone from Green Bay. No one from there, that I ever knew, had or has the sophistication to run a drug cartel the size of the one you describe to me. I do agree that Anna needs help. Jorge, I know I have told you I would help you here and I don't like to renege on my promises, but..."

He was interrupted by the entrance of Ramón, Eduardo and AJ, who carried a rifle.

Marnie gasped at the sight. He was not the brother she remembered at all. Looking older by far, bearded, browned by exposure to the sun, his face hardened, eyes distant, mouth turned down, he no longer was the brother she had known. He walked within a thick wall. An aura of sadness, despair and resignation surrounded him.

Alex stood frozen with shock. *I don't know him anymore.*

Cory was the first to move. "Oh, god, AJ! I'm so sorry! I didn't know how hurt you are. I can see the pain around you. I didn't know. I can see why you can't leave here. We shouldn't have come for you."

He walked to AJ and put his hand on AJ's cheek. "I'm so sorry," he repeated.

AJ remained very still, just looking at his brother. He reached up, took Cory's hand from his left cheek, held it, placed it on his forehead, shut his eyes, and shuddered through breath after deep breath. Slow tears began to run down his cheeks. No sobbing. No sound. No one spoke, waiting.

Finally, AJ gently dropped Cory's hand from his face, turned and offered the rifle to Jorge.

"I have to go," he said in Spanish.

"Sí. Comprendo, mi amigo, mi hermano. Please protect your mother. She is very loved by all of us here. Please will you tell her that for me? For us?"

"I will do that for you. For all of you. Yes." He looked at Jorge for long seconds. "Yes. For all of you." He turned to Jamie. "Are you coming too?" Jamie nodded.

"Then let's go. It's time."

Wisconsin

Forty-five

Anna paused, grasped the railing for support, stepped onto the escalator descending to the baggage claim area of Austin Straubel Airport and looked down to see Cait, Jenny, Sean and Mike, Aunt Carrie, and her brother Pat waiting at the bottom, their faces registering shock.

"She looks....awful," Cait breathed to herself, but the others heard her and gulped and tried to mask their reactions. Anna saw it and knew there was no hiding any effects of the ordeal she was experiencing—the horror and the loss and the anger and all that ate at her now.

There is no hiding anything anymore, if I ever did. Yes, I did. Years, eons ago I did, or tried to.

The escalator glided into the floor and Anna stepped off. Aunt Carrie wordlessly swept her into arms that held her tight. Then they all, one by one, hugged her. *Ok. This is home. No children. No home. But this is home.*

She felt tears run slowly down her cheeks.

"Get me out of here and some place where I can feel safe."

"I have just the place," said Jenny, linking her arm to Anna's. "Time for me to pay you back for your kindness to me."

Sean and Mike scooped up her luggage and they all trooped out the doors and over to the parking lot.

The Texan sat in a rented black Toyota Prius C in the fourth row of the parking lot watching the cavalcade of Anna's greeters enter and then, later, exit with Anna and her luggage. He was unaware he was muttering out loud to himself.

"Hell! It's damn sure if they were trying to get her here unrecognized, they ain't good at it. The only people not here are reporters and if they get wind of her comin' back, they'll be on her like crows on roadkill."

Now he mulled over in his mind whether alerting the media that she was back would work for or against him, and unable to decide, he let the matter drop. The thing he had to find out, he reasoned, was what she'd do now and how that would affect the plans he must put into place for El Capitán. The watcher had contacted him and, on his order, had fled the house many days ago. The man had turned the house inside out and found nothing more the Texan could use to rebuild the line.

Trailing carefully behind the two cars that made up her greeters, he was able to observe her as they arrived at and entered a home he was not familiar with—a very large old Victorian home on Chestnut Street on the near west side.

She looks like she's been through hell. Thinner. Really bad hair day. Tired-lookin'. Angry too? Yeah. She sorta looks like she wants to tear things apart. Damn scary!

Maybe we can get a bug into that house.

Greg was working. He was with a team that was scouring Anna's house from top to bottom, an exercise that did not net any person but did net prints on two leftover food boxes that shouldn't have been in the garbage container under the kitchen sink. It also netted a close examination of the tunnel, now more carefully shored up than it had been. He ordered it kept intact. He set a 24/7 watch on the house but knew that bird had flown, probably days ago.

All his efforts to contact Stacy had failed, leaving him with the nagging feeling that she was in serious trouble.

At Jenny's, Cait made two phone calls, which blossomed to four, which brought Carolyn and Rob and their boys with Marthe, followed by Father O'Doul, and later, under cover of darkness and a back yard full of bushes, Ben and Greg.

Jenny had insisted on Anna taking a long rest so they could prepare food and drink for the anticipated longer night.

"It's time to meet and hear what we all know and what we all have been through," Cait insisted and she got agreement easily.

A sense of impending change, of the strangeness of it all, of urgency and tension and threat, infected them, oozing into their pores and creeping cell by cell to minds and hearts.

Jenny focused them back on the practical.

"We also need to eat. I don't want to send out for delivery because I don't want any more attention to this house than necessary. I have enough food here but I need help with the prep," and so food was prepared, eaten and cleaned up except for a plate for Anna. When she finally came down, clean, refreshed but still looking worn and pale, she thanked them for the food but nibbled politely. Everyone could see she had no interest in it.

Pat, seated next to her on the couch, put his arm around her and gently kissed her cheek.

"Ok, my girl, let's hear it all. Don't leave out anything."

Anna closed her eyes and pictured it all from the time she'd left Green Bay and told the story, all she knew.

"So when I was flown out, AJ and Jamie were still down there. I'm terrified something bad happened to Stacy. I don't know where Mac or Ramón or Adelina or Tomasita are, or, for that matter, Jorge either. I think the Crocodile is still in control. I don't know who the rumored other cartel leader is or whether it even operates down there for sure and I have no idea who got me here."

"And your money was returned to your account?" Greg asked.

"Yes. That was because Robert de la Vergne handles my money and he has lots of influence in European banking. But for some reason I can't get hold of Louie or Robert. I'm terrified for the boys and Marnie. I haven't heard anything from or about them, have you?"

She looked hopefully at the faces around her and met only disappointment.

"Well then, tell me what's been happening up here."

An hour and a half later, all in the room had given their stories. The surprise was the account of Father O'Doul. A tall, gaunt and thin man with salt and pepper hair, Tommy O'Doul was much, much more than he looked. Physically, he resembled his Irish father who had grown thin and died from tuberculosis, but there the similarity stopped. He had the fiery personality and energy of his Italian mother and she had never let it be said she was afraid of anything or anyone. The upshot of that, they were all surprised to learn, was that he too had been out and about collecting news of the neighborhood and town in the bars, homes, small businesses and other places where he was accepted as no one else would be and where no one would have thought to go.

"Well, you see, my mother had to contend with the Mafia in Chicago back in the day and we were her eyes and ears and, well, I learned the art of collecting profitable gossip early on. Now, you need to know that there's rot in the police departments, city and county. I think our two policemen here know about that, but they didn't say that in their stories, now did you, officers?"

He nodded at Ben and Greg. "We need to have all the facts, I think." He turned his ice blue eyes at Sean and Mike and they hung their heads.

"So, let's have that story too. Now."

Greg told the story.

"Good." He nodded in satisfaction.

"So we know there could be two cartels with connections in Mexico who are sending their merchandise through this area. We know some group or groups were organized and acting here at least fifteen, if not twenty years ago. We know the O'Keeffes and Art Kinnealy and other men and definitely Wentworth's secretary were involved. We know that members of local law enforcement are currently involved. We know that someone is trying to take over up here. Wait! That's a fact! I'll tell you how I know in a minute.

He turned to look directly at Anna. "You already know, Anna, that they, whoever 'they' may be, are not done with you and, if your kids are still at risk, it is entirely likely that there will be another ransom demand for them.

"Here's more fact. The drug addiction problem is worse, not better. I've been on the streets night after night and I've seen it. Crisis calls, assault and battery episodes, ER admissions, and three trucking accidents in the last two weeks where drugs were found in the truck or the driver was stoned. Bartenders are having to deal with more drug and alcohol-addicted customers who are obnoxious and sometimes dangerous.

"Last, but not least, last Saturday I had someone come in the confessional who begged me to go to the police and tell them to look at the trucking industry as part of the drug trade. Just that. No names, no further information, no confession at all, just came in, told me that and left. I didn't see a face. The voice wasn't familiar."

338

Small gasps came from some. Greg and Ben were silent but alert. Sean and Mike sat up straight, minds on gerbil wheel speed. Greg thought of telling them about the text from Mac but decided to wait. *I have no real information on the tip about the head of the cartel and don't know if Mac made it out of Mexico. We need facts, not ifs and maybes.* He mentally kicked himself for not contacting British police earlier that day. *I need their info too.*

Anna sat silent for a long time as the others found their voices and discussed the information.

Finally, she stood up.

"Jenny, I need to remain here tonight but tomorrow, first thing, I want to return home, with a police escort, if necessary, to make my return obvious. I'm doing it this way to attract attention to the fact that I'm back. Then I'll wait for contact, which I think will come, especially from Ardith if she's still on the loose. I also need to get news of my children. The last I heard they were her captives.

"I'm not aware of anyone else who would want anything from me but someone surely wanted the information in the files and maybe already has what they want. We don't know that for sure so, Greg, we need to discuss how we'll set a trap for that person or persons. I have had an opportunity the past few days to think about what has been happening to me. I have to tell you all that right now I suspect," she took a deep breath, aware of the impact of what she would say, "that

Art did not die in that plane, that he has been alive all this time and he may be part of this somehow. Ardith herself bragged that he wasn't in that plane. She didn't say much more but it is possible he survived."

She held up her hands to stop the storm of protest and disbelief.

"Why not? I'm being realistic. I've taken a good look at the facts. The body was unrecognizable. It was already burned and then I had anything that remained cremated. Nothing was left. But anyone could have put the ring on the finger of the corpse's hand. Art himself could have done that. I took that as proof then but I'm not so sure any more. There's a rumor in Mexico of a white man who heads a drug cartel. Why not Art?

"I beg the rest of you to let this happen. I have to know. I must end this. I beg you, Cait and Caroline, to back off and protect your families and get out of here. I'll give you the money to do it. Think of it as reimbursement to you for all of the money C & C Decorating has lost the last three months."

God! It's less than three months since Ireland! Anna shook her head slightly as a wave of lightheadedness hit her.

"Jenny, you and your mother have suffered enough. So have you, Marthe and Aunt Carrie and Pat. Enough. No arguments. I'm going to bed."

"Greg, will you see if you can get through to British police and get news from them? And again, we need to set some kind of trap so I want to meet with you as soon as possible to figure out how to do that."

She turned and went upstairs.

The group was silent. Pat got up and stood in front of Cait, his eyebrows high in an unspoken question. Cait nodded and shook his hand.

He made the rounds of the group and the gesture was universally repeated.

"She has to have help. You saw that. She was about to pass out. Or something. We meet here tomorrow night."

Forty-six

Cait had another serious matter on her mind. Home again and as settled down as she could be, considering events, Cait turned her attention to her youngest son. She had done all she could to keep Liam's name out of everything, even to avoid mentioning his name to his brothers. Vulnerable as he was, she wanted nothing to stop or interrupt his recovery from the sexual abuse he'd suffered. She had never told anyone how frightened she had been when she realized he had identified with his abuser, had "fallen in love" with that creep.

Now she drove into the parking lot of the treatment center, sixty-three miles from home, for an appointment, parked, and sat in the car, hands shaking, breathing deeply to try to calm her anxiety. *He was so brainwashed. What if he becomes an abuser? A perpetrator of the abuse of other boys? What if he becomes psychotic? What if...? What if...? What if...?*

Pictures of him as a small, darling baby...as a laughing schoolboy...as a terribly wounded and frightened child...ran through her mind.

With tears in her eyes, she pulled the key out of the ignition, dropped it in her purse, and reached to open the door. Liam stood there, looking scared.

"Mom?" She saw his mouth say the word. Pushing the door open, she jumped out and pulled him into her arms.

"Oh, god, I've missed you so much."

"Mom. I can't breathe. You're hugging me too tight. But don't stop. I miss you too. Just do it a little lighter, will you?"

Cait fell apart and began sobbing, rocking him back and forth. "OK! OK! OK! I've got you! I've got you!"

He let her comfort him for a few moments but then pulled away. "Mom, I'm cold. It's October. Can we go in now?"

Two hours later, Cait, reassured by his counselors he would not be a perpetrator, held him again, saying goodbye.

"Liam, I'm so glad you're doing so well. I am so pleased. I've been so afraid for you."

"I'm ok, Mom, really I am. My mind was so screwed up. Uh, sorry, I mean messed, not screwed. I mean..."

"Liam, it's ok. You've done so much for yourself. I just wish I could have helped you more. We've had some trouble at home. It's that whole drug scene. Me and your brothers helped out a bit but it's done now. I'll come down on the weekends. When you're ready to come home for a visit, we'll be ready too."

Liam shuffled nervously, gulped, and spoke.

"Mom, I don't want to come home very soon. I'm sorry. I can't. It's the memories. They're pretty fresh. My counselors say they can help me make the memories fade some and not feel so bad but until then I don't want to make them worse. I don't like remembering him, Mom. Green Bay will have too many memories."

"Ok, Liam, Ok, I know that. I'll respect that. Do you really like it here? Do you feel safe here?"

"Yeah, Mom. That's why I'm getting better. I feel safe. Mom, will you think about sending me to a boarding school when I get done here? Please? I love you and I love my brothers but...I can't go home."

"I will. I will think about that, and see what I can find on the internet and yes, I'll see. I'll see."

Cait pulled Liam into her arms again so he couldn't see the hurt and anger she was unable to hide. He had more on his plate than any young teen ever needed. He didn't need to see that she would cheerfully have killed his perpetrator at that moment if he wasn't already dead. *The creep! The coward!*

"I'll bring your brothers to see you on Halloween for sure. You better warn everyone here. You know how crazy they can get."

"Everyone will love it, Mom. I'm lucky. I've got really cool brothers. Some of the kids here don't have anyone. Or it was their brothers who abused them. Or..."

A tear escaped even though Liam had told himself he wouldn't cry. He kept the hug going until he felt back in control.

"I gotta go, Mom. I have group therapy in ten minutes. Don't worry, Mom, this is really working for me." He backed away and waved as he ran up the stairs.

Cait returned to the car, tears pouring down.

No amount of tears can wash away all this guilt and all this anger!

Across the parking lot a man held a phone to his ear.

"It's a treatment center for sexually abused boys. This is where her son is—the one who was abused by that lawyer. What do you want done?"

As the yacht rocked gently on the water, his caller listened, musing about what a fighter Cait had been when she was little.

The man continued, "I'll draw up a file on the boy and the whole case and fax it to you. This could be a good hold over the woman if you need it."

"OK. That completes the information on the Fitzgerald family. Now start on the Bradley family. Have you got all the Texan's financials? Fax that to me too."

"Yes, sir."

On the yacht in the Caribbean, El Capitán checked off another item on his list.

Yes. I am very thorough.

Inside the treatment center, Liam stood behind the curtain watching the man in the car who had been watching them. His stomach turned.

I'm not safe here! He's another one! Or is he? I don't know, but I'm not safe. I'm not safe!

Panic hit his chest, sucking air away. His gut jerked and his bowels cramped.

Someone called his name and he turned away and didn't see the man drive away, following his mother. What he saw had been enough.

Someone knows where I am.

Forty-seven

"Hey, Sean, you and your brother come sit in with the band tonight. We got a wedding gig on the east side at that country club out in Bellevue. It's a fast $300 for each of you. They pay real good so I can hire you guys to amp up our sound. How about it?"

"Sounds good to me but Mike's in class at TC tonight. He can come later though."

"That'll work. See you about nine."

Sean hit speed dial on his phone.

"It's what I've wanted for three weeks. This undercover stuff is getting to me. I need a break," he told Mike. "Will you come?"

"God, yes! Finally, some fun! It'll be more like ten, maybe ten thirty, before I get there. Take my trumpet with you so I don't have to stop back home."

"Done."

Sean headed for a shower and a change of clothing. He nuked a quick-frozen burger, slathered it with ketchup, gulped it down, grabbed his guitar and tuned it, snatched up Mike's trumpet case and took off.

The country club was buzzing, the dancing in full swing, and the band into "I Love Rock and Roll" when Mike came in. He shouldered his way through the crowd, noting that there were several men and one girl who he was sure would be passing out before midnight. At the back of the stage, he waited for a break. When it came, Sean filled him in on the gig.

"As you can see, it's a huge wedding. The families have lots of money. We've already been through the Bunnyhop and YMCA. We still have the Chicken Dance, the Grand March and I don't know what else Sid has planned. It's a good crowd. The drunks haven't been too obnoxious and a couple girls in the wedding party look good to me. In fact, there are some really pretty girls here tonight over all."

"I'll judge that for myself, thanks." Mike grinned and turned to the bandleader. "Hey, Sid. Thanks for the call. Fill me in on the music."

Two sets later the Chicken Dance and the Grand March were over, and the crowd was thinning. All the little kids who had been allowed to stay up late had been carried out by parents. The pre-teens and teens were still going at it as hip-hop and gangnam wannabes, but many were running out of energy. The older couples or singles were sitting out everything but the slow ones.

"You can tell the ones with ADHD. They're still dancing."

"Yeah. We go to one a.m., right?"

"Sid says we play one extra song to make them think they got more than their money's worth so it'll be about quarter after when we finish for sure."

The chair flew past Mike's head, slammed against the back wall, bounced off and landed on a nearby table, where it shattered glass. Shards hit Mike in the arm. He stumbled backward to the rear of the stage, then stepped forward again, angry, ready to take on a fight.

A man in formal attire staggered to the stage and yelled out, "Play the damn song! I told you what I want. Now play the damn song!"

His buddies reached for him. He shrugged them off, then turned abruptly and staggered across the floor to the bar where he loudly ordered another drink. The bartender looked for approval to a man in a suit standing off to one side, who nodded, and a drink was poured.

Mike watched as the man downed the full glass completely. *I know him from somewhere. Who is he? Oh, man, yeah! That's the guy whose dad just died of a heart attack. I saw that in the paper. They own some company, trucking or delivery or... man, he's totally wasted! He'll get alcohol poisoning if he slams them down like that.*

"Mike! Are you cut? Are you ok?" Sean tugged at Mike's sleeve. The band had paused briefly as a waiter came and swept the glass off the stage and floor.

Mike checked his arm. "I'm ok. No cuts. No glass in my arm. I can play. I know who that guy is. He's the son of a man who has a trucking company here. His father just died of a heart attack."

Sid came up. "You ok, dude?" Assured that Mike could play, Sid continued.

"I feel sorry for the bride and groom. He's their best man. He's spoiling their wedding. He's been bragging about how rich he'll be now that his father's dead. How he's got a new side to his business where he'll rake in lots of money. All that alcohol talking. He's being a real jerk. Looks like they're going to get him out of here. Good. Back to work, dudes. Another half hour to go."

Mike and Sean eyed the progress of the man out of the room, then looked at each other. Undercover work had followed them.

They met Ben in early morning darkness outside their apartment and quickly entered the small kitchen, a dim glow over the sink their only light.

"We think it's a possible lead. If he becomes the head of a trucking company, or is now, because his father is dead, and if he's bragging about making lots of money, it seems to us he could be making dirty money as well as the legitimate stuff."

Ben took a long pull from his soda. "Maybe. It's worth looking into because there's more to it. There's an autopsy being done on his father because the death is kind of suspicious. The old man was in perfect health. His medical records show no signs of heart problems. Never had any."

Mike, now having a nervous reaction to it all, stood leaning against the stove, breathing deeply to calm himself. Sean sat at the small kitchen table across from Ben.

"So," Sean said, "I'm going to be laid off my job for a few months. Why don't I see if I can get a part-time job with his company? Just see what I can see. I can use the money."

350

Ben frowned.

"Let me talk to Greg first and see what comes out of that autopsy." He grinned. "Looks like I'll have to go to confession again. I'm such a bad, bad boy."

The channel of safe communication they'd all set up was perfect. It amused him to report to Greg through the confessional at St. Pat's. It was working well. It kept Cait, her boys, Greg, and all the others up to date. They didn't need to sneak into Jenny's house. It amused Ben even more because he was the only non-Catholic in the group, except for Caroline and family.

Rob had pulled them back completely from all activity and told the others he would be their avenue to safety should they need it.

Forty-eight

Anna, alone in her house, remained isolated from them all, unaware of their efforts to aid her and the police. She was fully aware that she had made herself a target. No one could have missed her arrival. She had seen to it, even to getting out and walking around the house, examining the yard.

She had tried calling Stacy, Mel, Mac, Adelina, the school. Nothing! She had tried London and Vincent Grant and Louie and Robert. More nothing. Her instincts told her something, several somethings were going on. A meeting with Greg was postponed due to his schedule.

A dull gray cloud of loneliness enveloped her as she stood looking out her dining room window at the Bradley house. Caroline had brought her all the food left in their refrigerator and said a reluctant goodbye.

No more just running over there. No more Caroline dropping in with coffee. No more Marthe here to talk to. No Cait on the phone or visiting. No brothers. No sons or daughter. No Lindy. Ever.

Tears filled her eyes but refused to provide the relief of falling.

I might still have a husband.

The thought repulsed her. Fury shrank those tears as she thought of what Art might have done to them all. She left the window and began

352

to pace the long hall, anger surging to levels of rage and back to a low simmer.

He led a secret life for years. Lied to us. Abandoned us. For what? To lead a drug cartel? To do whatever he wanted? How could he have done such a thing? How can anyone pretend the way he did?

"If he wanted to have a life without me, why didn't he have the courage to divorce me? Coward!! Why abandon his children too? Why put them through all the hell they suffered?" she yelled at the walls.

He was in this long before he left us. Greg thinks possibly as much as ten years before. Father O'Doul thinks at least fifteen years! How could I not have seen this? What's wrong with me that I didn't see this? Denial? No! What would I have known about drug cartels? For that matter, what did police know? I had no experience of that. I had no training, no education on that. I was a mother, a housewife.

So now that I'm home, now what? God, there's cobwebs on the ceiling! I haven't been home enough to even clean this place. I want to clean this place. I must do something, anything. I can't sleep through the night. I can't sit still. I'm so tired I ache all over. I don't want to go near the Allouez house. It reminds me so much of Conrad. I miss him. I need his advice. I can't bear to think of Ramon and Mac and AJ and Jorge. I can't have my kids here. They'll be in danger here too. AJ is in danger.

I wish, dammit, I could shut down my mind!

Anna walked into her office and slumped into a chair where, finally, her mind came to an abrupt halt and exhaustion overtook her. She fell into a dreamless sleep for the first time in weeks.

The gaunt and thin white-haired person who had unlocked and entered silently through the back door, carefully locking it behind him, stood gazing at her for a long time and then climbed just as silently up the back stairs to one of the small rooms at the rear of the attic, unlocked that door, laid out the contents of a large and heavy backpack, opened the sleeping bag that was part of it and laid it on a mattress stored there. A store of food rations for the next week went on a shelf, the door was locked again and the person settled down to wait.

I have been waiting for years. A few days, a few weeks? Whatever it takes, I'll get him. He's set her up as bait for me. I know it. He'll come. And I'll end all of it...the last thing I do.

Forty-nine

Greg's cell phone rang until it went to voice mail. Seconds after that finished, it rang again. That cycle repeated four times before he finally surfaced from the dream that was hounding him. Literally. He had become a giant rabbit in the middle of a swamp and a hound with Arnie Schwartzkopf's face was after him. He grabbed the phone.

"What?"

He rolled to the edge of the bed and it slipped out of his hand. He retrieved it.

"Sorry, you'll have to repeat that. I dropped the phone. Who is this anyway?"

"It's Cait. I'm calling from Jenny's house. I don't trust my phone at home. Just listen. You know Pat's been prowling this neighborhood talking to people since he got here. Tonight, Pat made the rounds of the west side Broadway bars. He's got something to tell you. I'll put him on."

"Cait, wait a minute. What the hell time is it?" Too late. He fumbled for his watch as Pat's voice came on. *Five after three. Geez. Why is she up at this hour? The woman's nuts.*

"Greg, it's me. Pat. I think you need to know what I saw tonight. It was down on the south end of Broadway, down past where the Mason Street bridge goes over the street, and I was walkin' home to here and I ducked under the bridge to take a piss 'cause of the beers I drank— too many and I just couldn't make it back here— and I saw these two guys about a block away and it looked like they was fixin' a truck. One was under it and the other was standin' by the side but not really doin' anything but watchin' suspicious-like and then this black car pulls up and someone in the car hands out a package and the guy takes it and gives it to the one under the truck and they all wait and it's about five minutes or so and the one under the truck hands out a package in return and there's a few words and then the car drives off and the two men take off and go to another car parked down the street and drive off and I wait."

He paused and took a deep breath.

"Pat, get to the point. It's after three in the morning."

"Well, don't get so impatient now. I'm comin' to it. I waited to be sure no one was there. It was one of them rental trucks, like people rent to move their stuff, and I was just strollin' outside of this little house down there the other day and so I happened to have met the guy who lives there and I know he's movin' up north to Marquette, Michigan, tomorrow for a job there and he wasn't one of the men. So I decided to see what I could see and I went on the other side of the truck where it was darker and I slid underneath and I think you're going to want to see what I found. I think you ought to go to confession bright and early tomorrow...uh-h...I guess that's today. Father O'Doul has it under protective custody so to speak. That's all I got to say but you'd better contact Sean and Mike. They had a busy night too."

The phone went dead.

"Wait! Shit!" Greg fell back on the pillow and stared at the dark ceiling of his own apartment. Visits to Cait had ended. She had warned him off.

"If you're around here all the time, none of us will be able to gather the information we want to get. Yes, the good people will trust us, but they aren't the ones we want to connect with."

"I don't want you 'connecting' with the others, Cait. It's too damned dangerous! You're not trained for this. Except for Ben, none of you are."

"I know this place and these people and every house that's dangerous and every house that isn't. I've run through every back alley and shop and nook and cranny since I could walk. So have my boys. I'm a fighter, Greg. I won't sit back and watch and wait. We'll get you every bit of information we pick up."

There had been no further negotiation.

Damn stubborn woman!

The phone rang again. Greg barked out, "What?"

Cait's voice. "You have to see Aunt Carrie too. She's got photos for you." She hung up.

"Oh, god! What's Carrie been up to?" he groaned.

Greg hit the button on the bedside lamp, swung his legs to the floor, stood up, grabbed his glasses, and made his way to the toilet, his seat of meditation. Assorted bits and pieces of jumbled information made their way through his brain, at

357

first seeming unrelated to each other. He slowed them down and rearranged them across his frontal lobes, trying different patterns, new connections. When he was satisfied he had set his brain on some new paths, he returned to bed and lay in the dark, waiting.

Not totally clear yet—too many gaps in the bits and pieces, but they'll fill in. I can feel it. It's coming together. We're going to have to get everyone who isn't a pro out of this somehow, though. First Pat, then Aunt Carrie. If we keep that up, we'll have the whole damn west side in on this. I better talk to Arnie.

When, at 6:30 a.m., his alarm rang, he rose, took a long shower, dressed, and went to confession.

"Bless me, Father, for I have sinned. What did Pat leave with you?"

"You're supposed to tell me what sins you committed but I'll let you off the hook for now. Look down."

Greg heard a soft scraping sound and a package nudged his knee. He reached down and picked it up.

"Did you check it out, Father, or is it unopened?"

"We checked it. Feel for the small tape on one corner. I'm no expert but I'm pretty sure it's heroin."

"Damn! Sorry for the language, Father, but I wish Pat had called this in when it was happening!"

358

"And if he had? Would you even have heard about it or would it have been covered up by whoever in the department is dirty? Or would the poor man who is moving his belongings today have driven up north right into a trap? Or would the heroin have been delivered to the streets up there to kill more people?"

"You don't understand. If I walk into the station with this, that 'poor man' won't be going anywhere. All hell will break loose and he is the prime suspect. Whoever in the department is on the take will know about it and want to make sure he's blamed for it or worse yet, he'll never see another sunrise! And, if I bring this in and report you gave it to me, you and the others could end up prime suspects as accessories. If I don't bring it in, I'll be withholding evidence from a drug exchange. I'm not authorized to investigate totally on my own, you know. Shit!"

"Hmmm! I see what you mean." There was silence for a short time, then the sound of ticking. "I have to say mass in fifteen minutes. Pass me the package. Quickly, and don't ask questions."

Greg slid the package back.

"You have just received a tip from a confidential informer that the drug runners may be using U-Haul trucks to run their contraband. You can go to U-Haul, get the names of those who rent the trucks, find out destinations and search any trucks heading north from here. Of course, there will be at least one truck that has no problem today. It will all take time. Technically, you did not actually *see* a package, it being quite dark in here and in the church. That's Jesuit reasoning. Now get out of here before I unlock the front doors. And your penance for the swear words is five Our Fathers and five Hail Marys.

"Oh, and I'm sliding the pictures Aunt Carrie took to you. Men definitely not from Green Bay, lurking around in a black SUV and other vehicles, and she got the SUV picture from a distance but it's pretty good."

The sliding door between their respective sections of the confessional slid firmly shut. Greg heard the priest open the door to his section, close it gently, and walk toward the altar. Greg, swearing under his breath, felt for and found a small envelope near his knee and slipped out the side door of the church.

Captain Arnie Schwarzkopf had a pounding headache which had come on due to loss of much sleep. Part of that headache was how to get all Anna's friends out of the picture. Another portion of it was because officers in neighborhoods on the near east and west side reported new faces, male, and not the kind of faces a mother would trust.

When Greg Klarkowski walked in and informed him of the tip from the CI—he didn't tell him it was Pat—it grew worse. That information alone meant days or more of overtime and it would probably lead to nothing.

It didn't. Before thirty-six hours had passed, two vehicles were found to have packages, one of a considerable amount of money, and the other non-prescribed Adderall which turned out to be related to a pharmacy robbery down in Illinois. Not exactly a huge drug bust but enough to make the police look good.

At home, Cait sputtered with righteous indignation.

"I know there was more to it than that. Someone's covering up what you saw, Pat. I just know it. There was heroin in that package. Where is it?"

Cait went very still, her chest tight with pain, her body frozen.

"Oh no! Oh no! What if it's Greg? What if he's in on this? Could he be? Would he do this? Oh, Pat! What if he's the leak?" Her eyes narrowed. "I'll kill him, I will! He'll wish he'd never met me! I'll tear him limb from limb..."

"Stop now! Yer gettin' crazier by the minute! It ain't him. You don't know the police ain't got that package. They might be savin' it to lure out more criminals. You don't know."

"I know we need more luck like that. I know my boys say they got a sniff of a lead about a trucking company that delivers goods that might be doing something shady. I know we have to get more information from these streets, from these people. And I want to know about those photos Carrie took."

Cait jumped as the cell phone in her pocket rang. "Yes? Uh, sorry, hello," she amended. There was a long pause. Her eyes grew large, her face white, and finally she gasped. "I'll be there as soon as I can! I'm on my way!"

Pat saw a terrible fear in her eyes and on her face.

"Liam is missing from the treatment center. They think he might have been taken. I have to go." She turned, grabbed her purse and ran.

Pat ran after her as fast as he could. "Wait, I'll come with you! Don't go alone! Wait for me!"

He reached the curb as she drove away.

Fifty

"We're terribly sorry this has happened, Mrs. Fitzgerald. It seems that Liam has run away. We've called police, sent out our own people, but we haven't found him. He left a note."

The counselor handed her a grubby, wrinkled piece of paper. Police stood nearby.

"I hate this place. I just want to be left alone. I'm going home."

Cait read it and shook her head.

"I don't believe this. He told me when I was here last week that he couldn't come home, didn't want to come home because of his memories of what happened there. He wouldn't have run to our house. He was afraid to go back home. Have you questioned the other boys? He said he preferred to be here. He felt safe here."

"Mrs. Fitzgerald, we think he saw something when you were here. Since you visited, he's become intensely hypervigilant, always on guard. We think he thinks you're in danger and he might be headed home because of that. He did mention to one of the other residents that a man was watching this place last week when you were here. Did you see anything that might have been out of place, odd, or different? Did he say anything to you?"

Tears fell silently down Cait's face as she tried to remember anything. "Nothing. Nothing at all."

She rose. "I have to go back home and look for him. I have to get his brothers to look for him.

Now. Right away." She turned and headed for the door.

"Mrs. Fitzgerald, wait! We want to help too! Police want to..."

The door slammed shut.

Twice on the way home, Cait pulled over to cry. She wanted to stop and search every ditch. She did stop at convenience stores and gas stations along the highways and walk through them, hoping Liam would be there, stranded and needing help.

I need a picture of him to show people. Posters I can put up. I can put this on Facebook. Maybe he's at home already.

She phoned Greg and had to leave a voice message. She phoned her other sons and got Seamus and he promised to go check on all the other places where Liam had ever hung out. She left messages for the others.

By the time she got home, her migraine was so bad she couldn't turn her head. She sat, rigid, in the car, unable to move.

Greg was waiting outside.

"I'm taking you to InstaCare. You can barely see. You need something for your pain so you can think straight."

He moved her gently out of her car and toward his own but, as Mike arrived, Cait collapsed. Mike dialed 911.

Greg called Anna as he walked down St. Mary's Hospital corridor behind the gurney. No answer. He left a voice message, then a text.

One by one, Cait's boys—Seamus, Mike, Andrew and Sean—made it to their mother's bedside.

"Please," she pleaded, "find Liam! Please find Liam!"

The Oneida Reservation

Big Abe Lemke eased his large frame into the too-small chair. With his narrow hips wedged securely there, feet up on a desktop, hands on his head and eyes closed, he reviewed all the information he'd picked up during this month of October, including what he'd learned from Ben, Sean, Mike and Pat, but most important, what he'd learned from the contacts he'd set in place.

The call from his chief had come with the nod to proceed. "We've also got an alert from city and county on a young boy missing. They think he might be walking through the rez into Green Bay. Name's Liam Fitzgerald, no less. Brother of the guys you mentioned as helpers of that undercover cop. We've offered our help to both county and city. They accepted. Pull out all the stops."

His motivation for his own involvement had increased exponentially when his girlfriend had called last night with the news that two more members of the tribe were in the hospital for heroin overdoses.

"I know those families. I thought they were solid." He repeated the name of one of them. "He's been in recovery for years. I thought he was doing fine."

"Well, he was until that accident earlier this year. Then the pain started and he went from prescribed opioids to heroin real fast," she told him. "It's really, really sad. I put some tobacco down for them this morning."

"What's the word among the people about how they got it? Especially how they got it out here as opposed to getting it in Green Bay?"

"I haven't heard anything about that. People are just talking about how it's bad all over. You take care. Those who spread that stuff around are not nice."

"I know that for sure. I'll see you tonight."

So. Trucking is a part of it. That's a given. Bars, of course. I bet the old Atkinson marshes out by the bay are a meeting place for drug deals, or a place to shoot up. What about Pamperin Park and Duck Creek? Yeah. That could be another place to check.

His mind recalled other dark and usually unpatrolled areas that he knew of, where he had, in fact, sometimes hidden out during his using days. He made a list.

He then made a second list of people he knew who had spent at least part of their lives on the margins of society but, now in recovery, had the street smarts and could be trusted to scout out carefully anything not usual. When he had a clear plan, he set first one foot and then the other firmly on the floor, opened the telephone book to the yellow pages, wrote down all the trucking firms in the Fox River valley, certain bars in the Green Bay metro area, and a long list he called his "special tactics troops", called those scouts and went hunting.

As he left, Greg called and told him Liam Fitzgerald was missing.

"I know. I heard. We'll hunt for him too," he promised.

The West Side

Sean had gotten the part time job easily and was put to work doing maintenance on the trucks in the yard. Ben, armed with a Class A OTR license, applied and began driving for the same company, but then Sean, with Cait in the hospital and his brother missing, reluctantly withdrew. The man heading the company was no better sober than he had been drunk. He read Sean a riot act and ordered him never to come back. Ben, standing in the yard, heard it and later called Sean.

"Don't worry, Sean. I got this. In fact, that guy is such a jerk, I hope I do find something. Call me when you know more about your mom and your brother. I'm glad Greg is on it. Keep in touch with me."

"I will. I'll try to get a job with another trucking company. I still have to earn some money and that will cover one more possibility."

Jenny O'Keeffe, in jeans, a T-shirt and stockinged feet, sat perched in the middle of her heavy oak dining room table, legs crossed, gazing out at the side yard and the tall elm trees that lined the driveway. She blew gently at the surface of a large mug of hot coffee.

Pat sat hunched in her mother's favorite blue and yellow flowered stuffed chair.

"It's almost a year now that my father murdered my twin brother and almost murdered Anna too. Maybe it's a little more. No, it's less. Time has become odd. It goes on but I rarely ever look at a clock. I don't wear a watch any more. It doesn't matter what time it is to me. I measure time by how long it took to forgive my mother for marrying my father and putting up with his abuse all those years. I still haven't forgiven my father. I can't yet. He..."

She lapsed into silence, took a sip of the coffee, made a face and set it down.

Pat nodded several times. "Yes. Time is strange. I'm sittin' here old and yet I'm still that boy who ran these streets with my brother. God knows I'm a different boy now. Then I was so innocent. Now I know a lot about what humans do to each other, both the horror and the kindness. Way too much about that first part. Not enough of the last. This I know. You can't let yourself go to the dark side, girl. I keep myself in the Light. It's the only way. I hope you can too."

"I'm trying but it pulls at me. It's odd. The Darkness isn't black. It's grey and hollow and there is no feeling. I think of it, taste it on the edges of my life, and I feel sorry for my father and brother who never knew what they lost, what they could have had. If I let myself be sucked into the Darkness, I turn grey and dry and sere. All the warmth goes away from my heart."

"Speakin' of time," Pat said, heaving himself reluctantly out of the comfy chair, "it's time we take those posters and go out lookin' for information on Liam. We've got three more streets to cover."

Jenny slid down from the table top and picked up the pile of papers next to her.

"Besides distributing these, I want to talk to anyone I can about the heroin problem and drugs. What do you think about having a series of neighborhood meetings to find out what people think? We could get Father O'Doul and the police to come and listen to the people. I think that might put pressure on those selling it and distributing it if they think people are informed and watching for it."

"Good idea!" Pat picked up the coffee, sniffed, sipped, smiled, and downed half the mug of it. *Now that'll keep these old bones movin'!*

The East Side

Captain Arnie Schwartzkopf was fully aware he had been investigated as the possible leak in the city police department. He could not help but be aware—most of the men were—that they all had been under scrutiny. He knew the chief had been cleared by the FBI and IA. He knew the man who was DEA had also been

369

cleared, but he was uneasy when he was near the man.

When Arnie became uneasy, his armpits itched. It had happened over and over in his career. He would get a bad feeling about someone or some situation and the itching would start—just a bit at first, and then it would get worse. The closer he got and the more he knew, the itchier they were. It was extremely annoying and informing at the same time. So now he sat at his desk and watched the man and itched and wondered.

I have no proof and I'm not supposed to contact the FBI directly. Usually the chief's decision, but I think it's time I said something to the chief about bringing them in. More manpower to do more digging on the streets. Of course, we have Ben, and his CIs. I've stayed away from them to give them room. And safety. That may not have been such a good idea.

His phone rang and he grabbed it.

"Arnie," the chief barked out. "I have an assignment for you. We just got a request from a citizen on the West side for police to meet with people over there about the drug scene. It's Jenny O'Keeffe. If I'm not mistaken, she's the daughter of that O'Keeffe who shot his son sometime last winter. She's looking for police who would come to neighborhood meetings. I want you to go see her about it. I want you to be my eyes and ears there. And, by the way, you're cleared. I think you know that already but I want to make that official. What do you say?"

370

"I say yes and thanks for the official clearance. I want to talk to you too if I can. Right away. It won't take long."

"Yeah. Come right now."

When Arnie left the Chief's office, his itch was gone. The Chief, however, had begun aching across his shoulders. His own intuition had gone into high gear because Arnie's "intuition" had never, ever been wrong. He had agreed with Arnie on everything, FBI included. In fact, he'd been consulting with them for a month. He and they had agreed that, given the persons involved past and present, Green Bay and Brown County would be the focus if there was to be a showdown. They had also agreed that, if there was to be any showdown, it would be initiated and controlled by local law enforcement, but federal and international law enforcement would be a strong presence.

Now that she was home, he knew that, if anyone became the target, it would be Anna Kinnealy. *This predator will make her his prey. I'm sure of it.*

The chief could not tell Arnie everything yet.

Fifty-one

It had taken Liam three and a half days to get back to Green Bay. At first, he walked east through woods. He had read a story of an Indian man who walked out to South Dakota from Duluth, Minnesota, at night, singing his way through the woods and across the fields. He found an old shack to sleep in the first night when he got tired and the dark became too much for him. The next two nights were a blur of discomfort and frosty cold. Liam did not sing.

He wasn't sure how far from Green Bay he was, but he knew it would be far and he was mad at himself for not looking up the route on a computer in the library before he left. *I could have printed out a map.* He had been too scared. Planning as carefully as he could, he'd succeeded in hiding a blanket, his outer clothing, a warm cap, and food and bottles of water in a large backpack he stole from a storage room.

Liam's mood dropped to a new low and he became deeply discouraged when he got to Waupaca and realized there were many more miles to walk. Afraid of asking for rides from men, he wasn't sure how to approach women either.

Maybe if I wait for a really old lady, I can get a ride east from here. Even if it's not all the way, at least it's closer.

He let three old ladies come and go at a gas station c-store before he got the courage to ask one for a ride. She had looked him over very carefully, for what felt like a very long time, as she peeled and ate a banana.

"Well, you look pretty harmless, young man, but how do you know I'm harmless?"

Liam had no reply to that and gulped and almost ran.

She smiled. "I am harmless. You don't have to believe that but you don't have to run either. I'm too old to chase you down. What town are you headed for?"

"Green Bay."

"I'm not going that far but I can get you to Maplewood Shell gas station just west of Green Bay. You can call someone from there. Get in." She pointed to her car.

His feet ached. His head ached. His shoulders ached. He was on the verge of tears. He got in. He sat as far away from her as the seat belt would let him, holding his backpack in his lap as a shield.

One of the boys at the treatment center had been abused by his mother and grandmother. Only one. But...Liam held his breath to keep from shaking, then slowly let it out as they moved from the station onto the highway.

After a while, she asked, "Do you want to tell me about it."?

"No."

"Are you hungry?"

"Yes."

"See the plastic bag on the floor next to your feet?"

Liam nodded.

"There's food in it. Help yourself. Whatever you want."

Liam slid his backpack to his feet, drew out a bottle of water, a banana, and a bag of nuts and ate.

They wouldn't be poisoned. The bottle and bag were never opened and the banana peel didn't have any sign of being loose.

He relaxed a bit when his stomach had stopped growling and the heat in the car had warmed him up.

They rode in silence until she turned north.

"Where are you taking me?"

"Maplewood Shell is on Highway 29. I'm going to Pulaski which is just beyond there. I'll drop you off at the station."

She looked at him over the tops of her glasses. "I could take you into Green Bay. It's not that far off my path."

Liam shook his head quickly back and forth several times. "No. No. I don't want that. I can find my way. I'm ok. I'll be ok. Just drop me off."

In spite of himself his voice shook.

"All right. It's ok. I'm not going to hurt you, child. I just want you to be safe."

"If you take me there I'll be safe. I know I can get someone to come and get me there. I can call someone. I have four brothers who live in Green Bay. One of them will come and get me."

"Do you have money to call from a public phone? Do you have a cell phone? How will you call them?"

"I have money. I saved up enough." He dug out change from his pocket. "I have two dollars. That's enough. I know that."

"Ok, then. We're almost there."

When she pulled in, Liam quickly undid his seat belt, opened the door, grabbed his backpack and slid out.

"Thank you. Thanks very much. I'll be ok now. I'll call someone right away."

She watched as he walked toward the public phone, picked up the receiver, dialed and put money in.

"Well, child. I hope they come soon," she murmured to herself and drove off.

In Pulaski, she stopped at a local restaurant and the television showed a picture of the boy she'd just dropped off. She listened and called police.

When they arrived at Maplewood Shell, Liam was gone. When police called his brothers, they had not gotten any calls from Liam.

Fifty-two

The windows in the building were dark when the Texan arrived early for the planned meeting with his two police contacts. He was worried about the IA investigation and needed to know how that would affect them all. The import store downstairs had closed at five. Now, at nine in the evening, the darkened parking lot just behind the building was deserted. He pulled his car into the lot intending to wait in his warm car for others to arrive, but his impatience got the better of him. He got out, stood next to his car, lit a cigarette, and glanced around. The dark air was cold and damp. Cigarette smoke combined with his frosty breath as he stood there checking his surroundings. He noted two cars in the lot across the alley. A third car was parked down the block on a side street. Two more cars were parked behind the corner building in the next block. Tex dismissed them, threw his cigarette away, let himself in and climbed the stairs under the night light's soft glow.

Shipments are off and running. Payments are coming in. We lost that one but we can use that as a cover. I'd sure as hell like to know where that package is though. It didn't hit the streets. Someone's got it.

His skin began crawling as soon as he opened the upper door. The room was completely black except...silhouettes of the men he was to meet were outlined in the front window by the glow of streetlights and a blinking bar sign across the street. He relaxed a little, then stiffened again when he detected a familiar smell and heard the voice.

"Howdy, Tex," came that voice from a shadowy corner of the room. "You're looking good, man. Looking fine."

"Sir. I didn't expect you so soon. I thought you were going to wait until more was up and running."

"I was. Yes, I was. I love being out on that ocean. Hate to come on land. But this is very important to me and I want to give it my full attention—get it to the point it almost runs itself. Turn on the light, will you? Boys, draw those curtains now. We can get started. Glad you are early, Tex. Shows dedication, it does. Shows interest, a good work ethic. Don't you think that's right, boys? I like that. I do."

Tex, standing at the head of the stairs, flipped the switch and waited as his eyes adjusted to the light. One man, El Capitán, came into focus first. He sat at a table across the room, to the right, his long legs splayed out in front of him, his overcoat open, a bulge under his right arm where the holster was strapped, a cigar in his left hand. The other two, the officers who represented the police forces, leaned against the brick wall on his left. They all stared at him, unsmiling. The skin along his spine shivered another warning. *Tread carefully.*

"Tex, you begin. I want a full report. I want the dossiers on everyone too. I hope you brought those."

"Yes, Sir. I did." Tex moved into the room and walked to the table. He stood across from El Capitán, laid a briefcase on the table, clicked it open, pulled out files and slid them toward El Capitán.

Without waiting to see if the man would read those files first, he launched into his full report. Each police officer followed suit.

El Capitán was silent for a while. Then, looking directly at Tex, he asked, "Have you been able to find out just how the packet of heroin disappeared?

"No, sir. Not exactly, but there are three possibilities. First, the men who made the exchange took it. I followed up on that. They didn't. They are, of course, no longer working for us. They have disappeared permanently, if you know what I mean. One of them was the man you set up as the handler of that ex-cop, Ben. Black never did get rid of those Fitzgerald boys like you told him to. Ben is still selling for us but he's unstable. Looks for part time work. Then quits or gets himself fired. Plays in a band one night, doesn't show the next. I think he's using. I want to know what you want me to do about that.

"Second, the man who was to use the rental truck took our product. He didn't. The police got an anonymous tip and they investigated and cleared him. We also know he didn't do it because we made sure he had no idea of what he would have been carrying up north."

Both police officers nodded assent to that statement.

Tex continued.

"Third, someone saw the exchange and took it. One neighbor told police that there was an old man in the vicinity, but he didn't know who he is and he wasn't seen near the truck anyway. He was taking a piss about a block away under the bridge. Just some drunk, the man thought."

El Capitán stood up to his full height of six feet, four inches and began pacing.

"You must realize that this particular package is worth a million to me, to all of us. I expect it to be found, one way or another. Since the old man is the only current lead, I want you to find out just who that old man is, and where he is."

"That old man" was, at that very moment, standing next to the car he'd seen drive into the alley behind the import shop and park in that small lot. Pat had been coming out of a bar just down Broadway on the other side of the street when he saw the Texan drive past. He didn't know who the man was, but he knew he didn't live on the West side, and Pat, seeing the car, got curious about him because he knew the import shop was part of the police presence, courtesy of info from Ben. Pat stepped back into a doorway and watched, saw a movement in the windows on the second story, saw light go on through the cracks behind the curtains up there and decided it might be of interest to check out the license plates on the cars in the near vicinity.

Six cars back here—one here, two across the alley, one down the side street, two behind the building in the next block. He began to write down the makes and models on a small notepad and almost left the safety of the doorway he was in to get license numbers of each, but a sound spooked him and he faded back into the alley and into a crevice where two old buildings nearly met. Years ago, the hiding place had sheltered him when he had been chased by some bullies one night. He'd had to climb a fence to get into it then. Now he merely stepped over some junk, disappeared into darkness, scrunched down, waited and watched.

"I thought I saw someone here," came a deep voice.

"I'll search," came a quieter voice. The man walked all around the nearby cars, then down the alley, passing Pat's hiding place, footsteps crunching more softly as he got farther away and then getting louder again as he returned. He stopped just before he reached the crevice where Pat crouched behind a piece of old cardboard. After a pause, he continued, pulling out a cigarette and lighting it.

"No one that way. I'll cross the street and check the alley over there but I don't think anyone's around. There were a couple dogs wandering through when we got here. It could be them." Footsteps once again moved away.

Pat exhaled slowly into the collar of his jacket, hiding the steam his breath made. He didn't move, well aware it could have been a ruse to draw him out. That had happened once to him as a kid. He'd had to run for his life to keep from getting beaten up.

His old knees ached from crouching down. Hips too. He steeled himself for a long wait. *Sure and one of them must have seen me arrive and walk around the cars. I can't take the chance of movin'. And if they're police, I'll eat my shorts.*

It was a very long wait and Pat was in pain that escalated to agony the longer he was there. The air grew colder and he became chilled to his core. When he finally heard a car start and leave, he hoped the others would leave too. A bit later, one did. The others did not. Again, there was a long wait. Finally, a third car left.

That's three. Jaysus and Mary, I hope the buggers leave soon. I'll not be able to stand up without help if this goes on. I'll be frozen in this shape for all eternity.

Finally, he heard a door open, close, and footsteps in the alley that paused, then came closer, then passed Pat and walked, paused, walked some more, paused again. With each pause, Pat was sure the man would go, but no, the footsteps returned, stopped in front of the crevice, and the man lit a cigar. Out of the corner of his eye, behind a ripped hole in the cardboard, Pat got a long look at the face, and the cigar smell floated to him on the night air.

The man moved on by. "There's no one down this way. Whoever it was you saw is gone by now. Get our car and drive us down the next alley. We'll pick up Carlos."

"Yes, sir, El Capitán. We..."

"Don't call me that here! Don't ever call me that here!"

"Yes, sir. I'm sorry, sir."

Car doors slammed, a motor purred to life, and a car drove away. Footsteps sounded from a distance. Another car started. Then a third.

Pat slumped further into the crevice, slowly, painfully and silently stretching out one leg and then the other. His mind had gone back to the distant past where a memory nagged and tugged and fought to come to mind.

I think I know that man. How could I know him? Where did I know him? No. Maybe he just reminds me of someone way long ago. An old man's memory is not to be trusted, that's for sure.

Pat, exhausted by the whole ordeal, fell asleep, and was rudely awakened much later by a pair of dogs slurping his face. It was getting light. He dragged his body up the wall to a standing position, scratched the pooches' ears and staggered out of the crevice on shaky legs, looking like a drunk.

The man El Capitán had left to watch the place, in the car on the street behind Broadway, observed the staggering and hesitant gait, labelled the old man just another denizen of Broadway's many bars and returned to watching porn on his phone.

Pat staggered carefully through shortcuts to the rear of Jenny's house and sneaked in. He gave her the information on the cars and what

382

he'd witnessed and, it now being morning, she took it to confession for him.

Rewarding himself for a decent night's work, he soaked in a hot tub of Epsom salts, took two aspirin, crawled into bed and slept the sleep of the just and innocent.

Fifty-three

The closer Liam plodded through the trees of the Oneida Reservation toward Green Bay, the worse he felt. Memories of his abuse flooded his mind, made him feel like he was choking, and tightened the band of fear around his chest. The counselors had told him about triggers, those bits and pieces of smells and sights and sounds that kick-start anxiety which turns to panic. At the treatment center, it had not been so bad. He had believed they were no longer strong, had little hold over him. He was wrong.

He gagged. A memory of forced oral sex. His butt hurt. He quickly shut that memory down but felt a rush of diarrhea and had to stop beneath some bushes to relieve himself. He had nothing, no tissues, to clean himself afterward. Flooded with feelings of shame and degradation, he trudged and stumbled through the woods, avoiding the roads and open fields, but when he finally reached the other side of the reservation, he had to break cover. Still on the far west side of Green Bay, he faced a long walk down tree-lined streets, across Military Avenue, and into the west side neighborhoods he'd roamed freely before all this happened. His body ached. His face was numb. He no longer felt the tears running down his cheeks.

The black hoodie up over his head so he would blend into whatever shadows there were, Liam found Shawano Avenue and walked eastward, took Oneida Street south to Ninth, turned east again and walked into his old neighborhood. He melted into the thick trunk of an old familiar tree and slid down to the ground. A half block away he saw the light in the house where he'd grown up. He hoped to see his mother pass the window but it didn't happen.

Seamus and Andrew will be home. Sean and Mike live on their own now. I don't belong here anymore. I shouldn't have come here.

It was a long time before he decided on a place to go. The lights were going out in houses, one by one. His mother's house remained lit. He knew she waited for news of him. He took one last look at it and headed for the train tracks. Looking south when he reached the river, he realized the train bridge was open. He would have to walk over the river on either the East Mason Street bridge or the Walnut Street bridge. East Mason was closer but longer and more exposed. Walnut was farther away but a short bridge. Faster. He slipped through shadows in the back alleys and made it across Walnut Street bridge without incident. The smell of the river lifted his spirit but then, triggers came again. The man had taken him to an office downtown. It had been the scene of several frightening episodes of abuse.

Liam made his way behind Washington Street south along the river path until he came to Anna's house. Hiding in the bushes, he surveyed the scene. There was a light in her library. He crawled silently through the shrubbery and was surprised to find, as he explored it, that he could slip in through the old tunnel. There was a barrier but it was easy to undo. He got into the empty cistern, climbed over that wall and finally lay down inside the old coal bin, trembling with exhaustion and hunger.

He wrapped himself against the cold in all the layers of clothing he could get on, burrowed into the sleeping bag he had carried so very far, and softly cried himself to sleep.

Upstairs, Anna, sleepless, sensed something. She checked out all the bedrooms on the second and third floors, and made sure the door to the attic was still locked. She went down to the basement, flicked on the light, made a quick visual survey of the area, and flicked it off again. Her edginess had been growing. She resisted the urge to call Greg so late at night.

There is nothing I can tell him. I don't know why I feel this way.

Across the river, Cait, home from the ER and at her wit's end, prowled from kitchen to living room to bedroom and back. There was no news about Liam. She alternately read God a riot act and begged Him to protect her vulnerable child. All the stories she'd ever heard or read about child kidnappings ran through her head. No one had phoned her. She didn't know he'd been seen at Maplewood Shell. She had sent Seamus and Andrew through the haunts of the West side again with no success. When the phone rang she jumped a mile high.

"It's Jenny. Come over now. Right now." It was a command.

"Now? It's after midnight."

"Now."

Although she couldn't stop her hands from shaking, Cait drove to the house, which looked dark. Only a small glimmer of light cracked through a kitchen window. She parked her car in the alley. Jenny stood just inside the back door and opened it as Cait came up the walk.

"Go right to my living room. I think you'll be pleased."

Cait stopped in her tracks at the door of the room. "Oh thank god! Thank god!"

Mac and Jamie saluted her. Pat stood off to one side, grinning. Aunt Carrie laughed. Cait's disappointment flooded back. No Liam. *No. He wouldn't be with them!*

"But where's Stacy?"

"She was badly hurt in Mexico. She's in a safe house in Dallas. Melissa, the woman involved in security in Mexico, is with her. We don't know whether she'll be a target or not but we're not taking any chances," Mac explained. "We're going to help you and Anna."

There was noise at the back door. Sean, Mike, Ben, Greg and a very large and tall man walked in.

Another opening and closing and Father O'Doul arrived.

"Now all we need is Rob," Cait muttered under her breath.

Another opening and closing and Rob stood in the door.

"I have Caroline, Marthe and the boys safely hidden, Cait. If you want your kids with

387

them, I can get them there tonight. I just placed two men to watch your house. They're safe! They're safe!" he hurriedly assured her when he saw her eyes widen and her face fill with fear.

"What is this?" Cait asked.

"It's Anna's Army!" Pat announced. "Or as close as it can be to that. Yours too, if you want it. We're goin' to find that child of yours."

Fifty-four

"We are going to have a meeting now," Jenny announced to all. "It's time and we have work to do. The first thing is to introduce everyone. We'll begin with our guest from the Oneida Reservation and then our former neighbors, now from Ireland, and finally, all of you who live here. Keep it brief. We have a young boy to find. Officer Lemke, you're up."

"I'm from the Oneida Police Department and I have news of three sightings of a young boy trudging his way through woods on the reservation."

Cait jumped to her feet, hands to her mouth. A short cry escaped but she held herself in check, waiting.

"There's a possible sighting of a young boy crossing to the East side over the Walnut Street Bridge," added Father O'Doul.

Jenny lost control of the crowd until Greg shouted them down.

"Stop this!" he yelled. "We need to make plans carefully or we'll be too disorganized. Stop! Now!

"Cait, we don't know if it's Liam but if it is, why would he be headed for the east side? Why not for home?"

"I don't know. When was this? What time?"

"Hours ago. It's one-fifteen in the morning now. This was probably around ten or so, maybe eleven."

"Anna's. He might go to Anna's. We stayed there while our house was being redone. There's a tunnel into it but it was blocked. I think Anna had it blocked."

"It's not blocked," Mac interrupted. "I had it opened and I made it safe when I was there last. There's a barrier against animals like rats and raccoons but he could open it easily." Mac was pacing back and forth. "I want to get over there too. I don't think Anna's safe. We learned in Mexico there's someone from the USA, maybe even from this area, who is taking over this drug line. I know Anna won't be alone long either. Her kids should be arriving there soon, if they aren't already. And Louie, her Swiss friend."

Again, chatter and speculation began.

"Stop!" Rob stood up. "We're wasting time. Think about it. We have three main jobs here. We must find that boy. We have to see that Anna and her family are safe, and we have to find out who is threatening all of us. I propose we do exactly what Jenny asked and then we divide up into teams—one to find the boy, one to go to Anna's and the last, give what help we can to police so they can do their job. Now, one by one, say who you are, your interest in this, and any news we all need to hear.

"I'll start. I'm Rob, and my family and Anna's family have been friends for years. We live right across the street from Anna's house. I have my family safe and am here to get Cait's boys to safety too. I'm offering safety to anyone who wants or needs it."

When the rounds had been made, he pointed out that there were at least three interest groups. "Mac, Pat and Jamie, you three are concerned with Anna. You can go there.

"Ben, Sean, Mike, and Abe can take to the streets. Cait, you come with me. We'll pick up your two youngest and get them to safety, then come back here to help. Aunt Carrie, you can come too."

"Nope. I'm going to the police with pictures of more suspects," she declared. "I've been out there photographing with a telephoto lens everyone I don't think belongs here and I've got one or two I know they need to see."

"I've already got a crew out on the streets searching for anyone not from here who might be involved in mayhem," added Abe. "Liam is on their list, too. And if you," he nodded at Aunt Carrie, "have pictures, we should get that out to them so they'll find and keep an eye on those persons."

"Jenny, we need someone to keep us connected with each other," Rob said. "You're command central via cell phone and your home phone. And email too. ·

"Father, you and Greg need to get all this information to the police department. I don't know about the rest of you, but I think something is building. I can feel it."

In the end, Pat and Jamie decided they would join Ben, Sean and Mike to help find Liam first. Aunt Carrie gave her phone to Fr. O'Doul so the police could retrieve the pictures. She would stay to help search.

"We can cover more ground if there's more of us," Jamie said, "and then Pat and I will go to Anna's house. If Liam does show up there, Anna would definitely call."

Mac would accompany Abe, Fr. O'Doul and Greg to the police station and then go to Anna's house. Abe would fill Arnie in on the role his people were taking and then go back out with the others. Cait and Rob would get Andrew and Seamus to safety and then return to help the others. All would communicate every fifteen minutes with Jenny.

Greg's cell phone rang as they emerged from his car at the station.

"I need you here now," growled Arnie. "Besides the Fitzgerald boy being still missing, we've got another major problem."

"I'm right outside. Abe, Mac and O'Doul are with me."

They were buzzed in. Arnie waved them into a room off the hall and wasted no time.

"Just like I thought, DEA isn't DEA. His papers look great. He talks the game, but we've got confirmation he isn't one of theirs. We know who our traitor is too. We checked finances and found he's been carefully squirreling away a lot more money than his paychecks provided, withdrew most of his retirement money "for medical reasons" which do not exist, and his other behavior has been strange. Such as, it looks like he's planning on leaving this area.

392

"County knows who their officer is too. You know him, Greg. It's Rudmann. Our traitor is Hallenbach. We can't pick them up. If we do, whoever is controlling them will be alerted. We don't want that. But now that we know, we can feed them the info we want them to have. I let you know because I want you in on the trap we're setting. More about that later. Be wary who you talk to. Give all information you get to either Greg or me only."

Greg's stomach turned over and over and then sank. Shock and anger hit him.

"Oh, man! Aw, crap! Hallenbach was with us when we worked the Kinnealy case back when Art K. was killed. He had access to everything we knew. Shit! I never would have thought he'd be the one. He's always been so gung ho law and order. He had access to those files. Everything. And Rudmann? Rudmann? Shit! I trusted that bastard."

"There's more," Father O'Doul added. "You know this, Greg. You got the call but we weren't informed. I'm sure you have your reasons but I feel we all should have been told."

Greg saw Mac jerk to attention and addressed him. "Anna's brother, Pat, got suspicious the other night about a meeting above the store we use as a front on the west side. He saw a man who he thought he might know. The man lit a cigar near where Pat was hiding. Pat took car makes and models. Pat also heard someone call the man El Capitan. The guy got angry when that happened and ordered his man not to call him that here."

Mac nodded slowly. "I've heard that name before. Recently. Down in Mexico." His eyes narrowed, face tight, pacing, he tried to recall. "A bar in Felipe Carrillo Puerto. A conversation behind me I wasn't part of. They were talking about El Capitan. Someone shut the guy up fast and I didn't hear anymore. But there is more. Bits and pieces I heard down there begin to make some sense. The gringo who's rumored to be running a cartel. It's connected to that. If that person is up here, it could be Art Kinnealy. He could be the head of a major cartel." He looked around. They were all waiting.

"Sorry. That's all I know. Oh, yeah. Here's Aunt Carrie's phone, too. She said you'll want the pictures on it."

Arnie looked marginally pleased, if still grim.

"Glad to have that from you, Mac." He continued.

"Well, Father, we did know, but we've been a little busy. You can help us. I want you to find Pat and bring him in and get him with our artist, who at this moment is working on a computer picture of an aging Art K.

"Greg, just so you know, I've pulled in Iron Mike Delorme to go back in all the old files looking for anyone who might have been a trouble-maker back then. He may be contacting you since you both worked that case."

394

Abe signed for attention. "I've got something you should know. I have a crew of scouts out looking for anomalies and strangers and things that don't fit in, and they're picking up some new faces in town. At least five, maybe six, and they think more are here. These aren't locals. They definitely aren't boy scouts. They are not just new Packer fans. They're packing. They are laying low now but I think something's up."

"Good! I want you to keep in touch with me on that," Arnie said as he scratched an armpit. "I'm going on the assumption that Anna will be the focus of any contact. Greg met with her when she first got back and she believes she'll be contacted in some way. She's expecting it. We could be wrong but I don't think so. In any case, as of two hours ago I've been setting up additional 24/7 surveillance on Anna's house. We'll be watching from the school across the street, Rob's house, the house that's kitty-corner from Anna's, and maybe that historic house next door. I have men watching the footpath as well. I'd have that completely done now but I can't get hold of Rob for some reason."

"We know where he is," Mac said. "Call Jenny O'Keeffe and she'll connect you. He's getting Cait's two younger boys to safety. Cait's with him."

Greg explained the arrangements.

"OK. Good. Greg, you and Father meet with Rob as soon as he gets back and bring him here. Abe, thank you so much and keep me informed, please. And one of you find Pat. I want that sketch before morning.

"In the morning, I'll be at the school. One more problem. I'm definitely not happy with the prospect of having so many at Anna's house. If someone wants to get to her, anyone else who's there become targets too. We have to find a way to get them all out of there. I'm torn between making it look like she's completely unguarded or placing obvious protection around her. I'll be talking to the chief about that."

He ran his fingers through his hair and scratched the beard appearing on his chin.

"I'll go watch Anna's house now," Mac offered. "I was going to go there anyway. Can you wire me up to you, Captain? I can report what I find. I'll move in fast through the tunnel and not let anyone know I'm there."

Schwartzkopf looked somewhat relieved.

"Good. I was going to ask you to do that. I want someone to contact Ben too and I'll have him follow you in. If this guy is Art, he might contact Anna. Maybe he has already. We don't know. Then I'll probably have to make it look like she's not being watched by police so maybe having her kids and that Swiss woman there will make that point. It will look natural. But then we really have to come up with a way to get them out fast if all hell breaks loose." Arnie's mind was going off in all directions.

Mac interrupted. "Don't underestimate the Swiss woman. She's highly trained too. Her husband was with her in Mexico. They were both spies at the end of WWII and during the Cold War. I don't know where he is now. He's probably in Europe. Maybe she knows. She'll be a real asset. Him too, if he can come."

"Good. We're talking to the Brits. I'll have London send me what they've got on both of them. For now, my orders to all my men are to stand off and observe, watch and report. And by the way, her kids and that Swiss woman should be arriving today. Having you inside, Mac, will be another set of eyes and ears. I'm going to ask you not to connect with Anna or the others. Can you keep to the basement if you have to?"

"Not a problem. There's a cistern and an old coal bin, each at opposite ends of the basement, roomy enough to camp in them. The tunnel opening is in the cistern. I can even sneak up the rear stairs without her knowing, like when they're all asleep."

Mac continued, informing Arnie about the fate of Melissa and Stacy.

"God! If that was Stacy's fate, I can imagine there will be no mercy if Anna is taken hostage by the person responsible for that."

Torture. All were silent for a long minute as they realized the implications of that news.

"Can you have someone take me back to Jenny's?" Father O'Doul broke the silence. "I'll contact Ben through her and tell him what you want. Besides, I know there are residents who have been recruited to be informers for the drug pushers and I don't like leaving her alone there. We also need to get all the records we kept of our activities out of there. We'll turn that stuff over to Ben and he can bring it here for you. If I think there's any danger, we'll be at the rectory," Father O'Doul asked.

"Good idea about Jenny, Father, and I appreciate the help contacting Ben. And Pat. Don't forget Pat. There's a car outside for you. Greg, stay for a bit."

Greg waited until the door closed. "What's up?"

"We have a high-level informer. This is international. I can't give you any details yet but keep in touch with me constantly."

Earlier in the day Anna, half asleep in her favorite library chair, and fighting vague sensations of dread for her children, thought she was dreaming when she heard Marnie's cry of "Mom, Mom, where are you?"

The dream became astonishing reality when she saw all four of them, one after another, walk through the door of the library. She burst into tears.

A group hug ensued and parted to show her Louie, waiting with a big smile on her face.

"Oh, how wonderful! I'm so glad to see you." She pulled Louie into the hug. "Why are you all the way here? Never mind. I'm glad you are. I need to hear the whole London story. I'll make tea, coffee, see what I've got to eat for you all! Oh, this is wonderful! Such a relief! You're all safe!"

"Mom! Mom! Settle down." Marnie gave her a little shake. "I've got the food and drink thing. You just sit back down and we'll tell you the whole story."

Anna stood in front of AJ and quietly continued crying. "I thought you'd die. I thought you didn't want to be in this world. I know you've been so hurt. I saw that in Mexico. I still see it but something's changed. What changed?"

AJ took a deep breath and brushed her tears from her cheeks. Slowly he let his breath go. It bought him time. He was in shock at how she looked. He felt a strange edge to her. He could think of no words for it but he felt fear.

Fear for *her? Fear* of *her? Both. Why? Thick energy coming from her. Survival? She's fighting for survival. And I have been too. Still am. Primal, this fight for survival.*

Louie saw and thought *I would not want to be her enemy right now. I know this look, this place. I have been there. And he has no words.*

"I could not help but come, mon cherie," she broke in. "The story we have to tell is too good to miss watching you hear it. You will be impressed with all our parts. Your children are heroes. They have been so brave. The queen of England has herself told us so."

"It's true, Mom," Cory said. "And Marnie was flirting with Prince Harry.

"Cory! Enough! Get in here and help me get this food out to the dining room."

Fifty-five

She spoke softly at first.

"My dear, you must send them away. They are in danger, just as you are. I can feel it as strongly as you do. And you, not they, are still the primary target."

Louie sat in a chair in Anna's bedroom watching Anna brush her hair. Anna looked up at the sound of Louie's voice, surprised. Most of her mind had been shut down while her senses prowled the atmosphere of the house, now alive with five more humans. *Maybe. There is something more. More what? I can't pin it down. I'm not used to all these...these...*

"Anna!" Louie put an edge in her tone.

"Oh. Sorry. My mind was off somewhere. What did you say?"

"Your children are in danger. Do you not feel this? I am feeling this very strongly."

"Yes. Yes of course, from out there," she gestured vaguely toward the windows, "but not in here. Not in the house. I feel we're all protected here. I can feel it. There's protection here. This is my safe place, our safe place."

She paused, her attention drifting again.

"I'm feeling protection around us. Have you noticed all the interesting smells here since you all arrived? It's amazing! I love the smells of my children. And you too, of course. Don't you?"

Louie didn't answer.

400

Safe in the house? Yes. But something is threatening. Something wants into this house, something that is thriving on hate. She's not tuned in to it. The number of people in this house—we're overwhelming her senses, her common sense, if there's any left. I must call Greg.

Her call to Greg never got to him. She had left a message and he had fallen far behind on answering his phone at the station. She took the gun from a secret place in her luggage and hid it on herself, and then, wanting an ally, sought out AJ.

"Something is building, AJ. I can feel it."

"I agree. I wish I had a gun. There are none here. If I go out looking for one, it will raise all kinds of questions."

"I have one, but only one, and I'll use it if I need to. I left a message for Greg at the police station but he hasn't returned my call yet. I'll call Jenny and see if she can get through to him. She must have his cell number."

But Anna walked in. "What's up with you two? What do you want for supper?"

"Mom, we need to talk." AJ was exasperated. "You know and I know we're targets here. Sitting ducks. What are our plans to protect ourselves going to be? What are we doing to prepare for someone threatening us? I want to do more than just wait like rats in a trap. We have to do more than just decide what's for supper."

Anna stood still, looking from AJ to Louie and back. Her face and body became statue still

401

to the point where she did not seem to even breathe.

Finally, she spoke. "I am fully aware we are targets. I invited that. I expect someone to come and I expect to have someone demand a huge ransom. Or, I expect that the man who comes, and it will be a man, will make other demands on you and I, AJ, which we will have to decide whether or not we want to follow. I expect that your father is the one who will come through that door.

"Stop!" she held up her hand. "I am certain of that now. He's the only one in all this who is left who could want anything from me. From *me*. Not necessarily you, but certainly from me. I don't know what and I don't care. I'm prepared to face him. If you want to leave before he comes, I wouldn't blame you. He's been out of our lives and has no claim to returning to it, and certainly has no place in yours, AJ. He gave up that right years ago. But I am determined to face him. I will, absolutely will, put a stop to this now."

"Louie, I love you dearly and if you choose to go, my love goes with you. This is not your fight.

"AJ, if you go, take your brothers and sister with you so they don't have to see the side of your father I now see." She turned and walked out of the room.

A long silence pooled around them as they stood and looked at each other.

"I won't leave," AJ said.

"Neither will I. One of us should stay with her as much as possible. I'll take nights, you take days."

"Done."

The call to Greg was forgotten.

In the attic, the man gazed out of a small window at the river, waiting. *I've waited for years. Now it's a matter of days. I'll end this game of blackmail and revenge if I die trying,"* he vowed again, as he had over and over for years. *"He's made her his bait. And that will make him mine."*

Shortly after he'd gotten himself situated in the basement Mac heard quiet snoring in the coal bin. He pulled himself up and peered over the wall. *So. I thought so. Let the poor kid sleep. He'll wake up to more nightmares soon. I hope I can get him out before all hell breaks loose.*

Quietly he retreated to the tunnel where he texted Arnie. *Liam is safe here in the basement. If I wake him now, he might run. I'll contact you tomorrow. Send Ben or someone with food. If I steal from the kitchen, she'll know.*

Liam had awakened, fed, been questioned and adamantly refused to go. Mac and Ben had gone along with that after they found out Liam knew the house like the back of his hand and could easily squirrel himself away in various nooks and crannies. And, that he had one other skill that might prove very useful.

"Besides, he's safer where we can see him. No telling what he'd get into out there."

El Capitan deemed his plans almost ready. He had decided on the house as his site of confrontation.

I will make sure her brothers are with her. The Fitzgerald woman as well. She knows too much. I want them all there.

He had kept tabs on the police and his informers told him police were currently more interested in other aspects of the drug scene, such as an intense ongoing investigation on the west side, a search for a missing child, and meetings with citizens about that drug scene. Tonight he would send men into the Bradley house, the museum house. And the house kitty-corner from Anna's where, his spies had told him, those people, an elderly couple, were conveniently gone to Florida for the winter. The Bradleys were gone as well. The museum had been closed for pre-Christmas season staff vacations. He could get someone in there easily. He had ruled out the school. Too many people to deal with. Too much risk of interference.

He had walked the streets of the neighborhood several times. He had observed auto and pedestrian traffic on Monroe and the other streets around. He had runners on the river path and watchers across the river with binoculars.

He had watched as Anna's sons had come and gone on errands. He had counted windows and doors and chosen the fastest ways in. He had a basic floor plan of the house. He had three escape plans in place.

I am very thorough.

Fifty-six

"Do you see the black car up on the hill just off Emily Street?" Schwartzkopf's voice came through Greg's earpiece. Arnie was in an unmarked car on the side street behind the school.

Greg, in the school, moved to an east window.

"Got it. How long has it been there? Is it actually related to this or just someone visiting the house on the corner? By the way, someone moved into Rob's house, the museum and the one kitty-corner from Anna's."

"The car's come and gone over the last week. We ran the plates. Out of state. We've got nothing so far. At first it seemed just a visitor to the house up there. I put someone on it full time and no one has ever emerged from the car when it's there. Ergo, I think someone's watching Anna's house.

"And yes, I know about the other houses but, as you know, we already had our people in them, waiting. Of course, his men searched but it was cursory. We're holding off. We can take them out quietly and very efficiently when we're ready. The trap is set. The FBI have internet and phone surveillance set up. The entrance to the tunnel is watched too.

"Here's the update on the pictures. Pat's description and three of Carrie's photos are enough of a match that we believe they are the same person. FBI sent the pics out worldwide.

We're waiting for an ID and any other info we can get.

"Mac is still in place in the basement. For some reason, he's not responding to my texts at the moment. Ben is back in there after some sleep and food. Probably giving Mac a sleep break. We're keeping communication to a minimum. Abe's guys gave us all the information they could get from the streets. They are running surveillance on the strangers, keeping them in their sights. We'll be informed about any of their movements."

"Who is it in the black vehicle? Art Kinnealy or someone else?"

"Definitely not Art Kinnealy. The pictures are not Art. Even an aged Art. Iron Mike is still digging. We're running computer comparisons to any known criminals or troublemakers from this area as far back as we can. No results so far. I want to buy us as much time as I can so I'm holding off while we wait for those results."

"Let me check this with you." Greg pulled a sheet of paper from his shirt pocket as he returned to the west window. "The people in the house now are Anna, her four kids, Louie, Mac, and Ben. Have I got that right?"

"Yes. And, don't go ballistic on me now, so is Liam. Right after he went in, Mac found him in the basement sleeping in the old coal bin. He was starving. Mac fed him and he's keeping him down there. He's stubborn, unpredictable, and impulsive. He's safer there than out here. Actually, he's an asset. Liam, apparently, has total knowledge of the layout of that house. He's a fund of information. And it seems he's also a dead shot with a slingshot. Learned it from another kid at the treatment center 'just in case' he told Mac. Mac will keep him safe.

"When we round them up, the rest of Anna's Army will be taken to St. Pat's. We'll let them know Liam is safe but not where or what's in progress. O'Doul offered the church and priest's house as sanctuary. Jenny's there now."

"So, OK," said Greg, "eight people and a kid. Cait's kid. I'm trying very hard not to yell at you to get him the hell out of there. On the other hand, I want to be there when Cait learns this just to see her give you hell.

Greg was silent for long minutes as he thought about it.

"It may not be the worst thing. He does know the house, including the tunnel. He can hide easily. He can get out fast and safely if he has to. At least he's not wandering the streets.

"But that's a lot of people around Anna," Greg continued. "Four people in there are trained fighters—Ben, Mac, AJ, and Louie. I think whoever wants connections with Anna will wait until she's alone, though, until the others have gone. Also, I can't see this guy going in alone. He'll have backup somewhere. Can you send a few others in through the tunnel?"

Another long silence.

"OK. You need to know the whole plan. Our confidential informer is the DEA guy. We've done a deal to get him out of here alive and disappear and, in return, we've know we've got the head of an international cartel in our sights. We know there'll be an attack on the house. Greg, all agencies are saying we've got a *very* big one here. We will be sending more people in as relief for you and Ben, and we have four teams on standby while we wait for this guy to make his move. We believe this guy's backup may be the men Abe's people have in their sights. We're playing a wicked waiting game here, a nerve-wracking one, but one we have to play now."

"Why can't we just get Anna and all of them out of there? Just get them all out through the tunnel? Or something?"

"First, any movement like that will tip this guy off. Second, Anna made it clear she refuses to go. Third, the rest won't let her face this by herself. And fourth, we have to..."

"Never mind. I've got it! I've got it! But I have a real bad feeling about this. I don't see how we can get in in time to prevent casualties."

Arnie was silent. Privately he agreed. His underarms were itching like crazy as he returned to headquarters to review the entire plan.

"The SUV is gone again." Greg's voice came quietly over the radio.

Both men had the same thought.

It's our opponent's move now.

Fifty-seven

They waited hour by hour...a day...a night...another day...before the move came.

Greg, sleeping in an empty school room on an air mattress, was shaken awake by another officer. He dressed himself for armed combat and moved through the moonless night to his assigned position.

It was Saturday. School had gone on as usual the past week. All of the students and most of the teachers had been unaware of the police presence. Now the windows were dark.

Greg, in an oversized black hoodie and dark pants, crossed the street one block north and returned by back yards until he was in thick bushes in the shallow ravine where the yards dropped to the river between Anna's house and the historic house. Two men joined him and they waited again...

The black SUV, melting into midnight darkness, again sat high up the hill facing downward to Anna's house. Early in the day, the man in the rear seat had given instructions on the phone.

"It will be tonight unless there is any sign of police. Then it's all off. There will be complete technical silence until I give the word. That will be tonight after nightfall. The inside teams in the houses will remain in place and, as you have so far, will maintain silence. The outside team will carry out the assault. I have another team looking for her brothers and the Fitzgerald woman. As

410

soon as I know they are captured, I will give the command to begin."

That had been mid-morning. Then came a long day's wait. In late morning AJ and Cory drove away and came back with bags from a grocery store. In late afternoon pizza was delivered.

In early evening, Marnie, Cory and Alex received a phone call. Could they come down to the station for more questions? Just for about an hour? They left in sweats to run the river path and back streets to the police station—less than a mile.

He punched another number on his phone list.

"Have you found her brothers?"

"Yes, they were in a bar on Broadway and we had to wait until they left to pick them up but we haven't got that Fitzgerald woman yet. There's no one at her house. We're in control of the O'Keeffe house except we can't find the girl. I'm not getting any signals from our man in the Bradley house. Nor from the house kitty corner."

"Right. They're still under my command for silence. Keep searching for her. Where are you holding Anna's children?"

"The ruse worked. We're holding them in our van."

"We don't move until we have them all. I want them all."

He dropped his phone into an inside pocket.

An hour later a text came. "Done. We found the Fitzgerald woman."

"Bring Anna's kids back first, wait ten minutes, then bring the others."

The black SUV moved quietly down the hill and glided to just outside the back door as his men crashed through back, front, and cellar doors.

"Take all but Anna to that third floor. Move fast. I do not want any fighting. If anyone fights, use chloroform."

Anna, Louie and AJ, sitting at the dining room table, had jumped to their feel as loud noises crashed around them. Back and front doors slammed open and Anna watched with open mouth as armed men entered the room with swift and silent steps, four from the rear hallway and two from the front. She was shoved roughly back into her chair. Louie and AJ had no chance to act as guns were pushed into their ribs. Another noise was heard at the back and Alex's voice yelling, "Look out, Mom! They've got us!"

Within minutes Anna was left alone in the room, except for one man who held a gun to her head. She listened and counted the steps as the rest trooped upstairs. *They're up on the third floor. It's got to be Art. Who else could have told those men about this house? How else could they have known how to enter this house so easily?* A slow seed of fury took root, broke open and began creeping through her.

Outside, El Capitan smiled, left the car and entered the open back door. He walked slowly and deliberately up the stairs, down the hall and turned into the dining room.

She waited, listening to his steps, anger inching up through her stomach, watching the hall door. A man in a black overcoat, with a broad-brimmed black hat, brim low over his eyes, came around the opening. Her jaw dropped. White-haired, tall, heavy around his middle, long slightly puffy face, ice blue eyes.

"You're not Art!" Anger turned to complete astonishment.

The man took his time looking her up and down, then slowly moved to the dining room windows, glanced at the darkness outside, noted the light in the Bradley house, and turned back to her.

"Good god, I hope not! I consider any comparison of myself to that piece of trash an insult. No. You may consider him well and truly dead. I should know. I killed him. I had his plane sabotaged as he sabotaged me. However, that was not, of course, his body you brought home. I left him where the animals could have their feast."

Again, he slowly looked her up and down, contempt on his face.

"So. I finally meet the dear wife, Anna. He spoke of you...now and then."

"Who are you?"

"You don't recognize me? Well, that both surprises me and then it doesn't. You may have been too young to remember. I assure you that I know you well."

He pulled out a chair at the head of the table, his back to the windows, and speaking into a small mike clipped to his collar, ordered a man to join another across the street at the Bradley house. Anna heard the person descend the stairs and leave from the back hall. She could see a dim light in the kitchen window of Caroline's house grow brighter and then blink out.

Rob got them out of there, thank heaven. That means at least five men here. Maybe more.

Her anger rose another notch.

"What do you want of me? I don't know you. I'm sure I don't know you."

Anna reached for her cup of tea. The man pulled out a gun with a silencer on it.

He motioned her guard away.

"Guard the front door."

He removed his hat and a thick head of curly white hair tumbled around his ears. His face was tanned, hung with fleshy pouches, square-jawed with heavy black brows and thin lips twisted in a cynical smirk.

"I would suggest you do not move without my permission. I have no problem killing anyone, least of all you. Your family has been an irritation to me for years. It will not bother me to kill all of you. You may drink your last cup of tea but I would advise you to remain seated and not move out of your chair."

Again he spoke into the small microphone. "Bring the two old men and the woman into the house now."

414

"Shit! Did you see that? His men broke the cellar door! Damn! They're in now." Greg and the other officers crouched in the small gully.

Arnie's voice came back, "We saw it. He's going in now. He's got her kids and they'll be in soon. He's just ordered two of his men to bring in Pat, Jamie, and, stay calm now, Cait. Don't blow this, Greg! We're fully prepared to go in after them. We have eyes through the dining room window and we're going to do this very carefully. He's got a gun on Anna.

"Ben and Mac are on the second floor. They sneaked up before this came down. Mac will see that windows aren't locked or blocked. They listened to everyone being moved to the third floor. You know they can access first and third floor from both front and back. You should be able to see our people climbing to the second floor porch roof. They'll go up and take the third floor, hopefully without alerting the enemy there. It's out of this guy's line of sight. I'm sending Ben up to third from the front and Mac will go down with orders to take out the guard at the front door. I want you and your men ready at that front door but be careful not to be seen or heard by that guy until we can get him. All of you, everyone, will wait until I give the signal. We want everyone in place and total surprise here."

"Copy that."

Greg moved through the bushes and shadows of the side of the house and, keeping low, crept to the edge, slid himself over onto the porch floor, two men behind him.

415

They slithered across the floor and lay just outside the door, waiting.

The night had turned cold. Greg was sweating.

Maybe we can do this without firing a shot.

Yeah, right!

Fifty-eight

Liam, awakened by a loud crash, had peered carefully over the coal bin wall. He watched men break through the cellar door and run with swift, silent steps to the stairs. He heard the back door slammed open and footsteps moving upward. He knew something was very wrong, but what?

This isn't right. I think I'd better get Mac.

Mac was not there. *He told me to stay down here if anything happens but...*

He waited for seconds that felt endless. Then the back hall erupted with commotion—loud orders, angry voices. People stomping and walking, then a silence. Voices upstairs.

Anna's there. She's in the dining room. One of those voices was Cory. He's mad. Alex too. I have to do something. I can't just wait here.

A second commotion came from the back hall. *That's Mom's voice!* He sucked in his breath and waited and listened as his mom yelled and others yelled and footsteps faded upward.

With great caution, he crept up the basement stairs, paused just inside the basement door and carefully peered into the back hall. No one there. He continued past a slightly open back door, up the few stairs to the first floor hall. No one there. The stairway door to the upper floors was wide open. He was about to sneak a peek into the dining room to see who was talking when he heard his mom yelling upstairs. He bolted up the

417

stairs and waited, breathless, at the second floor landing, listening. A hand went over his mouth and he almost cried out but Mac signaled him to keep quiet. He nodded, Mac removed his hand, pulled him out of sight and they waited. More yelling. Footsteps coming down.

"Yeh bloody bastards! What do you think you're doin'? Get yer dirty hands off me."

"Just get down the stairs, old man."

"Do as he says, Pat. Maybe we'll finally get to meet Art Kinnealy again and make him pay for all the grief he's given Anna all these years."

Jamie, shoved into the dining room, stopped abruptly when he saw the man.

"Well, shite, that's no Art Kinnealy. Who the hell are you?"

Pat stood still, his mind moving swiftly into the long past, into watching his stepfather die of alcohol poisoning. The face of a much younger man, a blonde, curly-haired man in his early twenties maybe, loomed into his mind.

"No. That ain't no Art Kinnealy," he said, "but I knew you. Yes, I did. Your name was..." he paused, thinking, remembering. "William. Fourth grade! William Regan. Billy the Bully! That's you, sure enough! Billy the Bully Regan. You and my old man had a helluva fist fight. Jamie, you remember! We weren't the only ones who had to leave town. He had a big fight, not only with our Da, years earlier, but Anna's as well. He owed money to Anna's dad and didn't want to pay it. A lot of money."

Jamie frowned. "That's right. By god," he breathed as memory dawned, "that's right!"

El Capitán rose, gun ready. "Finally. Here's who I've been waiting for. The only man who can put me in prison. Jamie O'Reilly, as I live and breathe. Too old to beat the shit out of me anymore. I've got the gun and I've got your sister and brother. And her kids. I've got the upper hand now, Jamie, old man."

"Jamie, what's this about? Who is this man? How do you know him?" Anna demanded.

Jamie hooked his thumbs in his belt and stood, legs apart, sneering at the man.

"Meet the man who really killed your father, Anna. It wasn't alcohol poisoning that killed your father. It was poison *in* the alcohol. This man sold that alcohol to your father. Oh, yeah, I poured alcohol down your father's throat to keep him so drunk he wouldn't be able to abuse you. But this is the man who provided alcohol, the drug of choice back then, to anyone who wanted it and then some.

"His father owned one of the bars on Broadway. A very rough bar where gambling was going on in the back room. So, if anyone couldn't pay his debts, or if anyone won more than the Bully's dad wanted to pay, which your father did, why, he'd just get sick and die of alcoholism, or so everyone believed. Alcoholic poisoning, the death certificate would read. Father and son both, they'd go after anyone by putting poison in the alcohol. No conscience, no mercy. That person paid with his life.

419

"Then, ah, yes, then, the debt would be 'collected' from the widow and her children. As in, your mother and us. And you. Quite a pair they were back then, father and son.

"So you're still alive, Billy boy. Your father's fryin' in hell and that's where you'll be goin'."

Jamie walked, unafraid and arrogant, around the table to Anna.

"He had plans for you, too. He was going to do to you what he did to so many women and girls. Rape them as part of the payment.

"I thought I killed him. That's why I ran. I vowed I'd never go to prison for killin' the likes of him. If I thought he'd survived, I'd have stayed to be sure he couldn't inflict any more pain on others. I got a letter about a year later from a friend, sayin' he hadn't been seen since we left, so I thought you were safe."

Motioning to the two men who had herded them in, El Capitán gestured to Jamie and Pat.

"Take them upstairs again. When I give the signal, kill them all. Make this man the first." He pointed at Jamie.

They were removed, Jamie protesting loudly. "You aren't going to win this one, Billy Boy!"

"Well, Anna. Does that answer your questions? You are my bait, but I haven't been after you. Jamie, and his sidekick brother Pat, been my focus from the very first. It was serendipitous, my meeting AJ in that bar in Felipe Carrillo Puerto. Hurting badly, he was.

420

When he began to talk about his family and I heard his name, well, it was easy to pump him for information. Thanks to your son being a drunk like his grandfather, I have my revenge. I've surpassed my father a hundred thousand fold," he gloated.

El Capitán began walking down the other side of the table, relaxed, gun held loosely.

Anna's mind had been sliding and shifting as anger rose second by second while El Capitan and Jamie talked. It became fury when he ordered all killed and passed beyond into rage when he talked of meeting AJ in a bar. Bolts of lightning cut through her. She felt her consciousness fading away. Then she lost awareness.

Fifty-nine

With that surge of immense rage, Anna, her face red, mouth open in a snarl, rose, kicked her chair backwards and shot upward, hit the tabletop on all fours and sprang at the Bully's throat where she bit into it and did not let go. She tasted blood, metallic and warm. Her hands clawed and gouged at his eyes. Instinct ripped through mind and body.

Kill!

El Capitan hit the wall on his gun arm and a shot went wild. The gun dropped. He clamped both hands on Anna's throat and squeezed.

On the second floor, Mac and Ben heard the chair fall and the shot and bolted into action.

Liam, on his own, started sneaking down the front staircase, slingshot in hand with a sharp stone in it. He paused at the landing, leaned over the railing, aimed down and fired. The man at the front door dropped his gun, clutched his eye and fell to his knees. Mac dropped past him, jumped over the bannister, landed in the hall and sped toward the dining room. Liam got off another shot into the man's neck, slid down the bannister, kicked the gun away down the hall and passed the man in a flash.

He rounded the dining room door, saw a man choking Anna, pulled back the rubber as tight as he could and discharged an arrowhead through the air, hitting the man in the temple. The pointed rock stuck in the side of the man's

422

head. Liam unleashed another which hit the eye and stayed there and, following Mac's yelled order, dived into the office for protection. Billy staggered and lost his balance but kept his hold on Anna's throat, his hands spasming tighter and tighter. Mac threw a knife as Billy turned and it caught him in the nearest upper arm. Still he held Anna's throat.

Louie, intent on saving Anna, had also raced down the stairs, shot the still-writhing man at the front door, continued into the dining room and shot Billy in one leg, the only part of his body not covered by Anna. At that, he screamed, let go of Anna with one hand, grabbed for his leg and slid to the floor. Anna's body collapsed on top of him. Mac tried to pull Anna away and yelled "We want him alive if possible, Louie!" he yelled. "We need his information!"

Mac looked up as one of Billy's men, gun raised, rounded into the dining room from the back hall.

"Look out!" he shouted, rising and throwing his body into the line of fire, crumpling as a bullet hit him in the shoulder. Louie turned, fired and took the man out.

When the third floor guards had heard the first shot they hesitated, confused, expecting a vocal command, and then two raced down the back stairs. They were followed by the white-haired man who appeared from the attic, pursued them down the stairs and shot at them from behind. One man tumbled forward and stuck on the second floor landing. The white-haired man, smiled, nodded, calmly stepped on and then over him and continued in pursuit.

He took out the second man in the hall as he reached the first floor, jumped over him and stepped through the door into the dining room. He stopped abruptly, calmly surveyed the scene, moved directly above the man choking Anna and shot him through the head. Then the white-haired man staggered backward, dropped his gun, and sank down against the wall, coughing uncontrollably as blood flowed from his mouth.

At the sound of the shot, Ben had sent the text signal to Schwartzkopf—NOW—and raced upstairs to the third floor, worried other officers wouldn't get there in time. He reached the ballroom, stopped as he came face to face with one of the Bully's men, gripping Marnie by her arm. He fired point blank and the man went down.

AJ had heard the first shot and had lunged at the nearest guard, took a bullet and fell to the floor. Jamie and Cait attacked the man, wrestling with him and Jamie was hit. Ben fired and missed, then fired a second time as Cait held the man's gun arm upward. That man went down.

Marnie and Cait remained with AJ and Jamie. "Stay with me, AJ. Don't die! Not you too! Please stay! Please stay!" Marnie begged as Cait pulled her cell phone out of her bra and called 911 for an ambulance.

When they heard the first shot, Cory and Alex had turned and jumped down the front stairs two and three at a time, passing Ben as he came up.

At the front door. Cory found Greg stepping over a dead man. Other police were behind Greg. More police poured in the second floor windows from the porch roof and the back window from the garage roof.

Greg arrived in the dining room door just in time to watch a scene he was never to forget.

The dining room table was on its side. Chairs were tumbled about. Glass from the breakfront glittered on the floor.

Across the room, Louie was disentangling Anna from a strange man whose hand was still clutching Anna's neck. Anna's mouth, chin and shirt were bloody. She seemed frozen and was unresponsive. Louie pulled her to the far corner of the room, away from the others, checked to be sure she was breathing, making soothing sounds and finally, just sat on the floor beside her, arms around her, rocking back and forth.

On the floor across the room, an old man slumped against the wall, bleeding from his mouth, gun still in his hand.

Mac swayed above them, blood pouring from his shoulder and then collapsed to the floor.

Cory, in the door behind Greg, stared in shock at the white-haired man. Alex, standing just behind him, blinked and shook his head. Both gasped, pushed Greg aside, ran and fell on hands and knees by the old man, whose whispered words were, "You're safe now, boys.

Tell the others they're safe. Tell Anna she's safe. There's a letter..."

His words were drowned as he coughed up more blood.

Sixty

Arnie had made the decision to allow the Bully's men to enter the house with their captives with great reluctance and trepidation. He had informed the chief of police of the full situation.

"Here's the thing, Arnie. We've got an international crook here, the controller of a monumental network. My orders are we get him now. Do it! That's an order!"

"Understood, sir, but there will be casualties," answered Arnie. Rescue squads were on alert. He could only hope the casualties would be few.

He had heard the first shot, thought "Oh shit no!" and ordered his men into the house.

Afterward, Greg had to replay what he saw, and what he heard from witnesses, again and again for Arnie, until they could piece together the details of the chaotic scene. Fragments stood out. The tall white-haired man shooting a stranger through the head...Louie dragging Anna, her face bloody, off the dead man and into a corner...Mac on the floor bleeding...his own extreme relief when he realized Ben, Cait, Pat, Cory, Alex, and Marnie were alive...his fear for AJ and Jamie when they found them wounded on the third floor.

The tally after police invaded and assessed the entire scene included seven wounded—Anna, Jamie, AJ, Mac, the white-haired man and one of The Bully's men. Most of El Capitan's men were dead. El Capitan was dead.

The white-haired man was Art Kinnealy.

It was an hour before Greg, having checked out basement and all four floors, and seeing the wounded off and clearing the way for crime scene people to get to work, found Liam hiding in the library, his slingshot in his hands, and, with no time to question him, called Sean and Mike to come get him, which they did.

When his brothers found out what he did—"You attacked the guard at the front door and the Bully with your slingshot!?!"—they took him to Burger King to celebrate. Then they took him to Jenny at the church and called Cait, waiting to be examined at the ER, because he'd begun to cry uncontrollably after eating half his hamburger.

Questioning took days.

Crime scene investigation took much longer.

Jamie died in the hospital three days later with Pat at his side holding his hand while Fr. O'Doul gave him last rites.

Art Kinnealy lived, unconscious, his sons at his side, for three days, then gained consciousness for two more days, hovering between life and death, but unable to give any information to police, except to whisper hoarsely, "Attic."

The doctor told Greg he died of advanced metastasized stomach and esophageal cancer. He would have been dead within two weeks or less.

Marnie had waited as AJ, unconscious and in the operating room, held a conversation with

Sheila's spirit while doctors removed the bullet which had collapsed his lung, caused much internal bleeding and nearly killed him. He told her he loved her and would love her always but he wanted to live, to build the clinic. She apparently agreed because after three hours the doctor came to tell Marnie that AJ would recover.

Louie waited by Anna's side as, even though sedated, her body tossed and turned and shuddered. Her breathing was shallow, labored. The doctor told them all, after a thorough examination, that her neck was deeply bruised, that she would have trouble breathing for a while, and should not talk. He put Anna on oxygen.

Caroline, notified by Jenny, called Louie to say she and Marthe were on their way to the hospital to relieve her. Robert called from London to say he was on his way.

The rest of El Capitan's men had been rounded up from the houses and neighborhood even before all the mayhem in Anna's house. The Bully's command for silence from his men and his focus on Anna and the others had worked beautifully for police and FBI. Those men had been subdued and were removed to jail even before the sun came up in the east.

On the third day of the crime scene investigation, when they had removed the blood and bodies and the detailed search finally reached the attic, Greg found out what "attic" meant when he emptied out the duffel bag Art had carried. He called Arnie, the chief, and the FBI man.

"You've got to see this! I think Art Kinnealy just gave us our early Christmas present. There are dozens of cute little animal key chains that are, actually, small jump drives. We have Thanksgiving, Merry Christmas and Happy New Year too."

The key chains carried massive amounts of evidence of years of the activities of drug cartels. It took DEA and FBI weeks to download and organize it all.

"It will blow apart cartel lines in Europe, the Middle East, Africa, and the line through here to Canada," Greg told Anna when, a week later, he could finally take a break to visit her in the hospital.

"Also in the duffel bag there was this letter to you and your kids. I'm sorry we opened it. We thought this would be more evidence and we did make a copy. You'll see why when you read it."

"Cory, you read it," Marnie said.

It turned out to be an apology to Anna and them all, telling how, while in the Yucatan, he'd stumbled onto Billy, who had betrayed everyone years earlier, how he had confronted him, how Billy had bragged about having both Soderberg and Moss killed and threatened to kill Anna and the children. The Bully had become a murderer.

There was also a sealed letter to Anna, which no one had opened. Anna said nothing and put it aside.

Greg didn't tell her that Art had been on massive doses of painkillers, a large stash of which had been found in the attic, along with medical marijuana. A Mexican oncologist told them Art had refused treatment and his file had been closed months ago.

"I want to know about Mexico," she croaked, her voice still hoarse.

"I'm sorry, Anna. I haven't had time to get news from there," Greg lied.

Anna stared silently out the window.

"You're a lousy liar, Greg."

Mexico, she knew, was another story.

Sixty-one

The headlines, translated into English on the internet, from a Monterrey newspaper, read, "Cartel Raid in Campeche State". It was a brief story. Mexican Federales had attacked the drug cartel, the story said, acting on information from local indigenous people. They had successfully freed thirty-four people intended for slavery, confiscated over six hundred pounds of heroin, and returned animals to a wildlife sanctuary in Guatemala. Four police officers had been wounded. Six Mayans had been killed and three wounded. The officers' names were listed. The names of the Mayans were not.

In Dallas, Stacy and Melissa read it and wept. They called Adelina.

Adelina did not need to read it. She had known that her nephew was dead as soon as he crossed over. She wept for her son she had never found, for her nephew, Jorge, who had fought for his people and died for that, and for her nephew, Ramon, in the hospital with a severe brain injury.

She had no medicine for that.

Tomasita, a widow, wept for her dead husband and their unborn child.

The newspaper reported that the Federales believed someone from Colombia is taking over the Crocodile cartel.

At Buckingham, the queen shook her head, took out her handkerchief and dabbed her eyes. Her friend, as his pipe bubbled and burned, had told her the whole story.

In France, Lindy's mother still wept for her daughter at the graveyard of the small church in a Paris arondissement. The whereabouts of Lindy's father are unknown and her mother has no plans to change that.

Louie needed comfort. It had been touch and go with Anna, and old memories of death and destruction had surfaced inside her own head and heart. She had not thought she would ever kill another human being again. She had not been prepared for what it was doing to her spirit and burst into tears when Robert reached her side.

Three weeks later, Anna, her children, Pat, and their friends wept for Jamie and Art at their funeral. They will take the ashes to Ireland when Anna is fully recovered. The ashes of the unknown man who died in Art's place will be scattered there too. There was no DNA to test to find out who he was so Anna decided to make him part of their family.

Louie and Robert flew home.

Greg Klarkowski moved back into Cait's house. Liam and his brothers were reunited. Liam is their hero. Being a hero has done a lot to relieve his post-traumatic stress symptoms but he will be returning to the treatment center to finish the program. Cait is looking for a boarding school for him. The publicity brought ugly harassment on the internet and in town. He wants to go where he feels safer.

Ben went home to reassure his parents he was unharmed, that he is still a policeman and is no longer working undercover. "We are so proud of you, Son. So proud." They beamed.

Mac, wound bandaged and healing, met with Greg to process his part in it all and then left. He said he would be going to Dallas to let Stacy and Melissa know what happened. He did not visit Anna.

On the reservation, Abe Lemke went out in the winter cold of November and put tobacco down, praying to the Four Directions, Father Sky and Mother Earth. He thanked Them for the two families on the reservation who now had three more people in recovery, and the closing of several sources of heroin.

He thanked Them for all who aided in making the world a little safer.

Sixty-two

My dearest Louie and Robert,

No texting, no email, no Skype. This is a real old-fashioned letter. However, I am typing it on my computer and printing it out. No writing by hand. I'm not that old-fashioned! I have a lot to tell you. It would take too long to write by hand.

Finally, we have spring. I'm feeling much better now that forsythia and crocuses and daffodils and tulips are blooming. Not as depressed.

First, Robert, I'm so happy to hear you are recovering from your heart attack. It's a relief this was all over and that you got home before that happened. Please know I send love to you both, and Louie, please give him a big hug for me. I know your loving presence will help him heal. Feel free to use the London apartment if you need it and thank you for finding permanent staff for it.

Next, I want to apologize again, Louie, for what you had to go through. I know! I know! You said you've experienced worse, but my behavior was so bizarre. Just know that I am not the same woman I was when you pried me off that man's throat. I have this terrible image of him bleeding to death into me, a gruesome image. My doctor told me that if I had bitten just a fraction of an inch more I would have severed his carotid artery.

I became an animal. I was and am horrified at what I did. I've had to be told what happened again and again. Even when I'm told, I forget parts of it, except for the taste of blood. I can't get that out of my mouth.

Still, I can't make myself feel any remorse that he's gone. His life was a long tale of evil. I hope I can get to remorse so I don't turn evil. That's what I'm most afraid of. I know you said that will never happen, but there's that part of me that's glad I killed him. I'm afraid of that part. I'm so sorry you had to see that.

But, to better news...

Soon I'll be able to leave here and that will be a relief. Green Bay is no longer my place. As much as I loved my house, I'm going to sell it. I'm selling the one that Conrad had in Allouez too. Marthe doesn't want it. She's living with Jenny now. And traveling. She's off to England soon with an over-sixty group of sightseers going to all the pre-historic sites.

Aunt Carrie moved in with Jenny too. She's the fun mother Jenny never had. Jenny's mom lives on in the nursing home, of course.

I'll be moving to Ireland. Pat will come with me. He doesn't feel this is his home either.

I'm so glad you've set up my Lake Como house for Marnie and her fiancé, Rene. He'll make a great husband for her. Even though I've only met him once, I feel good about him. I was worried and I'm still worried that she got into this relationship too soon after all that happened. Rebound or some sort of quick comfort. Of course, I trust your instincts. If you and Robert approve, I do too. Besides, I know you. You've had him checked out very thoroughly, haven't you?

She calls me several times a week to keep me up to date on her career. Thanks also for the references you gave her.

Cory is in the High School for the Performing Arts in New York, finally finishing high school. And—I'm so proud of him—he tried out for an off-Broadway production of *Equus*. He got a part but, thank heaven, not the part where the actor is supposed to get naked. I don't quite want that visual in my head. He's found his first real boyfriend. Donald is sweet. I just hope they can make it. They are both awfully young. Of course, since all that's happened the last year and a half, Cory's grown older inside.

It's only months since all this ended. I ask myself if my children are healed from all this. I can't believe they are but I trust they'll ask for help if they want and need it. I remind myself they're not children anymore.

I hope this is ended. It will be a long time before I stop looking over my shoulder.

Their father's apology went a long way to help all of them let go of anger and sadness. I read his letter to me. Then I burned it. I'm not the woman he married and the man he became is not the man I married. Still, I do wish we could have talked in the hospital before he died.

AJ is back in Mexico. He's setting up another hospital. I don't think he'll ever leave

437

there. Her spirit is still with him. Sometimes, though, he can smile and laugh at jokes. I cling to that as a hopeful sign.

Alex is at Harvard. He'll be learning to take over the family money, which was seriously depleted to get us all through this, but he'll make it grow. My children will have money to help them through life, thanks to Conrad. And to Robert. Give him another hug for me.

This past month Ramón has been in the United States so we could have a neurologist evaluate him. He's never going to recover from his brain injury totally but he is improving. He'll live with his children in Dallas. I had their mother moved into a group home for mentally ill in Dallas too. I've made sure they both have all the medical care they need. Because of the injury, he doesn't recognize me or her but he does know his children.

You asked what I feel for Ramon. I care for him. I did fall in love with him but that seems so long ago and far away and I think, if I'm honest with myself, it was a reaction to all the years of no sex and no man's love at all. Ramon opened up that side of me. I love him for it.

His children have been here to visit me but we must all return to Mexico tomorrow for Adelina's funeral. She has been called over. In truth, I believe she wanted to be with Jorge and simply decided not to stay here in this reality any longer. I understand that kind of connection now. When I thought AJ would die, part of me

438

wanted to go with him. If not for my other children, I wouldn't be here.

But, after all that happened in Mexico, it was Jorge I felt closest to. There was something about him that pulled at me, deeper than any other attraction, more like our souls are twins. I don't know how else to describe it. I never had any experience like that before.

You asked me if I miss him. Yes, I do. But I feel him. When I'm totally alone, I feel his arms and his warmth and his love. His presence is helping me heal from the madness my counselor calls posttraumatic stress. It took over my mind and spirit so totally.

Nightmares still come.

Well! That was a lot! Again, I want to say that I am so glad Robert is better. His kind heart needs all the love you give him now. All this excitement has been too much for him, and even for you. We're all too old for this. I'll see you both soon, when we scatter Art's and Jamie's ashes over the Cliffs of Moher.

Oh! One more bit of good news! I bought that large home in Galway I sent you pictures of, where I plan to spend my time nagging my children to fill it with grandchildren.

You and Robert will be welcome there anytime.

With love, Anna
PS I don't know where Mac is.

PPS Stacy lives in Dallas and she runs the non-profit safe haven I set up for the refugees affected by the cartels.

...journal...

The letter from Art confirmed for me he was part of the men who ran a cartel back then. He ran the illegally captured animal trade. Jon was trading in gems. Art tried to get out when he found out about slavery of children and women. When the cartels threatened the families of those involved—and that included Jenny and her mother, Anne Soderberg and her children, as well as us—he and Jon O'Keeffe went down to end the threat. Jon betrayed him. Big John was in on it too. Art didn't tell me how he escaped them all. There's a whole lot he left out. I'm glad. I don't want to know.

I do wish I could have told him how grateful I am for what he did. He saved our lives. But then, because he was gone for so long, and because he was dishonest about what he did, I could never have told him I love him with any honesty on my part. He asked for that in the letter, but no. No way.

Art spoiled our lives with his illegal dealings, and he lost the right to come back. In the letter, he apologized profusely. For me, his remorse is just too little, too late but I am glad he came to feel that remorse.

Bill Regan not only threatened our lives, he even had us watched. My skin crawls when I think about that. It horrifies me that he was responsible for the deaths of Soderstrom and Moss. I can understand why Art kept hunting him down.

I remember Regan's Tavern but I don't remember Billy. I was too young to be involved with the older teens.

I suppose I should have handed the letter over to police. More evidence. I burned it.

...two days later...

I met with Abigail Woodman today. The houses are listed for sale. I visited them the other day and there is a thick miasma of pain oozing its way through the air in them. I don't know how to clear that out. Maybe others don't feel it. She found me this condo way over on the far West Side, away from that old neighborhood.

She says I'll not have to testify at any legal meetings or trials. That's a great relief. I was so totally sick of questions and telling the story over and over in the month after everything happened.

Caroline and Rob and their boys moved weeks ago to The Ridge, south of East De Pere. He takes them away whenever he can and Caroline says they're thinking of moving out of the area entirely. She and I are close but it's not like before.

Cait took over C&C Decorating and found a decorator who helps her. She called this morning to keep me up to date on their business. She's determined to pay me back for my investment. I told her no but she's so stubborn! Her boys are fine. I'll always keep in touch with her. She's still mad because she couldn't deck Billy herself. She likes what I did. My horror and shame at what I did creates a barrier between us on my part.

Mac. Well, whatever hope I had of being with him died when he walked out on Stacy and me down in Mexico. Mac is a wanderer. He always will be. He's on another job for his government. He calls me from time to time but we're both realists. I suspect that he and Melissa are sometime lovers. Good. I wish them well. I have no idea where Mel is either.

It's time to go to counseling now. Part of me is still crazy. I still have no memory of what I did. I bit his throat? I bit his throat! Insane!

I have very little memory of anyone else's part in it either.

I keep one secret. I've told no one, not my counselor or Cait or Louie, of the animal I see often. I'm afraid of being locked away.

He comes to me and purrs and rubs against me and then dissolves into his own world. At first I labelled this a hallucination, but I know it isn't. I feel his fur!

Maybe I am hallucinating but I don't care. He's part of me. He'll always be part of me. I've named him Jorge.

Ok, Anna, you really are crazy!

Sixty-three

This afternoon Big Abe came to visit. Just to see how I'm doing, he said. That was kind of him. He joked that the condo I'm in is, in fact, Oneida land and so I'm now part of their tribe. He has a hilarious sense of humor and it was good to laugh.

I told him about the animal. I don't know why. I just blurted it out. Abe didn't bat an eye!

He pulled out a package wrapped in red cloth and took some kind of braided grass and some loose leaves from it and showed me how to purify myself and my apartment. He told me I should do this in the houses too. He said that in his culture, the animal who comes is my guardian, and that I will never be alone, that what I've seen is normal and not a hallucination. I burst into tears when he said that. I've been believing I'm so abnormal. After I stopped crying, he told me he came to see me because he can see the animal too. He said the animal came to me because I'm brave and to protect me and that I'll always be protected.

I told him, through tears, "My mind has been in pieces. This is such a relief! You can't imagine how you've helped me!"

I shared with him all the dreams and the sensations and the premonitions and all that I've never told a living soul. He told me that it's a gift from the Creator. We talked for a long time.

I'm not crazy after all. And if I am, there's an awful lot of other humans in hundreds of other cultures who are just as crazy as I am!

Now, finally, the constant fear and shame I've lived with for years is gone.

Maybe I can live in The House after all. I can go home.

Yes? No? It doesn't matter.

I am my own Home.

ABOUT THE AUTHOR

Judith M. Kerrigan is the pen name of Judith Kerrigan Ribbens, a visual artist, amateur photographer and writer. She holds a Bachelor's Degree in Human Development, University of Wisconsin-Green Bay; a Master's Degree in Expressive Arts Therapies, Lesley University, Cambridge, MA; and is a Licensed Professional Counselor in Wisconsin. She has been a counselor for over twenty-six years, including thirteen years as a crisis counselor. She now specializes in working with cases of complicated trauma.

Born in Green Bay, Judy was a longtime resident and has an extensive family background there. A mother, grandmother and great-grandmother, she now resides in the Wisconsin countryside.

The Jaguar Hunts is her third novel in the Anna Kinnealy series. The first two books in this series, *Betrayal by Serpent* and *In Crocodile Waters*, are available on Amazon.com in paperback and e-book forms. They can also be ordered through Barnes and Noble.

***

Book signings may be scheduled at least one month ahead.
Contact information:
judirose@tds.net

Websites:

For much more on the writing of her books, the characters, settings, and events, go to
www.judithkerriganribbens.com

***

To purchase prints, canvases, totes and other gifts reproduced from selected works:
www.fineartamerica.com/judyribbens

***

Other connecting points include LinkedIn and Facebook.

A big thank you to all who have purchased my work. It is the great reward of my old age to be able to use every talent I've been fortunate enough to have received, and to give back to the world some little bit of what I've received from others. Most especially, I give thanks to the many mystery writers out there whose works have entertained, thrilled, and inspired me.

67452526R00251

Made in the USA
Charleston, SC
13 February 2017